**The Public Library
of Nashville
and Davidson
County**

KEEP DATE CARD IN BOOK
POCKET

TIME BURIAL

The Collected Fantasy Tales of
HOWARD WANDREI

TIME BURIAL

The Collected Fantasy Tales of

HOWARD WANDREI

Illustrated by the Author

Edited and Introduced by D.H. Olson

FEDOGAN &BREMER

Minneapolis, Minnesota
1995

ACKNOWLEDGMENTS

"Don't Go Haunting" and "The Hexer" copyright 1939 by Street & Smith Publications,
Inc. for *Unknown*, June 1939.

"Macklin's Little Friend" copyright 1936 by Street & Smith Publications, Inc. for
Astounding Stories, November 1936.

"The Glass Coffin" copyright 1937 by Culture Publications, Inc. for *Spicy Mystery Stories*,
November 1937.

"Here Lies" copyright 1937 by the Popular Fiction Publishing Co. for *Weird Tales*,
October 1937.

"Exit, Willy Carney" copyright 1935 by Culture Publications, Inc. for *Spicy Mystery
Stories*, September 1935.

"The Wall" copyright 1934 by Street & Smith Publications, Inc. for *Astounding Stories*,
May 1934.

"The God Box" copyright 1934 by Street & Smith Publications, Inc. for *Astounding
Stories*, April 1934.

"The Black Farm" copyright 1940 by Street & Smith Publications, Inc. for *Unknown*,
March 1940.

"Over Time's Threshold" copyright 1932 by the Popular Fiction Publishing Co. for
Weird Tales, September 1932.

"Master-the-Third" copyright 1937 by Culture Publications, Inc. for *Spicy Mystery
Stories*, August 1937.

"The Hand of the O'Mecca" copyright 1935 by the Popular Fiction Publishing Co. for
Weird Tales, April 1935.

"The Missing Ocean" copyright 1939 by Street & Smith Publications, Inc. for *Unknown*,
May 1939.

"O Little Nightmare" copyright 1939 for Culture Publications, Inc. for *Spicy Mystery
Stories*, December 1939.

"In the Triangle" copyright 1934 by the Popular Fiction Publishing Co. for *Weird Tales*,
January 1934.

"The Other" copyright 1934 by Street & Smith Publications, Inc. for *Astounding Stories*,
December 1934.

"After You, Montagu" copyright 1971 by August Derleth for *The Arkham Collector #9*,
Spring 1971.

"The Monocle" copyright 1939 by Street & Smith Publications, Inc. for *Unknown*,
November 1939.

ISNB: 1-878252-22-4

Interior layout and design by Felix Bremer

A Note Regarding the Texts in this Volume

Producing definitive texts of any author's work is a difficult business. Such a task is made even harder when the manuscript record is incomplete—as is the case with the Wandrei materials. In the case of some stories there are no manuscripts at all. In others the only manuscripts are early versions that were later expanded; but for which the later versions are no longer extant. In most cases the manuscripts used in the preparation of this book were early typescripts that were then holographically overwritten. These were then obviously retyped prior to publication, with those typescripts now lost.

Editorial decisions regarding the textural purity of the contents of *Time Burial* had to be made on both a story by story and line by line basis. While this method is obviously less than ideal, it has nevertheless resulted in texts which are much truer to the author's intent than those in any previously published versions. In the end the editor's goal was to produce the best, clearest, and most definitive texts possible. To what extent I have succeeded or failed, I leave to the reader to decide.

Fans of the Spicy Pulps should also be forewarned that the versions of those stories reprinted here (with the exception of "O Little Nightmare") are appreciably more risqué than those which were actually printed in *Spicy Mystery*. Howard Wandrei, it seems, was a writer whose erotic scenes were simply too hot for the pulps.

Contents

Illustrations

Introduction

In the fall of 1972, there appeared in the mailboxes of many collectors and readers of pulp-era fantasies a most intriguing catalog from Arkham House Publishers of Sauk City, Wisconsin. Along with a description of Arkham's latest release, *The Rim of the Unknown* by Frank Belknap Long, this catalog included an interesting array of forthcoming books including no less than eight titles by Howard Wandrei: *Time Burial, The Collected Mysteries* (Vols. I & II), *Radial Symbolism: The Phenomenal Art of Howard Wandrei, Catalog Index: The Complete Art of Howard Wandrei, The Diaries* (in one or more volumes), *Selected Letters* (in one or more volumes), and *The Circle of Pyramids* (with Donald Wandrei). None of these titles were ever released and in time they, and the Donald Wandrei books listed with them, became among the most legendary unpublished books in the history of specialty publishing. In the years that followed the credibility of the listing, as well as the very existence of the titles themselves, has been repeatedly called into question. It is only now, more than two decades later, that the facts regarding these long lost books are starting to emerge.

Arkham House was established in 1937, the brainchild of August Derleth and Donald Wandrei. Both men, in spite of their youth, were authors of some note in the pulp magazine market of the time as well as long-time friends and correspondents of the recently deceased H.P. Lovecraft. Concerned that Lovecraft's work would be forgotten if not collected in book form, Derleth and Wandrei founded Arkham House specifically for the purpose of preserving his legacy for future genera-tions. Shortly thereafter, they branched out and began to collect the works of other pulp-era authors in book form. Collections by Carl Jacobi, Henry S. Whitehead and Clark Ashton Smith, as well as the publishers themselves, soon began appearing under the Arkham House imprint.

Upon the death of August Derleth in 1971, Donald Wandrei travelled to Sauk City to assume control of Arkham House, but rifts quickly developed between himself and the estate of his late friend. During his brief tenure as Arkham House's chief operating officer, Wandrei appears to have completed only two projects that were not already prepared for the press. One was *From Evil's Pillow* by Basil Copper. The other was the now infamous catalog of 1972.

Whether Wandrei truly intended to publish the books he'd listed remains a matter of conjecture. The listings for his own books (*Colossus* and *Of H.P. Lovecraft, August Derleth & Arkham House*) seem to indicate that he was, at best, preparing a long-term "wish list" that combined uncollected works with stories that appear never to have been written. In spite of Donald Wandrei's apparent willingness to treat his own unwritten works as extant, there can be little doubt that the Howard Wandrei titles listed in the 1972 catalog were not only possible but, in at least two cases, already partially prepared for publication.

As early as 1944, August Derleth had contacted Howard Wandrei regarding the possibility of producing a collection of his stories for Arkham House. This collection, entitled *Orson Is Here*, was never published by Arkham, but it was announced by Derleth in Arkham's 1949 catalog. Howard Wandrei himself seemed to have a rather lackadaisical attitude towards it; an attitude often expressed in letters between the two men. Initially, Howard provided Derleth with nothing more than a list of his published fantasies, with the expectation that Derleth would select the contents. Later, after being pressured by his friend and would-be publisher, Howard went so far as to produce a rough for the dust jacket. Whether a completed version of that jacket was ever executed remains unclear. What is clear is that the book itself never progressed beyond the talking stage, with Howard sending Derleth occasional manuscripts and Derleth commenting on their possible inclusion in the book. When Howard Wandrei passed away in September of 1956, the contents of *Orson Is Here* were still not set and any prospect of the book's release quickly evaporated.[1]

Yet, among the papers remaining in the Wandrei home at the time of Donald's death in 1987, there *was* a complete manuscript for a collection of Howard Wandrei stories. This manuscript, consisting almost entirely of photocopies taken from the pages of various pulp magazines, was itself a rather curious item. For one thing it had been put together, not by Howard Wandrei or August Derleth, but by Donald Wandrei.

The two pages of copyright information at the front of the collection were in Donald's handwriting. Moreover, there were several curious omissions. None of Howard's unpublished fantasies were included, nor was there any mention of the story "Don't Go Haunting," a tale that had been published under the pseudonym of Robert Coley and which was apparently unknown to the compiler. Adding to the mystery were two other curious facts. The first was that the manuscript, although undated, appeared to have been produced sometime during the late sixties or early seventies, at a time when photocopying was becoming inexpensive and the technology advancing beyond its more primitive stages. The second item of note was the existence of the original typescript of the unpublished "Time Burial." While this was not part of the large book-length manuscript discussed above, it was in close proximity and may have been connected. If so, the presence of this manuscript seems to indicate that Donald Wandrei's 1972 stock listing was not that far off the mark after all.[2]

Further explorations among the papers of Howard Wandrei turned up other surprises as well. While there is no evidence that Donald Wandrei ever began work on either volume of the art books or the *Collected Mystery Tales,* the material for such projects was clearly in existence and close at hand. A similar situation exists with the *Diaries,* which are extant even if no editing of them was ever begun. Most interesting of all was *The Circle of Pyramids,* the very book whose description in the 1972 catalog led many people to reject it as little more than a hoax. Long thought of by collectors as something akin to the fabled *Necronomicon, The Circle of Pyramids* was in fact compiled for publication by Donald Wandrei sometime during the early seventies. A collection of correspondence between Donald and Howard Wandrei, it relates primarily to Howard's studies of Gerald Fosbroke and William Blake, Blake's artistic structures, and the brothers own adaptations of those structures. The title derived from Donald Wandrei's own Blakian version of design.

If I have spent an inordinate amount of time discussing Donald Wandrei and his relationship with Arkham House in the introduction to what is, after all, a collection of Howard Wandrei stories, it has not been without reason; for the relative obscurity of Howard Wandrei as a writer is directly tied to both.

This not to say that Howard Wandrei doesn't deserve some of the blame for his lack of name recognition among modern readers. Even during the prime of his career, while selling ten or twenty stories a year, Howard seemed to go out of his way to avoid achieving the sort of name recognition experienced by many of his peers. Besides writing almost exclusively under pseudonym, he all too often tied his fate as a writer to that of editors he liked; thus limiting the number of markets open to him. He also took a laissez-faire attitude towards the idea of book publications of his work. This was true, not just of projects like *Orson Is Here*, but other, more mainstream efforts as well. His lone attempt at a mystery novel, *The Key to Trouble*, made the rounds of several publishers but was never completed, while attempts by friends like August Derleth to urge Howard into the science fiction boom of the 1950's met with little success.

These problems were further exacerbated after Howard's death by Donald's apparent indifference to any markets other than Arkham House. It's not that Donald Wandrei didn't care about his brother's work, it is just that, after years of mostly futile efforts to succeed as a mainstream novelist and playwright, Donald was himself burned out; content to devote his remaining creative efforts in the direction of the publishing house which he had helped to form. When August Derleth died, Donald's interest was rekindled for a time, only to be quickly extinguished in the bitter litigation that followed. When the dust had settled, the fate of *The Brothers Wandrei* and their literary legacy had been sealed. They, like many of their contemporaries, were left to languish in obscurity, little more than a footnote in the history of a long-forgotten era.

Howard Elmer Wandrei was born on September 24, 1909, in St. Paul, Minnesota. The youngest son of Jeanette Garnsey and Albert Wandrei, he was raised in the relative comfort of the family's Portland Avenue home. Albert Wandrei was a prominent St. Paul lawyer, Mason, and later, chief editor of West Publishing. Howard's two older brothers were David, born in 1907, and (apparently) adopted soon thereafter, and Donald, born in 1908. Howard's younger sister, Jeanette, was born four years later in 1913.

As parents, Albert and Jeanette Wandrei were tolerant and supportive. Their love of art, literature, fine music, and the uncommon appears to have passed on to their children at an early age. As youngsters, both Donald and Howard were what can only be described as precocious. Donald's knack for poetry was early in evidence, his first book of verse having been published when he was just 19. Howard first achieved a level of family notoriety by way of his artistic tendencies. As a child, he had taken up drawing, often in conjunction with, and under the inspiration of, classical music played on the family's phonograph. His skill in this area soon brought him to the attention of many of St. Paul's most famous artists.

Unfortunately for Howard, the permissiveness of his upbringing, while conducive to his artistic development, had its drawbacks as well. In 1923, Howard and several friends founded a neighborhood group called The Triangle Club. Innocent enough at first, the gang soon degenerated into something more unsavory. Club rules against swearing, smoking and theft were quickly repealed. In reading the organization's minutes, kept and preserved by club secretary Howard Wandrei, one can almost see the transformation; as though the Little Rascals had gradually mutated into lightly-armed Vice Lords with a taste for ice cream and candy. The Triangle Club disbanded within less than a year, but many of the associations lived on.

In 1927, Howard completed his freshman year at the University of Minnesota and moved, for a time, to Yellowstone National Park where he worked in a gift-shop and restaurant at the West Thumb of Lake Yellowstone. The job didn't last long. His low sales figures and often testy relationship with the shop's owner, coupled with continual till shortages—for which Howard was suspected—soon got him fired.[3] In the fall, after an extended trip to the east coast, he returned to the University where, as the son of a prominent lawyer and younger brother of the school's reigning poet laureate, great things were expected of him.

It was then that Howard's earlier associations with The Triangle Club came back to haunt him. Young, rich and bored, Howard, a like-minded underclassman named Wendall Whaley, and a number of 15 and 16 year-old associates began to practice the fine art of burglary. Their purpose was not to raise money, but rather to experience the "thrill" of the crime. At first things went well for the young bandits, then, on December 28, 1927, they made a terrible mistake. During a break-in at the home of a young woman who had jilted him several months earlier, Howard was suddenly overcome by a desire to "avenge" himself. He removed all of the clothes from her closet and cut them to ribbons with a pair of shears.

The bizarre nature of this burglary, coupled with its having been committed in the home of Clifford L. Hilton, a sitting Justice of the State

Supreme Court and former Minnesota State Attorney General, spelled the end of what would soon be known as "The Thrill Bandits." The finger of suspicion fell firmly on Howard Wandrei. Police raided the family home and confiscated Howard's diaries and revolver. Questioning of his accomplices soon netted even more conspirators. Within two weeks the entire ring of sneak thieves was in jail. Twin Cities newspapers had a field day with the story, as did several St. Paul ministers who used the events as a springboard to attack the "materialism of the modern age" as well as the young felons' "lack of parental attention." The University of Minnesota was especially embarrassed by the publicity surrounding the case and went so far as to issue a press release which called the affair, with typical bureaucratic understatement, "unfortunate."

Howard was incarcerated in the St. Cloud Reformatory. Still, wealth does have its privileges—especially when one has been tagged with the label of genius. Several of Howard's instructors continued to correspond with him throughout his imprisonment. More importantly, arrangements were made to insure that Howard Wandrei's artistic and literary development would continue in spite of his confinement. Paper and art supplies were sent to him. Over the next three years, he not only refined many of his artistic techniques, but managed to produce a body of work that was, by any measure, phenomenal. Much of the artwork praised by H.P. Lovecraft in letters to various correspondents, as well as that shown at various exhibitions, was work completed by Howard Wandrei during this period.

In late 1930, Howard was released from prison. He immediately returned to the University where he continued his studies in both art and literature. Of special note during this period were his sudden interest in the art of making batiks—for which he received numerous awards—and his increased involvement with the U's student literary magazine, *The Minnesota Quarterly*.[4] Howard first appeared in this magazine, through the auspices of his brother Don, in 1927. During the early 1930's he contributed to its pages several more times. *The Quarterly* published one additional story by Howard Wandrei as well as three essays and several drawings.

In 1932 two things happened that were to have a profound effect on Howard Wandrei's later life. The first was his introduction, through his brother Don, to Constance Colestock, a young woman who later became his wife. The second was his sale of "Over Time's Threshold" to *Weird*

"A Mythological Phantasy" (1933). Batik by Howard Wandrei.

Tales. Originally written for a creative writing class, it was Howard's first professional sale and forever changed the path of his career.

After graduation in 1933, Howard Wandrei and Connie Colestock moved to New York to begin their careers, he as an artist and writer, she as a retail sales manager. In keeping with the mores of the time, they lived separately, Connie sub-letting a modern apartment, while Howard, more strapped for cash, leased a room in an old longshoreman's boarding house at 320 W. 11th Street. Times were hard for both of them, especially Howard. His fiction sold slowly, if at all, while his artwork won high praises and even a few awards in gallery shows, but netted him very little income. By 1934, things had improved somewhat. Two of Howard's stories found their way into *Weird Tales*, where the Wandrei name held a certain magic due to the high esteem in which Donald was held by readers of that publication. Howard also managed to place five stories in the pages of *Astounding*. Four of those were written in collaboration with his friend Mike Smola, a doctor, and published under the pseudonym of Howard W. Graham, Ph.D.[5] The fifth, a solo-effort entitled "The God Box," was published under the rather transparent pseudonym of Howard Von Drey.

In late 1934, Howard and Connie moved back to Minnesota to prepare for another assault on the Big Apple. For Howard, it was the turning point of his career. On his first expedition to New York he had gone as the younger brother of Donald Wandrei, whose reputation among readers of horror and science fiction pulps was already well established. He had written for the same markets, covered similar themes, and even adjusted his prose style to match the perceived tastes of his brother's editors. Then, just before leaving New York, he'd tried something different. Virtually abandoning science fiction and horror, he'd started writing mysteries. His first known effort, "Finishing Touch," sold to *Detective Fiction Weekly*. More sales quickly followed. By the time he was ready to return to New York, Howard Wandrei's future as a writer was beginning to look up.

In January of 1935, Howard and Donald Wandrei moved to New York together, sharing an apartment at 155 W. 10th Street. In spite of their close proximity, their differences as writers were becoming readily apparent. Donald, in spite of his desire to make it in the mainstream, saw himself primarily as a fantasist and looked upon his mysteries as hackwork, done to make ends meet and nothing more. Howard, on the other hand, found a new freedom in writing mysteries. For one thing, they allowed him to produce tales in which characterization was often as important as the plots themselves. For another, they gave him an opportunity to loosen up his prose. Howard quickly adopted the hard-boiled style of Hammett and Chandler as his own, while Donald, clinging to the style of an earlier era, produced mysteries that were anachronistic even at their time of publication.

Howard further divorced himself from the role of "Donald Wandrei's Younger Brother" by effectively changing his professional name. After the first appearance in *Detective Fiction Weekly,* he adopted the nom de plume of H.W. Guernsey, a name which was to become his primary pseudonym from that day forward. From 1935 until his death in 1956, Howard would use his real name only twice more in connection with sales to magazines.

By mid-1935, H.W. Guernsey had become a mainstay with Detective Fiction Weekly, his stories appearing at regular two to four week intervals. He'd even begun to branch out and explore other markets. With a steady source of income, Howard Wandrei finally began to feel secure in his finances and, on September 24, 1935, he and Connie were married in a civil ceremony in Connie's apartment at 20 West 8th Street in Manhattan. They set up housekeeping in an apartment at 42 Perry Street. Shortly thereafter they moved to 21 Bethune Street. By May of 1937, they'd leased a basement apartment at 319 West 14th Street, where they remained until their separation in 1944.

In the summer of 1936, Howard's career underwent a sudden, albeit temporary, nosedive. For reasons still unexplained, although probably due to the departure of a favorite editor, Howard Wandrei severed his personal connections with *Detective Fiction Weekly*.

It was a bold move on Wandrei's part. In the fourteen months between April of 1935 and June of 1936, he'd sold 21 stories, 19 of which had gone to *Detective Fiction Weekly*. Now he had to find other markets—and fast. He returned to *Astounding* for one last fling with a tale entitled "Macklin's Little Friend." Then, in 1937, he hit pay dirt, placing no less than 16 stories with 8 different publications.

Part of Howard's success during this period was due to his sudden willingness to once again follow in the footsteps of his older brother. Having established H.W. Guernsey as a legitimate name in the field of pulp fiction, and confident enough in his own ability to make use of the openings provided him by his brother's contacts, Howard made a brief return to *Weird Tales* (under the Guernsey pseudonym), and cracked the previously unexplored markets of *Black Mask* and *Esquire*.

From Howard's point of view, the *Esquire* sale was especially fulfill-ing. Like every pulp writer, his dream was to break out of his existing markets and into the higher-paying and more socially accepted "slicks." *Esquire* seemed to present him with that opportunity. They loved his story "The Eerie Mr. Murphy" and wanted to see more. Sensing a chance at a "legitimate" writing career, Howard dropped his Guernsey pseudonym and allowed "Murphy" to be published under his own name. He wrote more stories with an eye to *Esquire*, a market that had shunned him several years earlier when he had approached them as an aspiring cover artist. Unfortunately, the $125 paid for "Murphy" was the only check Wandrei ever received from *Esquire*. In the years that fol-lowed, he received many encouraging rejection letters from them—but never made another sale.

1937 is also an important year in Howard Wandrei's life in that it can be seen as the branching off of a road not taken. On March 15, H.P. Lovecraft passed away in Providence. Wandrei, who'd met Lovecraft several times and had corresponded with him for a number of years, dutifully informed August Derleth of this fact in a letter mailed the next day. Derleth, upon reading the letter on his way to a favorite place in the marshes, immediately decided that Lovecraft's work needed to be preserved for posterity and wasted no time in enlisting Howard Wandrei's assistance in securing access to Lovecraft's papers. Over the next three weeks letters passed rapidly between the two men as Wandrei, Derleth, Frank Belknap Long, and other members of the Kalem Club actively conspired to separate Lovecraft's literary papers from the hands of his literary executor, Robert H. Barlow. In the end they were largely successful, and Howard returned to a writing sched-ule so overloaded as to make further involvement with the Lovecraft estate impossible. Impossible, that is, except for one thing. By April 1, little more than two weeks after H.P. Lovecraft's death, Howard Wan-drei had been enlisted as cover artist for a book of Lovecraft stories to be entitled *The Outsider.* During rare, free moments over the next year, Howard worked sporadically on his design, eventually producing a sketch entitled "The Street of Green Eyes." Unfortunately, the piece was never completed and, by the time it was actually needed in 1939, Howard's heavy work load and hectic social schedule had landed him in the hospital, suffering from the second of several severe bouts of pneumonia.

So it was that Virgil Finlay, rather than Howard Wandrei, became the cover artist for one of the most famous and collectible books in the history of fantastic literature.

More important to Howard's eventual career, 1937 brought him into increasing contact with Wilton Matthews and Trojan Publications. Two years earlier he'd sold a Guernsey story to *Spicy Mystery* entitled "Exit, Willy Carney." The story had simply been too "hot" for him to place in any "legitimate" markets. Now, feeling a financial pinch, he succumbed to the repeated requests of his friend Matthews and began submitting stories to Trojan.

The Trojan publishing empire was an interesting corporation with editorial offices based at 125 East 46th Street. Owned by Harry Donenfeld and managed by Frank Armer they were, by most standards, a rather shady outfit. Because their most notable publications were the Spicy Pulps (*Spicy Mystery*, *Spicy Detective*, *Spicy Adventure* and *Spicy Western*) they were always in danger of running afoul of New York's notoriously strict anti-obscenity laws. To avoid problems with their more "risque" publications, they maintained a second mailing address, in the name of Culture Publications, Inc. in Wilmington, Delaware. In the early 1940's, after New York's moral guardians finally caught up with them, Culture Publications was disbanded and then reestablished, with the same staff and editorial offices, first under the Trojan imprint and, later, under the new name of Arrow Publications. At the same time, publication of the Spicy's was curtailed and, when they resumed in 1943, the entire line had been renamed Speed (as in *Speed Detective*, *Speed Mystery*, etc.).[6]

Despite their less than savory reputation, Trojan was a good market for writers of the day. Besides the Spicy's, they produced a flotilla of publications: *Private Detective*, *Hollywood Detective*, *Candid Detective*, *Romantic Detective*, and more. None were as scandalous as the Spicy's, but all allowed a degree of sexual freedom unheard of by other markets. More importantly, they paid well, at least by pulp standards (one and one-half cents a word to start, slightly less on stories over 6,000 words). They also took care of their authors. As an established contributor, Howard was soon being paid well above their standard rate. His blossoming friendship with editor Matthews and his close proximity to Trojan's editorial offices held other advantages as well. When money was short, Howard and Connie were often able to obtain advances against future payments through the simple expedient of showing up at the office and asking for them.

With the exception of E. Hoffman Price and Robert Leslie Bellem, few of Trojan's authors were willing to appear under their own names. Pseudonyms were the rule rather than the exception. This posed a special problem for Howard Wandrei. H.W. Guernsey had appeared widely and achieved some small reputation among editors and readers. Afraid of damaging his primary pseudonym by linking it to Trojan, Howard set about to develop a new name. In the end he chose Robert A. Garron primarily because, as he later explained to August Derleth, "the initials spelled R.A.G." As Howard's involvement with Trojan increased, and his sales to other markets diminished, more and more of his fiction would be published under the Garron name.

In 1938 Howard and Donald Wandrei started work on what was to become their only literary collaboration. In their late teens and early twenties they had collaborated, in at least one sense of the word, in that Donald had written a number of poems "inspired" by his brother's artwork. Yet, it wasn't until January of 1938 that they'd tried anything on the scale of *Come To Life*. Why they'd waited so long to attempt such an effort, and why they never tried again, are both mysteries that remain to be solved. Both men were familiar with collaborations. Donald, in his attempts to become a playwright, had done many such projects with New York writer Douglas Wood Gibson and, later, collaborated on screenplays in Hollywood with Henry Borsha. Howard, for his part, had already written collaboratively with "Doc" Smola, Harold May, and Connie Colestock. He would later collaborate, anonymously, with Trojan editor Wilton Matthews and long-time friend Kay Holmes-Smith.[7]

Come To Life was a play aimed at a Broadway audience. A comedic fantasy about the managing director of a department store who wakes up one morning and finds that the mannikin he's passed out next to has come to life during the night, it is in many ways reminiscent of a French farce: people pop in and out, drunken friends and lisping policemen drop by unexpectedly, and so on . . . At one point the Wandreis passed the script to a man named Dailey Paskman who was supposed to turn it into a musical and shop it around New York. Several years later Paskman resurfaced, this time in Hollywood. Any chance of a movie deal fell through when Howard Wandrei and Paskman fell to squabbling over ownership rights. *Come To Life*, like Howard's semi-autobiographic solo effort, *Garden Apartment* (1937), was never produced.

By 1939, most of Howard's income was coming to him courtesy of Trojan Publications. He did, however, resurrect his Guernsey pseudonym for one last stab at the science fiction markets. Donald had recently landed a story with John W. Campbell's *Unknown* and Howard, sensing a fresh market suitable to his new, mature style, decided to test the waters. His first submission to them was "The Missing Ocean," a heavily rewritten version of the earlier Howard W. Graham, Ph.D. story "Time Haven" (*Astounding*, Sept. 1934), that also incorporated many elements of Howard's later, unpublished, vignette "What Happened to Rudolph?" It sold immediately. Inspired by its quick acceptance and *Unknown's* more than acceptable payment rate, Howard wrote six more stories for them and rapidly became, along with L. Ron Hubbard, one of the magazine's star writers. Unfortunately, for reasons still unclear, his association with Campbell lasted for less than a year. After April of 1940, Howard wrote exclusively for Trojan/Culture and H.W. Guernsey had, for all intents and purposes, ceased to exist.

The 1940's brought other changes as well.

Suzanne Elizabeth Wandrei was born on October 25, 1941, the first and only child of Howard and Constance Wandrei. Unfortunately for her, the home into which she was born was wracked by instability. Although they appear to have cared a great deal for each other, Howard and Connie had problems almost from the beginning. By the late 1930's, Howard's heavy drinking and tendency to overwork, coupled with infidelities committed by both parties, had driven the couple to the brink of divorce. Connie appears to have found a place of her own and, for a time, may have even stayed in one of L. Ron Hubbard's "communes." Howard, always a heavily auto-biographic writer, took out his frustration in prose; producing not just the aforementioned *Garden Apartment*, but also stories like "Don't Go Haunting," "O Little Nightmare," and the lost "Orson Is Here."

By 1940, the couple had reconciled, but it was only a matter of time before the strains would build up again.

As with many young couples, especially those with children, money was a major source of conflict in the Wandrei household. In 1943, Howard attempted to solve this problem by expanding beyond the confines of the pulp market. Overtures to Hollywood went unreturned but two other options presented themselves. One was an offer from a "pocket book" company that wanted one 50,000 word novel a month and would not have objected to Howard's expanding or combining pre-existent material.[8] In the end, the deal fell through, partly due to a war-time paper-shortage and partly due to Howard's preference for a second offer; that of a radio program featuring Boris Karloff.

It was a speculative venture, but one for which Howard had high hopes. Put together by Frank Armer of Trojan Publishing and DC Comics fame, it paired Karloff's famous voice and image with the writing team of Howard Wandrei and Bob Maxwell, two men who had previously worked together on some *Superman* radio scripts. Alas, the deal appears to have fallen through, at least as far as Howard was concerned. While reimbursed for his time and paid by Trojan for stories he later wrote from ideas developed during their meetings, a Wandrei-scripted radio program featuring Boris Karloff was not in the cards.

Ironically, the biggest beneficiaries of this failed venture appear to have been August Derleth and Arkham House. In an early production meeting Howard suggested dramatizing some of H.P. Lovecraft's stories as part of the program and was amazed to find his suggestion met by nothing but blank stares. None of those present had ever heard of Lovecraft! The next day Howard brought in his copy of *The Outsider* and loaned it to Karloff's agent, a man named Weiss. Weiss, in turn, passed it among the other principals including, presumably, Karloff himself. Within a matter of days, the decision had been made to include at least one dramatization of Lovecraft in the schedule. Howard, who'd suggested it and then worked as a go-between to bring it off, was not around to see it. Overwork and a rapidly deteriorating home-life had driven him to the brink of collapse.

Throughout 1943, Howard had often seemed to be on the verge of a nervous breakdown. Depressed for long periods, he'd been drinking heavily, questioning his own abilities as a writer, and becoming increasingly irritable. On the night of April 10, 1943, the tension in the Wandrei home had reached the breaking point.

Although some of the facts regarding this evening are open to dispute, the basic chain of events went something like this: Howard and Connie started quarrelling. Connie left Suzi with neighbors and then returned to the apartment. The fight escalated for a time, after which Connie left again. When she returned, the fight began right where it had left off. Sometime in the middle of it all, Howard left the apartment—naked—to take out the trash, and Connie locked him out. When the police arrived a few minutes later, they found an unclothed Howard Wandrei standing in the hallway, smashing milk bottles, and trying to break down the door of his own apartment. By then, calls to the Wandrei's 14th Street apartment had become routine, and the New York police seem to have found this incident particularly amusing.

Howard and Connie's marital problems continued well into 1944. After another near-fatal bout with pneumonia (apparently induced by a combination of over-work, exhaustion, and over indulgence), both Howard and Connie seemed to be looking for a way out. With invasions of Europe and Japan looming on the horizon, Howard found himself hoping he would be drafted and even conspired with Wilton Matthews to "pull some strings" that would put them both, together, in the Coast Guard. In the end even, this dramatic form of escape was denied him; Howard's prison record rendering him unfit for military service.

Not wishing to remain in New York, Howard pursued other options, the most viable of which seems to have been a project bank-rolled by the Associated Chambers of Commerce in Florida. Had it panned out, Howard would have been able to travel around Florida writing articles on "fishing in wartime" for the *Atlanta Journal*.

On October 13, 1944, Connie left for good. She returned to Minnesota where Suzi was already staying with her maternal grandparents. Howard stayed in New York for a few more months. Unable to write, he seems to have spent his time drinking and trying to come to grips with the dissolution of his marriage. In March of 1945, he packed up his suitcases and moved back to Minnesota, intent on effecting a reconciliation with his estranged wife.

The last ten years of Howard's life were spent in an on-going morass of legal action, emotional turbulence and, ultimately, physical dissolution. In spite of his attempts at reconciliation, Connie's decision had been made. Not long after his return to Minnesota, Howard was hit with a restraining order. In 1946, Connie, citing the milk-bottle incident among others, filed for divorce on the grounds of mental cruelty and adultery. Howard fought hard to obtain custody of his daughter but, in the end, even that was denied him. On December 4, 1946 a Ramsey County Court granted Connie's petition for divorce and awarded her custody of Suzanne as well as most of the couple's furniture. Howard was further ordered to pay all attorneys' fees and child support of $50 per month.

The issuance of the divorce decree should have been a positive development in Howard's life and, indeed, it probably would have been had other factors not intervened. By the end of 1946 Howard was writing again and seemed to be adjusting to the reality of his failed marriage. Then, in January of 1947, new disasters struck.

When Howard Wandrei had left New York, he'd maintained the lease on his 14th Street apartment and sublet it, fully furnished, to Mort and Thelma Weisinger. When the Weisingers suddenly decided to move into a new home on Great Neck, Long Island, Howard found himself forced to return to New York once again. He arrived on the morning of January 9 with $200 to his name—all of it borrowed from his mother—and raced to his old apartment. The reason for his haste was obvious. He and Connie had left many of their belongings, including all of their furniture, behind when they'd moved to Minnesota and Howard, learning from friends that Connie had gone to New York to claim them, wanted to be sure she took nothing beyond those items granted her in the divorce settlement. Howard, in spite of his late start, arrived first—primarily because Connie, not realizing he was on his way, stopped to have a drink with Wilton Matthews.

Howard was appalled by what he saw. The apartment was a disaster. Virtually everything in sight was broken or damaged in some way. Doors were off their hinges. Howard and Connie's furniture and lampshades were pock-marked with cigarette burns. Even the carpeting was destroyed, saturated with urine from the Weisinger's new baby who was, as Mrs. Weisinger explained, not being trained, "until they moved into their new home." Howard was furious, but it was only the first of many aggravations to confront him on his third New York sojourn.[9]

For the next few days, Howard's time was spent repairing, as best he could, the damage done to his apartment, visiting old friends, and inquiring into his ex-wife's alleged infidelities with a number of persons, most notably his good friend Wilton Matthews. Matthews, for his part, was quite forthcoming over his role in the affair, as was Wilton's wife, Hilda. But then Matthews could afford to be, for he had bigger things to deal with than any problems caused by a jealous ex-husband.

For several years, Wilton Matthews and fellow editor Kenneth Hutchinson had been running a lucrative scam out of the offices of Trojan & Culture Publications. They would buy stories that didn't exist by authors known to the company and instruct the accounting department to cut checks for them. They would then forge the authors' signatures, cash the checks, and pocket the money. In January of each year, the pair would intercept all the affected W-2 forms and destroy them prior to mailing.

In 1947 something went wrong. With Matthews and Hutchinson out of the office, someone, acting on their own initiative, dropped the authors' tax statements in the mail. One local writer, by the name of T.W. Ford, who had sold stories to Trojan in the past but had sent none to them in 1946, was astounded to receive a statement saying he had earned $2,850 from the company during that same period. Ford wasted no time in contacting general manager Frank Armer for an explanation. Armer, in turn, wasted little time in contacting the district attorney's office.

Wilton tried to head off the investigation as best he could. When that failed, he burned every bit of evidence he could lay his hands on and proceeded to drown his problems in the bottom of a bottle. On January 23, Wilton was taken into custody. On his way to the courthouse, the district attorney's men allowed him to stop in the bar where Howard was drinking with Wilton's wife Hilda and say goodbye.

The Trojan scandal touched Howard Wandrei in more ways than one. For one thing, it threatened the very company upon which he had become dependent as an author. More importantly, Wilton's attempt to destroy evidence had destroyed a good portion of Howard's work as well. Many of Howard's manuscripts, both published and unpublished, were reduced to ashes in the company's incinerator. Along with them went the majority of the firm's file copies and financial records. With Hilda's assistance, Howard searched the Matthews' home for anything that might have survived, eventually finding but a single manuscript, the original draft of "Exit, Willy Carney."

Devastated by the loss of so much of his work, Howard wasn't sure what to do. Worse yet, his friendship with Matthews, easy access to advance payments, and past prison record made him a prime suspect in a conspiracy charge. $96,000 was still missing and the district attorney's men, as well as the Internal Revenue Service, were determined to find it. Howard soon became convinced he was being followed. In between bouts of understandable paranoia, he spent many hours in police inter-rogation rooms, being questioned over his authorship of certain stories. Connie was not above suspicion either. On more than one occasion during their marriage, she'd stopped by the Trojan offices to pick up one of Howard's checks, signed his name to it, and gotten it cashed. With investigators poring over every canceled check they could find, and well aware of her relationship with Matthews, it was an arrangement that raised suspicions.

In the end, Matthews and Hutchinson went to prison while Howard and Connie went on with their lives, finally freed of suspicion or, at least, not charged with any crime. Still, the Trojan scandal marks the essential end of Howard's career as an author. He continued writing, but would never work for Trojan again—even when Frank Armer asked him to.

Howard stayed in New York for several months, living with old friend Talbot Southwick in an apartment over a funeral parlor.

His days were spent meeting fellow writers, editors, and agent Des Hall, but little came of it except *Key To Trouble*, an unfinished novel featuring detective Vik Mlada, that the Chambrun Agency was unable to sell. His nights were spent in the Village, drinking with old friends like Southwick. On May 13th, 1947, his New York affairs finally settled, Howard returned home to Minnesota where he immediately suffered a nervous breakdown.[10]

From the Summer of 1947 on, Howard Wandrei's life, while increasingly rooted to the old family homestead at 1152 Portland Avenue, became, if anything, even more complex and convoluted than before. This is not to say that Howard was *doing* more than he had previously. Rather, it's more a matter of the threads of his life and art merging together and entwining themselves in ways that are difficult to decipher, let alone describe.

The first step in this process was Howard's suddenly renewed interest in the works of the English mystic/artist/poet William Blake. He'd been introduced to Blake nearly two-decades earlier by fellow University of Minnesota and Central High School alumnus Virginia Bohan, then a member of the Board of Directors of *The Minnesota Quarterly*, as well as an occasional, albeit peripheral, member of the Wandrei social circle. What rekindled his interest in Blake is unclear, although it may have been the result of his breakdown. Whatever was responsible, Blake's influence was continuous in Howard's work from that time onward.

The first effects of this interest may be seen in the novel *Key To Trouble*, the first draft of which, written amidst the formaldehyde stench of Tal Southwick's second floor apartment, was a straight mystery, aimed at the developing paperback market of the day. The second draft, written soon after his breakdown, is a complete rewriting of the first; a version that attempts to meld Blakian symbolism and design (Howard's version of which was dubbed "Radial Symbolism") to the hard-boiled fiction of his past. In this second version, the first of a projected trilogy, detective Vik Mlada, Howard's main "series" detective, must solve a puzzle involving a curious key. The key is a map, leading to a spiral cave that represents, in Blakian terms, a "Vortex of Power." While never completed, the novel and its accompanying illustrations show the direction Howard's later work was to take.

Soon after laying this novel aside, Wandrei embarked on a period of intense creativity. It began with a burst of artistic production the results of which he referred to as "Series IV." The drawings from this period are an eclectic mix. Some are incredibly detailed miniature landscapes in sizes ranging from two to three inches square. Others are, at first blush at least, intricate line drawings of mundane or even mainstream design—quite different from his earlier style. Still others are models of Blakian, or rather "Radial Symbolic" structure. This later group of drawings are the most curious of all as they represent a unique form of artistic design: that of artwork as outline; drawings bordered by plot elements or featuring signposts of character traits and events.

In addition to the drawings, Howard also produced a number of short stories and novellas. Most, like "'Tis Claude," "The Lunatic," and "Daddy Smells of Gasoline" are models of symbolic design and, as such, intricately tied to their pre-existing illustrations.

Howard's interest in William Blake was soon to receive another boost as well. In the early thirties, Virginia Bohan had married David Erdman, yet another product of St. Paul Central. They'd begun dating at the University of Minnesota and, on one of those early dates, had attended a party at the Wandrei's Portland Avenue home. There, Virginia had introduced her husband-to-be to Howard Wandrei for the first time. In the early forties, the Erdmans visited Howard and Connie in New York and, several years later, after Howard's divorce, their paths crossed again when David Erdman, now a professor, took a position in the English department at the University of Minnesota.

Some years earlier, at Virginia's instigation, David Erdman had himself become intrigued by the work of William Blake and started down a path that would soon make him one of America's foremost Blake scholars. In the period of 1949/1950, several years prior to the publication of his landmark *William Blake; Prophet Against Empire*, Erdman had written an article on Blake's London entitled *"Lambeth & Bethlehem in Blake's Jerusalem."* Needing a map to accompany it into publication, he turned to Virginia's old friend Howard Wandrei, who obliged after a great deal of painstaking research of his own. The result, both article and map, were published in the February 1951 issue of *Modern Philology*. Howard's map was later reproduced as an illustration in Erdman's book where it has remained through three editions and a number of reprintings.

Howard's painstaking research on the map led him deeper into William Blake and eventually soured his relationship with the Erdmans. The problem was that their visions of Blake were different, not just in terms of background (Howard as artist, Erdman as academic), but in terms of outlook. Erdman, like many academics of the day, had a number of socialist leanings and, in Howard's view at least, these sympathies caused him to effectively misinterpret much of Blake's message. Howard, on the other hand, was moving in a quite different direction. Up until the Korean War, Howard had remained essentially apolitical in spite of his strong Republican leanings. By the early 1950's he had become a radical anti-communist who hated Truman and loved Eisenhower—but not McCarthy. While much of Howard's anti-communist rage, such as his lengthy poem "Tart Red Cherry Pits for A Child," are almost laughable, other aspects, such as his prediction, in the early 1950's, that the Soviet Union would collapse of its own economic weight, seem positively prophetic. In any event, his views were hardly typical of academics or artists of the day and, in time, they caused him to drift away from, or totally break with, such old friends as the Erdmans, Grace Holmes (the Communist Party candidate for Vice-President in 1948), and Joseph Weinberg, an atomic scientist and U of M professor who assisted Howard Wandrei in researching "The Rydberg Numbers," a Solar Pons story by August Derleth.[11]

The radicalization of Howard's politics during this time also brought him into increasing conflict with his brother Donald. However, most of the problems between the two men had little or nothing to do with politics.

The relationship between Donald and Howard Wandrei—and, indeed, between all of the Wandrei siblings—had always been unstable, if not downright dysfunctional. In 1949, for instance, Howard made what appears to have been a "final" break with his brother David. After an

Donald, Constance and Howard Wandrei enjoy a quiet dinner in New York during the 1930's. Photograph taken at the Café Shangri-La, corner of Lexington and 47th Street.

A rare example of Howard's advertising art, which originally appeared in the March, 1936 issue of *House Beautiful* magazine.

altercation in the family home, police were called and David was banned "forever" from the confines of 1152 Portland.[12]

Actually, from 1947 onward, there seem to be few occasions in which the Wandrei household was not in some kind of uproar, whether by visiting friends, relatives, or feuds between the siblings. Of all the difficulties between family members, none seem to have reached the levels attained by Donald and Howard Wandrei. Between 1947 and 1956, the brothers battled over any number of items and often went for extended periods without speaking to each other. On at least one occasion, a disagreement became so violent that it resulted in a physical altercation. Interestingly enough, the main point of contention between the brothers does not appear to be either politics or their long-running rivalry. Rather, it seems to have been Howard's divorce.

While the full details of Donald's relationships with both Howard and his sister-in-law may never be known, some intriguing details are starting to emerge. In the early 1950's, Howard confided to both Virginia Erdman and Gerald Fosbroke that his marriage to Connie had, in fact, been Donald's idea. While the reasons for Donald's interest in Howard and Connie's marriage are unclear, it does go a long way toward explaining his reaction to the divorce. While the rest of the Wandrei clan rallied around Howard, and Howard struggled to decide how to proceed, Donald came down firmly—and none too subtly—on the side of the Colestocks. In fact, during late 1949 and early 1950, at a point when the Howard-Connie feud had reignited and threatened to return to the courts in a new round of litigation, Donald started returning his brother's letters unopened. At the time, both Donald and Connie were living in New York and seeing each other on a regular basis.

In fairness to Don, it must be said that he may have had good reasons for his actions. Howard, after fighting hard to win custody of his daughter, never really knew how to deal with her after the separation. Like many children of divorce, she was often used as a pawn in the ongoing battle between her parents; and it seems unlikely that either Howard or Connie were totally innocent in the matter.

An effective and lasting truce between families was finally established in 1950. In January, a meeting in the offices of Rudolph Low, Howard's lawyer, effectively ended the threat of further legal action. Then, in June, Donald returned from New York and reestablished residence in the family home. Two months later, when Connie flew into town for a visit, Donald acted as intermediary and, somehow, managed to bring the two of them together. After that meeting, Howard and Connie were able to establish an increasingly peaceful and positive relationship, much to the benefit of all concerned.

In late 1950, Donald moved to California and took a job as a Hollywood songwriter. During the next few months, in between working on screenplays with Henry Borsha and writing lyrics for songs like "Bananas, Bananas, Bananas," Donald kept up an intense correspondence with his younger brother. In one letter, dated January 20, 1951, Don put forth his idea on the interconnectedness of artistic design: that of a circle of nine pyramids, joined by ramps and bridges, and representing "the relationship of form and structure and technique in all Fields."

Howard, deeply versed in the symbolism of William Blake, the character studies of Gerald Fosbroke, the metaphysical musings of Tal Southwick, and his own version of artistic interconnectedness (Radial Symbolism), jumped into the correspondence with both feet; accepting his brother's basic design while, at the same time, adapting and expanding it along his own lines. The result is the now notorious *The Circle of Pyramids*, a curious cycle of letters, heavily dominated by those of Howard Wandrei, that discuss not just Blake and Fosbroke, Circled Pyramids and Radial Symbolism, but also such apparently unconnected elements as H.P. Lovecraft's cosmic vision, the sex-life of pulp author Steve Fisher, and *Dianetics* by L. Ron Hubbard. While Don's later plans to publish these letters in book form seem almost inexplicable, they are quite illuminating in many areas. Most importantly, they shed light on just what Howard was up to in his later work; as he tried to blend fiction, sculpture, graphic design and symbolism into one unified whole.

The entire surviving text of *The Circle of Pyramids*—all 80,000 words of it—was written in less than six weeks.[13] After February 10, Howard's enthusiasm for writing long letters on the subject seems to have cooled. Instead, he was moving rapidly to attempt a come-back as a writer.

In early 1951 Howard seems to have been trying to do everything at once. In addition to writing at least two stories, a poem and a couple of songs (using a coded musical notation he'd developed himself), Howard returned to his hobby of "inventing" things—some of which he tried to market through commercial channels, others of which became short articles aimed at *Popular Mechanics*. He also changed agents, moving from Des Hall at the Chambrun Agency to Fred Pohl of the Wylie

Agency, and somehow managed to get roped into a TV project in Austin, Texas that involved old friends Eric Rolf and Gerry Fosbroke.

Then, in April, Wilton Matthews was released from Sing-Sing. Having nowhere to go and little cash, he called Howard to ask for a loan. Howard wired him some money and, before he fully realized what was happening, Matthews had boarded a train bound for St. Paul and taken up residence on the Wandrei's couch. Whether out of pity or a remaining residue of friendship, Howard decided to help his old friend get back on his feet.

An attempt to get Matthews a job at Bigelows fell flat, but he did start doing some free-lance work for Gene Colestock, Connie's father.[14] Howard soon came to see Wilton Matthews as little more than a drunken con-man and, possibly, a thief as well. After his wallet disappeared, Wandrei became increasingly concerned that his former in-laws were about to be taken advantage of. He threw Matthews out of the house and, after May of 1951, appears never to have seen him again.

Not surprisingly, the return of Wilton Matthews succeeded in opening some old wounds. By September, Howard was again in trouble with the IRS, and it's likely that some of their questions involved the still-missing money from the Trojan Scandal. By October, Matthews, continuously drunk and addicted to Hexadrine, was phoning Donald Wandrei from Las Vegas and begging for money—the $500 he'd taken from Connie and the contents of Howard's missing wallet obviously long gone.

In spite of the disruptions caused by Matthews, Howard continued to work at a fever pitch. His passion for inventions continued unabated and he became involved in yet another television project, this one involving Clement Haupers, Eric Rolf, and a local station. The death of his uncle Lou in North Dakota also began to take up a lot of Howard's time. With Donald still in California, the disposition of the family inheritance became Howard's responsibility. The resulting oil speculation, centering on Uncle Lou's holdings in the Williston Basin, appear to have paid off handsomely. After 1952, neither of the Wandrei brothers ever had to work again.

In early 1952, Howard Wandrei flew to California and he and Donald embarked from there on an extended road trip. Howard flew into San Francisco where he stayed for several weeks with Kay Newton and her "husband" Ken. Then, flying down the coast to Los Angeles, he spent time with his old U of M mentor, Dr. Malcolm MacLean at UCLA and linked up with Don and his girlfriend, the actress Dorothy Hart, to tour the RKO studios.[15] Heading east they passed through Tucson and El Paso on their way to the town of Alamo in the extreme south of Texas. There they spent several days with Gerald Fosbroke, author of books like *Character Reading Through Analysis of the Features*, and his wife Josephine. After accompanying the Fosbrokes on a brief excursion into Mexico, the brothers packed up the car and headed for home. What sounds to be a pleasant trip was anything but that. From Los Angeles on, the brothers were at loggerheads, with Donald in a hurry to get home and Howard preferring to spend more time visiting his seldom-seen friends. Worse yet, on the drive back Howard became ill and, by Kansas City was, in his own words, "bleeding like a stuck pig."

Bad news of a sort also awaited Howard upon his return home. After several years of failing to get any of his fiction published, *The Mysterious Traveler Magazine* had reprinted his old *Detective Fiction Weekly* story, "Smot Guy" under a new title. This was bad news for two reasons. One was that Howard had not been paid for it. The other was that, like a number of his early mysteries, "Smot Guy" was at least semi-autobiographical, and Howard feared that its reprinting might cause some unpleasant ramifications. Howard sent several letters to both Bob Arthur, the editor, and his new agent Fred Pohl. Obviously unhappy with the results, he later dropped Pohl as an agent.

In the Summer of 1952, Howard went traveling again. This time he went east, and he went alone. As with the first trip, details are sketchy. The only thing certain is that it ended with Howard Wandrei, once again, fighting for his life in a New York hospital. This time it was not illness that felled him, but rather a car driven by a hit and run driver. When he was well enough to travel, Howard returned home and continued his recuperation in Minnesota.

Howard Wandrei had no doubt as to his own mortality. Twice before, he'd been hospitalized and near death due to pneumonia. As early as 1946, he'd taken to referring to himself as being on "borrowed time." Now, in the aftermath of his New York accident, the shadow of eternity began to close in on what was left of Howard Wandrei. Still suffering head and shoulder problems, Howard tried to start a mail-order business with an old friend, an interior decorator named Warren Rogers. Nothing came of it. Less than six months after returning from New

York, with his injuries not yet healed, Howard was back in the hospital again.

After ten or eleven transfusions and nearly a month in the hospital, Howard returned home, weak, feeble and unable to walk even a short distance without the aid of a cane. Among his diagnosed problems were heart disease, kidney disease, cirrhosis of the liver, pernicious anemia, yellow jaundice, and arthritis. With such a list of illnesses, it is hardly surprising that no one in the hospital expected him to survive; but survive he did. Still, when Howard returned home it was with the full and certain knowledge that he would be dead—if the doctors were right—in two years at the most.

While very little has been written of Howard Wandrei, most of what has mentions his death from cirrhosis of the liver and paints a picture of Howard as a drunken invalid; a man who drank himself to death in much the same way that a laboratory rat, given a choice between food and cocaine, will eventually starve itself to death. Howard Wandrei was no white rat. Nor, in fact, was he the increasingly dedicated alcoholic that some have imagined him to be. In fact, Howard Wandrei's alcoholism, and his eventual death from it, are questions that need to be looked at in some detail.

There can be no doubt that Howard Wandrei was a heavy drinker during his New York days. This is as true of Howard as it is of Donald or, for that matter, most other writers of the period. Amazingly enough, Howard's drinking appears, from all available evidence, to have been heavily related to place. Or, put another way, removed from New York and the circle of friends that he and Connie had acquired there, Howard seems to have been no more than a moderate "social" drinker. Moreover, Howard's returns from New York were often followed by long stretches of total abstinence (at least eighteen months in the case of his 1947 mis-adventure). This evidence seems to indicate that, whatever damage was done to Howard Wandrei's liver, most of it can be blamed on events prior to May of 1947. During Howard's 1944 hospitalization for pneumonia, doctors had diagnosed him as having an enlarged liver (an early sign of cirrhosis) and encouraged him to lay off the booze. Howard had obliged—at least for a time. His two later trips to New York, in 1947 and the Summer of 1952, coupled with medications taken to relieve other conditions, may have simply pushed his already over-taxed liver over the edge.[16]

In spite of some wishful thinking and hopeful medical speculation, fueled by his old New York City collaborator Doc Smola, that a properly regulated diet might help to regenerate his liver, Howard had no illusions about his future. His attitude is summed up best by his journal entry of July 25, 1953, in which he states quite simply, "Back at work again on drawing, carving, writing. I hope to finish a lot of stuff before I kick off . . ."

True to his word, Howard continued his drawing and carving, albeit on a smaller scale than before. He also wrote several stories, including "Measure of Infinity," a somewhat altered version of his much discussed, but never written, "The Return of Timothy Murphy." August Derleth's intense criticism of this story in 1954 appears to have limited—but did not wholly eliminate—Howard's literary production from that point forward. In any event, Howard had found new interests; writing, drawing and carving took a back seat to jewelry-making and the business of buying and selling antiques. Contrary to his image as an invalid, Howard was as physically active as ever during 1954 and 1955. His jewelry designs and occasional finds at auctions and rummage sales were offered for sale through a number of Twin Cities antique and consignment stores. Additionally, he did watch and clock repair as well as occasional electroplating for a friend in the trade named Fifi Johnson. He also developed several methods of turning a fast buck. Sometimes when he needed extra money, he would go to Minneapolis, buy broken typewriters, and then drive back across the river and resell them at a quick 200% profit. Occasionally, if a machine of particular quality caught his eye, he would repair it first, and then either sell it at an increased profit or keep it for himself.

Ironically, if any of the Wandrei brothers had a drinking problem during this period it appears to have been Donald. By 1954, Howard had become a strict teetotaler with ample reason to be sensitive where alcohol was concerned. Donald, on the other hand, had been broken both creatively and romantically during his Hollywood tour and appears to have gone through an extended period of heavy drinking. At one point, the situation became so bad that Howard was driven to contact Clem Haupers, then vacationing in Mexico, and ask that he "have a talk" with Don about his drinking. Haupers, who'd known the boys since childhood, was aware of the situation and acceded to Howard's request.

Howard's apparent recovery from cirrhosis was only illusory. In February of 1956, after starting a new story called "The Sleeper,"

Howard was felled by "a bug" that was going around. Recovery was slow and incomplete. His weight fell to 125 pounds, 35 below where his doctors wanted him, and when Connie visited in June of 1956, he had assumed an almost skeletal appearance. Worse yet, he was beginning to have problems with his eyes. Not only had he gone from farsighted to nearsighted, he was experiencing almost perpetual double vision. Diabetes was suspected but remained undiagnosed for nearly a month.

By July 27, Howard was down to 119 pounds. Then, in early August, he contracted a serious case of blood poisoning. Massive injections of penicillin knocked out the infection, but Howard found himself unable to use his right hand for a time. Meanwhile, his weight had dropped to an even 100 pounds.

On August 18, 1956, the day after his diabetes was finally diagnosed, Howard suffered diabetic shock and lapsed into a deep coma. In the weeks that followed, as Howard fought to make yet another miraculous recovery, family and friends rallied around and lent their encouragement. Minor surgery to draw off an excess of edemous fluid relieved his discomfort somewhat, as did his eventual removal from the oxygen tent.

On September 4, Howard, now out of his coma, described his status in a brief handwritten note to old friend Kay Newton:

Quite weak; it has taken me a couple of days to read your letter of 29th Aug. I can't read at all except by using double loupes I made for watch repair, and these pinpoint, allowing no peripheral sight. No change as to this trouble. Very depressing.

Got hit with virus infection, have been fighting it with its agony in solar plexus three days. Can hardly breathe.

My hands cramp without letup also.

Everyone has been *swell*. Spectacular flowers in room always. People, even neighbors. Carton cigarettes from Fifi. Don in sometimes twice a day with real love, and I await his visits. Yes, he has the genius label; is most widely read scholar I know, much my superior. Thanks lots for your letters.

Love,
How

On September 5, the end finally came. At 10:00 a.m., while visiting with his brother Donald, Howard suffered an esophageal hemorrhage. Within an hour he was dead. Donald, badly shaken by his brother's death, would later report to August Derleth that Howard's last words were, "You know, Don, I've always wanted to write a play with just a song or two."

Funeral services for Howard Wandrei were held on the afternoon of September 7 at the Willwerscheid Mortuary in St. Paul. Afterwards his mortal remains were entombed in the family plot at Acacia Park Cemetery on a wooded hillside overlooking the Minnesota River.

Donald Wandrei was hit especially hard by the death of his younger brother. In spite of their almost continual problems, they had also been soul-mates of a sort. Within weeks of Howard's death, Donald had begun giving serious thought to what he might do to preserve his brother's legacy for future generations. One idea was to prepare a volume of Howard's Selected Letters, drawn primarily from his correspondence with August Derleth. The other was to drop the still unformed *Orson Is Here* in favor of an omnibus collection of Howard Wandrei stories entitled *Time Burial*. Little if any work appears to have been done on either project until at least 1959 when Donald, suffering the further shock of David Wandrei's sudden death from cancer, was inspired to begin work in earnest. Over the next few years, Donald saw five of his brother's drawings into print through the auspices of Arkham House and began organizing Howard's letters to Derleth with an eye toward publication. *Time Burial* itself, while announced as forthcoming on the jacket copy of *Poems for Midnight*, does not appear to have been started until sometime later. Ironically, the rise of Howard's underground reputation as an artist of unnatural skill and originality—driven by the publication of only a few of his earlier and less intricate drawings, and Donald's own nearly worshipful statements regarding them—completely overwhelmed what remained of his reputation as an author. During the late 40's and early 50's, Howard Wandrei had made a number of appearances, under his own name, in anthologies edited by Groff Conklin and August Derleth. Then, after 1956, his fiction disappeared from print for over fifteen years; only to re-emerge briefly in the 1970's with one story in *The Arkham Collector*, and two in Damon Knight's *Science Fiction of the Thirties* (1975). Since then, Howard Wandrei's work has been completely unavailable to all but a handful of collectors.

In 1987, Donald Wandrei passed away leaving an incredible cache of material behind. Included among these papers were boxes of material related to his younger brother. Besides Howard's surviving artwork, manuscripts and magazine file copies, Donald had also retained nearly all of his brother's other papers. Included among these were Howard's diaries, journals, address books, and thousands of pages of correspondence. Eventually disposed of by the Estate, parts of these archives may now be found in the Wisconsin and Minnesota Historical Societies, the John Hay Library at Brown University, and the Special Collections of the Temple University Library.

In preparing *Time Burial* for publication, the Editor has had to make several tough choices, not the least of which were those regarding its contents. As a result, the direction and scope of this project has changed several times. Initial contacts with the Estate in the late 1980's envisioned a single collection of Howard Wandrei fantasies. Subsequent acquisition of Wandrei's magazine file copies and the Estate's loan of the original *Time Burial* manuscript in 1990 expanded the project, at least conceptually, to include a multiple-volume collected works of Howard Wandrei. A verbal "agreement in principle" on the first book was reached with Rudy Low, the Estate's lawyer, but had to be placed on hold until such time as a final disposition of the Estate could be completed.

This final dispersal of the Wandrei papers in 1993 necessitated still more changes in the Editor's plans for the book now known as *Time Burial*. The sudden availability of over a dozen previously unpublished and/or unknown stories made it clear that, the initial preferences of both Donald Wandrei and the current Editor notwithstanding, *Time Burial could not* be a true omnibus collection. There was simply too much material available to fit comfortably into a single volume. The result is the book you now hold in your hands, a volume quite accurately subtitled "Vol. I of the Collected Fantasies of Howard Wandrei."

The division of Howard Wandrei's genre fiction into two books obviously precludes *Time Burial* from being considered a true omnibus. Still, in spite of the necessary omissions, including most of the unpublished material, this volume may be read as an amazingly thorough retrospective of the author's work in the triune fields of horror, science fiction and fantasy. In fact, with the exception of some bits of pure juvenalia, *Time Burial*, as it has finally developed, includes stories from every stage of Howard Wandrei's professional and post-professional career.

The earliest tales in this book, chronologically speaking, are "Over Time's Threshold" and "In the Triangle." Early versions of both were written in 1931 and 1932, apparently in conjunction with a creative writing class at the University of Minnesota. Like much of Howard's early work, they derive their strength not from plotting or characterization but rather from their odd power of description. Nightmare images and hazy vistas of dreamlike unreality predominate. It is hardly surprising that Howard's early stories are often confused with those of his brother Donald. The similarities are more than coincidental.

In a similar vein is "Time Burial," the story from which this book derives its title. Completed soon after Howard arrived in New York, it represents his first true attempt at making his way as a professional, self-supporting author. After being rejected by both *Weird Tales* and *Astounding*, the manuscript for this story went back into Howard's files where it remained until his death. Why Donald Wandrei chose it for use as a title story is unclear. One reason may be that its plot has more in common with Donald's work than it does with most of Howard's later efforts. At least part of it had been written in Donald's apartment while Howard searched for a place of his own and, as such, Don may have felt a greater proprietary interest in this story than his brother's later work.

The next group of stories, like "Time Burial," date from the period of Howard Wandrei's first New York adventure. While the plots still bear an unmistakable similarity to some of his brother's work, Howard was already beginning to show flashes of the techniques that would serve him so well in his later career: a sense of black humor, and a knack for creating flawed yet sympathetic characters. Three of these stories ("The Wall," "The God Box," and "The Other") appeared in *Astounding* and are typical of Howard's work, both published and unpublished, during this period. The fourth, "The Hand of the O'Mecca," is more of a throwback. Stylistically it has more in common with earlier tales, such as "In the Triangle" than it does with anything else he was writing at the time. "O'Mecca" is also a throwback in terms of its plot, being little more than a variation on several old folk tales, some of which can be dated back as far as Petronius—if not farther. While this type of "borrowing" was common among pulp writers, most of whom were struggling just to put food on the table, it was rare for Howard. In this case it seems likely that "O'Mecca" had its genesis in the writings of Montague Summers, a writer whose work was not unknown to the young Wandrei.

"Here Lies" (*Weird Tales*, Oct. 1937) and "Macklin's Little Friend" (*Astounding*, Nov. 1936) are, in a sense, transitional stories, in that they bridge the two main bodies of Howard Wandrei's work as a writer of science fiction and horror. Written during a period of time in which virtually all of his attention was being spent on detective fiction and the odd story for the Spicy's, they show a polish often lacking in his earlier genre efforts and foreshadow some of his best work. This is especially true in the case of "Macklin's Little Friend" whose most graphic scenes serve as a precursor to similar grotesqueries found in stories like "Danger: Quicksand" (*Unknown*, Sept. 1939).

"Macklin" can be seen as a "bridge" story in other ways as well. An early version of this story was written—and rejected—during Howard's first New York excursion. The story was later rewritten so extensively as to make it, essentially, a brand new tale. It was then rewritten at least once more before finally finding a publisher.

During the late 1930's, Howard was putting more and more of his efforts into stories for the "Spicy" pulps. While most of these were detective stories, a fairly large number were also fantasy and horror stories aimed at *Spicy Mystery*. Four of these tales, "Exit, Willy Carney," "Master-the-Third," "The Glass Coffin," and "O Little Nightmare" are included here.

The first, "Exit, Willy Carney" (aka "Exit"), is noteworthy primarily because it was the first story of his to be published by Trojan/Culture Publications. Too weird for the hard-boiled markets, and too hard-boiled for any of Howard's normal genre markets, all it needed was a little "sexing up" to make it perfect for the Spicys. A later, de-sexed version slated for an August Derleth anthology does not appear to have been completed.

Hard-boiled is also a good description for "Master-the-Third" (aka "Something in the Air"), a story noteworthy for its use of an old Wandrei haunt (Horatio Street) as a setting, and its rather lengthy explanation of the linkages between Greek mythology and the "red-skinned" people of Atlantis. These Red-Skinned Ancients appear in a number of Howard's stories and are probably derived from the Theosophical mythology of H.P. Blavatsky, but they are never "explained" elsewhere.

Another item of interest in "Master-the-Third" is, strangely enough, its sexual interlude. Included primarily to add an element of sexual titillation in an otherwise non-sexual story, its essential idea—that of an invisible sexual predator—was later used to great effect in "The Molester" (*Spicy Mystery*, December 1937).

"The Glass Coffin" (aka "Orchids of Death") is, in some respects, the most atypical of Wandrei's work in the *Spicy's*. In spite of its quasi-science-fictional elements, it's a story best described as pure weird-menace; more at home in the pages of *Horror Stories* or *Terror Tales* than in the magazines that Wandrei normally wrote for.

The final *Spicy* story, "O Little Nightmare," is in many ways the most notable of the four. Primarily this is due, not to the plot itself, but rather to its characters. Rodney and Ursula Quist, while somewhat fictionalized, are clearly caricatures of Howard and Connie themselves and, if Howard's correspondence is to be believed, highly accurate caricatures at that. Some internal evidence, such as the character of Betty Orson and the use of infidelity as a sub-plot, suggest that this story may, in fact, be the long-lost "Orson Is Here." Unfortunately, the manuscript for that story is not extant and was probably destroyed by Matthews in 1947. Because of this, not to mention Trojan's annoying habit of changing the title on nearly every story they published, we may never know if "O Little Nightmare" was actually a heavily re-written or edited version of that earlier tale.[17]

Perhaps the best stories in this volume are those taken from the pages of *Unknown*: "The Missing Ocean," "The Hexer," "Don't Go Haunting," "The Monocle," and "The Black Farm." Produced within a one-year period, they show a writer at the height of his creative powers and on a professional roll that must have had him feeling invincible as he racked up acceptance after acceptance.

"The Missing Ocean" was Howard's first sale to *Unknown* and was, in fact, cannibalized from two earlier Wandrei efforts. Captain Amandus Rudolf began life as the title character in the unpublished thousand word vignette "What Happened to Rudolph?" a story that appears to have been inspired by a real event and colored, much like H. Beam Piper's "He Walked Around The Horses," by early immersion in the writings of Charles Fort; especially those portions of *Lo!* that dealt with the strange disappearance of Benjamin Bathurst in 1809. The latter portions of "The Missing Ocean" are taken, almost verbatim, from an earlier published Wandrei story: "Time Haven" (*Astounding*, Sept., 1934).

Within a month, Howard had placed two more stories with *Unknown*, both of which appeared in their June, 1939 issue. The first was an odd little vengeance story entitled "Don't Go Haunting," a tale that Howard would later forget about until reminded of it by August Derleth. Memorable primarily for its occasional bursts of comic detail, "Don't Go Haunting" is also noteworthy for its elements of fictionalized auto-biography. While it is always dangerous to read too much of a writer's life into his work, there can be little doubt that Dolf and Kay Ornstein, like Rodney and Ursula Quist in "O Little Nightmare," are thinly dis-guised—and rather nasty—caricatures of both his wife and himself. Likewise, Wilbur Huron and Hogie McCaffery are obviously Wilton Matthews and another, less clearly identified acquaintance of the Wan-dreis. Count Lonczewski is, in reality, the Polish-born Count Stephan Colonna Walewski, a Zoroastrian magician and sometime dinner com-panion of both Wandrei and Matthews. Two years later, Walewski—or rather, Lonczewski—reappeared as a character in yet another Wandrei Atlantis-based fantasy, "The Persuader" (*Spicy Mystery,* January 1941).

In that same issue was "The Hexer," a story so highly regarded by Campbell and his editors that they later chose it for inclusion in their "best of" anthology, *From Unknown Worlds. Unknown's* readers, while they liked the story, were somewhat less enthusiastic. Typical was this critique from a young science fiction fan named Isaac Asimov:

> "The Hexer," by H.W. Guernsey—Four stars.
>
> Interesting and humorous, but I thought it was rather mean of Guernsey to allow the story to end with everyone still under the spell. It gives you a feeling of frustration because, of course, I was looking forward to an ending where everything was hunky-dory again.[18]

Readers upset by the irresolute and non "hunky-dory" ending of "The Hexer" were probably equally annoyed by Howard's November 1939 offering. Like "The Hexer," and "The Eerie Mr. Murphy" (*Esquire,* Nov. 1937), "The Monocle" is now generally considered to be one of Wandrei's best, although for quite different reasons. Humor and hard-boiled elements are not excluded from "The Monocle," but they are minimized. In their place is Ardanth, an enigmatic red-skinned sorcerer from ancient Cebes, a land long since lost to history; a civilization whose ruined temples lie buried and forgotten beneath the shifting sands of what is now the Sahara Desert. The plot, such as it is, concerns Ar-danth's quest for immortality, Constance Ydes' quest for Ardanth, and an emerald monocle with the power to foretell the future. All in all, a strange and indescribable story that manages to be both entertaining and disquieting at the same time.

The final story from *Unknown* to be included in this volume is "The Black Farm," a tale that essentially lifts "The Damned Thing" straight out of Bierce and plops it down in the middle of a Robert A. Garron hard-boiled mystery. The result is an odd combination: a farm on which everything has been painted black, a crazy farmer, an unsolved murder, a dangerous gun-toting sister-in-law, a state-wide man-hunt for a vicious gangster and, oh yes, an invisible man-eating monster. Howard seems to have had a lot of fun with this one and it shows. At one point he even puts himself, or rather his pseudonymous alter-ego, directly into the story; as "Art" Garron, a city detective in hot pursuit of mobster Tommy Mishaw.

The two remaining stories in this collection date from what might be called Howard Wandrei's "post professional" career. The first, "After You, Montagu," is a silly little vignette for which an intelligible description is as ill advised as it is impossible. The second, "'Tis Claude," is a serious work from Howard's Radial Symbolic (or Blakian) period. As such, some further background is probably needed.

As with many of Wandrei's Blakian works, "'Tis Claude" was written in the late 1940's, not long after he had put the second draft of his novel aside. While outwardly a poltergeist story, "'Tis Claude" is in fact the tale of a man, abandoned by his wife and caring for a young child, who has retreated into the safety of his past and is simply biding his time until "something happens." In a sense, Ballardi is himself a ghost, a routine-driven automaton whose existence finds validation only in the past. The old family homestead. His childhood memories.

Like most of his later stories, "'Tis Claude" is also highly autobiographical and there can be little doubt that Ralph Ballardi is, with only minor alterations, none other than Howard Wandrei himself. There's even a reference to deep-sea fishing off Chincoteague, a real-life vacation that, if references in Wandrei's letters are to be believed, seems to have been a sort of turning point in his relationship with Connie. Likewise, the symbolism in this story is pretty basic, with the exception of the cork-screw-shaped tunnel which has its roots in Blake's "vortex of power."[19]

Whatever weaknesses this story may have, there can be little doubt that Wandrei considered it one of his best. In *The Circle of Pyramids* he writes:

> I started reading through one of the carbons, for a story called "'Tis Claude," and cussed to myself and got up and walked around after a few paragraphs, because the story is "in there." I know this is an unusual thing to say, but that job is extraordinary and is jampacked with what we have been discussing, whether anybody else can see it or not. That's the one that Maggie Cousins at *Good Housekeeping* referred to for the "strange power" of pulling you into it. It is not popular writing it is obvious.

Perhaps not, but August Derleth, one of the harshest critics of Howard's post-1946 work still liked it enough to want it included in *Orson Is Here*.

Like all of Howard's stories from this period, "'Tis Claude" was preceded by an illustration, several elements of which may also have doubled as an outline.

If so, the drawing for "'Tis Claude" (page 115) is more subtle than most on this point; lacking as it does a progressive scale of sign posts or a bordering of plot elements. There are, however, several oddities in the drawing which, indecipherable though they may be, were meant to serve as some form of key. Specifically, curious readers will note the number and/or letter sequences in the upper right and left hand corners and, in the upper-center, the six-handed clock upon whose face the numbers have been replaced by the letters: R-E-C-O-R-D-E-D-T-I-M-E.

The illustration for "The Hand of the O'Mecca" was done at around the same time as the story itself (*i.e.*, 1934 or '35). Howard, who originally had dreams of illustrating his own stories, quickly abandoned the idea when he discovered that pulp editors had little use for writers who could also draw. This particular drawing was rejected by Farnsworth Wright of *Weird Tales* on the grounds that it would not reproduce properly on the magazine's pulp paper stock. It was later used as a dustjacket on Donald Wandrei's *The Eye and the Finger*—much to the dismay of Howard Wandrei, who had preferred a different, and no longer extant, drawing of Captain Rudolph.

The illustration for "The Other" is, in fact, a full-color ink and water-color portrait entitled "Jongkovski's Wife." Dated July 17, 1930, it was produced while Howard was incarcerated in the St. Cloud Reformatory and has no connection to his 1939 story of the same name (*Detective Fiction Weekly*, April 8, 1939).

Accumulations of personal and literary papers comparable to those of the Wandreis are rare. Even rarer are situations in which such materials become part of an Estate whose Executors exercise caution in regards to their disbursement. Fortunately, both have proven true of the Wandrei Estate. The Wandreis themselves never seem to have thrown anything away; their life-long habitation at 1152 Portland Avenue thus producing an archive of material almost incalculable in size and importance. The Estate, facing a truly daunting challenge, nevertheless took its responsibilities seriously. Moving slowly and methodically, they eventually effected a disbursement of the archives along organized lines. Perhaps the most unusual aspect of this disbursement was that the material was divided amongst an incredibly small, and geographically condensed, coitteriere of institutions and collectors.

With the exception of a small amount of illicit material that made its way to California, the vast majority of Howard's surviving papers remained in Minnesota; divided between the Minnesota Historical Society, a Minneapolis-based collector, and a couple of area bookdealers. *Time Burial*, and its lengthy biographic introduction, while primarily a result of the efforts of the Editor, can, in some ways, be considered a collaborative effort between all of these desperate parties who, through their love of the genre and respect for the Wandrei legacy, conspired to make this book possible. Special thanks are accorded to Tom and Kathy Stransky who were there at the beginning. Kudos also to David Miller and Judy Reynolds-Miller of For Collectors Only for their early research into, and organization of, Howard Wandrei's correspondence. Additionally, thanks must go to Todd Daniels-Howell, Patrick Coleman and Dallas Lindgren of the Minnesota State Historical Society for providing easy access to that organization's files even as they were being indexed and sorted. Beyond that we must acknowledge those without whose assistance and cooperation this book would not have been possible—in ANY form. Namely, Harold Hughesdon, executor of the Estate of Donald Wandrei, Philip J. Rahman and Dennis Weiler of Fedogan & Bremer, and Steven Stilwell of *Murder for Pleasure*, who planted the charges, handed the timer to someone who knew how to set it, and stepped back. The result, for better or worse, is the book you hold in your hands as well as those that are to follow it.

Additional thanks are also due the following:

James P. Roberts and Kay Price of the August Derleth Society, Virginia Bohan-Erdman, Richard L. Tierney (professor emeritus of the Secret Wandrei Society), Clark B. Hansen, Rodger Gerberding, Dick Wald, Stefan Dziemianowicz, Will Murray, Scott Wyatt, David Schultz, Rusty Hevelin, Lynn Rahman, Kathy Youker, Hugh B. Cave, R. Dixon Smith, Gerry Schattenberg, and the photocopying crew at the Minnesota Historical Society.

Finally, the editor would like to extend a special thanks to Cindy Rako, without whose keen secretarial skills the production of the definitive texts found in this book would not have been possible.

Fans of Howard Wandrei will be pleased to know that Cindy is already hard at work on the manuscripts that will eventually make up *The Last Pin* (Vol. I of Howard's Collected Mysteries) and *The Eerie Mr. Murphy* (The Collected Fantasies, Vol. II).

D. H. Olson
Minneapolis, Minnesota
July, 1995

NOTES

1 The 1949 catalog included a partial listing of contents for *Orson Is Here*. Of the fifteen stories listed, ten are included in this collection, one, "The Last Pin," will serve as the title story in Vol. 1 of Howard Wandrei's *Collected Mysteries*, and the remaining four are scheduled for reprinting in a future horror and science fiction collection tentatively titled *The Eerie Mr. Murphy*.

2 The title *Time Burial* was not original to the 1972 stock listing. It was first mentioned in 1964 as part of the jacket copy for the Donald Wandrei poetry collection *Poems for Midnight*.

3 In fairness to Howard, it must be noted that his diary entries for the period , while discussing the shortages and his employer's suspicions, also vehemently deny any guilt in the matter.

4 The art of batik making originated in Java and only reached the United States in the first two decades of the twentieth century. In essence, batik making involves covering a cloth in wax with a "tjanting pen" and then dipping it in dye. The dye stains any area of the fabric left unwaxed. The cloth is then rewaxed and dipped in another color of dye. This process continues until all of the desired colors have been used. In especially intricate designs, like those created by Howard Wandrei, as many as thirty separate waxings and dippings may be required.

   The traditional tjanting, or wax pen, is a primitive instrument that allows heated wax to be applied directly to the cloth by means of a hollow spout. Howard developed, and patented, a vastly improvement version. It included such innovations as an adjustable stylus, clog-proof spout, and an internal heating element that allowed the artist to adjust the temperature of the wax to within one-tenth of a degree.

5 As of this writing, the true nature of the Smola/Wandrei collaboration remains unclear. There is, however, some evidence to suggest that the actual writing was left entirely to Howard.

6 It would likely take an entire book to explain the full workings of the Trojan Empire and their connections to other publishing affiliates like DC and National Comics. Until such a book is written, interested readers will have to make do with Chapter 7 of Ron Goulart's cursory but entertaining study *The Dime Detectives* (Mysterious Press, 1988) and Will Murray's excellent article "An Informal History of the Spicy Pulps" in *Risqué Stories* (March, 1984).

7 Kay Holmes-Smith later went by the name of Kay Newton, and some of her collaborations with Howard may have appeared under that name. The reason for the name change was that she was living with a man named Ken Newton. Kay assumed the name of Newton simply to keep up appearances and avoid unsavory gossip.

8 Possibly Dell. Wandrei's letters to August Derleth in June of 1943 cover the proposal in some detail, but never mention the name of the publisher.

9 The details on this incident, as well as for most of Howard's other New York experiences during this period, are taken almost exclusively from Wandrei's Diary. Some supplemental information has also been gleaned from Howard's later letters to August Derleth.

10 Besides stress, detoxification appears to have been a major cause of this breakdown. A detailed, first person account of this breakdown - hallucinations and all - may be found in Howard's journal.

11 Weinberg, if he is remembered at all today, is probably best known as the famous "Scientist X"; the alleged Soviet agent named, but never formally charged, by the House Un-American Affairs Committee (HUAC).

12 The words "final" and "forever," while common in the correspondence of both brothers, were seldom either. While David appears to have had little contact with his adopted family after 1949, he is known to have visited Howard during his final illness in 1956.

13 Since writing the introduction new material has come to light which makes this statement somewhat questionable. It now appears that some of the letters may have been written as much as a year earlier, while Donald was in New York, and included in *TCOP* by mistake. Nevertheless, the bulk of *TCOP was* completed between January 1, 1951 and February 10, 1951.

14 Howard's contact and "friend" at Brown & Bigelow was its president, Charlie Ward, a local millionaire and former inmate at Leavenworth. Some recent researches into St. Paul's Underworld suggest that Ward also had close ties with Meyer Lansky, Benjamin "Bugsy" Siegel, and New York's "Murder Incorporated." (*John Dillinger Slept Here, a Crooks' Tour of Crime and Corruption in St. Paul, 1920-1936* by Paul Maccabee, Minnesota Historical Society Press 1995, pages 54 & 55.)

15 Miss Hart's first big break in the movie business coincided with Howard's arrival. Interested readers may find her playing the female lead, opposite George Raft, in *Loan Shark* (1952).

16 Wandrei appears to have suffered from hypochondria along with everything else. Because of this he was often given to self-medication and, for long periods, took regular doses of everything from calcium to iodine to odd vitamin supplements.

17 There is also conflicting evidence to suggest that "Orson is Here" is a completely separate story which just happens to have a plot similar to that of "Nightmare." Further research among Howard's surviving papers may yet turn up the answer.

18 From the letters column of *Unknown* (August, 1939).

19 Vortices were also important elements in the cosmology of Tal Southwick. In a letter to Howard Wandrei dated 3-1-48 he explains vortices thusly:

> "All conflicts. Clash of time against position . . . The Vortex can be any whole unit of moving and solid parts . . . Friction results. But friction can be negative or positive. The friction is the intermediate between action and reaction; cause and effect. . . . In summary: Any unit. Divide it into position and time. These clash. There is thrown off either a positive or negative . . .
>
> "Vortex involves a constant whirling or confusion. Out of the whole superior or inferior forces emerge: excrement, ideas, atomic particles, planets, reason, structure, specimens, ad infinitum."
>
> The full explanation covers three pages and includes two diagrams. The above excerpts will have to suffice for our purposes.

TIME BURIAL

The Collected Fantasy Tales of
HOWARD WANDREI

The Hexer

OXBORO *ENQUIRER* JUNE 2. —at the departmental hearing on the Kramer case, Patrolman Brian Daugherty insisted stubbornly on his original version of the odd affair. Off duty and in plain clothes, he was walking home. He was nearing the deserted intersection of Dale Avenue and Fourth Street shortly after ten o'clock last Monday evening when a man "come helling around the corner." Asked what he meant by "helling," Daugherty explained, "Like mad, like a banshee. He was traveling like a bat out of— I mean he was really traveling."

Commissioner Hopkins asked: "Are you familiar with banshees, Daugherty?"

Without cracking a smile, Daugherty said: "My old lady told me about a couple of them she saw in Ireland, but I never saw one myself."

Mayor Anderson said impatiently: "Let's get ahead."

Daugherty recited, "Another man busts around the corner almost as fast as the first one who I was shagging."

"Got eyes in the back of your head?"

"I heard him. The first guy was running light; the second guy was running heavy."

"The second guy. That would be Heinrich Kramer?"

"Yessir; only I didn't know who he was then, though. He come boiling around the corner hanging onto his head. Like this." Daugherty demonstrated, grabbing his head like a basketball and making a face. "He looked nuts, with his eyes glaring that way. I had my gun out, and when he saw it he stopped. I asked him what was his hurry, and he said his head. 'My head,' he says, just like that. The guy he was chasing was gone already, so I went for Kramer, just walking easy toward him. Right away he ducked back around the corner, and when I got there, he was halfway down the block already and picking up speed all the time."

Jan Kupra, representing the *Enquirer*, asked: "Aren't you pretty handy with your gun, Daugherty?"

"I'm a good shot," Daugherty admitted modestly. "I got him when he was over a block away."

"You just took aim and shot him. If you'd killed him, it would have been murder."

Daugherty got red in the face, and said: "He'll tell you so himself. First I yelled him to halt and he—"

"You yelled him to halt?" Kupra mimicked.

"Get along with this," the mayor ordered.

"I yelled him to halt, and he kept on going. Then I fired over his head, and he still kept on going, so I brung the aim down a little bit."

"And you got him," said Kupra. "And he skinned his nose and his knees, and might have cracked his skull and died, and it would still be murder. Do you like to shoot men in the back, Daugherty?"

"Shut up!" Mayor Anderson shouted, "or I'll throw you right out of here myself!"

"I was shooting for his legs," Daugherty said, "but the way he was running, I had to aim higher. He ain't hurt much, except he ain't comfortable sitting down. What the hell, I thought he was trying to hold up that other guy, and I had to stop him.

"When I got to him, chief, he was cussing around like I'd have to throw him in the klink if there was anybody listening to him but me. He was calling me names that—"

"Never mind. Mr. Kramer is noted for his vocabulary outside of Oxboro."

"Yessir. Then he started talking wild about his head again. He said that guy he was chasing done something to his head. I asked him what, and he clammed up. I took him to the hospital on account of that little puncture, and that's all, sir."

Heinrich Kramer, of course, is the bard of Oxboro. He is as well known for his several great novels as for his own almighty opinion of them, classing himself with Hardy, Maugham and others. He has long been considered the leader of Oxboro's café society. It was ascertained by police that on Monday evening Kramer the Great was drinking in the exclusive Number 400 and holding forth to companions, when he was annoyed by a stranger staring at him and chuckling. Kramer made a comment to his friends about the stranger, abruptly clapped his hands to his head and knocked over a table on his way to reach the man who was staring at him. The man got up hurriedly and left, with Kramer in chase.

Mr. Kramer has confined himself to his home, refusing to be interviewed, refusing in fact to bring charges against Patrolman Daugherty.

"There's no sense in it; it's whacky," Kupra said. "What's all this business about his head? There was nothing wrong with his head except for its size. You can't go around shooting prominent citizens indiscriminately, Daugherty."

Mayor Anderson said: "I warned you, Kupra; you're only here to listen. Now GET OUT!"

The mayor screamed the way he does whenever he gets the chance, and everybody in Oxboro knows how he gets grapefruit-purple in the face and sticks his hammy ears out, and hikes his shoulders up so that it looks as though he hasn't got any neck.

The mayor then told Daugherty, "You, too, patrolman. Get out, and take your banshees along with you. Get back to your post, and next time don't be too handy with your gun."

Why the famous Heinrich Kramer acted as he did, is a mystery. But he chose to run when arrested, and he didn't stop when Daugherty fired a warning shot.

The only description of the man whom Kramer was chasing is that he was slight, elderly but athletic, and well-dressed in a dark suit, black topcoat, hat and shoes. As yet no clue to this individual's identity has been found—

A few days later in his column, *The Banana Stem*, Jan Kupra wrote:

There is something funny going on in Oxboro. The secret won't last long, because the mortality among secrets shaves one hundred percent pretty close. For the time being, certain people are acting with suspicious furtiveness; they jump up and beat it out of restaurants while you're talking to them, snub old friends on the street, and some of them stick inside their houses as though there's a plague on the loose. Maybe it's a secret society, and maybe it's political, huh? If you don't think strange habits and unnatural actions and secret plots are dangerous, remember what happened to Heinrich Kramer. According to the way they're behaving, we could name a few names who belong in the bughouse down the river. Names you've seen in print before, too—

The streetcars in Oxboro are way longer and wider and more powerful than the trolleys in New York. They are painted bright canary-yellow, and the seating accommodations consist of lengthwise seats in front and rear, crosswise seats in the middle. In the crosswise seats passengers look at the backs of heads and study dandruff, coiffures, and types of ears. In the lengthwise seats passengers sneak looks at pretty legs, succumb to the hypnotic interest of blemishes and deformities, and shorten the ride with successive mental sneers at all those hopeless, idiotic specimens of humanity lined up across the aisle.

Kupra owned an expensive sedan which he used for pleasure; he took the streetcar to the shop and elsewhere during the day, because it looked democratic; besides, being a born snoop, he never tired of studying faces, strange or familiar. He liked to analyze, to sift all the fascinating details which make up a countenance, to take a face apart and put it back together again like God. An old hand at the game, he was able to say, "That man has the eyes of a murderer"; or "Well-dressed as he is, the man's ears are more animal than human." On the 7th of June, Kupra was riding in the rear section of a streetcar on the Hill Park line, and practicing industriously his refined, private brand of cannibalism.

The sky was all blue, and the sun was shining particularly on Oxboro. Some of the green lawns and boulevards were splashed with dandelions in beds, like microspores of pollen each expanded to giant size. Having finished his covert inspection of Passengers Number 1 and 2, Kupra went to work with his eyes and mind on the third individual from the left. Kupra read from left to right.

This person was an old man of perhaps seventy winters. Whatever his stature was in its prime, he had diminished to gnomelike proportions. Height: five-feet-four; weight: a hundred to a hundred and ten pounds; white hair, fashionably barbered. He was a neat person, and sat with his knees close together, his spine straight, his slim, girlish hands folded asleep composedly in his lap. His necktie was correct with his shirt, whose collar encircled his slender throat with accurate, soft dimensions. He wore a dark-gray hat, a suit of hard gray worsted that was immaculately pressed and tailored, sheer socks that were snug around his ankles, shapely shoes which were narrow and short and pointed, painstakingly carved out of solid ebony and polished with oil. His lips were compressed to a thin line, and he was so smoothly shaven that his face was a girlishly fresh cameo. His ears were Puckish, close to his head. Kupra observed the observant stillness of the stranger's eyes, and afterward he could never remember what color they were. All told, the dear little old man who was riding on the seat across the aisle was a diminutive aristocrat whose lips smiled subtly about something.

Kupra looked along his nose with great dubiety, then slowly raised his face to the varnished, hooded architecture of the ceiling, just to make sure; his nose was a yard long, or longer. He sighted along it, in the manner of a hunter centering on a deer with a .351 rifle.

None of the other passengers observed the casual lifting of his eyebrows.

Kupra brought his attention down again and the attenuated schnozzle wabbled elastically. When he turned his head too suddenly, his newly acquired deformity wagged obscenely, like the tail of a hairless dog. He lifted his hand to his face with a careless gesture, and made sure that the long, nude proboscis was there. It was there, all right, equal in length to four or five frankfurters joined end to end, about a pound in weight since it was boneless. It was his own secret, obviously invisible to all the other passengers. Save perhaps one. He stared hard at the beautifully tailored old pixie across the aisle.

He was shaking with some private mirth. When Kupra's eyes returned to him, he rang the bell abruptly and reached the back platform as the car arrived at an intersection. The back gates opened and he got off, and was gone at a brisk, catfooting walk after a glance through the windows at the stricken Kupra.

The broomstick of nose was the old man's doing. It was he who had escaped from Heinrich Kramer, chasing him because he had made the Oxboro bard's big head a private actuality. And now he had hexed Kupra, hanging a pole of a snout on his face, giving the keyhole-peeper a branch of anatomy which he could really snoop with.

Appalled by the indecency of the fate that had overtaken him, Kupra turned his head to look out the window at the green lawns riding by and get rid of the whole idea. There was a man sitting beside him, and the gun barrel of Kupra's nose batted him across the Adam's apple.

"Glob!" exclaimed the man, and took hold of his throat. He glared suspiciously at the columnist, who sat with hands folded, staring innocently across the way. Frowning with puzzlement and worry, the man kept swallowing experimentally and gently massaging his gozzle.

As for Kupra, he refrained from stroking the pain out of the marvelous beak where its architecture had bent across his fellow-passenger's neck.

For the duration of the ride he kept the phantom schnozzle gently clamped between his knees, anchoring it out of harm's way and pondering the immaculately dressed old Hexer's malicious talent.

He got off at Ashland, his street. Big elms were spaced along the boulevard, and the warm shadow under their canopy of foliage was conducive to thought and experimentation. With no citizens in sight, he explored the ghostly sniffer from end to end as though playing a dirge on a flute, and there was not the least doubt about its authenticity. It was a hell of a quandary to be in.

A housewife interrupted the chore of sweeping off her porch to watch the rapt, sleepwalking exercises which Kupra was doing with his arms.

"Hello, Mr. Kupra," she called, in the tone of a person addressing a drunk. "Is something the matter?"

"Just exercising, Mrs. Jefferson," he lied resignedly. "You know how your arms get stiff."

He continued on his way with his hands in his pockets, shaking his head slowly with dull disbelief. His nose wagged; it had the same flexibility as its length in garden hose. He was the proprietor of a phenomenon which would baffle surgery. No wonder Kramer had run from Daugherty; if he had divulged what the Hexer had done to his head, the authorities might have consigned him to the nuthouse down the river. On Kupra it was a terrible punishment to visit for his crimes of reporting. With a stroke of his eye the old man had done it, the mischievous devil.

When he reached his number, he observed two cars parked at the curb, empty. He had guests as usual. He had loaned his keys a couple of times, and the girls had had duplicates made; he hadn't gotten around to having the locks changed; the girls were sources of information as to who was having babies, when, what guy or gal was breaking up whose home, and so on.

There were five people sitting in his living room, drinking Collinses made out of his fancy gin. Morosely he looked around at Johnny Pollet, Jeannette Shires, Dave Martinson, Anne Pryor and Betty Turner.

"Want a drink?" Anne asked.

"Yeah, will you mix me one?" he asked. "I'll be taking a shower; I'm all sticky."

Perspiring and shaken because of what the Hexer had done to him, he closed his bedroom door, stripped and stepped under the shower for a quick one. He forgot about the nose until the last, soaped it then and wagged it under the spray to rinse it. The magnitude of the unmerciful disaster which had overtaken him numbed his wits; he moved like an automaton, stepping out of the tub and toweling himself. He made a complete change of clothing even to shoes. As he selected a new shirt from a bureau drawer and got into it, he hung a new necktie temporarily on his bugaboo of nose, about midway along. In the mirror, the necktie looked as though it were suspended in midair. In spite of its stick-out reality, the nose didn't reflect.

He closed the drawer, fortunately not hard because his nose got caught in the crack. He clawed the drawer open. Pain streamed up the schnozzle into his skull and nearly blew off the top of his head. Shuddering, he screwed his eyes up; tears trickled, tickling, down his olfactory extension.

Dabbing at his eyes, he gained control of himself and joined the chattering party in the living room. A drink had been made for him.

When Anne tendered the glass she performed in a most peculiar manner. Instead of turning around and going back to her chair in a normal way, she backed warily with a very odd smile, passing a hand behind her and making a gesture as though catching something up. Kupra, who had held his head aside with an absent-minded expression to keep his nose out of the way, stared speculatively at her while she smoothed her dress with singular extravagance and drew her legs up onto a window seat. Anne was a brunette, choicely rounded and graceful; she had the right height and heft and resiliency of anatomy, and cultivated a pronounced ability to pose. She was feline in her exact graduations of movement, and her voluptuousness was contained this afternoon in a handkerchief-linen dress opaqued with a satin slip. The wrinkling across the hips and in the skirt behind did not diminish her attractiveness, and she didn't need to worry about showing an amount of knee and a moon-gleam of thigh, because she was among friends.

Wondering why she acted as though she thought he would give her a kick if she turned her back on him, Kupra went to a chair and sat on its arm, keeping the lengthy quiver of his nose away from his drink so that he wouldn't knock it out of his hand himself.

"Well, what's the important word?" he asked at large.

Around the room he got serial answers, "Nothing happens," "Mh-mh. Hm-m-m," "I don't know a thing." "What have *you* got?" and "There's nobody in town but us."

"Oh, you just dropped in," Kupra commented. He tried his drink, and it was pretty good for a girl's work. No taste of gin. He arrived at the conclusion that there was no gin in the drink, and repaired to the kitchen, returning to hear a lot of conversation about nothing going on. Anne was highly decorative and posey, and was strolling about for effect as usual. Kupra observed that now and then she gave her hips an inexplicable galvanic twist as though she were muscling an appendage, like a cat. A cat she was, of course, and eventually someone stepped on her tail. She let out an agonized caterwaul, grabbed behind her and snatched to her breast the injured member, which, of course, was just as invisible as Kupra's nose.

Everyone jumped and Kupra asked: "What was that for?"

"Why, nothing," she said breathlessly. She forced a laugh. "I just wanted to see you all jump."

"A fine sense of humor you've got," Kupra remarked. "Don't do that again; it's too hot to jump."

He let the party go on as it would, just listening. Being host was never any exertion to him, because if anyone wanted a drink the person made it himself. He kept an eye on Anne, remembering the torment in the screech she had let out. When he had a chance he told her: "I want to talk to you."

She agreed, and they drifted unobserved into the bedroom of the bungalow. When he had closed the door he asked: "What's on your mind, Anne? Come on, what's the matter?"

"I don't know what you mean. Honestly, I haven't got anything for you. Please." She was out of breath.

He stared at her, and there was fright in her eyes. "Maybe nothing I can print," he suggested, "but something else?"

"Always the snoop," she bantered, "It might be something very personal, none of your business at all, you know."

"I can almost guess what it is," he hinted.

"You couldn't possibly."

"Listen, Anne," he urged. "Haven't I always been a mommie and poppie to you? Have I ever done you dirty? Gimme."

"All right; it's just this. Well," she groped, "I . . . I think I'm going crazy. Really bughouse, I mean."

"What makes you think you're going bughouse?"

"I've got a tail," she said shakily.

"What kind of a tail?"

"A cat's tail. I mean I really have," she said in a rush of words. "It was trailing on the rug, and Dave Martinson sank his heel into it."

"Well, I'll be a son of a gun," Kupra mused. Anne looked as though she were going to cry. He saw her wet eyes and said hastily: "Don't worry, Anne; you're no battier than I am. Just a minute, though. If you've got a tail, how do you get a dress on over it?"

"I don't know," she said, with a shrug of despair. "It just works that way."

"Line of cleavage," he muttered.

She turned, and he made a pass at the supposedly empty air. She said: "There. Oh, damn it!"

Rooted to the base of her spine was indubitably the tail of a cat, its proportions proper for her size. It was covered with fur, and flexible, and she could twitch it, having full muscular control over it. He let it slip through his fingers to the end, ascertaining that it was a generous five feet long. Experimentally he tugged, and she was compelled to back up protestingly.

"It's there beyond a doubt," he said. "Now guess what I've got. A nose." He had her stand just so, and gave her a gentle bat across the side of the head.

With awe, after feeling along its length, Anne said: "For heaven's sake." She laughed uncertainly.

"I guess," he said sardonically, "that he wanted to bring home the idea that I was sticking my nose into other people's business, like the feline streak in your case."

"I'm not feline."

"You've given me some pretty catty gossip."

"But how can such a thing happen? It's utterly wild!"

"Very utterly. When did this tail grow on you?"

"Just a couple of days ago. I was having cocktails with a couple of the girls down at the Casino, and we were chatting—"

"Cutting each other's throats, and snickering at your friends, maybe telling a nasty story about some Hollywood actress because you're not in Hollywood."

"Gee, you've got a mean tongue," she said. "Anyhow, all at once it happened. Umph. As quick as that. I left right away, of course, as soon as I was sure. I'm positive the girls didn't suspect anything, because they had engagements and were in a hurry, too."

"I wonder what he did to them."

"What did who do?"

"Hoodoo is right," Kupra cracked. "Did you happen to notice a pink-faced shrimp of an old man anywhere in the Casino? A skinny old geezer all barbered and manicured and tailored up."

"Oh! He was all alone at the next table, and he bought all our drinks for us. He looked charming, but I wondered if he wasn't senile and thinking he was going to get something out of it."

"Rest your mind. That old monkey is the one responsible for this. He got me on the streetcar only a little while ago on the way uptown."

"Oh, no!"

"Oh, yes!"

"Why, that devilish little mummy!"

"Sure. He gave Henny Kramer a head the size of a beer barrel; Kramer was quick on the trigger and chased the buzzard who hexed him up like that. Damn that cop Daugherty. Henny was just about grabbing the old guy's coat tails."

"Kramer was a fool to run."

"Sure he was. But are you going to go around advertising the fur job he did on you?"

"You won't tell on me, will you?" she begged. "It's so devastatingly ridiculous."

"As long as you don't give me away about my nozzle."

They regarded each other strickenly, and with the baffled compassion of companions in misery.

"I wonder if the condition is permanent," she hazarded. There was a wail in her inflection. "People are beginning to think I'm queer. I have to positively sprint into a room so that I don't get a door closed on my tail. And I get tired of keeping it curled in the air all the time so that it doesn't get stepped on. Besides, it's nervous; it's got a tic in it that's driving me out of my mind. And it gets matted the way fur does and feels terrifically uncomfortable. I'm combing it all the time. And even with an electric dryer, after I give it a bath, it's ages before it's all fluffy again."

"I just closed a drawer on my beak when I changed my shirt," Kupra chimed in somberly. "When I go to bed tonight I guess I'll have to lie on my back and do a juggling act. And I never was able to sleep on my back."

"You know," said Anne, "I think there's something wrong with Jeannette and Betty, too. They've been acting as though they've eaten a goblin apiece."

"There's something screwy about Martinson, too."

After kissing Anne, just to see whether it could be done with the handicap of his nasal equipment, Kupra eased open the latch of the bedroom door and looked through the crack. They rejoined the party which had formed through the usual happenstance. People who had nothing important to do in hot weather, collecting in comfortable surroundings in which someone had snitched a key—Betty or Anne or both.

The drinking went on through the afternoon past twilight. Kupra found things out. Across the room, Dave Martinson was getting himself soused. He was a lawyer, somber in appearance, dark and devious in the ways of his mind. His forehead was smooth, white, as unblemished as a boy's. Absently, he was tracing with a forefinger an invisible mark, a certain letter which the Hexer had branded there above his eyes. The habit of tracing the letter revealed it in pinkish outline. Martinson caught Kupra staring, and the lanky lawyer jerked his hat on, sat staring morosely at the rug, inevitably to raise his finger to his forehead again.

Jeannette Shires spent a couple of hours a day on her marvelous complexion; she had gardenia-petal skin, its purity accented by magnificent black hair in a carved coiffure of gleaming curls. During the evening she got Kupra aside and asked to borrow his razor. She had a whim to shave her legs, she said. Kupra told her they didn't look as though they needed it.

"What do you know about it?" she retorted.

"The more you shave your legs, the hairier they'll get," he warned.

"That's all right with me," she retorted. "All I've got to do is keep them shaved."

The Hexer had got her. He had given her a heavy black beard, and she had to shave twice a day.

That made it five out of six. If this group was representative of the town, the Hexer had already distributed his wares among five-sixths of the citizens of Oxboro.

Keeping his eyes skinned for the next few days, Kupra found plenty of evidence that such was the case, that the Hexer had spared very few in squeegeeing the town. Some of the deeds were good; most appeared to have been committed with the most greedy malice.

There was a certain loud-mouthed cop, notorious for his insolence of manner in writing out tickets, who had mule's ears. From the length of the stroke, for he was continually feeling them to see if they were still there, it could be determined that they were a full eighteen inches of botheration. A certain blind beggar, who had salted away something like sixty thousand dollars at his profession, really went blind and got run down by a truck. That was how the money turned up.

The best-dressed man in town started growing flowers back of his ears. The narcissus scent was unmistakable. A listener could detect the snap of stems when he picked them daily. He got round-shouldered and ceased wearing a gardenia in his lapel.

The meanest man in town had a face like a saint. Overnight a caprice of paralysis struck his benign countenance into an iron mask of virulent detestation of the whole human race.

And so on down the line.

Mostly, the Hexer avoided repetition in his works, indicating interest in his profession, or hobby. Not everyone was affected by the potent gleam of that gray eye, but his goal was not necessarily a hundred percent. Too, it was presumable that only he could take back his gifts; widely as he plied his mischief, however, none of his victims saw him more than once; he returned no more, deaf in his mad glee to prayers in whatever humility or rage pronounced. What he did he would not undo.

All Kupra found to do was hope futilely that his particular curse would wear off; while the phantom schnozzle might yield to surgery, he had the dark conviction that another one would spontaneously sprout. At the typewriter, when he knocked off his daily column for the *Enquirer*, he kept on printing capital letters, quotation marks and the like on his beak. Sometimes he wondered whether mass insanity had hit town. Otherwise he wondered where the little old man had come from, and where the little old man had gone.

He certainly did his cussedest in Oxboro.

Oxboro *Enquirer*, June 25; Public Notices. WANTED: Works on black magic, secret doctrines, hypnotism, Tibetan mysteries, ancient lore, occult and mystic sciences, and the evil eye, with emphasis on lifting spells. Premium prices paid. Phone Jan Kupra, *Enquirer*, or Oxboro 2748.

The Black Farm

URROUNDING THIS FIELD was a worn fence whose rails had been split and laid by Anton Bulik's grandfather. Mr. Zero remained where Anton had spotted him early of the humid morning, before milking—down there in the grassy corner of the field nearest the woods. This morning it had been no trouble at all; the whole area—all this low, rich, drained section—could be scanned from the woodshed of the ugly farmhouse. Anton had acquired the habit of smoking before breakfast. He owned five pipes. One corncob for tradition, two sweet briers which were most superior and expensive.

With the stem in his teeth Anton had opened the woodshed door guardedly, then incautiously stepped outside and smoked, speculating. At first there was no evidence of Mr. Zero, but then Anton's dark, worried eyes came back to that corner of the field. And he had looked, and wondered if the thing was asleep, if it ever slept. But, at any rate, he didn't have to go hunting for it as he had on previous occasions. Over the ridge and down to the lake, taking only a few steps at a time, slowly and watchfully.

He had brewed coffee and loaded his pipe again. As long as he knew where it was he wasn't worried, because Mr. Zero was slow-moving. Anton had eaten a cold Idaho potato that was in the refrigerator from last night. That was breakfast. When he mounted the tractor which was cuddled against the corn crib he had some peculiar equipment.

In a canvas knapsack hung thick slices of Virginia ham wrapped in waxed paper, sandwich slices of cabbage wrapped likewise, two apples from the orchard, a few slices from the loaf of bread. Nothing unusual about packing a lunch, but most irregular were the bulky, powerful binoculars and the rifle—a .30-30 lever-action holding seven shells, eight with the one in the chamber.

Anton's accuracy with this weapon was most uncommon, and quite well known to the natives of Hurley, a few miles away. A few of them had been sniped at, and hit, at impossible distances. That was quite a few months ago, following his wife's death and the finding of her bones. The muttering had died out when the natives, with few exceptions, reached the conclusion that Anton Bulik was mad in the most thoroughgoing and hard-working manner. His derangement manifested itself in various fascinating forms, but it had become evident that he was not homicidal until compelled to defend himself.

Since the death of his wife had driven him batty, it was horse sense to argue that he hadn't murdered her, and he wasn't pulling a fast one that time he stood up Chris Christopherson in My Brother's Bar. Chris had been a fellow Martha went with at first.

True, Anton hadn't killed Martha because of Chris. And though he suspected, there was nothing he could prove at that time. There was no doubt about it now, that it was Mr. Zero; for the time being, Anton was keeping the information to himself. There was no thought of vengeance in his mind, for it was at once obvious that vengeance could not be inflicted on the thing that moved secretly, browsing with bovine placidity in satisfying its tremendous hunger. Anton talked to himself sometimes, consciously; he got to calling the monster Mr. Zero just as he addressed his collie as Smoke, the black stallion as Nigger. Mr. Zero had gotten Stripes, the cat, and her litter of five.

The thought of Martha's being encompassed in that thing's fatal embrace and unhurriedly eaten alive made his flesh crawl. He guessed he had nightmares more horrendous than any man ever had before. No, it wasn't to be regarded as animal at all. What he had to deal with every day was an unpredictable menace which fluctuated in form and perhaps in size. Its dimensions could not be found by rule. He didn't hate it nor was he afraid of it. It was an engrossing, difficult, highly dangerous problem, as clueless for solution as a cunningly manufactured puzzle delivered with the key piece missing. Possibly there was no way of lifting the strange hoodoo from the place, but he wouldn't wish it off on anybody else. One day his own bones would be found in a white, clean-picked litter in the field, if he got unwary.

Row by row he returned toward the farmhouse, having started at the far end of the field. All he could do was give Mr. Zero quick glances with increasing nervousness, having to thread the rows of green corn shoots, four at a time, through the pairs of cultivator shovels.

The situation was complicated further by the person watching him from a distance up the slope, twenty yards down from the woods. Up there was a log, the trunk of a good-sized oak hung around back of the tree's low stump so it wouldn't roll. Some time ago he had painted them black, as though he wanted to preserve them. Reclining behind the log and watching him was Irene Leigh, Martha's younger sister. It wasn't the first time, but this was the first time he had seen her.

From the adjoining Leigh farm Irene would take the old Indian Trail, the drag marks of the poles still discernible after all these years, and cut through the woods to one point of vantage or another, covering the place where Anton happened to be working. What her purpose was he couldn't properly guess, and he would have been wrong at any try. He had found evidences

of her visits—a couple of apple cores with her even teeth marks the time she hid in the orchard, a piece of ribbon, a handkerchief, the prints of small feet, marks on the grass made by the weight of a light body.

Anton had met both girls at the State University, in the Agricultural College. He had liked Irene much the better of the sisters, but she was taking a lot of courses in the Arts College and wasn't marrying any farmer, as far as he could make out. At first he had been laughed at for his scientific farming, then there was Martha's disappearance and death, and now he was just holding his own, if not, in fact, imperceptibly but surely going under. He couldn't work the whole blasted farm alone.

That conviction recurred to him as he came riding the slow roar of the tractor down the field to take the turn and the last four rows which would bring him back to the road near the crib and machinery sheds. "Betsy, you stinking pile of scrap iron," he muttered, referring to the formidable, efficient invention he was driving, "I don't know what I'll do."

Up there on the slope behind the black log, unaware of how conspicuous she was with the sunlight on her yellow hair, Irene watched intently. He had the advantage of her in knowing she was there. What he didn't know was the fact that around her middle was strapped a man's broad leather belt, against her stomach the tight belt held an old, long-barreled revolver. It was a .32-caliber Harrington & Richardson, and as soon as she decided something in her own mind she was going to use it on Anton Bulik.

Smoke came to a rigid standstill, his legs apart, tail drooping, head low and thrust forward. Anton was thinking he would risk a glance up the slope at Irene as he made the turn; he grabbed, and braked the tractor to a halt just in time to avoid running down the dog. Smoke would have stood there, idiotically defending the tractor as well as Anton. He was a large dog and looked like a wolf, all wolf instead of being only partly so. His pelt was flowing iron-gray, unmarked except for accents at the ears and a stripe on the plume of tail. He was strictly obedient, fearless, and ferocious in his transcendental allegiance to one master.

Mr. Zero had remained where he was for much too long a time, and finally was on the move. Anton shut the motor off as he grabbed for the rifle. Low to the ground now, Smoke prowled a few slow paces forward in a direct and angry line toward the corner of the field where Mr. Zero had been satisfied to remain quiet all morning.

Anton still couldn't hear the dog's snarl, low and continuous and ominous, as though Smoke thought he was good enough to tear a pair of tigers to pieces. Anton himself couldn't see any movement, but the dog had detected it. Then some grass went flat; and there was no wind whatever. The dog quivered with impatience and sneaked a paw forward, breathed and uttered more of that advancing, determined growl.

Upon the steep slope, Irene was frightened by the crazy thing she was watching. When Anton had stood up on the tractor she jumped to her feet, and jerked the revolver from her belt when he picked up the rifle, she thought he was going to shoot at her, because there certainly was nothing in the corner of the field down there. There couldn't be. It was just a corner of a field, grassy, with nothing there. Unless it was something small, like a snake or a gopher. But the two of them, the dog and the man both, wouldn't look and act like that about any thing small, as if they were mad.

There was a blur, and she blinked a few times, rubbed because she thought she had gotten something in her eyes. And the rubbing made the blur worse, especially in that corner of the field. She was not as good a shot as Bulik, but she was accomplished and the bullet would have gone through the middle of his chest, and heart, if her finger had tightened a little more on the trigger of the old, accurate revolver. The weight of it brought the gun down to her side as she watched incredulously.

It was preposterous—Anton standing up on the tractor down there, the beautiful dog creeping over the young corn, the two of them performing as though this were as important as hunting big game in Africa.

The dog yelped, and she had never heard a sound like it before. It was a sound of fury, sudden but musical, lunging with eagerness. Watching the dog above all else, even at this distance she saw Anton brush the magazine release of the rifle with his thumb. He was wagging the gun as though he didn't know what to aim at, but doing it watchfully.

Thinned by distance, his voice reached her, commenting in the imperturbable manner she knew: "All right, pal, you've got me." He was talking to the gorgeous dog. "Where the hell is it? Smoke!"

The dog's head came back for the briefest instant, the tongue acurl and dripping.

To Irene, Anton's voice sounded elfin and far away when he ordered, "Get him, Smoke."

Instantaneously, with its fur rippling like magic, the dog bolted in a diagonal for the corner. With all its abrupt speed and power and savagery it could have scared anything. Just as abruptly it turned at right angles, skidded on the ground and acted as though it had gone mad. It snapped at something invisible, snarled, barked just once, circled and kept on circling a patch of grass which the dog worried but never entered.

Anton hung a leg over the big wheel of the tractor and sat; he drew aim, let the barrel of the rifle drift a little to the left. He fired, moved the barrel up and fired again, and once more. The dog sniffed over the grassy corner, bristling; turned, and leaped the fence and resumed its tactics—snarling, snapping at something invisible, worrying the thin air, going through all the motions of driving a herd of tired, dumb cattle.

On the wheel of the tractor Anton sat watching his incomparable dog, the rifle aimed at the ground and his shoulders sagging. He wasn't worried about Smoke, because that dog was alert enough to terrify a ghost. Anton watched the grass, and the other manifestations, his eyes quick in tracing the progress of the thing; Mr. Zero followed the fence at the speed of a man's walk, turned and at the same rate of locomotion ascended the steep slope, a hundred yards to the left of the black log on the side hill. A tree on the crest of the hill shivered, the foliage making a soft, distant, wet sound in the quiet afternoon as it stirred, as though some blundering, immense creature had butted the trunk with elephantine power in passing. A juggernaut.

Way up there on the crest of the ridge, Smoke swept his tail back and forth a couple of times with sheer *joie de vivre*—with yanking abruptness, triumph. Zero was going down to the lake, where he would probably make a meal of frogs, turtles, fish, and the wet green grass. Perhaps a martin or two flying too low to the ground. This was a wet year, and there was an abundance of frogs and small coral-marked toads which Anton hadn't seen before. The dog turned and came down the hill laughing, all rippling gray, and back to Anton.

Irene was wearing a printed cotton dress which her rounded body fitted snugly. The skirt was full, and she didn't have to catch it up to run. Her skin was golden-brown and she wore no stockings, and the broad leather belt made her waist look slim. She ran as though she were scared crazy; Anton watched the strained, rapid rhythm of her tanned legs until she disappeared into the woods, dodging along the Indian Trail. His lips quirked; it looked like a smile, but it wasn't one.

A glance down at the dog showed him that the dog was so satisfied with his conquest that he didn't need his ears held and gently tugged at, nor even the commending sound of Anton's voice. He was absolutely certain of how Anton felt about him, and they didn't advertise the regard in which they held each other. Bulik looked hard at the dog, which was facing the ugly farmhouse and panting from the session with Mr. Zero, and this time he grinned to the point of laughing aloud. The savage, conceited dog was an actor. Smoke drew his tongue in and sniffed scientifically at a large stone polished by the last rain and hail. Then he set off down the houseward boundary of the field at a beeline canter. It was like an order. Anton got back to the seat, started the motor, swung the tractor and headed down the last four rows of corn, feeding the rows of lusty green shoots between the shares, and jerking an upward look now and then at the leading, parading plume of Smoke's tail.

At the road he used the lever which raised the wicked, bright-steel shares, climbed the embankment. Smoke stood and looked back, panting. Anton followed the dog for the distance of a short walk along the dirt road, and again parked the tractor alongside the corn crib, below the house. According to the weather report over the radio, and it was reliable now, it wasn't going to rain tonight. For a change. And it was a difficult drive over rocky ground to the machinery sheds since the flood. He was still amazed that mere water could roll down that obstacle of boulders, big fellows, and shear away his pen of squealing pigs.

Anton took the sweat off his brow with his forearm and looked down at the barn. The black paint was holding pretty well. So was the paint on the silo. Brick. Painted black up to fourteen feet high.

All black. All around. He turned his head with impatience, and there was nothing to be seen but the things he had painted black, and he felt drunkenly unhappy. All the fences were painted black and so were the pens, machinery sheds, the granary, the farmhouse itself. The shade trees were black up to the bottom branches, and so were trees at strategic points in the woods, chiefly along the trails. Likewise boulders on the hillside, an outcropping shelf of granite, everything paintable on the Bulik farm was made startling with this calamitous color, "the badge of hell, the hue of dungeons and the suit of night." Everything to which he had taken the paint can was a pawn in the grim game he was playing with Mr. Zero. Bulik ascended the slope to the sprawling house and let Smoke in. After getting a glass of beer from the icebox, Bulik sat at the kitchen table. The stillness was complete and unfriendly, await with the unimaginable things that haunt an old, old building. If a man is alone there and thinking.

Saturday began by drizzling, and Bulik guessed it would continue all day. It wasn't rain. The air was filled with a mist of pin-point beads of water which didn't seem to fall, but rather drift along the rolling ground in shapes. The stuff silvered the hair on his forearms and brushed an elusive taste on his lips. Overhead the clouds hung unusually low and moved so slowly that their direction was indeterminable.

With Smoke trotting ahead, they cut back through the orchard and went on in a line as direct as the terrain would allow. They went to the easternmost part of the farm, where it was bounded by the highway running north to the city. Here there was quite a stretch of pasture lying in a long slope. At the north end, a barbed-wire fence ran at right angles to the road along the edge of the woods, which got increasingly dense as a man entered them. Where the highway swung through the woods the embankment was steep, but it was fairly easy to enter through the pasture up there in the corner. Hunters from the city, after mushrooms or game, had beaten a path across that corner.

Anton hadn't minded in the least until young fellows started coming with girls, and snipping the barbed wire so they could get through without snagging their skirts or skins. Even that was all right, because he rarely had anyone to talk to. Nevertheless, he posted the place lavishly. The neat signs couldn't be missed: "No Trespassing." The variety was emphatic: "Absolutely No Hunting," "No Game, Mush-rooms, Nor Flowers," and the simple "Keep Out" along with the lie, "Mad Bull."

The signs were only to prevent the hunters and trespassers from being hunted by Mr. Zero; but some sorehead was writing letters about getting the State to take title to the woods, which was one of the largest stands of virgin timber in the State, and turn it into a park. There was a pair of pliers in Anton's jeans. Someone had ignored the signs and cut the fence again, and he guessed that when he had the time he'd have to put up gates.

To the right and out of sight on the highway, two cars and then a third went by at blockhead speed after slowing up for the curve below. Trying to pass each other at seventy and eighty and more, as usual, even with the road slick from this mist. When he had followed Smoke only twenty yards in a diagonal across the pasture, he heard another car coming fast, and this one didn't slow up for the turn.

Anton could see it as vividly as though he were down there watching the frightening rapidity of it. The driver's speed took him far out, way out on the wrong side of the curve as he almost but not quite negotiated it. The wheels touched the shoulder of the road, and the shoulder was slippery from the weather. The machine skidded. Whoever was driving kept his head and didn't use his brakes. He stepped on the accelerator. Because of the motor principle involved, if it had been a left turn he would have made it by a hairbreadth. There was a slosh of gravel against the embankment as the car plowed long burrows along the shoulder. Then some ground broke away and the machine crashed into the ditch. Freakishly it bounced back onto the highway, but skidding sidewise with the tires squealing, and this time went back down with a slam and rending of metal. The ground shivered under Anton's feet as the car corkscrewed and bounced a couple of times.

The ditch was full of boulders, and Anton swallowed, thinking of the mess he was going to see.

But before he could move he was astounded to see the scrambling figure of a man pop into view and grab hold of the fence at the edge of the pasture, a quick-mannered, bantam-size individual in unpressed clothes. His hat was lost if he'd had any, and his forehead and cheek were torn open and bloody. Down the highway was the hum of another car, speeding; the fugitive glanced down, snarling, before he stepped on the wire close to a post and jumped awkwardly. The barbs of the top wire snagged his trousers leg and tripped him, and he bellyflopped into the pasture. It was lucky for him, because someone shot at him just then, and the shot missed. The gunman was in the approaching car, which screeched to a stop down below on the highway, behind the wreck of the first.

Anton watched dumfounded while the little man picked himself up and went pelting for the woods. Jackrabbit in style, he was making excellent time when he first noticed Bulik, and promptly snapped a shot with the revolver in his hand.

Anton threw himself to the ground and ordered the poised, whining dog, "Down, Smoke."

The little man was dodging eccentrically to make a bad target of himself; he was a generous fifty feet from the fence along the woods when the two pursuers clambered into sight from the highway. One of them exclaimed, "There he is!"

But before either of them could fire, their quarry was gone like a pricked balloon. They looked mighty silly there at the fence, wagging their guns as they searched for something to shoot at. Their man was fifty feet from the fence, at least, and couldn't have made it, disappeared like the sound of a finger's snap.

"There's a hole up there or something he dropped into," one man suggested.

"Must be," the other agreed. "Them weeds aren't tall enough to hide anything. Take it easy now, Art."

They rolled under the fence in turn and at a wary crouch headed for the spot where their man was last seen. Both of them jumped when Anton got to his feet and asked, "What's the trouble, gentlemen?"

"Where the hell did you come from?"

Anton answered literally, "That fellow fired at me, and I hit the ground."

"He was firing at us," one of them said, but they weren't really paying any attention to him. They were sneaking forward with their guns ready.

"All right, Smoke." Anton made a go-ahead gesture, and the dog barked and passed the detectives at a smooth trot.

"That's the idea," Art said approvingly. "Scare him out with the pooch."

But Smoke stopped at a safe distance from Mr. Zero and stood with legs planted; his tail didn't wag, and his jaws were shut. He looked at the woods, then back at the approaching men. By this time they could see that there was no hole, no depression in which the fugitive could fall or throw himself. The weeds weren't more than a foot high. There wasn't any hiding place between here and the woods.

"Well, what the hell," Art commented, and both paused momentarily with arms akimbo and stared around.

Smoke sidled against one of them and snapped his jaws, so that both were compelled to tour safely around Zero. The dog acted none too friendly, and Anton was ordered, "Mind your dog, farmer, or I'll plug him between the eyes."

"If you did, you'd get it in the same place yourself," Anton said matter-of-factly. He shifted the position of the rifle on his arm.

He got a long, ugly stare from the man, and then they went up to the fence and looked into the woods.

The more talkative of the detectives, Art Garron, stated: "It's impossible. Only a bullet could travel that fast. Why, he was down there where that damned dog is, it seemed like."

Much similar in build to Garron, Floyd Sharpe said: "I never had my eyes off him, but he was dodging around, and there's this fog. He must 'a' been closer to the fence than he looked."

"I don't see any tracks. That ground in there is spongy. I—" He was going to say that he had done a lot of hunting in the big woods, in spite of the signs; he caught himself.

"He'd get lost if he went in there," Anton drawled. "Been lost in there a couple of times myself."

"You again," said Garron. "You watching him?"

"I was watching him."

"Well, did *you* see where he went?"

Peaceably Anton said, "It was as though you winked just as something you were after ducked behind a tree."

Both detectives were angry. "Listen, Art," said Sharpe. "There's no sense in us going in there, just the two of us. This is a hell of a big woods, goes back for miles. We'd be shooting at each other if we got separated and started circling around. He's in there all right; let's go down and give the wreck a look, and come back with some men."

Garron cursed with regret and added: "I thought we had him. How the hell could anybody get out of a smash-up like that alive?"

Smoke was casting back and forth and moving slowly down the slope the distance of a pace at a time. Mr. Zero was on the move, retreating like an animal with freshly caught prey from the attentive, silently worrying dog.

Smoke went halfway down the pasture before coming back, and Sharpe inquired, "What's the dog after?"

"Playing with a gopher, possibly," said Anton.

"You don't talk much like a farmer to me," Garron said.

Anton shrugged. "Farmers go to school."

"That dog can smell tracks, can't he?"

"He's not going into the woods and get shot at for you, or by you, or anyone else," Anton said flatly.

"Going to be wet as hell in there, Art," said Sharpe.

"Yeah, I never forget a guy who does me a favor," said Garron, with another of his baleful stares.

Abruptly Garron pointed his gun at the dog, and Smoke crouched with a snarl. Anton didn't bring the rifle up; just aimed at Garron from the hip.

Garron relaxed, chuckling, and holstered his gun. "Just kidding," he said. "Just kidding."

"That ain't no dog," Sharpe said suspiciously. "That's a wolf."

"I don't care what he is," Garron retorted. "I don't want to see him around when we come back. I don't like him."

"He doesn't like you either, and neither do I," Anton commented.

"Come on, Art," Sharpe urged. "We're getting nowhere, unless this guy's got a phone."

"You're closer to town than my phone."

If the fugitive was in the woods, there wasn't too much hurry, those woods being what they were with a serpentining swamp and a multitude of sink holes and brush like barbed-wire entanglements. Garron lingered to indulge in a moment of gnawing frustration, taking it out on Bulik.

"You missed a golden opportunity, rube," he said, and his face was congested with his feelings. "You know who that was? That was Tommy Mishaw. All you had to do was plug him, and you let him get away. They want him in three States, and there's about five thousand dollars reward for him, and we'd 'a' given you a nice split on it. Think of that. Five thousand!"

"I don't see why I should have shot at him."

"He shot at you, didn't he?"

"You said he was shooting at you."

"What's the difference? He come busting through here, didn't he? And with all them signs you had a perfect right to shoot at anybody."

"In that case I have a perfect right to open fire on you right now."

Garron had his mouth open to say something more. The best he could do was a strangled sound of disgust, and he started back to the highway with Sharpe. First they had to circle the dog, which turned in its tracks to point at them, a soft growl issuing between the bared teeth.

Anton heard something that sounded like "Crazy farmer," and observed to himself, "What a couple of low customers!" and started down the hill to locate Mr. Zero. His face was hot, but he couldn't help it if he had taken such an instantaneous dislike to those men. Before he had gone very far he heard the sound of a car being started and shifted rapidly. Sharpe and Garron going for help, or perhaps one of them had remained to investigate the wreck down below. The men weren't from Hurley, but from Waterloo, the larger town off to the east.

In the newspapers Bulik had seen the name of the shrimpy man they had been chasing. If ever the law shagged a man bowlegged it was Tommy Mishaw, more often called Sleepy and Shut-eye. He robbed banks and committed various similar crimes of violence which are regarded as gainful in the underworld.

He got his first name by starting out with a Tommy, or submachine gun, as a weapon, and earned some money that way until the apparatus jammed one time and he had to junk it. He had the artillery rigged inside a suitcase, the front and back ends of the luggage being hinged and connected to swing open simultaneously when he stuck his fist in the rear, and with this thing he walked into country banks and up to tellers' cages. He took to sidearms, but on the whole his style didn't change and he was no hand at disguising himself, no matter how hard he experimented with hirsute adornment and haberdashery. The hunt for him got kind of cruel, like a householder planting poisoned mice along the back fence to take care of the cats that keep him awake at night.

The law came upon and all but caught Mishaw a dozen times, and thus he acquired his other nick-names. In hotels or barns, and once in a tavern booth with his chin in his beer, he was always asleep, grabbing his forty winks when he decided the opportunity was at hand. He had never failed to shoot his way out, and there were a couple of dead men besides the three accredited to him in the actual holdups. Once Mishaw got going in one of those shooting matters, he could really scamper.

What with the wrangling among the banks, the law and the insurance companies, Mishaw was very much sought after for a little fellow like him. The only reason he hadn't socked a bullet through Anton there in the pasture was because, besides being hurt and in a hurry after he wrecked his car, Anton loomed and was just one of those things that get fired at wildly in a fog and turn out to be unsubstantial. Either that, or Mishaw had killed another man, the way Bulik had flopped to the ground. Ordinarily, Mishaw could peg a bullet through a target with the accuracy of a carpenter driving nails on his own time.

Anton hopped in order to avoid kicking something on the grass. It was a pistol, and it had been dragged, because a tuft of green grass was sticking up through the trigger guard. Down on hands and knees, Anton sniffed, and the dog sniffed at his hair. The gun was warm with a reek that Anton considered pleasant. Mishaw's gun; dropped from nerveless fingers, proving that Mr. Zero had him. Anton got up, butting Smoke's nose with a jerk of his head. He plucked the dog's ear, fingering it at the roots, and they continued down the slope of the pasture through the fog until Smoke turned across Anton's way and leaned hard to stop him.

How the dog knew where Zero was baffled him. The dog's senses were sharper than his, of course; but, extra sense or not, Smoke merely seemed to know where danger was. Anton got the rifle ready, seeing nothing. He looked down at the silken-silver weight of the dog against his legs and backed up.

There was a little hollow here, and Mr. Zero was in it and wasn't moving. Anton walked well around, backed up and sat on a rock. Smoke sat on his haunches alongside, alternately opening his jaws to pant and then closing them alertly.

With the rainy fog there was nothing to be seen; Anton could make out nothing at all, but he knew Mr. Zero was there. He couldn't do anything but peer because he had nothing to go by. He didn't touch the dog now, nor speak to him, because it would be Smoke who would scent danger first. Anton used his shoulders as though in revulsion, and very slowly got out tobacco and filled his pipe.

There wasn't a sound unless it was that of the grass growing, but he turned his head as though he had been called. He puffed on the pipe a couple of times, and then he located her. The girl down there. In the corner of the field diagonally opposite the cut wires was a cattle gate, and perched on the top wooden bar was Irene Leigh. It was funny how a person could remain still in this drizzle and fog and not be observed. He held the warm bowl of the pipe in his hand, and she stared back at him steadily. She was wearing a costume that reminded him of the tennis courts up at the university: silken gabardine shorts as white as the cloth could be bleached; a pull-over sweater, also white; and over that an expensive light-gray leather jacket in suede. Around her waist was a broad leather belt which looked like one her brother used to wear, and tucked in the belt was a revolver.

Anton told himself that he would be snag-dabbed, and got up off his rock. Leaving Smoke to look after Mr. Zero, he went down there, not very fast, and not shambling either.

"Hello, Irene," he said, and looked back swiftly to make sure that Smoke was minding. The dog wasn't bothering, so Zero kept to the comfortable hollow, a nothingness in the nothingness of fog.

"Hello, Anton," she responded; her voice was musically throaty and assured. The way she lingered over words was seductive; he distrusted her, because he was unable to tell whether she was sincere or whether she was just holding her laughter in. Her eyes were always so wide that it might have been either, and he couldn't forget the laughter he had left behind, long ago, after he had asked her to marry him, and he had started running through the dark because her laughter followed him.

His gaze fixed glumly on the butt of the revolver. He asked, "For me, maybe?"

"Uh-huh," she admitted casually. "It's perfectly silly saying it. I—had to do something about it if you killed Martha, or if I thought you were—"

"Insane?"

"Uh-huh." Casual again, inspecting him with her indecipherable eyes.

"Do you think I'm a lunatic?"

"No, you're not crazy," she said thoughtfully, with their eyes searching each other's eyes. "Anton, what's it all about? I got here just as that man came running through the pasture and shot at you. I just nearly pulled the trigger when he was gone." She snapped her fingers. "Like that."

"Mr. Zero got him," Anton said succinctly.

After a pause she asked gravely, "Who's Mr. Zero?"

"I'll show you." He nodded at Smoke and turned away.

They ascended the slope to the point where Smoke was standing guard. Anton directed, "Come around here."

He maneuvered her a little to the side and behind Smoke, and indicated one in the line of fence posts, all of them painted black.

"I don't see anything," she said, after staring and searching all the ground between.

"Keep looking," said Anton. "It's hard to get the knack of it in this mist. Blurs everything."

"Oh!" she exclaimed in a moment. The post was bigger than the others, and curiously blurred and vague in silhouette, like a streak of lamp-black painted against the mist.

"Come down here now." They descended a little way and sighted through that area guarded by the dog at another post. It jumped in size, and its solidity, like the other, took on the insubstantiality of something like a plume of dirty vapor.

"That's Mr. Zero," Anton stated. "He got Martha, and he's got that little fellow right now." He told her who Mishaw was.

Irene gasped and laid her fingers on his forearm. She was trembling and stammered: "I don't know what to say."

"There isn't anything to say. There he is, that's all."

"But what is it?" she demanded, shocked.

Anton shrugged. With a single sardonic syllable of laughter he remarked: "All I know is that the blasted thing won't get off my farm. Good foraging here so far. It came from somewhere up north."

"How do you know that?"

"I'm not the only one who's lost cattle. I got to wondering what was killing them off, and made a trip up to the agricultural college. Asked them for reports on farm animals killed, and game. This hoodoo has left a track of skeletons running straight north on up into Canada. Don't know how far up."

She breathed the words, "It's fantastic," but what she meant was, "It's horrible."

Irene asked: "Isn't there something to do about it?"

"What?" he demanded, with restrained rage. "I've painted the whole damned place black to spot it easier, so it won't get me. You can't kill it; bullets don't hurt it much more than mosquito bites."

He gave her all the information he had been able to wring out of the mystery. What material it was made of he didn't know; it had tremendous weight, and the solidity of flesh made invisible. Its means of locomotion couldn't be discovered, but its progress might be described as the sluggish roll of a huge, resilient ball of dough. It couldn't move very fast, or hadn't found the occasion to so far. Certainly its progress down from the north was a loitering one—browsing speed.

It could bear extreme cold, for during the winter the temperature had gone as low as forty-two degrees below zero.

How long it could go without food was indeterminate, but while it was Anton's guest it ate enormously. Into its maw went a whole cow at a whack. It had no ferocity itself; it was an ambush with the lumbering temperament of a tame bear. To all intents and purposes invisible in itself, it possessed the extraordinary talent of rendering invisible whatever entered it. That was the only way of describing the way Mr. Zero fed. An animal would enter the area occupied by the unknown creature and would not reappear except as a débris of bones.

In size, Anton guessed it was from twelve to fourteen feet in height and perhaps as much in diameter. A big, sinister blob. The first he saw of it, he related, was the blur which he thought was a fault in his vision; but the blur remained where it was in the landscape, while he thought, while gooseflesh covered him, while he made certain of the thing's existence with growing disbelief and dismay. But he still thought that he had discovered Mr. Zero's fatal handicap—that, while he was practically invisible to the human eye—if not, possibly, to the dog's—the very nature of the material composing him effected a certain amount of magnification of objects behind him.

There were a few other things, one particular characteristic of Mr. Zero's which was most fiendish and subtle, but before Anton could speak of it there was a groan as though a man had made a furious effort and failed.

Smoke pricked up his ears and uttered a prompting bark. Anton, and Irene breathing hard, watched the area from which the groan originated. There was another cry from that mysterious prison which had swallowed up Mishaw, this time almost a squeal as the gangster threw every ounce of clawing, frantic strength into the try.

Anton put his arm against Irene and cautioned: "Don't go any closer. This is as close as we can go."

He called, "Mishaw!"

After a moment Mishaw's voice responded, hollow and bodiless as an echo: "All right, hayseed, how does it work? Let me out of here."

"I can't get you out of there," Anton answered. "Quick! What's the trouble? Can you stand up?"

"You can see, can't you?" Mishaw snarled. "What kind of a gag is this?"

"We can't see you."

"What?" Mishaw yelled, outraged, and he wailed, "What kind of junk is that I'm stuck in, anyhow?"

"What do you mean?" Anton asked anxiously. "What sort of stuff is it? Mishaw!" He waited and called again, "*Mishaw!*"

Mishaw made a strangling sound and moaned, "God!"

It was brief and devastating.

From the oblivion of Mr. Zero came an unbelievable, siren-high, bloodcurdling screech. Mishaw screamed: "My hand is gone! I can see the bones of my hand! Help!" It was the yelp of a mad animal. They could hear him battling around in there, and from the rattle of bones more than his hand was gone. He screamed continuously, shouting incoherences of maniacal, babbling horror. He *was* insane now, but still hideously alive. The gibbering diminished into a slobbering, watery gurgle, into silence.

"Mishaw!" Anton called.

Irene couldn't stand it, and Anton caught her as she slumped in a faint. Unsteadily, shaken, he swung her up with an arm under her knees and walked down the pasture, and she didn't open her eyes until they were on the route back to the farmhouse. He started to set her down, but she clasped her arms around his neck and held so tightly that it hurt, shuddering. Her breathing made a sound as though she were crying.

Sharpe and Garron returned with a dozen others, and five days were spent in systematically searching the big woods. Naturally no trace of Mishaw was found; Anton figured out that the only reason Mr. Zero didn't help himself to a couple of the posse was that he didn't like too much activity in his neighborhood. It had been demonstrated that he didn't like Smoke's attentions, and on the way down from the north he had invariably avoided cities and towns and kept to the open country. The hermit nightmare. Then Mishaw was falsely reported to have been seen up in the city, and the hunt moved elsewhere.

Anton found Mishaw's bones on the following Saturday, on the shore of the lake below the sand cliff where the martins nested. The skeleton was disarticulated, as usual. Along with sopping wads of clothing, he found a thin platinum watch which had stopped but started going again with an inaudible tick when he wound it. Farther on was a shiny long wallet which contained a thousand and some dollars. Anton reflected that he would turn over Mishaw's worldly goods to the Hurley authorities when he got around to it—say, after the next election on the chance that an honest police chief got in.

It was a hot day, and along the beach the air was stagnant and stifling. He threw a stick out into the enamel-smooth water for Smoke to retrieve, and the dog abandoned it on shore, knowing perfectly well that there would be another stick farther on. When the dog shook himself off, the spray felt good on Anton's skin, and he decided to have a short swim for himself in the inlet.

Ahead, around a little hook of land, was a sand-bottom pool, into which fed the cool water of his brook, surrounded, except for the channel into the lake proper, by woods. He left the beach and cut directly up and over the thumb of peninsula, and then he proceeded cautiously, because he heard splashing that wasn't the sound of water gurgling over stones.

Out in the pool, swimming lazily in the sunlight, Irene was so lovely to watch that Anton stole down to cover where he could see her without being discovered. She must have been here a lot, because she was toasted an even golden tan. Smoothly she went under water; after a couple of strokes she rose and broke the surface, but held her lungs inflated to float on her back. Her momentum carried her slowly toward shore. She kicked a couple of times, then stood, sprang as high out of the water as she could with delight. Paddling at the water with her hands, she unhurriedly ascended the sandy slope of the bottom toward the beach where her robe was folded.

When she had come out until the water was thigh-deep, she halted and turned her head as though with suspicion. Anton made no attempt to hide.

But she didn't see him. She took another step beachward, and from then on acted as though she were hypnotized, sleepwalking. One languid step after another, the water breaking at her knees and then below the knees.

Anton jerked his attention to the beach, and for an instant was paralyzed with horror. A little distance beyond her robe was a boulder that had been rose granite but which he had painted black. The rock was bigger than it should have been, and its contours were as hazy as an object seen through tears; because Mr. Zero was parked there, reaching for the girl with his invisible webs—the scent or numbing emanation of power or whatever it was, the means by which it was aided in catching prey.

Early in the game, Anton had narrowly missed being sucked into that trap and then only by a violent effort of will. What made Smoke so valuable was that the potent, beckoning influence only enraged the dog. Smoke recognized it as something that required full obedience, and he obeyed nothing living, no one, not even the pull of hunger, excepting Anton Bulik alone.

Anton's command was a low, terrified groan. "Smoke!"

The dog got going as though it had been catapulted. Jaws laughing wide, it went down in a flowing silver streak, a magic of silent savagery. Smartly it took the headlong flight straight down to the beach, and then cut right and skimmed over the sand.

Anton had jumped to his feet, and shouted frantically without realizing it, before plunging down through the brush after the dog like a madman. Irene didn't hear him. She was walking slowly ashore, smiling raptly, and set foot on the sand, packed hard by the water. It was so close that Anton's wits were numbed with fear; nothing that happened registered, and what he did was purely automatic, only vaguely remembered afterward.

The dog left the sand in a spectacular leap and struck the girl amidships, knocking her back into the water with a resounding splash. Smoke somersaulted over her into the pool, churned, and came out again in an explosion of water.

Anton came pounding down the beach, avoided the hysterically angry dog and plunged into the pool. Grabbing up Irene, he floundered out until he was waist-deep with her and watched. Inch by inch, Smoke's murderous rage forced Mr. Zero up the beach. Nothing else could happen. The dog was too quick to be caught and was absolutely without fear, whether Mr. Zero was just a cowardly hulk or not. The retreat accelerated until Zero was going away at the speed of a man's walk, entering the woods and laboring over the point down to the shore of the lake whence Anton had just come.

He carried Irene ashore, left her for a while and came back, to find her sitting on the black boulder, dazed. She couldn't remember anything that happened, and he had to tell her.

That scent of Zero's could be detected at a distance of twenty or thirty feet. It wasn't an animal odor, perhaps not an odor at all, but it was damned effective. It was an inexplicable condition of the air, and was as satisfying as a cool drink to a man going mad with thirst on the desert. Its very elusiveness was hypnotizing, with the elusive suggestion of perfume worn by someone beautiful, of great tranquillity or the satisfying weariness preceding sleep without pain, a tormenting glimpse of the

Elysian Fields. Within his area of operations Mr. Zero exercised the fascination of something which had to be explored once that ineffable glow ascended into the victim's brain.

"It was something like that," Irene murmured.

They were sitting on the woodshed steps of the farmhouse in the late afternoon, and Anton suggested that he might walk over to the Leigh farmhouse with her.

He thought she hadn't heard him, but she announced, as though no contradiction were possible, "I'm going to stay here."

Gently he rubbed the back of his head, and she reminded him: "You asked me to marry you one time. Remember that night? I laughed, and you got up and went away and didn't come back. I was laughing because I had you. When you didn't understand, there was nothing for me to do but keep on laughing."

"Well," said Anton.

"We can go into town and take care of the license and things."

Anton could hardly breathe, but managed to say, "I guess so." He pondered on an excuse to get inside and make his bed, because he didn't want her to see it that way, because he really wasn't sloppy. And then they were discussing Mr. Zero.

Irene startled him by saying: "We ought to celebrate, maybe, but that makes me think—why don't you feed him?"

"Feed whom?"

"Mr. Zero. As far as I can make out from what you've said, he's just an enormous stomach. Never satisfied. He's never refused anything that can be digested. Like a permanent Thanksgiving dinner."

"Hm-m-m. Suppose I drive a couple of cows into his neighborhood," Anton suggested ironically, and chewed on a straw.

"Suppose you do. He'll get them sooner or later."

"Nope. I'm keeping them in the barn. Zero will go up to a building, but he won't go inside, or else he doesn't know there is an inside."

"When he gets hungry he might find out."

Anton took the straw out of his mouth and sat with his elbows on his knees for a long time, motionless with thought. He turned his head and looked down to where Mr. Zero was, beyond the corn crib.

Suddenly he got up and stretched and laughed. He snapped his fingers at Smoke, and Irene got up and followed along. At first Anton thought of having Smoke do the job, but decided on something more direct. He took a chicken from a coop and killed it, Irene watching. Going down within range of Zero, Anton let some blood splatter and dragged the flopping hen on the ground the short distance down the road to the granary. There he left the headless bird to accept its destiny and entered the two-story black building. With the door open, he stood with Irene on the platform until Zero followed the trail of blood and scent and took the flapping chicken into his private nothingness. The hen simply vanished off the ground.

Anton picked up a hundred-pound sack of grain and tossed it off the platform. It disappeared before it reached the dusty ground. In midair it was gone.

Promptly he seized another bulging sack and tossed it, and the same thing happened as to the first. And again, and again. Grimly he continued until his shirt was plastered to his skin with sweat. Outside, Smoke sat on his haunches, head cocked aside and watching with interest.

At last Anton leaned against the door jamb and said: "My God, what's the use? How much can the beast hold?"

But Smoke got up, sniffing, because slowly Mr. Zero was moving away from the granary. Very slowly, ponderously. The dog wagged his tail with contempt and jumped up in the granary to stick his nose in Anton's hand.

"Can you see him, Smoke?" Anton asked.

In the darkness they trudged back up to the farmhouse.

There was no sign of Mr. Zero the next day, nor the next. But on the third afternoon Smoke came back from a ramble, and his actions, whining and running off, and whining while he waited, persuaded Anton to follow him.

What was left of Mr. Zero was deep in the big woods. There was an irregular clearing here, and in it, on the ground, was something which would have been inexplicable to anyone except Anton and Irene. There was a broad circle about forty-five or fifty feet in circumference, of some crisp, black stuff that crunched to powder underfoot like eggshell—like the rim of a huge mushroom that had dried to powder in the sun.

In the middle of this ring was a huge pile of wet yellow grain which gleamed like billions and billions of wheat-size grains of solid gold.

Macklin's Little Friend

THE OLD, SUBSTANTIAL residences on Lincoln Avenue stood in blocks of secret, dark masses against the swiftly failing green pallor of the western sky. A fleet new coupé slowed, slipping forward close to the curb. After crossing the intersection of Mills Lane it stopped at the corner residence as silent as destiny. The powerful white beams of the headlights went off. Out of the car staggered the muscular, personable, but now nearly furtive figure of Willard Macklin.

Light from the corner lamp reached his face. His gray eyes were ablaze. Somewhat lean, and intense with years of determined study, his dark features were extraordinarily accented by his glistening paleness. He wore no hat. But the huge and perplexing turban of bandages surmounting his head seemed to be as great a burden as he could support.

Shakily mounting the steps like a drunken man, he paced laboriously up a red brick walk dividing panels of level green velvet lawn.

Above the doorbell in the brick wall, partially hidden by vines which swarmed over the house, a browned brass plate carried in modest relief the name of THEODORE KLEY, M.D. One year following Macklin's imminent marriage to lovely Barbara Kley, allowing that time for the honeymoon and their getting settled, old Kley meant to retire and Macklin would assume his moderate but rich practice. Macklin inclined the sickening weight of his head for a moment, then stumped the bell with his thumb.

After a moment old Theodore himself drew the door wide. A stocky, heavy-boned Dutchman, grizzled, he still had his penetrating and infallible blue eyes and big but neat hands that were marvels of surgical skill.

Macklin had those same muscular, unerring hands. Sight of the huge bandage drew a grunt of surprise from old Kley. He hooked the slim, fragrantly reeking cigar out of his mouth, wet his broad lips and swallowed. Then he said gutturally and angrily, "Don't stand there. Come inside!"

Macklin blundered in, smiling shakily. "Where's Barbara?"

"Upstairs finishing her bath; she'll be down directly."

Macklin indicated his head, and said jerkily, "This—this thing has been driving me crazy. Wait till you see it! You've got to do something about it, sir, before Barbara finds out about it."

Scowling at the mysterious turban, Kley closed the door and said softly, "We will go into the study."

They heard Barbara's bare feet hurrying down the hall upstairs to her room. Her door didn't close, so Kley closed the door to his office. This was half-study, half-laboratory, and occupied the entire ground floor of a wing which had been added to the east side of the house. Heavy walnut shelves built against two walls to the height of Kley's reach were jammed to the heads with a valuable medical library.

At the rear wall stood a large, windowed cabinet with a murderous and glittering array of surgical instruments on glass shelves. There was a patent chair fixed to the floor, used for minor operations. Alongside it, a metal standard equipped with a variety of electrical instruments— sterilizing apparatus.

Near the front windows stood Kley's big desk laden with typewriter, the open volume which he had been reading, notes on his own third work, and accumulations of papers and correspondence.

He gestured Macklin into an easychair beside the desk, and lowered his own bulk unhurriedly into a swivel chair back of the typewriter.

Macklin's lips parted, but he couldn't say anything. He was plainly in the ripest kind of funk.

Kley put his cigar out in an ash tray and reflected gruffly, "We've been wondering what you were doing these last two weeks. We knew you were working hard to get the house ready before the marriage, but—" Indicating the bandage with a nod he asked, "What's that?"

"I don't know." Macklin shivered, and his gray eyes were bright with fear. Abruptly, as though he were committing a reckless act, he began to unwind the gauze from his head. Kley watched. In the end, the bandages protected no slightest wound nor head injury. But there was something contained in the bandages which rendered Kley's ordinarily placid face stiff with stupefaction. He let out an explosive breath. Rising slowly from his chair he stared with as much disbelief as though his dead wife Anna had abandoned the rotten mahogany of her coffin and walked into the room. Medical impossibilities.

"For Heaven's sake, what is it?" Macklin asked in a shattered voice.

Kley swallowed with incredulity; his heavy lips worked soundlessly as he bent far over the desk for closer scrutiny. He was plainly aghast. "Keep hold of yourself, boy," he rumbled gently. "It isn't anything. It's nothing at all."

Macklin laughed, a tortured, one-syllable sound. "I'm not a child," he gasped. "Do something about it!"

Bound twice around his sweating head under the many turns of gauze, and now depending from his right temple into a nest of coils on the floor, was a fifty-six-inch length of limp tentacle—a slim, easily tapering rope of flesh.

Kley had never before seen nor heard of anything even remotely resembling it. Formed in general like a serpent, but without any recognizable head, this dangling obscenity was studded from root to tip with close, even rows of hard, rugose nodes or nipples graduated in size from about that of small peas down to pinheads.

At its base, the frightful appendage was horny. More phenomenal still was its partial translucency, within which seemed suspended a complex and fine network of ruby veins stemming from one main dark artery like a backbone. The artery did not seem to continue into Macklin's head.

Kley took hold of the dreadful tentacle, tugged gently. There was no pulse. And the thing was like flexible horn, tough, sinewy, like the tentacle of an octopus save in it tapering roundness.

"Be quiet now for just a little," Kley cautioned in a strangled voice. He circled to the operating chair, selected a tubular chromium instrument from the standard alongside, and returned drawing fine electric cord from a reel under spring tension. The chromium tube was closely jointed, for flexibility, and terminated in a glass capsule which produced a tiny intense beam of white light. This needle of light Kley directed at the juncture of the tentacle with Macklin's head. He played the beam raptly, pushing at the horny root experimentally with his thumb. The light snicked off.

Kley made a clucking sound and muttered, "Damnedest thing." Aloud, to Macklin, "Where the devil did you get this little friend of yours?"

Macklin shook his head. "It sprouted from that cut I got two weeks ago. At first it was just a bud, but it's been growing like—like this. I've been holing up because I didn't want to scare Barbara out of her wits."

Kley made a sound of comment. "The only reason she isn't down here with her arms around your neck is to show you that she can make you wait, too." Soberly, "Tell me about that cut again."

"Why, Barbara and I went picnicking. There's a spring-fed lake on the Joel Spinney farm, north of town. We were going swimming, and I dived in first. The lake has rocky banks, and I grazed my head on a jagged rock under the water, I guess. We drove right back here."

Kley had dressed the wound. "There were three deep slashes, like the work of a knife or fangs," he remembered. His accent had become strong. "Something bit you."

"What, sir?"

"You want this to come off, don't you?"

"Good Heavens, yes! But—"

"There is a perfect line of cleavage at the temple. If the blood vessel is articulated there the way it looks, there won't be any trouble. Relax, boy. We'll dock this fellow in a jiffy." Kley returned the chromium light to the fixture, headed for the cabinet and selected a lean and hungry-looking scalpel and a strong and ugly pair of forceps with ridged jaws.

"No local. Nothing!" Macklin burst out. In a groan, "Lord! I've had this thing in bed with me for two weeks!"

"Is there any feeling in it?"

"No, but the whole side of my head is numb. I don't think I'll feel the knife."

Kley nodded. For a moment the tentacle held his perplexed regard, and then his hands went to work as though there were brain fiber in his finger ends. Macklin paled as the scalpel flickered in a ribbon of light and the ropy growth fairly peeled from his temple.

He remained motionless, but his pallor turned faintly greenish. With a grimace, Kley dropped the limp amputation on the desk in a heap of convolutions and proceeded to sterilize and bandage the raw circle on Macklin's head. Following the line of cleavage with absolute precision, he had not drawn a drop of blood. The membrane protecting the source of the growth remained intact.

In conclusion, he produced a bottle of hoary old brandy and brimmed a slender, soap-bubble glass of it which he urged on Macklin. Kley had one for himself. After it was down he remarked somberly, "I didn't tell you that I've been investigating the small lake on Spinney's farm. You know it's the only one of its kind."

Macklin's hand strayed to the neat bandage on his temple. "How do you mean, sir?"

Kley listened for sounds of Barbara's coming, then said, "About the way it was formed, I mean." His voice was idly musing, putting Macklin at ease. "Ten or twelve years ago a meteorite fell on Spinney's farm. You might say Heaven did Spinney a good turn. The meteorite smashed through a shell of granite south of the farmhouse, the only worthless ground on his land. It opened a reservoir, and the water climbed to form this remarkable lake."

"Oh, I remember something about that." The brandy was bringing a flush into Macklin's lean face. He kept his eyes away from the thing on the desk near Kley's elbow. "There were some men from the university who went down there to take soundings and raise the meteorite if they could. But they thought it must have blown up under water. What did you mean, sir, when you said that wound of mine was a bite?"

Kley shrugged heavily. With slight reluctance he asked, "You don't really think you cut your head on the rocks, do you?"

"But there's nothing in the pool, sir," Macklin argued. "There never has been."

"I'm not so sure of that," Kley stated ambiguously. Slowly, "I've been talking with Joel Spinney. He had lost a fine dog, cattle, and many of his chickens. This has been going on to some extent for years."

"I don't understand."

"His animals disappear. He has found packs of feathers caught in the rocks at the water level in his lake. What's more, there isn't any small game, no squirrels or mice or anything on four legs, in the woods and pasture near the lake. There used to be plenty."

Macklin laughed uncomfortably. "That doesn't mean anything."

"Spinney and I think it does. The crows raise Ned over the wood several times a week. Spinney has come running, but never got anything but a splash in the pool. You can find the bones of game in the woods. Spinney thinks a big snake is killing his hens."

"A snake? There aren't any snakes around here big enough to carry off a dog. His dog must have run away."

"He told me about hearing a heifer bawling in the pasture one evening. When he got there the ground was plowed up with hoofs, and no heifer. There was also a groove, like the track made by an oversize bicycle tire, hitting through bushes and weeds straight to the pool. And he said he thought the water in the pool looked reddish, but it might have been the reflection of the sunset."

Macklin held himself from shivering, though the night was sultry and without breeze. He remembered his deep dive into the crystal water, and the solid, wholly unexpected blow his head had received. If some problematical water snake were lurking there, it might have been startled from a nest in the rocks and struck him a glancing blow before retreating to the bottoms. But no such reptile was indigenous to this middle-Western State, if indeed it existed at all. Nor was there any ready accounting for the phenomenon of the abominable parasitic growth which had been developing with mushroom speed and sapping his strength for these many days.

Papers rustled surreptitiously on old Theodore's desk.

Macklin's gaze went rigid and Kley turned his square, massive head with a jerk. The tentacle lay serpentined and still. The air was dead, and Kley thought the thing's convolutions must have disturbed the loose papers in settling. But the suggestion in the sound was gruesome.

"It moved." Macklin couldn't keep the hysteria out of his whisper. His lips were like a scar.

"Nonsense," Kley snorted in his heavy bass. "It has only just settled a little. I'll get rid of it."

The butt of the growth, the root which had been covered with a fine pink membrane after the amputation, was now whitely, gleamingly denuded. Interested, Kley picked up the scalpel and tried the exposed surface with it. The microscopic steel point slipped off. Kley took hold of the firm flesh of the butt and again tried to score the rounded enamel with the steel. But it was of such tight, resistant texture that even the scalpel's wicked sheerness couldn't find a flaw.

Faint markings in the bright enamel were discernible. The lines zigzagged closely as though two parts had knit, or like small, wonderfully perfect, needle-toothed jaws rigidly locked. The suggestion of close rows of teeth girt with a fold of leathery lips was increasingly obvious.

Kley muttered something under his breath and poised the scalpel to make an incision in the specimen just behind the blind head. Before the steel touched it the thing moved fluidly, the coils turning as smoothly as flowing oil. It stopped, and Kley was still with a vast surprise. Abruptly and violently he brought his powerful left hand down and seized one of the coils. With the contact the blood drained from his face. He ripped his

hand away and sprang to his feet with a hoarse, convulsive oath. Starting, his eyes were blind with agony.

Macklin shouted, "It's alive!"

That hideous, tapering tentacle with its rows of tough studs streaked
over the edge of the desk with a heavy, burring sound. As luck would
have it, the horror shot down into the wastebasket beside the desk. All
sinew and electric nerve, it moved with lightning velocity and piled up
in the wastebasket with the force of a falling club. Simultaneously
Macklin erupted from his chair, overturned the steel basket on the rug
and knelt on it. He looked up, breathless.

Kley's breath hissed. The palm of his left hand was flayed in a neat
strip denuding knuckle bone, muscle and tendon. His palm was a cup of
bright blood which brimmed over and pattered on the rug like ghostly
little footfalls.

Kley glared at his hand as though he didn't comprehend what had
happened, then broke for a washstand at the end of the room. His hand
hurt as though seared, but his face was merely grim. He washed the
wound and kept swabbing it with brownish stuff from a bottle he
snatched from the cabinet. The spring of blood lessened, and at last he
was able to bandage the numb hand. His bull voice came over his
shoulder, "That devil! Don't let it get away!"

"For Heaven's sake, what is it?" Macklin asked frantically. A commotion in the wastebasket shook him, magnifying his horror.

"There still are forms of life that we have never dreamed of," Kley
said with a kind of cold passion. Then, his eyes quirked with realization,
he added, "You know, that hellish thing was mature. That's why there
was such a plain line of cleavage. In a few hours it would have detached
itself from you naturally if I hadn't cut it off. Ah, if I only had had the
brains to cut it in two!"

"But, Dr. Kley—"

Scowling, Kley turned and snapped with a kind of sinister intelligence, "Something in Spinney's Lake bit you, and impregnated the
wound. Nature tries all methods of reproduction."

Which meant that another nightmare like the one imprisoned under
the basket dwelt in the bottoms of Spinney's Lake. The fact that the
monster was of an unknown species did not make it less appalling. In a
race of thought Macklin played with the possibilities of the monster's
origin. It could not have been indigenous to the subterranean reservoir
on Spinney's farm. But the seed of it might have been carried in by the

meteorite out of the vastness of space. Cultures of unknown bacteria and fungus life capable of withstanding extremes of heat and cold had been obtained from meteoritic bodies before this.

It happened before Kley got back to the desk.

Macklin's hundred and eighty-odd pounds shivered and bucked above the upended wastebasket as though he were trying to hold down a series of explosions. He cried out, "I can't hold it down!"

Abruptly, he sprawled headlong into Kley and knocked him off his feet. A litter of waste paper and cigar butts and ashes went flying. They scrambled to their feet at once and in the following frenzied, futile moments they ransacked the entire floor area of the room, on the rug and the tiles and under furniture, but Macklin's little friend had gone into good hiding.

"Well?" Kley exploded gutturally, baffled. "Where did that devil go?"

"It—it just disappeared," Macklin stuttered. He felt like a complete fool. Still dazed, he wiped the perspiration from his throat and face. His temple throbbed. The prodigy having vanished, it seemed now to have been only some gruesome figment of the imagination. He piously wished it were.

But there was Kley prowling tensely about the room with the breathless industry of a big mastiff. Macklin fought down the hysteria that was beginning to shake him and kept searching, too—futilely. His breathing had accelerated raggedly.

The door of the study swung open, framing Barbara Kley's loveliness. She was blond, with hair like molded honey. She had a challenging, fresh, oval face, velvet lips, her father's blue eyes, a boyish and statuesque figure in expensive green silk. She looked from Macklin to her father, at the overturned wastebasket on the sumptuous rug, and alarm jumped into her eyes.

"What have you been doing down here?" she asked sharply. "What's the matter?"

"Nothing!" Kley boomed. "Quick! Close the door!"

Barbara stepped into the office; the door closed heavily behind her. She saw her father's bandaged hand and Macklin's temple and said worriedly, "You're hiding something. Tell me what's wrong. Why were you making such a racket?"

Kley softened his voice. "Wait for us in the den, Barbara." His gaze shifted restlessly, searching the floor. "We have a little work to do; it won't take long."

She appealed to Macklin. "Have you stopped loving me? What's the trouble? How did you hurt yourselves?"

"It's a—a specimen I brought," Macklin said rapidly. "We were examining it, and had an accident. It got away. That's all."

"Oh, that's all!" Barbara mocked. "What kind of specimen was it, then?"

"A leech," Kley blurted irritably. "A giant amphibious leech."

Macklin thought of the spontaneity with which the thing's bloodsucking apparatus had flayed Kley's hand, and looked as sick as he felt. He pleaded, "Wait outside for us, Barbara."

"I'm going to stay right here," she said determinedly.

"Stay close to the door, then," Kley warned. To himself, "Lord! We can't let that hellish thing get loose!"

A stealthy, rubbing sound originating from the bookshelves drew the attention of all three.

"Listen!" Kley ordered in a whisper.

The silence was enormous, and then the leathery studs of that thick, whiplike nightmare were again rubbing against one of the walnut shelves behind the books.

Kley ghosted soundlessly to his desk and quietly drew open the shallow middle drawer. In the course of his profession he had had to deal with maniacs and criminals, and therefore kept at hand the seemingly clumsy but wonderfully efficient automatic which he had used in the War. With this deadliest of small arms he was an infallible shot.

Macklin advanced with him to the bookcase. The slight sound of their approach made the leech still. But it flinched, behind the books, in response to the click of the safety button on the automatic rooted in Kley's fist.

They located the leech. It had retreated behind the books on the third shelf from the bottom, having entered through the space between the tops of the books and the shelf above. When it sprang free from the wastebasket it must have shot through the aperture like an arrow. At a nod from Theodore, Macklin cautiously took hold of half a dozen books on the shelf, suddenly whipped them out and leaped aside.

Barbara saw the head of the thing and screamed with the report of the ugly gun. It was a miss. The leech disappeared backward in motion too quick for the eye to follow. But there was a bullet hole in the backboard where the head had been.

"Quick, eh?" Kley ejaculated. "Don't let it get near you. Those rows of buttons on it are suckers; you saw what fast work they did on my hand." Blood was seeping through the bandage now.

In that brief glimpse they had seen the amphibious worm's frightful jaws. The jaws were supplied with long, curving, murderous fangs anchored well back in the head by sloping roots. Such blind ferocity in any living thing was enough to shake any one's nerve, but Macklin stole vengefully, crouched over and listening, along the wall of books.

At the end of the shelf a length of the blind tentacle issued like a snake striking. It stabbed half a dozen times, in a blur of motion, at the books on the shelf above. It shot through the aperture above the books on the fourth shelf before Macklin could get out of Kley's line of fire. He cursed and looked back at Kley with his lips twitching.

"Never mind," Kley grunted. "Just so it doesn't get out of the room."

Still at bay, the monster no longer advertised its exact position by prowling behind the books. One way of locating it would be to jam one book after another against the backboard, on the chance of pinning the creature momentarily.

Kley had the idea too. "But it's too dangerous," he advised. "Think of how powerful it is and how fast it can move."

"You're not going to do anything as crazy as that, Willard," Barbara chimed in, terrified. "Where did that horrible thing come from?"

"From Spinney's Lake," Macklin said shortly. He mopped the perspiration from his face and said to Kley, "Do you suppose that damned thing can hear? It acts as though it can."

"We can find out."

Macklin whistled piercingly, and was rewarded with a spasmodic slurring sound near the end of the shelf closest to the door.

"So," Kley rumbled, gluing his eyes to the spot. "Tactile hearing. Tough as they are, those suckers must be sensitive enough to pick up sound vibrations. Lord, what a foul thing! All mouth! In that case we do it this way."

With his lips straight, Kley nosed the gun against the back, low, of a clothbound work on forensic medicine. He squeezed the trigger. In the closed room the report of the gun was stunning. Simultaneously a block of books erupted in Kley's face, knocking the pistol from his fist as he staggered backward and recovered his balance.

The monster's tail lashed out, a quivering, tortured whip of living sinew. Barbara was speechless. As Macklin dropped to all fours and scrambled for the gun, the monster raged down the shelf. In a boil of whipping steel it catapulted more of Kley's prized volumes from the shelf. The thing's coils thrashed powerfully in plain view for an instant, and then it appeared to dissipate among the splashing pages of Kley's books.

Kley held his battered jaw and gasped, "My! My, dot's actif!"

"Active!" Macklin snapped, mocking Kley's guttural understatement. "Not any more, though. I think you put a shot in it that time." But doubt and excitement had accelerated the beat of his heart to a continuous murmur of pain. And he was no stronger for his two weeks of sickness. The leech might be injured, but it wasn't dead, and he couldn't find it. He moved the books on the floor aside with his foot, and flirted glances along the disordered shelf of books. They listened. There was not the least stir of movement. With a puzzled grunt, Kley stooped and made the wastebasket clang with a rap of his knuckles. There was no response from the bookcase to this new sound. Macklin passed the gun back to Kley, hunched his shoulders and without a word began emptying the fourth shelf. Nothing there.

He asked Barbara, "Did you see where it went?"

Her eyes were wide and brilliant, and she couldn't speak; she shook her head.

Macklin unloaded the third shelf, stacking the books on the floor. He was wet with perspiration. So was old Kley, who stayed close beside him with the ready gun.

Then it had to be the fifth shelf. Damn the thing's silence!

"Careful, now!" Kley warned.

Macklin's eyebrows were laden with sweat and he felt dizzy. He mopped his whole face and neck, mentally gearing himself for another encounter with the giant leech's ready fury. He hoped that it was dead, that the effect of Kley's shot was the hideous worm's dying agony. An idea occurred to him. The leech was a blind and deaf thing, but the one sense with which nature endowed it made it as formidable as a tiger. If it could feel sound, conceivably it could feel light. Tactile vision, as in plant life. Its first act upon coming alive was to streak for protective darkness. The aperatures in the bookcase were the darkest shadows in the room. They had taught it not to answer to sudden sounds, but sudden light might goad it.

"What's the matter?" Kley asked.

"I've got an idea," Macklin answered. "I think light bothers that thing. You know, the way a shrill note hurts a dog's ears."

"Good!" Kley nodded. According to Spinney's information, the curse of his lake went abroad pillaging chiefly after dark. If it slaughtered stray chickens during the day, it was a dark day, or else it was driven into the sunlight only by its unappeasable hunger. It was, as Kley expressed it, all mouth.

Macklin got the chromium peep light which Kley had used and bent the flexible end so that light could be directed downward behind the row of books. He wet his lips and asked, "Ready?"

"Ready," Kley grunted. "Try it here at the end, first."

Macklin slipped the slim but powerful torch deep into the shelf and directed the bent end downward. Kley stood woodenly. The automatic was like part of his fist.

From the door came the soft rush of Barbara's breathing. Against her white face her lips looked like a bright scar.

Macklin snapped the button on the torch and a beam of light spurted down behind the books. The sudden impact of the light must have tormented the cornered leech just as much as the bullet. At least, the spontaneous fury of its reaction took both Kley and Macklin by complete surprise.

A section of the big medical books burst from the shelf as though dynamited. A book caught Macklin across the throat, filling his head with fire. He dropped the torch and it snicked back into the fixture beside the operating chair.

As though it had been shot from a gun, the maddened leech struck athwart Kley's body with a sickening, clubbing sound and all his breath left him explosively. The thud of impact was sharpened by the clean crack of bone. The gun sounded with three mighty reports in quick succession.

Drawn up stiffly, as though in insupportable pain, Barbara parted her lips to scream, but the sound was only a long, searing whisper. Her eyes looked mad.

A frantic gobbling sound issued from Macklin's throat. He hurled himself at the doomed Kley and tried to rip off the leech. But he snatched his hands free instantly with blood running from his finger tips. Kley blundered backward into the bookcase, his massive body warped.

Like a spiral of steel cable the leech bound Kley's body. Its blunt, horny head had gone through his jacket and was half buried in his breast. Studded with ravenous suckers, the leech bound his left arm crushingly against his side and continued around his waist, feeding. Kley's chest was in an inexorably closing vise and his blunt features fast empurpled with the stoppage of circulation and lack of breath. Veins stood out on his face in knotted violet cords. When the thing went around him like a steel hose his left arm had been broken. But what shocked Macklin and Barbara to the point of insanity was the way in which that spiraled length of ferocity was melting into Kley's helpless body—feeding, through fabric, deep into his flesh.

Macklin had snatched up the scalpel and was back with it. Kley brought up the gun in a trembling arc and half unconsciously prodded the leech with the muzzle. His broken arm dangled. He tried to say something to Macklin, but his lungs had collapsed and his lips scarcely quivered.

Holding the scalpel like a dagger, Macklin attacked the leech just behind the head, cramping Kley hard against the gutted bookshelves. Severing that tough sinew was like trying to cut tempered rubber. Kley shook his blackening head in a wordless negative. Macklin got the blade of the scalpel under the leech and jerked with all his strength. The crazy violence of that effort severed the leech's head from its body, but it was too late. The gun roared, jumped in Kley's fist. His arm dropped and the gun fell on the floor. The bullet had passed through his heart; his body relaxed and he pitched forward.

The leech was dying. It worked convulsively, freeing itself in bursts of nervous reflex from the dead surgeon's body. Scarcely knowing what he was doing, Macklin reached down and snatched it entirely free. He whipped it high over his head and smashed it down on the floor with the bitterest passion. Then, aiming deliberately with the gun, he discharged the five remaining bullets into a twitching length of blind sinew that was still trying to crawl. He continued pulling the trigger after the clip was exhausted, until Barbara ran sobbing to him and stopped him.

Called by neighbors, a squad car had stopped in front of the house; two uniformed cops were hammering on the door.

The police limousine passed the city limits, heading for Spinney's farm. This was early on a brilliant and hazeless afternoon five days following the death of Dr. Theodore Kley. Beside Detective Joseph Waller, who was driving, sat Detective Sergeant George Brehm, with a bomb in his lap. The bomb consisted of numerous sticks of dynamite roped together, with a cap, and a coil of fuse like a whitewashed spring. Hence no one was smoking.

In the rear seat rode Barbara Kley and Will Macklin, who also carried a burden. This was five pounds of beefsteak wrapped in brown paper. The paper was getting wet with meat juices.

The limousine was brought to a stop at the edge of Spinney's woods, a moderate sprint from the roughly elliptical lake. Macklin compelled Barbara to remain in the car and accompanied the two detectives.

In a land of lakes Spinney's Lake could be called only a pool, however deep and crystal-clear. The water was of unquestionable purity, but some vestigial instinct deterred the farm animals from picking their way down through the garter of rocks to drink at the water's edge.

The three men halted on the brink of a granite table overhanging the untrembling mirror of water—a surface of breathless innocence that was, but just as false as a spoken lie. The overhead sun, now inclining more appreciably from the perpendicular, penetrated to an unusual depth. No moss grew on the rocks, submerged or on the banks. And there were overhangs and labyrinthine caves in the depths where it was always absolute night.

Without delay, Macklin pitched the sodden package of meat toward the middle of the pool. The water geysered; but even while it was quieting they could see the package sinking, staining the water a little. Far off on a brown-black slope beyond Spinney's farmhouse crawled a team of horses with their black coats shining with sweat. Spinney sat hunched on the cultivator they drew, and from beneath him climbed a soft plume of dust.

Out of the pool's depths, while the package was still in sight, foamed a savage projectile of such proportions that the two hard-boiled detectives jerked backward, getting in the way of each other. The leech was a larger edition of the one Macklin had killed. More than a dozen feet in length, it seemed even more horrible with its maculations of dirty-tan and violet and inky-black flecks. A spotted nightmare, jaws parted in living murder. It struck and overshot the mark as its coils whipped around the package of bloody meat. Water burst over the pool in a glittering shower like broken glass.

The bomb had been set down on the granite footing. Macklin lighted a match and touched the petal of flame to the fuse. It ignited with a spurt; he lifted the bundle of dynamite stocks with both hands and heaved it into the pool.

"Run like hell!" he blurted, and was sprinting for the police care before the bomb hit the water.

Waller and Brehm weren't far behind him. At the car the two detectives plugged their ears and turned around to watch, but Macklin piled inside and took Barbara in his embrace.

She buried her head in the hollow of his shoulder and sobbed. "Don't ever leave me." Her voice was blurred. "Can't we get married to-morrow?" Do we have to wait any longer?"

"No, darling, we don't have to wait any longer."

Then the earth vibrated as the bomb went off. The jagged granite walls of the lake acted like the bore of a cannon, and earth and steaming water smoked up into the sky with thunder like a volcano. The echoes rolled back in deafening concussions, and the banks of the lake caved in, completely sealing the reservoir. Where the lake had been was a shallow crater with saffron smoke and dust hanging over it. In the distance Spinney's team broke and stampeded down the long slope.

Detective Waller lighted a cigarette nervously. "Say," he asked, "did you see what snagged onto that hunk of bait?"

Detective Sergeant Brehm cleared his throat. "Yeah."

"What the hell was it?"

"I don't know," Brehm said forcibly. "And so help me, I don't ever want to know."

The Glass Coffin

THE LAST SEEN of lovely Kathleen McQuade was some time between twelve-thirty and one o'clock, shortly previous to the time she had set for her luncheon-bridge. She had complimented the maid for the artistically set luncheon table in the sun room. After a glance at the two bridge tables with their equipment of cards, pencils, cigarettes, and trays, and apparently satisfied that all was perfection, Kay had left the house. The old McQuade house was located in Maxwell Heights, at the highest point of the bluff overlooking the river. The finest residential district in the city, Heights once had been a city unto itself, and still had its shops catering to the rich, theaters and a playhouse in its small and rather quaint business district.

Three blocks from the house Kay passed a shop dealing in fancy groceries. She was a conspicuous girl. She wore a dress of formal outline, with a richly draped skirt that caressed her splendid legs as she walked, and a floppy straw hat that made her look like an animated poppy. She had a gorgeous body. Under clinging silk her exceptional breasts were secrets more than half revealed and no man, possibly not many women, who saw her so could think of anything but girls, girls, girls. The point was that she was as lovely as all that, the embodiment of all feminine allure, that she drew the eye as only beauty can. Yet, after the white-aproned grocer greeted her ingratiatingly, and in response she gave him free of charge a smile that made him forget his garden-variety wife and two children and dream of the impossible for a time, Kay swung around the corner and vanished into the unknown.

Not immediately. For the grocer strolled casually past his luscious display of vegetables to the corner and looked after the doomed girl, dwelt on the perturbing motion of her hips and the arousing shapeliness of her legs as she walked. It was in his mind that she was on the way to Zuchet's, the florist's, and he could have kept her in sight all the way to Zuchet's on the lower bluff. But a limousine pulled in to the curb in front of the grocery store, one of the snooty old hens of the district who shopped personally because she distrusted her cook or butler, and the grocer had to descend from the pearly clouds to the sordid reality of ringing up sales on the cash register. So he didn't see Kay McQuade reach the end of the block.

At the house, Kay's maid waited until a quarter of two, when luncheon wouldn't keep any longer. Some of the hors-d'oeuvres, especially the pate on little toast rafts, were beginning to look deadly.

At three-thirty Kay had still not returned, so her brother Arnold fourthed at one of the bridge tables for her after shaking up a couple of batches of cocktails. For the moment, as far as Arnold McQuade was concerned his sister's absence was a bit of good luck. Of the seven girls on hand, his, Jeanne de Winter, was far and away the most beautiful and McQuade couldn't get enough of her. He thought she was more beautiful than his own sister, and wasn't far off in his belief that she was one of the most rapid methods ever devised by nature for raising a man's temperature. And keeping it raised. Jeanne had a closely-molded glory of dark, silken hair, wide, alert black eyes, and incomparable red lips that seemed always at the point of smiling but seldom smiled save for Arnold McQuade. The real beauty of her soft lips was the most important thing about her; her slim body, her athletic torso with the suave hips and the firm, twin thrills of her breasts, all of her splendid youth and gay personality was summarized in her velvet lips, inexpressibly delicate lips that always looked kissed. They had a sincere, thorough understanding, Jeanne and Arnold. When they got around to it they might marry, but there was no hurry, and being young they set a high value on stolen sweets.

The other girls at the bridge party knew about the affair and envied Jeanne more or less openly because Arnold was regarded as a "catch." First of all, of course, was the McQuade money and position in society. A close second was his physique, combined with which was intelligence and talent. He kept tanned the year around, and if his slate-gray eyes weren't set so deep the gleam in them would have been mischievous. At twenty-three he acted like thirty or better, and could be regarded as more than a promising young painter. Most of his work went into portraits, because human beings fascinated him in their infinite variety. When he did a landscape it was unusual, and his nudes were startling. He showed only the nudes posed for by professional models, because in spite of his close, brilliant technical method with its hint of surreality, his subjects were easily recognizable. Jeanne had fought with him to persuade him to offer a flamboyant nude of herself for the annual City Museum show, and he had refused point-blank.

"The idea of a gang of foul-minded yokels ogling your body, even if it's only a canvas," Arnold said, "would gag me. Sure it's art! That canvas probably would take the first award, but the honor doesn't mean a damned thing to me, the canvas is not for sale, and the amount of the prize wouldn't begin to pay for what the scandal clubs would do to your reputation. Nix!"

"Why, Arnold," Jeanne mocked in her lazy, golden voice, "you don't think people would whisper that we were having an affair, do you? How old-fashioned!"

"You know damned well they'd say it!"

"They wouldn't be far wrong, would they, darling?" she laughed. "If you want to keep me a secret, you oughtn't to leave the canvas so well displayed upstairs in the studio. You know, your dear sister has shown a number of her friends through the studio when you've been out, several times. Everyone in our set at least knows you've done that canvas, and knows what a really swell job it is. If you don't exhibit it, tongues will start wagging about us anyhow. Darling, they've got us going and coming. Don't you see?"

"Damn that sister of mine anyhow!"

But the exclamation was scarcely more than rueful. He was genuinely fond of Kathleen, as was Jeanne. Before the first rubber of bridge had been completed this afternoon, the same dismaying thought occurred to him and Jeanne simultaneously, and their eyes met in a brief glance that was electric with apprehension. Within two years more than a dozen girls had been reported missing, and none had been found. Perhaps the monster had struck again, and Kathleen was gone from the world. Something had happened to her; she would not stand up her guests like this for any reason whatsoever. As the afternoon waned, the very sunlight became tawny and thick with something sinister and forlorn. After the bridge game broke up the usual conversation and laughter turned false with an undertone of anger and hysteria as the girls overcompensated for fear.

Fear of the unknown strikes in high places also. Of the missing girls, all but one had resided in Maxwell Heights. A terror was at large, close by. It operated even in the blaze of noon, even though the Heights had become as closely and efficiently policed as any district in the world. Notorious for their abhorrence of secrets and the supernatural, the police expected to capture sooner or later a sex-mad murderer. If such a man existed, his cunning was such that no trace of crime could be detected in any of the disappearances. None of the girls had any reason for dropping out of sight. But if they wanted to vanish utterly, their right to do so was undeniable, while it certainly remained a matter of hotter and hotter police inquiry.

From the maid, Arnold had received the belief that Kay had gone to the florist's for a corsage of orchids. Before reporting to the police, Arnold made a thorough investigation of his own by telephone. He talked with Emil Zuchet, the florist, who informed him that Kay had not visited his shop. He could state this positively because during the noon hour, when his two clerks were at lunch, he, Zuchet himself, took care of trade in the showroom. His two clerks said she had not been in before twelve, nor from one to five.

Arnold talked with the grocer, made numerous other phone calls, and at the end remained baffled by the fact that Kay had disappeared somewhere between the grocer's and the florist's. He reported Kay missing to an old friend of the family, Lieutenant Furness, who admitted reluctantly that the missing girls on the blotter numbered fourteen. Now fifteen.

Jeanne had remained for supper, after which he adjourned with her to the enormous studio upstairs. On the easel was another full length canvas of her, just begun, which he had intended to work on most of the evening if Jeanne didn't tire.

With no exhibitionism nor affectation she proceeded to disrobe near a princely lounge covered with *cafe-au-lait* chenille, whose whopping cushions were stuffed with down. Jeanne was wearing a button-down-the-front dress of uncrushable linen, which came off to reveal her sheathed in a whispering taffeta slip. She peeled the slip off over her head, remarking muffledly, "I love to have you watch me get ready, darling. Your eyes do things to me."

"I wish," said Arnold as she laid the slip across the foot of the lounge with the dress, neatly, "someone would tell me why you are so God-damned lovely the way you are now." She stood with her long legs close together. Her panties were the merest trifle of lace, and still in her high-heeled shoes and sheer hose she was breathtakingly beautiful. Call it a million dollars or so worth of curves which were not for sale.

She cupped the twin delights of her breasts in her palms and said, "when you look at me the way you're doing, something happens to me here."

"You're making things happen to me."

Suddenly Jeanne flung out her arms and whirled into a writhing, sinuous dance. She had studied under good teachers and could dance well, but this dance was something she hadn't learned in school. Burlesquing, she gave him a little of the grind with her hips; with her feet set well apart and her knees bent she bucked her hips forward just the right number of times, not mechanically but voluptuously, then writhed as she trailed her hands languorously up her thighs, her athletically firm torso, and as she held her creamy breasts hard she rotated them slowly as though they were twin aches of passion. If she was trying to seduce him, he thought, she was doing a first-class job of it. But what she was really doing was making him forget about his sister, stop worrying until it was certain that Kathleen was gone.

"It's no use, Salome." He tried to make his voice laconic. "Better stop before something gives way."

Jeanne shrugged and quit, sighing, "You can't blame a girl for trying, can you?"

"You know something's happened to Kay as well as I do. What's the use of trying to kid ourselves? We've got to do something!"

Jeanne indicated the dais on which she was to pose. "Let's you and I do a lot of work, shall we? Kay's all right. And even if she has been kidnaped or something, do you think you could compete with Lieutenant Furness and all the detectives down at headquarters? I'll pose, darling, and you go ahead with the canvas. There's no point in worrying until we're sure something's wrong."

Arnold flung down the brush with which he was making the figure drawing on the big canvas. "How are we going to be sure? Just wait? And guess? Not a trace of the other girls was ever found. Something horrible has happened to Kay, and I'll be damned if I can do any work tonight." He scraped the big smear of sienna, which he was going to use for brushing in outlines, off the palette again, put it back in his "junk jar" and clapped the lid on. With all the McQuade money, it was a funny trick of his to be economical with his pigments.

"Well, what are you going to do?" she asked. When he didn't answer immediately she idled over to the chenille lounge and flung herself on it, on her back, with her arms over her head.

"In the game of 'Murder'," Arnold mused startlingly, wiping his hands on a soft cloth, "which is played in the dark, all the players must tell the absolute truth in the mock court which is held following the crime, all the players save the man secretly designated by lot as the 'murderer.' He may lie."

"What do you mean?" Jeanne asked slowly.

"What do you think of Emil Zuchet?"

Jeanne went rigid, relaxed with a sigh. "Don't be silly, darling. That harmless little man? A florist?"

Arnold crossed to the lounge and sat on the edge beside her. Jeanne's use of the word "harmless" indicated that she too thought Zuchet was a peculiar man, the sort that a healthy young being like herself instinctively disliked but did not fear.

Zuchet was not taller than five and a half feet, but he was broad and perhaps weighed more than Arnold's hundred and sixty pounds. Zuchet's features were almost pleasant but not quite. There was a shade too much color in his lips, which could nearly be called sensual. Any sensitive person would have called his eyes evil. Perhaps obscene. They were round black eyes with a liquid jet glisten, and usually he kept them on the floor as though tired, or as though he could hear better than he could see when waiting on customers. He dressed very well and was clean, with his nails always neatly scraped. Mixed in with the fragrance of flowers in his shop was the elusive, cloying scent of an expensive, exotic perfume he wore. The chief thing Arnold remembered about Zuchet was the incident when he accompanied Kathleen to the florist's to order flowers for their mother's funeral. Arnold had happened to be in a position for observing Zuchet unawares, and Zuchet's eyes had crawled over his sister's body like a pair of spiders. More than the man's eyes, Arnold didn't like Zuchet's slow, caressing voice with its indefinable accent. It was a sexual voice, conveying to Arnold, now that he thought of it, insinuations of a rotten mind. It was the voice of a man who had seduced many girls and committed loathsome acts. A fat, lolling voice.

"Once before," Arnold remembered, addressing Jeanne earnestly, "Zuchet was questioned about one of the missing girls. He admitted she had bought flowers there, but said he was not in the habit of molesting or following girls, and didn't know which way she had turned after leaving his establishment."

"Yes, I know." Jeanne looked at him under the satin curve of an arm bent over her face, shielding her eyes from the light. "That was Elaine Betts. Her poor mother was sure that little Mr. Zuchet was an ogre who had attacked and murdered her daughter and buried the body in a flower bed. The police trampled through his gardens and greenhouses, ransacked his house from attic to cellar and didn't find anything. Zuchet started suit against the city for damages, but dropped the suit. I know that story."

Arnold rested his hand on Jeanne's torso, slipped his hand upward on the hyacinthine flesh of her body and chose her dainty right breast. Leaning over her, he kept squeezing the sweet, tight little breast unconsciously in giving emphasis to his words. "Here's the point: in these two cases at least, don't you see that we have only Zuchet's word? He says he knows that Elaine Betts left the store with her flowers *because he was alone and waited on her himself.* When I called him before supper, he told me he was positive that Kay had not been in the store during the noon hour, *because he alone was taking care of customers in the store and he would have waited on her if she had come in.* I think Zuchet is lying."

"But, darling," Jeanne said softly, breathing faster, "a man can't murder fifteen girls and not get caught. You're letting your imagination run away with you."

He caressed her torso absently, as a man might with his wife, and hooked his fingers under the elastic band of her panties. He snapped the band against her stomach a few times; it stung, but she lay quiet. He slipped his hand between her thighs, squeezed the thick of her right thigh hard and said abruptly, "I'm going down to Zuchet's."

"I'm going with you. When you see how wrong you are you're going to feel pretty silly."

"You stay right here and wait for me."

Jeanne sat up and wrapped her naked arms around him, and he felt the eager resilience of her breasts against him, and her cool, wet lips parted against his. He yielded for a moment, thinking that her tongue was a soft, perfumed rapture, stood up suddenly and headed for the door.

"Arnold!" she exclaimed commandingly, and he halted, turned. "You're being foolish. Give me time to dress and I'll go with you. You won't find out anything alone. Let me go in to buy orchids all by myself; if you want to set a trap, that's the only way to do it. You know it. Only girls have disappeared."

"You're not going to disappear!" Arnold snapped.

"Don't be crazy!" she protested; she leaped up and ran to a closet door. She was so beautiful as she ran on her high heels, with her proud young breasts dancing, that Arnold waited, attentive and moody.

She offered a good argument. In the closet hung about a dozen of her dresses, two of them formal for evening wear. Kathleen had probably opened that door at some time or other and smiled, knowing that her brother had chosen the loveliest girl in the city. Jeanne chose a dress which had yards of rippling satin in the skirt, but which was extremely economical in the way it sculptured her hips, waist, breasts; in this creation most of her back was bare, and she had a perfect, delicately tanned back. When she went into Zuchet's, the florist would think that she was on her way to a dance in one of the downtown hotels and had stopped to pick up a corsage. In these crazy days, girls might drop in alone to buy flowers and there was no breach in etiquette. Etiquette is personal. Very. Zuchet's wide mouth might smile, and secretly his gleaming, spidery eyes might crawl. Against his will, Arnold was convinced that Jeanne was right, that as a decoy she would have far more chance for success than himself.

The Zuchet Gardens covered most of the ground on the lower bluff. Aside from the rich terraces, there were the greenhouses with their acres of glass spattered with whitewash, built out in three directions from the house. Connecting directly with the greenhouses, the front room of the house was used as a place of business. There were tall glass cases filled with fresh, dewy, cut flowers, and tables freighted with potted plants.

On either side of the house, the greenhouses extended away and were lost in the humid night. Only the "store" was lighted. Jeanne saw no one in the place through the plate glass windows, but when she opened the door a spring-switch in the jam either rang a bell or turned on a light that brought Zuchet from somewhere in the house.

"Good evening," he purred. His words were a little too slow, as though he were dwelling on some secret pleasure.

"Good evening," Jeanne responded, smiling engagingly. Even though it was such a short walk down here from the McQuade house, Arnold had taken out the roadster and was waiting in it, with the lights out, in the alley a half block up. He was going to wait exactly twenty minutes, time enough for Zuchet to give himself away if he was going to.

Jeanne could not have worn a dress which displayed her body to better advantage. What little there was of the bodice modelled her torso in detail. Her mother had called the dress indecent; under the gleaming satin was only her skin, because fashion wouldn't allow panties or a brassiere to show. Jeanne knew how delectably shaped she was and thought she was lucky to be able to wear a dress like this. Slim ivory seduction, she stood unaffectedly with her shoulders presenting the firm, girlish perfection of her breasts individually under the satin. When she inquired about orchids Zuchet mourned, "I have none cut. Would you care to make a selection from what I have? But no, you might soil such a lovely dress walking through my greenhouses."

"You grow your own orchids, Mr. Zuchet?"

"But yes; I am a florist." Zuchet gurgled with slow laughter. "Would you accept any variety, Miss, or would you like to see all the beauties. I would not like to cut one you do not like," —ingratiatingly— "because it would not live long and Zuchet must run his business at a profit."

"Good heavens!" Jeanne thought, "my twenty minutes will be gone like nothing if he keeps talking as slow as this." Through her head flashed another thought, "'Will you walk into my parlor,' said the spider to the fly. No, he doesn't really care whether I see his orchids or not. But what ugly eyes he has!"

This was a matter of the briefest hesitation before she decided, aloud to Zuchet, "Perhaps you had better let me make my choice. I think I can be careful enough not to soil my skirt."

"Certainly. I will show you the way, please." He turned unhurriedly, and she followed him from the store into a corridor which branched into the greenhouses. Hesitating, he suggested, "We can take the long way around through the gardens, but it is shorter to go through the basement corridor to where they are. You will not get soiled that way."

"All right," she agreed, thinking, "Hurry up! Hurry up! Before Arnold comes boiling in and makes a fool of himself."

Zuchet opened a door in the corridor, turned a switch that jumped the basement into view with bright yellow light. As she gathered up the extravagance of satin at one side of the dress and prepared to descend the wooden stairs after him, he was out of sight for a moment. She heard another click as though another switch had been worked, then a trembling vibration of short duration, as though the unit of an electric refrigerator had run briefly. Her high heels tapped the wooden steps briskly as she went down.

Halfway across the basement, Zuchet turned his head to smile at her, then proceeded into what seemed to be the entrance of a dark corridor. Jeanne glanced around swiftly at stacks of flower pots and garden equipment as Zuchet turned lights on beyond the entrance and waited for her.

On the threshold she stopped with an exclamation of rapture at what she saw beyond him. Smiling, Zuchet stood aside to let her run forward to a bed where grew stupendous blooms of unimaginable beauty. Watching her with eyes slitted, Zuchet flipped up a tumble-switch in the wall; he leaped on her with the velocity of a tiger as, with a heavy trembling, a section of solid masonry rose from the floor at the entrance to seal them in the subterranean chamber. She whirled to receive a solid, savage blow under the jaw that felled her, senseless, before she could utter a cry. The cry would have gone unheard.

The door to Dr. Zuchet's underground laboratory was cleverly concealed. What looked like parallel pipes half-embedded in the cellar foundation were two of the vertical tracks in which the false section of foundation was operated by concealed power machinery. Nature had furnished the laboratory with another exit, which was also well concealed.

Zuchet's slowness of manner was pretense. In the chamber, scented overpoweringly by the orchids, he worked with terrible, quick efficiency, like a surgeon with only flying seconds at his disposal. He was a genius. A florist by trade, he had been trained in foreign universities in physics and chemistry, and had earned his several degrees as a scientific wizard. In America he had made a richly paying business out of his hobby, horticulture, to which his scientific genius was wed in a most peculiar and horrible manner.

The rectangular orchid bed stood in the center of the chamber, whose floor was original, somewhat uneven, bedrock. Against the wall on the left stood an operating table, with a mass of scientific equipment near it. Anyone giving the equipment a casual glance would have thought, because of queerly-shaped vacuum tubes in a cluster, that Zuchet might be experimenting with radio or television. Over the table, equipped with wing-nuts so that it could be screwed fast to the table, was suspended a glass canopy about the size and shape of a coffin.

Doubly insuring the success of his assault, Zuchet gave the girl a hypodermic injection in the arm, stripped her down to the sheer knee-length hose and slippers, and laid the few articles of clothing aside to be destroyed.

Gloating over the loveliness in his arms he murmured, "Sixteen. You'll be immortal, too, the loveliest of them all." His lips caressed the thrilling, creamy swell of her breast; he bit gently, making a low growling sound in his throat...

Laying her limp body on the table, he arranged her arms and legs, and turned on the power in his apparatus. The vacuum tubes glowed, and a low whine filled the room. The last thing he did before lowering the glass canopy was take down a length of tubing which was connected through the metal framing the rim of the glass box. The tubing terminated in a hollow, fine chromium needle. Zuchet pricked her with the needle under the left breast, forced the needle into her flesh slowly and carefully between her ribs, in, in...

Jeanne opened her eyes. The drug she had been given kept her body numb and powerless to move. With parted, trembling lips and eyes wide with horror, she watched the canopy descend, heard Zuchet swiftly turn the wing-nuts that sealed her in.

He glanced at a stoppered glass flask into which her rich red blood pumped in regular spurts from the other end of the tube, nodded and hurriedly left the laboratory. The whole business of conditioning Jeanne de Winter for immortality had been executed with so little waste motion that scarcely twenty minutes had elapsed since she entered the store. A bell rang as he closed the basement door, meaning that someone had entered the shop. He opened the door communicating with the shop and recognized grim young Arnold McQuade, whose sister he had coveted for so long and whom he had disposed of so recently. The harvest of two girls in one day made him smile pleasantly, asking, "Yes, Mr. McQuade?"

"Where is she?" Arnold demanded.

"Who?" Zuchet inquired innocently.

Simultaneously, Arnold acted with maniacal speed and fury. Both his fists were solidly reinforced with bone, and he hung one on Zuchet's teeth even before the very capable Zuchet realized how insanely angry he was, that he had a quick temper and could move with explosive speed. Ten seconds later, consciousness returned to Emil Zuchet. He sat up with bleeding lips, his mouth full of broken teeth. Arnold towered over him with a bloody handkerchief whipped around his right hand; his knuckles were slashed open to the bone.

"Where is she?" Arnold roared.

Zuchet spat out broken incisors and blood and sneered quietly, "Young man, you are going to regret having done this all your life."

Arnold whined with blind rage. Powerfully he snatched the squatty Zuchet to his feet by the throat and smashed the side of his head with the bandaged fist. He flung the body of the florist, unconscious again, back to the floor and called police headquarters from the desk-phone on the counter behind Zuchet.

Besides squad cars, Headquarters sent cars of detectives and one of the police emergency trucks out to Maxwell Heights. The truck was equipped with two floodlight units: powerful, portable lights whose generators were driven by compact gasoline motors, good for twenty-eight hours to the three-gallon tank; the floodlights were set up in the gardens. Police and detectives, among them the police chief and Lieutenant Furness, who was no mean criminologist, scoured the gardens, stampeded through the hothouses and prowled through Zuchet's residence from gables to the cellar bedrock. They found nothing, and most of them thought McQuade had gone off half-cocked. Zuchet was a wealthy and respected citizen, a man who donated generously to the church to which he belonged. The fact that girls had disappeared near the Zuchet Gardens did not mean that those girls had disappeared in the angry florist's shop.

Zuchet was going to sue the city, and this time he meant business. Some time before the police had arrived, while Arnold was storming through the house in search of Jeanne, Zuchet had set a little stage in the front room.

He had rung up a sale for two orchids on the cash register, taken from his wallet enough scented money to cover the sale, and placed it in the drawers. He removed cut flowers from a crystal vase and put them with flowers in another vase, leaned a price-card reading "$3.00 ea." against the empty crystal vase in the showcase. Having worked himself up into a mood of righteous wrath, and convinced that police are stupid, he presented his little stage-setting to the police department with his compliments. Jeanne de Winter, he lisped through his broken teeth, had visited his shop and he had persuaded her to buy his last two orchids because they wouldn't last until morning. The sale was registered, and the perfumed money was in the cash register with a little change. He indicated the empty vase and the price card in the glass case; he didn't mention that he prepared his orchids for wearing with the stems sealed in glass capsules filled with water, so that the fragile blooms would last longer, and the impatient detectives didn't know any more about orchids than they could talk in archaic Persian.

They had to believe Zuchet. It had just happened that Jeanne had left the store without McQuade's seeing her from the alley where he was waiting. Zuchet swore she had told him that she was going to a dance in a certain downtown motel with "a new man." It looked to headquarters as though McQuade had been stood up, and that was all there was to it, and they weren't very pleasant about it. Not only was the battered Zuchet going to sue the city; he was going to sue McQuade for first-degree assault, and he was going to sue him plenty. Zuchet was outraged.

Lieutenant Furness hunted for McQuade through the Zuchet Gardens, but couldn't find him. At about the time Furness gave up and returned to his car to go back to headquarters, McQuade was making his way along the river at the very bank, at the water's edge, stepping deep into black muck. He remembered something.

As he floundered along, jerking his feet free from the ooze with sounds like a line of wolves smacking their jaws, he remembered exploring both banks of this river as a boy. Somewhere along here was a tunnel at the water's edge, a tunnel in which ran an underground stream about five-eighths of a mile long, spring-fed. Near Zuchet's house, almost squarely under the south hothouse, there was a shaft opening into the ceiling of the tunnel. A rusty iron ladder hung six inches from the shaft into the tunnel. The short shaftway connected with a spacious natural cave, scoured out by the spring in the dawn of time before it escaped into the river directly. The previous owner of Zuchet's house had filled the cave with beds of rich soil for growing mushrooms. As the boy-explorer, Arnold had wandered through the mushroom cave, awed, found a door, found himself in what was obviously the basement of the house up the river and departed forthwith. His father, being told of the adventure, had told him that the house was very, very old indeed, that the pioneer who built it had extended his cellar and tapped the tunnel in order to be provided with a possible avenue of escape in case of attack by Indians.

What had suddenly occurred to Arnold, after having searched Zuchet's house for Jeanne just now, was that the basement was considerably smaller than his boyhood memory of it. Part of the basement had been walled off.

He heard his name called in a shout made thin and eerie by the height of the bluff and distance. As he ignored it, he plunged up to his chest in icy, crystal water. Whooping with the shock, he headed into the tunnel under the bluff, thrashing against the slow, frigid current.

Before advancing very far, he pulled out his cigarette lighter, blew off water around the wick and snapped the wheel. He snapped it a half dozen times before it came to life with a tiny bud of blue flame. Enough to see by.

That other time, he had paddled a canoe in here and been able to reach the ladder easily. This time he had to spring from the clay bed of the stream with every ounce of strength in him and snare the bottom wrought-iron bar one-handed. He made it, the lighter going out. The ladder shuddered with his sudden weight, and sand sifted down on him with flecks of rust. With the dead lighter in his teeth he went up, trembling, and with his breath whistling from exertion. His knuckles were split open again, but his hand was too cold to bleed readily.

The stagnant air of the cave hit him with it's full weight of mustiness and corruption. The cave was still being used for cultivating mush-rooms. In the pale, thin radiance of the lighter they bulged from their beds of fertile mold like spheres of leprous flesh, like blind eyeballs. The cave was being used for something else, too. On one side were fifteen long mounds in a row, some of them swarming monstrously with mush-rooms, which was why there was no use dragging the river for missing girls. Here their lovely bodies slept in a subterranean burial-ground. The fifteenth grave was fresh, Kathleen McQuade's, and against the wall near it leaned a damp spade.

Arnold raced down the rotten board walk that extended the length of the cave from the door. It was an ordinary wooden door with three panels, and it was locked from the inside. Arnold had never been one to waste his strength in trial efforts. He backed off, held a good breath, and smashed into the door shoulderwise with everything he had, ramming into the portal just above the level of the latchbolt. Wood split and the door burst wide open, still on its hinges, with a crash that filled the cave like low thunder.

If the air in the cave was hard to breathe, the air in the orchid chamber was stupefying with the drugging strength of perfume distilled by the flowers. The perfume was sickeningly sweet, lodging in the throat like the taste of fine, poisoned candy. Already half-stunned, Arnold got up from his knees with the re-lighted flame and spent a preliminary glance on the bed of flowers. Fourteen of the specimens, one of them a vine, were in flower. The fifteenth was a naked bulb, freshly planted, with its upper part exposed and releasing a fat tongue of violet-flecked green.

Across the room, the vacuum tubes in the apparatus emitted a glow of soft red and there was a whine in the air. Reflected light on the glass case momentarily prevented him from seeing what lay inside. He could discover, despairing, no exit from this weird chamber into Zuchet's basement.

On a stool near the orchids a flask full of red liquid caught his eye. Glass tubing connected the flask with the box of soil in which the orchids grew, a box supported on heavy legs. The tubing, full of the ruby fluid, ran completely around the box. There were twenty-four stopcocks and connections, with auxiliary tubes running from fifteen of the connections through the sides of the box, one feeding tube for each orchid.

The orchid nearest him, a fantastic beauty of extraordinary size with crumpled chiffon petals weeping with golden tendrils, suddenly leaned toward him on its tall, curiously fluted stem. For a moment he stood rooted, while gooseflesh washed his whole body with icy hands, fascinatedly watching the great, fragile flower move on its flexible stem as though searching for him.

He stretched out his hand and touched the gorgeous thing. Instantaneously the tendrils twined around his hand and fingers, tightly, as the petals caressed his palm. His fingers were touching the stem, which was intricately veined like flesh, and the stem was pulsing. Arnold drew his hand free nervelessly and the golden tendrils reluctantly let go.

Sickened, he held his hand to his throat, and his fingers encountered leaves. All the tendrils of the vine had stolen upon him behind, unfelt because the leaves and tendrils were of the same temperature as his own body. The leaves had the peculiar, porous softness of human skin. Involuntarily he struck at the thing with a cry of disgust. The vine flinched free of him as he sprang back; it shrank into a compact mass of coils and foliage, visibly quivering with hurt from the blow he had dealt. These beautiful, foul things were alive with a horrible, sentient life.

In his present position, as he looked about wildly, he saw the outrage of Jeanne de Winter's white body in the glass box. His face convulsed and he reached her with a scream of horror. He didn't see how the box was fastened down, and the glass was too heavy for him to smash it.

"Jeanne!" he shrieked.

He was too late. She recognized him with the ghost of a smile on her lips, but her eyes were closing in death. The needle stuck into her heart just below the perfect left breast had drained most of the blood from her body. The flush of life was almost gone from her and her nymphean form had become a dreadful white ivory. On her jaw was the stain of a bruise, where Zuchet had struck her. Against the white hemispheres of her breasts the pectoral marks budded darkly. Her beautiful, stark things were somewhat apart. They trembled together, her breasts ceased their slow rise and fall with her breathing. She relaxed into a reclining sculpture lovelier than anything man ever cut from marble.

Her head rested on a plate of peculiar grayish metal which was wired somehow to the electrical apparatus near by. Suspended above the case over the plate was a glass bulb shaped like a cathode tube, also wired. Like a glass gun it was directed upon an egg-shaped flower bulb which was immersed in some perfectly transparent liquid in a crystal jar. On a shelf were several such jars containing bulbs of slightly different shapes and sizes. At the instant of Jeanne's death, a beam of visible light shot from the plate under her head to the cathode tube suspended above it, where the beam was condensed, brightened, and fired at the orchid bulb in the jar in a needle of light. Emil Zuchet had discovered how to capture and make use of that form of energy which is called "intelligence" or "the soul" in a living human being. The average weight of energy constituting the human "soul", as other scientists before Zuchet had discovered, was one quarter of an ounce, which is lost at "death" and according to archaic Indian mysticism returns to its source, the envelope of the universe which is fumblingly worshipped or scorned as "God."

A section of the chamber wall slid down in its shaft with a dull rumble. Overhead lights flashed on; Arnold whirled as Zuchet flipped the switch that sent the ponderous slab of masonry rumbling back up into place. There was a revolver in Zuchet's fist.

"You found your way in here, did you? When the door to the mushroom cave is opened, it rings an alarm in the house."

"Does it?" Arnold asked in a queer, flat voice.

"The police are gone now. And you and I," Zuchet sniggered insanely, "have business together, haven't we?" There was something about his lisp, caused by his broken teeth, that made him seem all the more deadly.

"Yes, we have business together," Arnold whispered, easing toward Zuchet imperceptibly. He was poised with the cold, merciless calm of a man who had gone insane with a fixed idea, the driving necessity of murdering the unspeakable Zuchet with his bare hands.

"How do you like my place, eh?" Zuchet crowed. "Before I kill you I am going to tell you a secret. The orchids I am growing here, they are not like other orchids. Oh, no! They are human beings, like you and me! They think; they feel; you can make them twist with agony. You know what I do with all those girls who disappeared?" His wide mouth slobbered. "All those lovely girls with their white bodies? I imprison their souls in those orchids, those splendid flowers. Their souls, man! Would you ever think of that?"

"Yes, I thought of that." With a guttural laugh of complete insanity Arnold charged.

Zuchet shot him through the stomach. Arnold was beyond feeling shock and advanced steadily, though he was a dead man. Zuchet shot him twice more, once through the shoulder, once through the chest; Arnold coughed blood and staggered, but kept coming. Zuchet backed away frantically, gobbling with fear, and emptied the remaining three bullets into his body. Only transcendent hate kept Arnold on his feet. He reached Zuchet's jaw with a clumsy blow of his fist as the last bullet tore through his heart.

The blow was enough to sprawl Zuchet on the stone floor, where he sat gasping, swallowing with relief as he looked at the dead man. A pleasant stupor overcame him so swiftly that he was unable to get to his feet.

Perspiration beaded his face; he wiped it off drowsily, wondering what was the matter with him. His ears began to ring, and a sweet weakness weighed him down. "Zuchet, Zuchet," he muttered. "What is happening to you?"

The overpowering fragrance of the orchids drugged his brain. His eyes closed with a dream of fair white bodies, of slender torsoes with firm young breasts, of shapely legs with the creamy thighs so soft, so soft between . . . At last the agony in his throat and wrists reached his brain, and he jerked his eyes open.

The flowering vine had stealthily snared his wrists and throat, his cheeks, all the exposed area of his skin. The tendrils of the vine were equipped with suckers, and the vine was getting fat with his blood; he was dying.

He screamed for help and struggled to free himself. But the chamber was soundproof, and the tendrils of that gorgeously flowering leech, fattening insatiably, or revengefully, enmeshed him even more securely with the tensile strength of flexible steel thongs. He gibbered feebly, and with all the power left in his barrel chest produced a scream that had no more volume than the drawn-out chirp of a cricket. A squat, helpless and dying cricket.

His round head struck the stone floor meatily as he fell back. With tremendous effort he blinked his glazing eyes, the prey of the verdant horror of his own invention.

Don't Go Haunting

THE APARTMENT WAS three steps below sidewalk level, low-ceilinged and, therefore, quite dark even on the sunniest days, like this one in the advanced spring. Ornstein kept two lights burning in the rear room all day long. It was a floor-through apartment; if the mailman wished, he could stick his nose into the grille protecting the front window and see all the way back into the garden if the French doors were open. It was a walled garden and once a jewel, with a marble fountain that played. The Carrara girl was gone now, and the curbing of the pool had been filled with soil to make a circular flower bed. Vines grew thick on the brick walls, and only the least stir of the heavy traffic on Fourteenth Street penetrated to the yard. There was a table with magazines and cigarettes, an ash tray, a glass of beer and a bottle; there was a comfortable weathered oak chair with a cushion, and there Adolf Ornstein sat—not exactly alive, and not exactly dead.

Properly, it was the flesh, the mortal envelope of Ornstein and nothing more—the thing slumbering in the chair. Because he, his conscious intelligence, his mental self, or whatever lubricant it was that oiled the mechanism known as Adolf Ornstein, was standing with arms akimbo looking down at his clothed clay speculatively, without surprise. It had just happened. The secret was known to learned men in ancient times, of course, but in this modern day there were few adepts, save for certain high lamas in Tibet, who in their inaccessible places study the occult gospels removed for safety before the burning of the library of Alexandria. Ornstein was a graduate student in both black and white magic, his particular bent being for the darkish variety, through acquaintanceship with the Polish Count S. Metonna Lonczewski.

Having broken the lock of his grandfather's trunk as a lad, in the attic of the family home in the Ukraine, the count had found an archaic work on magic, written on parchment in classical Latin. The count, being a prodigy, had digested a third of the book when his aunt came up to see what he was doing. He promptly hypnotized her and dispatched her to the kitchen to make him a plate of sandwiches to eat while reading. The book was a translation from an earlier work in Egyptian, which had been done in turn from the lost original in the language of the Atlantides, and was still in the count's possession.

Following Lonczewski's detailed instructions, at his own risk, Ornstein had performed the experiment successfully. The problem had not been especially difficult; it was a matter of will-power, concentrating in specific directions given in that particular chapter in the book, eliminating the directions one by one until what remained was an avenue of escape, exciting liberation from the slavish monotony of having a physical body.

The sun was shining down on his clay, but the free Ornstein didn't cast any shadow. He thought he had better report on his condition, so he went to the phone in the rear room of his apartment and gave Lonczewski a buzz.

"Hello, count?" he asked. "This is Dolf Ornstein."

"Hello, Dolf," said the count. The count had no teeth; resulting in his meticulous enunciation, his words sounded as though he were pushing them very rapidly through a keyhole. "Hello. How are you?"

"I am very well," Dolf said. "How are you?"

"I am in good health, too. What is on your mind?"

"I thought I would tell you that I made the experiment, and it is a complete success."

"Do you mean the one in Chapter XVII?" asked the count. "You do. Remember, I told you it was dangerous. You don't want to do anything that you might regret."

"I won't. You won't give me away, now, will you?"

"Give you away? I should stick out the neck of Lonczewski." The count laughed with a sound like the puttering of a small gasoline motor. "Are you in that condition now? Are you invisible?"

"I am completely invisible," Dolf reported, looking down at himself. "But the funny thing is, I have just as much weight as I always had. There's a hollow in the seat of the chair where I'm sitting."

"That is correct," Lonczewski informed him. "It didn't occur to me to tell you. How do you feel?"

"Well—call it exhilarated," Dolf decided. "It's a kind of tingling, or singing, like a mild current of electricity."

"That's the way I remember it," said Lonczewski. "I haven't done it for a long time—not since I had to go to that man's house for the book he borrowed from me. It was the only way to get it back. Where is your body?"

"In the chair out in the garden, count. From here it looks dead drunk. There's a glass of beer that I didn't quite finish."

"You were drinking beer?" the count demanded. "My friend, it's remarkable that you had any luck at all. There is not supposed to be any alcohol, or nicotine, or drug in the system, not even any food in the stomach. You had extraordinarily good fortune. Don't press it."

"I don't intend to. Now, about returning to the status quo. I feel a little nervous about that, I must say. Suppose I couldn't get back?"

"I felt the same way," Lonczewski chortled. "But it is simple as flipping a coin, unless you have a hard time getting to sleep. Remember, what you left out in the garden is an imbecile; it is a man, but it is mindless. It cannot take care of itself; it is scarcely breathing, and the pulse is so faint that you will have a hard time detecting it. That thing is senseless, and something might happen to it if you go away. I am taking no responsibility, you know; how long you want to leave your clay in jeopardy is up to you. When you want to reanimate the clay, all you have to do is to go to sleep near it and it will happen automatically. Reanimating the clay of course, is only a special kind of sleep."

"Well, I'll have to wait a few hours," said Dolf. "It isn't two o'clock yet, and I never had any luck going to sleep during the day."

"It is up to you. But if I were in your shoes, I would carry the clay in and make it comfortable on the bed. For one thing, it will get pretty dusty out there in the garden."

"Yes; but as you said, there isn't much of a heartbeat discernible. The weather is bright and fair, and the sun will keep the clay warm. If its temperature dropped too low, the heart might stop beating altogether. I wouldn't like that to happen. The thermometer in the back room here says that it is only 72°."

"That's something to consider," Lonczewski agreed. "But the clay might get sunburned."

"I think it has sufficient protective tan. During the winter I used the sun lamp regularly."

"I take it that you are going somewhere this afternoon."

"I certainly am going somewhere."

"I have two engagements, but I can break them for you," the count said. "Do you want me to come down to your place and take care of the clay until you are through with what you have in mind?"

"Oh, no, thanks!" Dolf refused. "I wouldn't even consider such an imposition. Everything will be all right."

"Ho-kay, then," said Count S. Metonna Lonczewski, who liked to use American slang. "If you commit any crimes, be absolutely sure that they can't be traced back to you, aside from the fact that you cannot afford to indulge in the least microscopic minim of conscience. Don't get caught!"

"I will consider and strain to the utmost, no matter what the temptation is," Dolf promised.

"No matter if you are invisible," Lonczewski said, "you still leave fingerprints. No one has to see you. Men have been hanged for crimes they did not commit. The quicksand, my boy, is circumstantial evidence."

"That," said Dolf, "I will avoid."

After hanging up, he paused on his way out to the garden to look at himself in the mirror over his linen chest. The mirror was empty so far as any reflection of himself was concerned. At his eye-level, through him, was reflected a watercolor landscape that hung over the fireplace behind him.

It was the damnedest thing, and it gave him a very odd feeling, this being bodiless. Totally incorporeal.

He continued into the garden, and was just in time to find his clay slumping, at the point of falling off the chair. He rescued it, pushing the shoulders back; the skull might have been cracked on the flagstones if the loose body had tumbled.

The clay presented the blanched appearance, along with the un-co-operative handling, of a corpse too new yet for the inevitable rigor mortis. Ornstein was somewhat scared. He felt the pulse and it was there, faraway and slow.

He arranged the clay so that it wouldn't fall out of the chair, propping it securely with the head comfortable, the legs extended, the arms draped in the lap. He tested it, pushing at it all around to make sure that it would stay planted just so. With thumb and forefinger he spread the lids of one eye, and the blue orb was as clammily blank and gruesome as a pickled nightmare. He jumped a step backward with a whispered oath.

Through the open gate in the rear wall trotted the superintendent's white terrier from the basement apartment on Fifteenth Street. The dog padded to one side, then the other, as though its moist and intelligent nose had sniffed a barrier. Then it stood planted on its four legs, pointing rigidly not at the recumbent flesh in the chair, but directly ahead at the spot where Ornstein wasn't casting a shadow. He looked at the dog, highly interested.

Her lips skinned back as her muzzle lowered, and the hair on her back bristled erect from her ears to her tail. With low, continuous growls she shifted her legs as though getting ready to spring, but she was inching steadily backward. In a flash she whipped around and bolted, yelping, through the gate and beyond into the cool safety of the super's apartment.

The super, overalled Archibald Agnew, stalked through the gate shortly to see what had scared the hell out of his dog. He looked at the open-mouthed, obviously unconscious body of Ornstein draped in the garden chair for a moment.

"Drunk," he muttered contemptuously, and went away.

Since his clothes garbed his clay, Ornstein was, of course, naked. Nor was it in the least unpleasant in the stagnant air outside. No one could see him and he couldn't see himself as he was now, but with twenty-odd conditioned years of behavior behind him he could be fairly certain of how he was displacing what amount of air. Habit. Visibility wasn't necessary in his knowing what his posture was, where his arms and legs were. Merely because he was invisible didn't mean that he would bark his shins on low furniture, because he could walk around or step over as he would in the flesh, without having to gauge distances. He still weighed a hundred and sixty-eight pounds in spite of the fact that he was invisible. That was the only difference; in shape and substance he was the same. If he spread his hand and whacked himself on the chest, there was a meaty sound. With invisible fingers he could comb invisible hair and scrub invisible teeth.

He danced in impromptu jig, and his bare heels thumped on the flagstones. He picked a yellow violet, just to prove that it could be done, and laid the flower on the table. On second thought, he threaded the stem through the buttonhole of his clay's jacket. Anyone watching would have seen the violet pick itself, adjourn to the table momentarily, then continue like a winged insect to his clay's lapel. Ornstein laughed heartily, because there were great possibilities ahead.

A swarthy man in shirt sleeves stuck head and shoulders out of a window on the third floor and looked down for a couple of minutes at the charming little garden. Then he threw down a cigar butt, whose coal burst in a shower of sparks, and ducked back into the apartment. Ornstein waited, and the man up there cautiously poked his head out again because the man in the chair was apparently sound asleep.

There was a moderate litter of matches, bottle caps, hairpins, milk-bottle stoppers, a garter, dead tendrils from a Wandering-Jew, glints from a broken milk bottle, scraps from a piece of pastry that didn't taste right and had been pitched out the window, and a few soggy stogy butts—the usual and continuous smattering of rubbish and garbage from the upper floors of the building. It was a puzzling thing, but the people living in the sardine-can apartments over him were jealous of him because he had a garden with flowers growing in it. At first he had let them come down to enjoy the privileges he was paying for. They sunbathed and picked his preciously tended flowers, and helped themselves to drinks in his kitchen, just as though he were a guest.

Then he folded up the deck chairs and put they away so that they wouldn't have any place to sit. Then they dropped articles of laundry, slips, dish towels and what not, as an excuse for coming down. He kept the French doors to his apartment locked for a while. Then he said, "This is a private garden. Keep out." They started hating him, and made it an active hatred by throwing stuff out of the windows. Every Saturday he had to give Agnew a dollar for sweeping up with his broom.

The man with the broad face and negroid nose up there on the third floor was Dino Ferronatti. He was a no good. He was nasty, was broad-shouldered, didn't like work, and made a practice of going out of his way for trouble; he liked to hit people. He had found out that if you knocked a man cold you could walk away with his wallet. It was a great and enjoyable novelty here in America, because in the old country you could brain a man with a rock and consider yourself lucky if you found a few chews of tobacco in the corpse's pockets. Ferronatti held a brown paper bag filled with garbage. He gave the bag a heave, and it plopped and burst on the flagstones, scattering orange rinds, coffee grounds, eggshells, and green stuff that looked like liquid spinach.

"Why, you stinking cheese," Dolf said distinctly. "How would you like to come down and eat this mess?"

Ferronatti, having ducked out of sight again, reappeared; with jaw mugged out a la Doo-chay, he demanded incredulously: "What you call me, punk?"

"Come on down here and I'll spit in your eye," Dolf said. He wasn't as big as Ferronatti and under ordinary circumstances never would have tackled him. On the other hand he was no weakling, and he took up a stand near the super's hall entrance with his heart beating with anticipatory pleasure. He didn't have long to wait. The door was yanked open, and out charged Ferronatti into the garden. He was breathing hard from running down the stairs.

"O. K., you!" he called belligerently to the form in the chair. Only a yard away from him, the invisible Ornstein fetched him a whistling right-hander squarely in the middle of his mush.

Ferronatti stood up straight, eyes popping with disbelief, and took a few little steps in a circle while he got his balance. Then with a growl he doubled his fists and crouched, looking around to see what had hit him, like an animal lost in the dark. His angry gaze fixed on the unconscious clay in the chair, suspiciously.

Dolf got set, wound up and fired his best Sunday punch into Ferronatti's teeth. Something snapped. Dolf thought he had broken his invisible knuckles and massaged them tenderly with his invisible left hand. Then he saw the tooth on the flagstones. Ferronatti had assumed a horizontal position in front of the doorway and lay supine with his eyes closed for a little more than the count of ten. Dolf watched; the eyes opened dazedly and the man struggled to a sitting position; he scrambled to his feet then, and fled back into the building hold his jaws. Dolf called after him: "Get the idea? No more throwing stuff out the windows."

"O. K.; don't get hard about it," Ferronatti snarled.

Dolf felt smug. It was the first time he had ever knocked a man cold, and the accomplishment, thanks to Count Lonczewski's able teachings, was gratifying.

He paid a last visit to his clay to make sure everything was all right, loosened the necktie and opened the top collar button for greater comfort in breathing. He also loosened the shoelaces, knowing that on every occasion when he slept with his shoes on he would awake with his feet aching as though they had been beaten.

Returning to the apartment, he took another look into the mirror. There was no reflection, but he felt of himself and he was there, all right. He pulled a drawer open and took out a handkerchief, unfolded it and blew his nose with it. The homely sound was convincing, and he got a childish pleasure out of watching the handkerchief cavort all by itself in the air. In short, he was unquestionably in a position to haunt houses.

"By golly," he said with quiet jubilation, "I've always wanted to haunt a few houses I know of, and here goes."

Leaving the apartment, which faced south on Fourteenth Street, he mounted the stairs to the parlor floor to perch a while in thought. First he sat down on the edge of the top landing, then got up to roost on the iron side railing.

There were certain disadvantages to being invisible. Neither standing nor sitting was very comfortable on the general run of surfaces, and forays like this one depended on weather conditions. Going around invisible in the wintertime would be out of the question. He wondered about his feet getting dirty. That would be a fine thing—a pair of bare footprints flickering along the sidewalk like shadows. He cocked a leg up to look at the sole of his foot; he couldn't see anything, and he had already walked around enough to get grimy. A fortunate development negatively.

His hunkers began to hurt on the thin railing and he stood up, watching traffic on the street and particularly pedestrians. No one looked up, though a fair percentage of persons rubbernecked through his front window. That was because the garden in back was a bright green in the sunlight, and such a tended garden as Ornstein's was more than somewhat rare on Fourteenth. He was comfortably warm; since his invisibility passed a hundred percent of the bright sunlight there was small likelihood that sunburn would reveal him.

His only worry then was that something might go wrong, that the term of invisibility might have a capricious limit and spontaneously he would appear naked in a public place. Lonczewski, however, had assured him that such an embarrassment could not occur. Control was absolutely his, Ornstein's, until he wished to terminate his condition by the mere expedient of going to sleep, when his conscious mind would again become automatically united with his subconscious. He was also assured that the clothed clay which he was leaving in the garden would not do any somnambulating and get itself into trouble. It would stay strictly put until he had further use for it.

With full confidence, now that he had gotten used to the true nature of his condition and was convinced of its advantages and foresaw the privileges and responsibilities thereunto appertaining, he descended to the sidewalk. He had to be careful. He could get run down by a taxi just like anyone else, in which event he wondered what would happen to his clay. Would it die? More probably it would continue living as a helpless idiot and would be put into an institution.

On the bottom step he paused to let a building-line hugger pass, the type of pedestrian who couldn't go anywhere without maintaining the maximum distance between himself and the gutter. During the brief delay Dolf rubbed the bristles on his jaw with his fingertips, and produced the familiar sound of soft chalk marking a blackboard. He clapped himself on the shoulder, and he was still there, just as solid as the horse drawing that rubber-tired milk wagon now passing in the direction of the Ninth Avenue El. For good measure he mussed his hair up properly. He could go about unshaven and with his hair unkempt, and it was no one's damned business but his own.

He walked down to the corner of Eighth Avenue and Fourteenth Street, feeling just a trifle deflated so early in the adventure. In a garage only five minutes' walk removed, he kept a little sedan in live storage, but he couldn't use it. A driverless car in motion through the streets of Manhattan would attract no end of attention, besides the fact that the license number would be noted more than once.

He couldn't use taxis. Either he walked, stole rides on the subways, or hopped rides on the rear bumpers of surface vehicles, like the kids. He didn't mind walking as a rule, but he hadn't gone barefoot since he was in breeches, and his feet weren't calloused any more. He had to weave in and out of pedestrian traffic unless he wanted to get bumped, and he had to watch where he set his feet down, to avoid cuts and bruises. But the novelty and exhilaration were such that he kept wearing his mischievous grin—diabolical grin.

He had a destination in mind, one chief destination among several, and a crime to commit—the major crime of murder. The thought of committing murder made his heart beat fast; with the cruelty that the most sunny-featured men keep bottled up with a disarming whistle, he realized that he would have committed murder long ago except for the consequences. He knew there is latent, cheerful murder in every human being's heart, and that he was no exception. That crimes go unpunished, that an individual is entitled to vengeance out of all proportion to original fault.

The address in which he was interested was on Waverly Place; the most convenient means of reaching it was by taking the Eighth Avenue

Subway, which zigged east from here, and getting off at the Washington Square stop. Not a long walk from there.

The cast of characters were few. There were two men, and the guilty one was either Wilbur Huron, the slender Englishman who looked like a spy, or the lusty red-headed Hoagie McCaffery. The girl was Kathleen Feles and she lived on Waverly Place. Until a year ago she had been his wife, Ornstein's.

Then she had said: "Rolfie, I am leaving."

"Why?" he had asked, being just as noncommittal about it as she was.

"Because I want to. When we were married, didn't we agree that either one of us could do whatever he wanted?"

"I guess so. But I sort of expected that I would have something to say about it. Can I ask any questions, like who the man is?"

"If you wanted to break off, would you answer any questions about who the woman is?"

"There isn't any woman, angel pie."

"I didn't say there was any man, darling. I just think that it would be better if I went away for a while to think things over. You don't think I'm going to walk right out and go and live in sin with somebody, do you?"

"Well, what the hell are you leaving for? I love you."

"Oh, no, you don't," Kay had said. "You just said down at the Municipal Building when we were walking around, 'Let's try it and see if it works,' and we went up and got married. You made a lot of promises, but all you've done for nearly a year is sit around and plant bulbs in the garden and pull weeds."

"Damn it! It isn't everybody in New York who can afford to spend most of his time weeding his garden," Dolf protested. "What have I done?"

"That's the trouble; you haven't done anything," Kay had said. "You were going to angel a play and have your name in lights; you were going to buy up a bankrupt store and make it pay; you were going to write a book; you were going to finance a man who had some machinery for getting gold out of the Atlantic Ocean. You haven't done a thing."

"Somebody's taking gold out of the ocean already," Dolf had said.

"So what? It's a big ocean, isn't it? And there's another ocean out West. All you do is sit around and live on the interest from the money you inherited from your crackpot uncle out in California, and plant seeds that never do anything, and pull little blades of grass out of the ground. Never mind; I'm going. You never loved me in the first place."

"Maybe I didn't," said Dolf coldly, because obviously she wasn't in love with him. She had married him for his money. The allowance he laid beside her breakfast plate every Saturday morning was as much as he got for section-managing in a department store before his uncle died, but she wasn't satisfied with it. Shoes and dresses and coats and crazy hats—she was always buying things. Five thousand dollars interest a year wasn't enough; she wanted to cut into the principal and take cruises to Bermuda, and buy diamonds and an imported car; she wanted a house in the country, and when they didn't go to Florida for the winter she almost stopped speaking to him; she was extravagant.

When the door closed on her and she was gone, she was gone for good. Both McCaffery and Huron were wealthier than Dolf was, and she could take her pick because she was a remarkably personable girl.

At the cost of a thousand dollars he had found out where she lived, and he had to pay the private detective for his meals and hack fares and room rent besides. He was quite piqued. Every time he thought about it, it was as though a bee stung him, and yet he couldn't do anything about it. She never telephoned him, and if he dropped in on her unexpectedly and both Huron and McCaffery were there, they would beat the living daylights out of him while Kay urged them on. When she said, "I am leaving," she meant, "I am never going to see you again in my whole life."

The idea of murder occurred to him even then, for he had added her up previously and slapped his forehead many times at the inevitable conclusion—she was a luxury. But he had not progressed in his studies with Count S. Metonna Lonczewski to the necessary extent until recently.

So he was going to commit a murder, possibly two murders, three at the outside depending on circumstances. He descended the steps to the subway, walking clear of gum and expectorations. He ducked under one of the turnstiles, and from the lower platform boarded a southbound local.

He took a frontwise seat, the most popular type. After him, a man and a girl spotted his apparently empty seat simultaneously. The man butted the girl aside with his shoulder and came on the run. When he presented his buttocks preparatory to sitting down in Dolf's lap, Dolf planted both feet on the chubby, inviting posterior and catapulted the stranger down the aisle at a mad run. Even the hugest strides couldn't keep up with the hurtling body, however, and the fellow bellyflopped magnificently. People laughed, and the man skulked into the car ahead. Dolf lost the seat anyhow, because the girl promptly claimed it. No lengthwise seat ever manufactured is as good as a crosswise one. He was tempted to sit right where he was and let her take the consequences, but you could never tell what a woman would do when she started screaming. If he was taken hold of, he could be held onto. So he got up disgustedly and rode standing, hanging onto one of the enameled uprights.

Out on the sidewalk again he breathed more easily. Coming down Eighth Street was a girl holding two dogs on taut leashes. She walked with the insolent superiority of a spoiled princess. Her complexion was as flawless as milky ivory, and her eyebrows were black and enhanced her features with the winged arch of their curves. She wore her hair up in short black curls, and looked more like a certain Hollywood actress than the original. He mouth was shapely, not quite pouting and not quite world-weary or knowledgeful in expression, and lipsticked in satiny red with jewel precision. Her stockings were as sheer as the merest trace of cigarette smoke. She wore a wool suit in somewhat grayed violet with a little felt trifle of hat to match, the hue of the stockings matching; her blouse was striped lavender silk, and there was a little necktie effect that only a woman could get by with and looked silly anyhow. She was gotten up with the exactness of clockwork, and Dolf Ornstein was filled with an instantaneous and violent abhorrence. The fragrant little witch was walking her dogs down Eighth Street from Fifth Avenue, slumming.

The dogs were spectacular Russian wolfhounds, and were extending their lean, laughing muzzles to get within smelling range of a yapping Pekingese up the way on Greenwich.

In the first place Dolf didn't like dogs in New York. It was hard on the dogs, and it was impossible to keep them a hundred percent curbed. Moreover, people like this million-dollar filly who kept dogs in the city felt, invariably, pretty damned good about themselves for no logical reason. The word was snooty, with a variable spelling. Besides which, Dolf might have been influenced by the fact that here was something he could never have, something he couldn't buy because he didn't have money enough and she was already purchased and paid for and not on the market any more, very likely—the most conceited morsel he had ever seen on the hoof.

So he walked around behind her and got into step, observed the way she was looking down her nose so that the enchanting shine of her eyelids might be publicly included among the items of her glamour. Dolf measured distance, cocking his arm in the manner of a man about to slap a mosquito. He took a terrific swipe downward at the hand gripping the leashes, and the impact of his masculine fingers produced a sound like a firecracker touched off.

"Yow!" the girl ejaculated. Her little ivory fist jumped open, the leashes escaped like whips, and the two wolfhounds bolted for the mean-faced fawn Pekingese as though shot from a gun. The girl went tearing after the dogs. She could run, too, though she probably hadn't indulged in such an undignified pastime since she was wearing cotton bloomers, and she looked just as silly as all women look when so engaged. Dolf followed along to the uproar. The China dog's owner was holding the yipping animal up in the air at arm's length and yelling; a cop bulled his way forward and demanded: "Can't you hold your dogs?"

"A man hit me and I let go," said the girl in violet, panting. She pointed at random to a young fellow in the gathering crowd. "That man there."

"You're a liar," said Dolf.

The cop swung around, and he was a poisonous, bucktoothed, red-faced customer. He barked: "Who said that?"

"I did," Dolf said. "Want to make something of it?"

"Wha-a-at?" Officer Delehanty demanded, outraged.

Delehanty's eyes bulged, and he probed face after face among the bystanders, hunching his shoulders. Dolf walked around and got into a store entrance, where he wet his lips, stuck his tongue out and blew a loud, insulting and satisfying razzberry. He added: "If you don't like it, you great big beautiful policeman you, you know what you can do about it."

Everybody was too scared to move a muscle. Delehanty was a smart cop and used his head; he plowed back and forth through the crowd, shouldering and pushing people and ordering, "Come on, come on! Break it up! Come on, walk!"

The crowd and dogs dispersed rapidly. After a period of looking wild-eyed up and down Greenwich, the cop headed toward some mysterious destination that cops have.

Dolf departed from the battle, and shortly was standing in the foyer of Kay's building. Beginning from the left, he pressed bells in succession until the lock buzzed. He entered, and proceeded to her apartment on the third floor. He expected that he would have to go over the roof and come down the fire escape, but to his surprise the door was unlocked. She was at home. He held the door open an inch and listened, but heard no sound. She might be reading, in sight of the door, watching the door. At the other end of the hall a door opened, and a woman came to the head of the stairs. She peered down into the stair well and returned to her apartment muttering.

Gently Dolf pushed the door open as though a breeze were doing it. He entered with a quick stride, closed the door again with only the slightest click of the latch. He was in a narrow hall connecting living room and bedroom. His footsteps were soundless on the carpeting. In the doorway to the living room on the left he came to a halt and stared, thunderstruck.

Kay's apartment was haunt proof. It was a place from which to depart with all possible dispatch. In fact, it probably had haunts of its own already. There was a man lying slumped on the sofa across the room; it was big, red-headed Hoagie McCaffery, and he was dead. There was no bullet hole in evidence, but blood soaked the sofa behind him in a patch like wine. On the floor lay another body. It was Kathleen and her toes curled as though trying to grip the nap of the rug. She lay with arms outflung in a stretching position; there was a bullet hole in her right hand, another one just below her right eye. Dolf ran to the front door, stood undecided and then returned to the scene of crime.

Looking made him realize how far murder had been from his real intentions; all he had meant to do was scare the daylights out of her, just haunt her house a little bit, and possibly get her back through some maneuvering. He wanted her back like everything. He trembled, and his heart was beating so fast that it was just a lump of pain in his chest.

That Kay had had lovers there was no doubt in his mind; he wondered which one of them it was who had beaten him to the draw in committing murder. It wasn't a common burglar's or any outsider's work, he imagined; the name that occurred to him was Wilbur Huron.

Kay and Hoagie had been drinking. There was a coffee table in front of the sofa, and on it stood two partially consumed drinks—Scotch and soda. The ice cubes in the glasses were not yet melted, indicating that the crime was fairly recent. There was lipstick—Kay's—on Hoagie's mouth and cheek. On the floor, Kay's body was clad in diaphanous, lusterless triple-sheer; the robe was belted at the waist, and modeled her slenderness revealingly in green shadows. Suspecting that she was two-timing him, Huron had paid a visit and found them preoccupied with one another. Probably the door had been locked and the jealous murderer came down the fire escape from the roof as Dolf had intended to.

He checked up. The escape window was closed and locked, but that could have been done from the inside. And yes, there were marks on the iron slats of the platform made by shoes.

The murderer had come through the window. Using either the route through the corridor or bathroom, he had taken a look into the living room and seen all he needed to see. McCaffery had seen Huron standing there with a gun in his hand and had opened his mouth to yell. The first bullet had gone down Hoagie's throat, right between his teeth before he could bite it in two. That was why there was no apparent wound on his face. Kathleen had jumped up, covering her face with her hands, and the second bullet had gone through her hand and head.

The gall, the effrontery of that man Huron, exercising the privilege of being jealous of Dolf Ornstein's wife! Dolf was appalled. He looked down and couldn't see himself except for the impression his bare feet made in the rug, but he scratched his head with marvelous indecision and got normal resistance. He was solid; he was still there.

Being invisible, of course, he was perfectly safe even if the cops came, but Huron must have departed very rapidly in case the two shots had been heard. Seemingly the two reports had reached no ears.

He was mistaken; the doorknob turned as he was reaching for it, and he jumped back, flattening himself against the corridor wall. A man stuck his head inside and looked in both directions, then came all the way inside, followed by another man—detectives. One headed for the living room and the other for the bedroom. Dolf made his exit between them through the door, which they had left open. At the head of the stairs he heard, "Hey, Tommy! Here in the living room; two of them!"

Dolf went down the stairs breathing fast to make up for the long one he had held in the corridor. On the sidewalk he started running lickety split for the subway. His heels took a terrific pounding, and his toes slapped down every time until they hurt like the mischief. They felt as though they were going to split open with the next stride.

Then he asked himself, "What the hell am I running for? I didn't do it."

Panting for breath, he stood with his toes hanging over the edge of the curb near the corner to give them a rest. No, he hadn't murdered Kay and Hoagie, but the cops would certainly consider him as a possibility. It wouldn't take them long to discover that she was Mrs. Ornstein and that she had left his bed and board. Then they would discover that he had hired a private detective to find out where she lived. The thing for him to do was get home and fall asleep as quickly as possible so that he could get back inside of his clay. But he couldn't fall asleep now; he was too excited.

It was turning somewhat chill with the setting of the sun, and goose-flesh crawled on him here and there as eddies of breeze stirred moistly. Out in the garden the temperature of his clay would decline degree by degree. It ought to be lugged into the apartment and covered up warmly. But all around the garden were back windows and random housewives rubbernecking out of them. It wouldn't do for anyone to see his body levitate and go coasting through the French doors into the apartment in midair. Such a sight wouldn't be forgotten by anyone who saw it. Further and more, as Lonczewski would say, the clay would be better left out in plain sight now. It was his alibi. As far as anyone else knew, that was Adolf Hermann Ornstein snoozing down there in the chair in the garden. That gangster Ferronatti must have looked out the back window a couple of time since, and stared stilettos at the man who had knocked him cold. Good old Ferronatti. Other people must have looked out, too. There was that old hag, that white-haired lovable gentlewoman, who threw bread out her window every afternoon for the sparrows whose raw, piercing chirping used to drive Dolf crazy. The flock of Manhattan-gray birds got bigger every day. And there was that fat slob of a woman on the top floor, who would run her laundry out to the line post on screeching pulleys, almost every day, then rest her obese elbows on her window sill and contemplate the soapy wet line dripping diagonally across the garden below with eyes squeezed to slits by her cheeks. She spoke just enough English to tell him that that was her hook on the line post, and if it dripped, what was he going to do about it? Come on up! Oh, his clay wouldn't slumber down there in the garden unnoticed.

But he was getting chilly. Directly in front of him, waiting for the change of lights, was a roomy sedan. It was this year's model, and its only occupant was the driver. Dolf opened the rear door and stepped inside, sat on the plush. The driver's head snapped around; all he did was scowl, reach for the handle and haul the door shut with a slam; the lights changed and he turned uptown, shifting gears as though he were in a hurry.

The lights stopped the car again at Fourteenth Street, and Dolf got out because he didn't want to go uptown. Another reason was that he had learned that car upholstery, if you are bare, is the most uncomfortable stuff in the world to sit on. It prickles like the devil.

There was a lot of pedestrian traffic on Fourteenth Street now, and windows were lighted, and Dolf had to keep on the jump. His toes got stepped on once when a man turned around without warning and walked into him upon some mysterious decision to walk in the opposite direction, and Dolf was momentarily nauseated by the pain. He slugged the pedestrian, who immediately swung at the nearest visible man within reach as his opponent. Dolf hopped along on one foot and leaned against a post, groaning and holding onto his mashed toes. Someone else wanted to lean against the post and watch the fight, and he had to move.

He limped to the corner, and crossed the street at a run while he had the lights with him, wishing that he had hit that fellow harder. Anyone who turned around suddenly without looking had a good sock coming from the person he bumped.

Suddenly it was dark. There had been light in the sky, but now there was only the luminous haze through which no stars can be seen. At regular intervals Dolf shuddered from the chill of the night air; he rubbed his shoulders briskly and embraced himself for the warmth provided. His feet hurt so much that he couldn't walk the distance home. When he got home he was going to have a good stiff drink, and fill the bathtub with water of the proper temperature, and laze in it. When he got out of the tub and scrubbed his invisible self with a Turkish towel, he would take a couple of sleeping tablets from the bottle in the medicine chest.

If his clay had caught cold already it was a small matter; he didn't like the idea of sleeping out in the garden all night, but there was no help for it. On the contrary, now that it was dark, he could lug his clay into the apartment unobserved. Well, drag it, because his hundred and sixty-eight pounds were a lot to lift. He might be seen, because the lights in the rear room were on, the front curtains up. People passing by could look into his apartment, but he would have to take chance on it. Pull the front curtains down first. Then lug his clay into bed, take a bath and swallow the tablets and lock the doors.

Probably the cops wouldn't get around to him tonight, anyhow. Poor Kay. But she had it coming to her, the conniving little money-hungry wench; he never would have got her back again.

He got into another car bound across town. This one had smooth cotton slip-covers on the prickly upholstery, and Dolf sat down in comfort. All the driver did was look back and scowl, reach for the handle and haul the door shut with a slam. But again he was out of luck and had to leave the car when it turned uptown. As he reached the curb a violent stab of pain shot through his head from temple to temple and remained at full intensity, like an embedded arrow. It nearly drove him to his knees; he staggered up to a store window and leaned against it, wondering what had happened.

The agony of it gradually lessened, and with a worried shake of his head he set out across town on foot. He couldn't take the normal pedestrian's chances ducking through traffic, and had to abide by the lights when crossing the avenues. He arrived at his address without further mishap.

All the lights were on in his apartment, and several unpleasant-looking masculine customers were pacing about as though awaiting further arrivals. The basement gate was open. Numb with alarm, Dolf took the steps with a bound and raced down the basement corridor. He didn't stop at his own door, but continued on through the super's entrance into the garden. Light from the back room touched the green of the garden somberly and turned the foliage into mysterious submarine growths. Men stood around the chair in which his clay was propped, and with bulging eyes Dolf danced about looking over their shoulders. A man stooped to pick something up from the flagstones, and another detective ordered, "Leave that there, Bridges; the photographer hasn't got here yet. The damn fool," he added, evidently referring to the clay in the chair.

There was a bullet hole through the clay's temple, and a dark spattering of blood on the flagstones produced when bullet and expanding gases from the muzzle of the pistol blew his brains out. The object which Bridges had almost touched was an object of dull, wicked gleams, a revolver which lay as though it had dropped from his clay's right hand.

Among the detectives' conversations he heard the comment, "Killed his wife and the boy friend down on Waverly Place, then came back here and bumped himself."

Horror filled Dolf. That was his revolver lying there at his clay's feet, his own gun, for which he had a license. He had never used it, thought little of it when Kay took the weapon along with her when she left. The murderer had known where she kept the gun.

Oh, that clever Wilbur Huron! That slim, gloomy bird who looked like a spy. After killing Kay and Hoagie he had come here, and through the front grille had seen Dolf apparently sleeping in the garden. Light from the back room had illuminated the clay after dark. Huron had sneaked down the corridor to the janitor's door, slipped up to the slumbering clay. Put revolver muzzle to the clay's forehead—pulled the trigger—dropped the gun simultaneously and sprang to the safety of the building before any of the heads sticking out of the windows now could pop into view. That was the pain Dolf had felt through his head down the street, so recently. As simple as that—pinning the two murders and "suicide" on the helpless clay. That sinister Huron, sitting in a bar somewhere and chuckling to himself now.

Involuntarily Dolf screamed. He was still invisible, of course, so they couldn't locate him. The wild yell of fear reverberated from the back walls of the buildings, deafening in his own ears and certainly enough to make the steeliest nerves jangle. But no heads turned, no one paid any attention. Invisible jaw hanging, invisible eyes staring, Dolf felt of himself; in a conniption of horror he grabbed his shoulder, clapped himself on the chest.

He wasn't there any more.

'Tis Claude

STANDING NEAR THE center of the high-ceilinged kitchen, Ballardi glanced about and was aware of the immaculate order of the place. His right arm was raised, his fingers were spread wide so that the span found the cord hanging from the overhead globe. Unconsciously he was listening.

There was still enough light from the front of the house, when he had given the cord its smooth little pull, so that he was caused to hesitate when he reached the hall-end or little room between the kitchen and the peculiar front arrangement, at least of the downstairs, of the rock-solid old home. Where he stood now there was a secondary ante-room or landing, and he looked down the five brass-bound steps into the grade-entrance landing.

"Potatoes," he said as a soft exclamation. At the moment he felt sure that his impression of something amiss had been concern about provisions; always with regard for the other person, he knew that the housekeeper couldn't keep track of everything, though supplies should have received attention first. The mesh bag of potatoes, in the usual place on the landing, was nearly empty.

He was not aware of the glass panes in the side door, as the boy had been, never once thinking that they acted as mirrors. Just now, he had caught himself speaking aloud, though it was only the single word, and the lapse bothered him; also, he did not want to awaken the boy. He was worried. Even though this way of living was routine, simply keeping the plant in order as he thought of it, he was aware of a growing alarm. An experienced man in his thirties, and not much given to looking for trouble, he had the feeling that "something more is going to happen next." The unpleasant feeling had been with him intermittently for weeks, and he could not be certain of decisions in his business, with the strain of waiting.

The problem of the boy really sickened him a little.

Well, time could not be speeded. Trying to think of some solution to the endless waiting and waiting, he nearly spoke aloud again, and wondered whether he had been doing it more than he thought. This time it was merely mocking himself for taking things so hard, putting his name backwards as "Ballardi, Ralph," for whatever perspective there is in cataloguing one's self.

Passing through the two doorways of the hall-end area, he stood in a space which had formerly been part of the main hall, but where a great deal of remodeling had been done.

On the left a music room measured nearly square, opening through a broad archway. Opposite through a similar archway stretched a living room which had been almost doubled in size through an addition to the front of the house. A large French crystal mirror in the living room showed him with his back turned, motionless for a full minute while he looked at the boy sleeping on the lounge in the music room.

The boy had his mother's classic features—not so much the expression of Gracia's mouth, but the resemblance was strong in the middle third of the face. There was a trace of aggression in the jaw, very much like Ballardi's. The boy's face was ashine, and his eyes with the closed lids seemed to rest in his face with the color of deep lavender satin, as though evenly bruised. The boy had been playing handball in the alley between opposite garage walls of smooth brick—the tan bricks were unusually long and narrow, with a fine line of mortar between—old-time and costly masonry. The alley was paved, making a fine court, and the sound of feet or the impact of the ball bounced elastic echoes between the walls. . . . He had played the whole afternoon, and more than an hour in the evening until his chum down the block gave up, finally the loser because of the boy's tenacity. Ballardi took a step forward automatically, because the boy hadn't removed his scuffed shoes; he would hurt all over from the constriction of the shoes and clothing, and lying in one position.

The father thought forcefully and with a flash of hatred, *She should come back!*" But he knew the anger would get him nowhere. He changed his mind about doing anything for the moment and continued to the front door, where he stood at the screen and looked across the way.

In the still evening the sound of footsteps intruded as they approached, offensive in their peculiar hardness. The man was walking very slowly, and though he was still at a distance of a few houses down the street, his leather heels struck the cement squares of the sidewalk with the weight of a heavy individual. The stranger walked as though with oblivious contentment, much as though he were retracing a way through old scenes. This estimate would have been correct, though Ballardi was not much aware of recognizing the characteristic gait of the man whom he hadn't seen for a dozen years or more. . . . Such recognition was easy and not much a stunt of mind, as Ballardi didn't know many people, the ladies excepted, who had that singular preference for hard leather heels. Ballardi had always connected the preference with those persons who were opinionated and vain, concerned chiefly with themselves and not with the rights of others. Just now he was a little sensitive to annoyance anyhow.

The large home on the property opposite, owned by railway people when he came to think of it, and frequently closed because of their travels, was not set directly across the street. Thus, through the perpendiculars of the elms, which had gone to height over there, he could see over a long level of land; there was an embankment at the front of the property, at the sidewalk, then the ground dropped away tumbled and folded in the distance for miles.

Transversely, the city opened into the country from here, as its arteries of traffic ran mostly north and south. In daytime, the scene Eastward was of rolling woodland in haze, the haze from random burning and from moisture in the air. About a quarter of a mile away was a spine of ridge, where box-shapes of inexpensive houses were being set in parallel lines, on that street. The houses were not bad in design, but they were all the same. The view which Ballardi had would not be obstructed until the thin little wands of trees on that boulevard had had a few years of growing. Nothing of the distance could be seen now except for a thin and softened resting of light on the horizon, where there was a little town on the route to Chicago. He had a stake over there.

It was not any drowsing little town, quiet as it might appear. It was in fact rather wide open; Ballardi had played the slot machines in the back rooms, entranced a little at the wall-cases racked with prizes of fine guns; there were double-eagles, and like premiums on the machines. He had something of a fondness for the lawlessness of the place, the liking of one who felt hemmed in by human laws; in the gold coins there was also the harking back to times when gold was in circulation, as a symbol of halcyon days.

Just beyond that village he owned a piece of land. This was mostly low, swampy ground except for the highway-end. Here there were gas pumps and a roadside store on the site of an old farmhouse. There were three other buildings, cabins for tourists, and in quite satisfactory shape but needing paint. The people running the place were local, oldsters, and Ballardi had no thought of making a change. There was a profit to him averaging a hundred dollars a week.

But the whole sink of land was being filled in with tons of earth every day, as a hill was being levelled off and he had granted the rights for the dumping. The bottom land was worthless. His end-third was integral with the highway and trucking-belt; very close to him a modern trucking and transfer station and truck garage were going up, just for trucks, and his place was a nuisance. . . . There was going to be a huge apron of concrete, and the present operations were fascinating to watch. Crews were pumping concrete through tubes into the fill, having found the bottom of the shallow sink on his farmland; this latter junk under the mud was broken shale, flowage emptying on a lower contour of valley known as the Driver-Tarrant Farm. When there was wet weather, there was a little stream. The arrivals of trucks pumping that concrete were literally erecting a permanent platform on a system of snaking concrete stilts forced into a thick bed of rock, and as manifold as a rigid sponge. The idea fascinated him, and he could not get over the team-energy of those rugged men working on the job. They seemed to know exactly what they were doing, they answered inquiries pleasantly, and the whole thing was proceeding according to some contractor's estimate, or the estimate of his engineers.

He had been friendly with representatives of the trucking outfit, and they had been very friendly, with the constant threat of truck tie-ups where the labor union was strong. Instead of trucking the whole hill off somewhere, bulldozers could shove it into the hole in the ground which Ballardi owned, right next. The truck corporation agents didn't care whether he sold out, kept his piece as an island, decided on a rental, or what. They wished to strip the end-third, and said so, along with the fact that there was plenty of time to decide, though it seemed that the fill was coming toward him pretty fast. It looked as though the hill would exactly fill the hollow.

The agent for the truckers had a kind of basic philosophy, giving Ballardi to think that most of the people he met were smarter than he was; this last fellow seemed to be a kind of lawyer's contractman, but Ballardi wondered what other talents and experience he had. The man suggested in a very absent way as though thinking aloud, "It is only a matter of security. The lease can be graduated, if you wish it that way." There was of course the matter of whose security. The truckers simply wanted the thing on the books; it did not matter which way. No hold-up of anyone was involved, though Ballardi profited.

The heavy screen door framed Ballardi, and he answered promptly when he heard his name called, in a spontaneous way, from the sidewalk over the green lawn. The figure had come past the thick hedge dividing the properties on this side of the street. "Ralph!"

"Hello, Billie," Ballardi answered. Just from the footsteps, there was no mistake about its being Billie Leverence. That family had split to pieces. Once they had lived a few houses down in this block, and Billie had come around that way to look at the homestead, now practically a new place since being remodeled by strangers; he had not taken the shorter route on the cross-street. Ballardi could not imagine what had gone wrong in that family, what had caused the center of it to crumble, any more than he could understand the reasonless disconnections in his own household.

He had a row of nicks down the frame of the screen door. He had been making these nicks with his thumbnail as the days passed, not counting, as there were only a couple of dozen, and going over them again and again, making them deeper as a kind of punctuation of thought.

There was a semi-hypnosis in the habit of standing there, though most of the day he was downtown, working about the estate outdoors, or the like. But here at the door he drifted off habitually into a mood of waiting and thinking, and trying to arrange his ideas into a system of operability, not thinking of the effect of fatigue on himself. He did not know how hard he worked, say in the cutting-small of a limb sawed from the tree in the back yard. The half-trance at the doorway was connected with familiar sound, in some manner with the fascinating race of noises of the trains speeding down the grade through the center of Marbury to the yards flanking the river downtown. He had sensed something wrong as usual before Gracia left; then she had said something sarcastic about his standing at the screen and talking to himself. All he had said was,

"Well. . . . I don't know." As though, if there was going to be another time of her going away, it was the last time, and then he was through.

The thought had not been as clear as that. When there had been some remark about all that he did not know, about a lot of things, he had looked at her and said, "Remarks like that always cut both ways. . . . I should have said something about wondering whether it was wise to dispose of the property."

"Why don't you?" she had snapped, and gone into the house with an indifference which made her unapproachable. It gave him a little smile, for it was just as though she had asked, "Why don't you wear your pants on backwards so the seat won't get shiny?" The thing was that he could have snapped a few of those sarcasms back at her, and torn her to pieces. Once in a while when he had felt the old flash-anger he had eased it off through a variety of means, all requiring physical effort, like switching the tires around on the car in the garage, or lugging blocks of cement for a walkway at the side of the house, and thinking up cusswords until the feeling was gone. He thought that women like that were hard to live with.

He opened the door for Leverence, and shook hands with him. The time was nine-forty in the evening, of a hot and sticky day, with the wind six miles from the south. The periodic reports on the radio, playing softly, registered automatically. The temperature at this late hour was eighty-nine degrees. The weather had been very sticky, with heavy downpours and quick showers for ten days, and the stifling days may have had something to do with the unease in this house. One could think that he actually smelled mustiness or jungle-rot outdoors in Nature.

The rapid assessment and preliminaries out of the way between Leverence and Ballardi—they hadn't seen each other for so many years—they proceeded through the house to the kitchen. Billie had brought a bottle of wine with him, carrying it in a briefcase filled with papers, correspondence, and a strange assortment of odds and ends mostly of memento character which he had picked up at his sister's, and where the valueless things had been dutifully stored.

Billie himself no longer lived in Marbury, but came through from time to time as he traveled for a manufacturer in the East. He was an erratic correspondent, and Ballardi thought, short on tact for any job in human relations, let alone being on the road. Some crude streak in the level of breeding, an analyst would say.

"The old place hasn't changed a bit," Billie remarked, with a meaningless laugh, and the contrary of his remark was the case.

"Things don't change much," Ralph agreed imperturbably.

It seemed the wrong weather for wine, and the wrong time; Leverence readily agreed to a tall drink. Ballardi had the same skill in home bartending as in everything else, being one of those contained persons with developed muscular sense, having a schooled precision of hand and eye. In particular he had developed a conception of the home as an efficient, smoothly-running plant kept in constant repair, on which was based a fairish and well-worked-out philosophy.

In passing through the hall to the kitchen, Leverence had sighted the boy sleeping. There was an inexplicably patronizing way about Leverence, and the idiosyncrasy of his stupid laugh was one of the irritants of life. This unique laugh was sounded not in the usual manner by the rhythmic expulsion of breath, but by sucking in a few short breaths with the throat closed, so that he contrived a remarkable, rutting chord of notes, not loud, but out of place anywhere; something of a negative accomplishment as a matter of fact. It was a sound which might be characteristic of a person having a bad dream, but was unexpected and disturbingly primitive from anyone awake and civilized. This time Billie asked, "Do you always let him sleep in there?" It was of course a stab of automatic, unconscious belittlement. . . . "No," Ballardi replied thoughtfully, in the kitchen, and stabbed back with finesse. ". . . Looking at your old family place down the street?"

It hurt, and he knew that Billie's face had darkened, without turning to see. "I thought I'd come by that way," Leverence admitted, after the briefest hesitation. The question popped out—"Is Gracia here?"

The drinks were made, so in turning Ralph observed the slight movement of the head indicating the upstairs.

"She's in New York," he answered, without revealing any emotion at all. But with the straight look at his old chum there was perhaps a little of thought-transference. Billie was an incurable chaser of women, with all the signs of it in his face—the musculature of the chin, the set of the lips and development about the eyes, even the nostrils, where the indulgence in sex leaves its signs in a curiously identical way with the heavily excised fancies which come in bottles; the two mostly going hand in hand in parallel respects. Billie needed a continual feeding of his vanity, with the little security he had as a self-admiring male. Ballardi's wife had always been a focal point of fascination for him, along with anything that was Ballardi's, back into school days. The mechanism of the interest was as lively as ever, no matter how carefully concealed.

"Is she coming back?" Leverence asked, with his glass in his hand. He was incapable of realizing how he had put it, and Ralph nerved himself to waiting out the evening and a well-dressed friend who had turned gross, when the passing years were thought of.

A little staggered by the question, Ballardi made a sound of humor, and guessed, "I suppose so."

It was said in exactly the right way, with an aloofness from Billie's kind of suspicion. He added, "She's a lousy correspondent, the way you are."

It was interesting, the way alarm and fear could be kept at a distance with an incessant and subtle attack, as though there was a parallel between the rules of warfare and ordinary social contact, though the latter might be refined to unrecognizability.

The accusation made Leverence apologize, "Well, you've got a desk here . . ." And he shut up, remembering class papers which Ballardi had done for him, while Billie pow-wowed with the girls in Coon Hollow, and Ralph had told his father defensively that he might as well get Billie through that final semester, since he had started.

All the same, Billie asked, "How long has she been gone?"

They had made themselves at ease in the long living-room, where at one side was a large library table covered with the papers which Ballardi had been working on. This was largely the real-estate material. On top was a stout abstract of title made thicker and clumsier with photostats. Billie had his eye on it all, the whole of the living room.

"About three months," Ballardi hazarded. "You weren't here in that weather we had, were you?" This was an inquiry, and another accusation that Leverence didn't keep in touch, when he was in town, and it was true that Billie would get wound up with some girl in some fashion, then have to eat his breakfast and catch his train West. He lied, and said that he had been in Texas at that time, when the thick slop of Spring in Marbury had been such, freezing to rock-ice overnight, that Billie didn't think twice about setting foot out of downtown Marbury, for anybody or anything.

Though there was a give and take in conversation, the main idea in Billie's head was that he had come here expecting to see a beautiful woman beautifully dressed, though the high-strung Gracia couldn't stand this dull "bloke"—her term—with whom Ralph had such patience.

The next interest aside from Gracia was her boy, sleeping crumpled in the other room as though poured out by exhaustion onto the soft leather lounge.

Leverence had five children of his own, three by his first wife; Ballardi had never met the second nor third.

Billie had a notebook, or journal or diary in his briefcase. Though it was hard to believe, Ralph watched with stilly amazement as his old friend took it out and wrote in it for several minutes which seemed a long space of time. With instant perception Ballardi knew that Leverence had been doing this at addresses around the town, checking on the people he used to know. Billie asked what Ralph's I.Q. was, and Ballardi answered blankly that he didn't know; he couldn't help a twitch of the lip, listening to the soft power of the radio. Billie had his head down and talked, saying that he had been sitting in the library reading books on it, for some reason unexplained, and stated that his older boy had an I.Q. of 180.

"I wonder if you have got that straight," Ballardi responded mildly. "You brought your boys here once before I was married, you know. There's no point in giving any amount of weight to tests of that kind." He didn't know what to say, didn't want to get into any lengthy explanations about genius selling shoes in department stores, blockhead millions, genius going haywire with wealth, or any angle.

"What's wrong with it?" Leverence asked, looking up, not blushing but only puzzled. Two of his boys were in school here. "Don't you really know what your I.Q. is?"

"I haven't the faintest idea," Ballardi said, without any real irritation. The man must be charting his friends, he thought. He suggested, "Those tests are made in school, and you aren't supposed to know what the results are. What is your I.Q.?"

"Why, 160," said Leverence. "Not as high as the older boy's," and he sounded his obnoxious laugh, which was something like a snigger in reverse. "What is the boy's I.Q.?"

"No test has been made, so far as I know," Ballardi said meticulously, trying to figure out his friend's system of cheating. Billie was setting his glass down here and there on the papers covering the library table, leaving wet rings because the glass was sweating in the humid air. Billie had shoved papers aside with his elbow, and the sheets damaged were only those, Ralph hoped, on which he had been doing his arithmetic. He said, "I'll get a coaster."

He came back with an aluminum tray, and blotted the papers with a cloth. There was a plate of canapés on the tray, these prepared by the housekeeper and left in the refrigerator. The purchases like potatoes had evidently slipped her mind while she was doing these, so everything was all right. The housekeeper was right in her choice. There were enough potatoes through tomorrow, the loaf of bread was sufficient in the slices remaining, and the woman had things closely figured, had actually done an extra job, and very well. Ballardi watched his friend eat the crackers and toast covered with the delicious things of the larder. Billie remarked, "I hate anchovies."

So help me God, Ballardi thought, here is a real oaf.

The telephone rang; it was his lawyer, about a signature, and he said that he would phone in the morning. The lawyer had called from his own house. When he hung up after the brief exchange, Ballardi's cast of thought automatically shifted to legal terms, and this house was his choice of venue, or decision, though the term was not entirely one of legal action or instrument. He gauged Billie's drink from where he sat at the telephone deep in the dining room, and another one wasn't needed yet.

"Is the boy afraid of the dark?" Leverence asked, as Ballardi returned with his head down and noticing that the thick rug needed vacuuming. It would need cleaning where Billie sat, anyhow, for if a paper stuck out over the edge of the table he would cut the ash from his cigarette on that, without thinking, with the motivation of a child-personality still learning.

. . . The boy afraid of the dark.

The journal which Billie kept was still on the table.

"His mother isn't upstairs," Ralph said. "And I'm not. He's been playing handball all day down the alley where we used to play. Funny echo down there, isn't there?"

The quick reference to two ideas or more set off a chain of recollection, and Billie remembered the handball games, Ralph tanning dark in the hot sunlight and Leverence blistering, in the savage competition. There was still a stable then, farther down on the opposite side of the alley from their street, and their hands always stank from a combination of rubber, manure and sweat, thought they kept the alley clean to avoid accidents of "hindrance."

Yes, it was a strange, springy echo between those walls which they used for a handball court, hypnotic in the same way as the trains sending the echo of rhythms of heavy machinery, smoothly running freight and passengers and equipment down that long grade a block away, or inching up the same grade with giant coughs from the stacks, the exhaust chattering when the pressure was lost, like a mechanical, deprecatory laughter. Then there would be a faint trembling of the ground, and a locomotive and tender would come running backward, dinging rapidly, to hook on, and the double-header would seem to heave and cough, getting its hind legs under for the effort, and pull away with the roughness of sound from the stacks going soft and smooth, just as they were doing now. This structure of sound was what Ballardi listened to in making those nicks on the frame of the screen door, aware that there were no sounds lonelier nor more filled with nostalgia than those connected with railroading. He had stood on the bridge, or rather on the cast-iron pipeline for gas which went over the bridge, watching the trains at night and feeling the tremor in his feet when they passed, seeing people dining in a lighted car, wondering who they were and where they were going.

"I guess all kids are that way," Ballardi said. He turned an ear to the radio, and continued, "You were afraid of the dark yourself, probably."

"No, I never was," Billie said promptly, and laughed. "None of my kids were, either."

Ballardi could not resist it, and was beginning to get a tightness in his chest: "How about that time you came home crying with Georgie Ferrold, right past the front of the house here, and my mother went out, the time you were supposed to be camping out on the Horsemills Road?"

"That was out in the country," Billie said. "That's just homesickness; everybody gets that." Referring to Ballardi's boy he asked, "Is he really afraid of the dark?"

"I imagine that he does have a fear of the dark," Ralph agreed, and he put some thought to knifing this line of inquiry in two. "He wouldn't be sleeping in there if he were sleeping upstairs. I don't know whether you remember when we were kids ourselves. . . . We used to go to movie serials every Saturday afternoon. There were things like THE VOICE ON THE WIRE, or THE MYSTERIOUS MAN IN BLACK. The character who slept in a coffin in a sub-basement. There was some trick photography when he was upstairs in the plot. He'd be standing behind draperies, and he could project phantom hands to strangle someone in the room. Or these phantom hands would come out of the bookshelves behind someone. As I remember it, the man in black was a prospector who had struck it rich in the desert, and blew his fuses because his wife welched. As soon as he was supposed dead, she married somebody else, and the hands were all vengeance."

It seemed to Ballardi that he had at least three serials combined, but Leverence said, "I remember." Then he added abruptly, "What was the name of that candy we used to get at the corner drugstore?"

"Lavenders," said Ballardi, with a sudden brilliant recollection. They were a vanished confection, of fluted tubes with pinched ends, which dissolved quickly in the mouth. With things and qualities no longer obtainable, there was also the reminder of a graciousness of living which was gone forever. "Anyhow, you remember the nightmares from those movies, and the way your dad used to holler at your mother about letting you go to them. I don't know whether there are such things nowadays or not—maybe in comic books—the kids just seem to have lively imaginations."

Billie was not going to admit that he didn't have any imagination, so he said, "Well, I guess I've had a few nightmares, at that." He produced his obnoxious laugh, humorless and unconvincing.

The big radio boomed softly in the background, music being something which would not awaken the boy; he went to sleep listening to music. Ballardi thought that there was nothing on earth which conveyed an idea of such terrific power as music did, and good performance either in the classical or popular was readily received by a man with ideas of precision and order. Also this was the only magic in the world, and there was the appeal to the strain of small-boy which is in all men. He had used to sit with his head inside the doors of the phonograph to shut the world away, and forget pain. The innumerable associations of happiness were the reason why he had the machine on now, though he did not think of it except as a quiet and sure means of threading the beads of time. He remembered that Leverence had little appreciation of music and had flunked in the snap-course of Music Appreciation in school. Another strange thing was that Billie had stated that he hated flowers, just about the most stupid thing which Ballardi had ever heard. Both in the dining room and living room stood bouquets of flowers from the garden, in the cut crystal of the modern Swedish artisans. Very fine.

The grandfather's clock with its German-made mechanism and the iron spiral which was the chime—Ballardi had taken it apart and adjusted it for its present tone—had sounded ten o'clock, and the single stroke of the half-hour was due, with the strange and spreading note that lingered in the air like a church sound, or a signal in a monastery in the heights of mountain fastnesses. It was a beautiful thing, or random visitors would not have said spontaneously, "I like the sound of that clock." The mechanism always whirred with a sound like a human sigh, a few minutes before striking.

In the kitchen to replenish the drinks, and without any waste motion, Ballardi shook his head in thinking about the man in the other room and how far Billie still had to go. Every last thing of skill and understanding which Ballardi possessed in his hands and mind had been acquired through bitterest experience; he did not merely *have* his abilities. He had been out in the world and done his traveling, tried his hand at every job suitable for his kind of build. He was a thin measurement over six feet in height, if he stood barefoot a few minutes, which he did, often enough; he was medium in bone-structure, firm in musculature and not sedentary, in general was strong in the tenacity of the American, and in all respects and in the type was an example of the fact that the American is the killingest soldier on earth when he is aroused.

One of the questions which Leverence had asked was whether Ralph still had his stamp collection. That had caused the shake of the head just now. Ballardi had said that most of it had been sold, only the U.S. issues being retained; the collection was the boy's simply from handing it down as soon as the idea of the hobby was grasped. . . . When he was so observant, it was peculiar that Ballardi didn't glance down the stairs to the side door and its panes of glass, except to note again the nearly empty mesh bag of potatoes. Nor did he think of raising his glance just that little angle, on his return. . . . The rustle of paper had probably taken his attention, and he thought that Leverence might be looking through the interesting abstract on the library table, or the accounts. It made no difference, or Ballardi wouldn't have left the material there. On the return, it simply appeared that Leverage was writing in his journal again. No matter how much he wrote now, he was going to write some more later on this evening when the afterthoughts had been put together. Ballardi set the drinks down and excused himself, seeing that his friend was intent on scribbling in the journal with his pen, and Billie made his acknowledgment absently.

In the music room Ballardi lifted the boy from this massive leather lounge which Gracia had insisted on buying, and the boy's head dropped as though he had a broken neck. The shine of lips parted, showing the teeth; the lashes looked stuck. . . . There had been a lot of violence in Ballardi's experience, before he ever thought of marrying Gracia. In the whole range of experience the present situation was dead wrong, but he hated so much the violence he had known that he had an automatic check on that black anger against anyone. He had seen the whole works of human passion, had seen murder.

He walked past the clock and up the stairs, and put the boy to bed in the boy's room off the northeast corner of the square upstairs hall. In its way that was the best room in the house, and had been given the youngster with some idea of sunlight in the morning through those windows. This had been the grandfather's room. The most remarkable furnishing in the place, aside from the bedstead, was a lampstand made of three ancient muskets. . . . Ballardi was surprised to find the smallish professional handball in his hand when he had put the boy on the bed, not remembering that he had picked it off the piano keys downstairs. . . . The boy was sticky, and he smelled like a small boy. Ballardi dressed him in pajamas anyhow, with swiftness; something for wonderment—the boy simply turned over, sighed, and slept soundly on. Totally dead to the world. Wonderful.

This was a long room, and Ballardi wondered where to put the handball; he set the boy's shoes a little farther out from the bedstead, and placed the ball on the rug alongside. He stood for an instant with his hand closed on the carving of the footpost. A glance showed him that the screens were secured; the windows were open for ventilation, with very little air stirring. He pressed the wall-button that turned off the musket-light.

Through some jump of mind from the boy's weariness, he thought of the hopelessness of waiting in the morning. Really, of waiting for the mail that never came. He hated to lift the lid of the old iron mailbox, and the boy knew of his waiting, always hanging around in the morning, waiting in the yard until the mailman had passed, leaving the magazines or whatever, but not what was wanted. Ballardi had only the choice of gently cussing, or keeping silent. There was nothing on earth that he knew of which would make Gracia communicate, which she would only when she got ready to. Once, he remembered his father writing him when he was on a venture in the West which looked promising, and failed, "There is nothing more discouraging than hope." Ballardi didn't remember whether that had been a quotation or not, his daddy having been a reader of books.

Downstairs he switched off the stairwell light, and the setting was still of Leverence writing persistently in his book. Ballardi could not imagine what was being written, supposed it was in the nature of a report connected with the man's travels. Also, Billie showed a liking just for sitting in a comfortable home.

Ralph sat at the radio until the writing was done, adjusting the machine slightly, and listened to the slow and quite fascinating modern arrangement of an old tune. It was done on harmonicas by experts, faultlessly, and he remembered reading something about the inventor of this instrument thinking that his invention would be an addition to the orchestra. Periodically Ralph recalled coming upon such arrangements or performances, or music he liked, when the lower levels of despair had been reached. It seemed the luck of exact timing, whether he had happened to be in a New York hotel, or whether it was a juke box in the South. However, his sense of humor had come to the rescue in the same way.

In an analysis of music, which seemed to be integral with his whole self-reliance, it seemed to act constructively. Without any attempt at diagramming, one might be in a rotting of gloom, and here in examples of music he liked was assurance of something permanent, and according to his idea of beauty. He had always thought that music was a system of the only pure magic in this world.

The piece ended, and the music continuing without a break into another done in a primitive jungle rhythm, Ralph made a trip to the front door patiently, and had a look at the giant elms. The little wind stirred the foliage and made it whisper multitudinously as though with the syllables of many people talking softly among themselves. One could imagine hearing fragments of gossip, earnestness, and traces of sarcasm. The boy received those sounds, seemingly coming at the windows with folds of darkness in waves. Ballardi returned from the doorway, and took the chair nearer the library table.

In a moment which was like total silence, though there was always the rosined high-note of the crickets, there was suddenly a sound and vibration in the large house, as of a huge and hard peg turning in its hole, and little clinks as though from dishes touching in the china cabinet. Ballardi blinked his eyes, trying to think of the source of the sound, or the series of sounds.

Everything was as before, in fifteen or twenty seconds. But their eyes met as Leverence looked up from his journal and asked, absently, "What was that?" He had finished, and now he put the book away in his briefcase.

Ralph resisted the temptation to say that it was the "poltergeist." Leverence wouldn't understand such humor; at the same time Ralph couldn't figure out where the sound had come from, except that it had come from below. He knew all the seeming accidents of sound in the house, and when something fell, he knew what, and where.

"The house settling," he suggested, because it was a sound of stress on wood. "It probably came from next door at Dixon's. He's doing something out there in the yard."

"That was right here in the house," Billie said, in the way he had of popping out his certainties. "I could feel it in my feet." His feet were on bare floor. There was no further sound when they listened, and there were no trucks passing. It was just as though all other sound had quit so that they could hear that one sound.

"Then it's probably down the basement," Ballardi said, smiling. "Right under where you're sitting, there's an eight-by-eight supporting post, and it's split. If it has split any more, I'll have to jack up the center beam and get some iron straps around that post. I can put those hands to work down there," he added, as an afterthought.

"What would make it split?" Leverence asked.

"Weight," said Ralph. "Those beams are solid oak and they weigh a lot themselves. The same stuff supports the upper stories, and there's always been a lot of weight up there. Right over us is the boy's room; my grandaddy read a lot, and he had his whole library up there, and piled all around."

The suggested job in the basement wasn't for any one man, and Leverence asked, "You mean Dixon is going to help you down there? I didn't get that about putting somebody's hands to work."

"No, that was just a figure of speech," Ralph explained carelessly. "The boy wanted to know whose hands those were in the basement. Like a glass of jelly standing there empty, and you ask whose hands have been at it. There are always explanations for things like that. A friend might borrow, with the door open, and forget, and there's plenty down there."

"Was the boy down in the basement?" Billie asked.

"No, he was in the kitchen with me," Ralph answered, and swallowed. He sipped his drink for a real swallow, and lighted a cigarette after giving Billie one. The remark on the hands had seemed self-explanatory, in the way children mingled the imaginary with the real. Leverence had children of his own, and should know. At the same time, the peculiar noise they had just heard was the strangest, slow, shuddering sound that Ballardi had ever heard. He had to take into account the fact of ingenuity of kids. They had a trick of drawing a rosined pole across the edge of an upended plywood crate, and it would make the windows shiver if well done. What they had heard was a deeper sound, and Ralph's mind was on that, not the fantasy of the hands, because his concern was with the house.

"I don't get it," said Leverence bluntly, staring, and always with a suggestion of ruddiness and anger in his manner.

There was no reason why Ballardi should go along with this, but he took a breath to clear his throat, set down his glass, and explained, "It's like this: The boy asked me whose hands those were in the basement, because he had seen them down there."

There seemed to be some kind of subtle insult involved, as though there were the suggestion that Billie's kids weren't smart, or Leverence himself wasn't, but Ralph had no evidence that Billie ever got belligerent when he had had a few drinks. A good guess was that he went to sleep if he was smart about it, might get into minor accidents if he drove a car. He was the opposite personality type from Ballardi's.

Ralph didn't trouble to straighten out the fact that he had told the boy to keep out of the basement for the time being, where his daddy had the workshop. This, because there had been some trouble with the former housekeeper, whom Ballardi had discharged. This woman had been an uppity Virgin Islander, black as a cat and sarcastic, and who entered the house talking in a loud way about what was going to be found wrong today. She had chipped all the hollow-ground knives opening cans with them; never put things back where they belonged, but simply out of sight somewhere. This maid had come through Dixon, and he fired her in turn for similar reasons. She was good for small apartments, nothing larger, as she got excited when questioned about anything elaborate in arrangement. . . . It did not occur to Ballardi that the boy hadn't been in the basement for some time; and the boy had asked that question about the hands when he was standing in that little room at the head of the basement stairs. Upper and lower rows of hooks set in the wall, on the other side of which was the stairs leading to the second story. The lower row of hooks was for the boy's things, and he kept tools for his bicycle behind the door, which concealed everything when it stood open, and leaving the basement stairway unobstructed, with the old panes of glass in the door in view, at the eye-level of a small boy. Otherwise there was a cross-beam because of the upstairs landing, and habitually Ballardi hung on this, which had a wooden crosspiece at the corner, to swing down to the landing when going to the cellar. The boy had gone through the kitchen with what seemed like a damaged flute, for there was one in the collection of junk behind the door. The boy had sat on the back steps for a while, whittling a piece of wood to spread the mouthpiece of the flute, and then he had hammered on it with a piece of wood because he had been told not to go into the basement for tools. It was one of those things to feel mean about long afterward, but Ballardi had told him the right way. And the boy had made the flute work, without any resentment that Ballardi could see. With the shavings left on the porch, the aimless tootling of the flute had gone through the yard and down the paved alley out of hearing. Ralph had made the mouthpiece for the flute because the boy couldn't learn to blow it, and some youngster had used the mouthpiece for a screwdriver when the boy wasn't looking.

It was understood perfectly well that there were only the two men in the house, and the boy sleeping upstairs. Leverence asked persistently, "He asked you whose hands those were in the cellar?"

There was something vaguely wacky about the idea, going back to childhood and those movie serials; along with that, there was his friend's matter-of-factness about something strange and horrible and unnatural, which went back to Ralph's telling him of things which he had experienced when he lived in the Village in New York years ago. In all Ballardi's travels the memory was of a chain of violence, no matter where he was. There was the time he was in Jersey City, and an ordinary man in front of him suddenly whipped out a pistol and fired spaced shots in the air. Behind Ballardi had been a scuffle, one man knifing another, and the man with the gun had been a private detective, firing those shots for effect and to attract police, and the police got there fast, on the jump. It had given Ballardi the snakes, the gun going off repeatedly, so close. That private detective had thought fast, and hadn't been involved; neither had Ballardi, continuing past out of range. The brawls in apartments and restaurants he would as soon forget. Someone in a fury would raise his fist and smash it down, breaking the glass on the bar and cutting his hand open. Or some woman would start yelling for her husband and taking her clothes off, mostly, when Ralph thought about it, because the lady felt sick and clothes stifled, and there was the distraction of a little exhibitionism. There had been a murder on his own corner, and so on and so on. All of these things had been spaced in his experience, but he had gotten fed up on noise and things happening, on the kind of people he had to deal with, and most of all, vermin. He abominated the constant fight against bugs in the house, the dozens of cockroaches peering down over the picture molding; in the sweltering summer, when the doors were open, the Croton beetles or whatever they were would come flying in as big as eagles. These things all of them were why he had decided to come back to Marbury, one day on 8th Avenue when he had suddenly smelled a florist's fresh lilacs. There was a breeze on 14th, and he thought that the clear scent might have come all the way from Jersey across the Hudson, just by some fluke. And then of course his thoughts continued West to here, where lilacs were massed on the roads in the springtime, where there was lush grass, and there were still streams running with clear water. The country was wooded, and there was virgin forest within a short drive. It was still an idyll to Ballardi, though his household was now split because of Gracia's leaving, and the boy had not yet betrayed his feelings except by playing too hard. One night Ballardi had been delayed, and the boy had made an attempt to prepare dinner, the housekeeper having gone. The boy had fried eggs so hard that they had seemed covered with plastic, and the fried potatoes rattled around. Both had eaten the meal calmly, and it just took a little longer, though it was pretty gruesome.

Right now he wondered what to do with Leverence, who evidently had no train to make, and might wish to stay, though he had his sister's place and his hotel room. Ballardi said in his usual way, "I guess so," shielding his annoyance, and simply wishing that it was tomorrow. "Just a pair of hands lopped off at the wrist, and'fooling around' down there; 'staying in the air,' he said. Kids have ideas like that. They make things up."

"I should think that he'd be afraid of those things instead of the dark," Leverence suggested, intently.

"I don't think it's the same thing," Ballardi said. "They make things up or exaggerate, in connection with what they've done, but fear of the dark is connected with the unknown. Wake up in pitch darkness in a strange place, yourself, and if you've been using your eyes a lot you might wonder whether you'd gone blind. I'd call that fear of the dark."

Billie drank an ounce from his glass, and blinked thoughtfully at an oil painting of Gracia on the wall above Ballardi. The artist had painted her in a dress fitting snugly, frilled or fluted in the material so that with the bare shoulders the breasts were given a natural spring of youth, with wit just within taste. The back was straight in the portrait, with a patrician dignity which Ralph and the artist knew that Gracia did not have. The artist knew his business, and had given the right emphasis to lips and eyes, where all the fine musculature of character was located. He and the artist knew each other's mind. Gracia had been delighted; Ralph had given the artist a look because of the brilliant job; if the artist had said anything aloud it would have been, "There is no loyalty in her. My friend, she is a bitch."

The peculiar muscles in Billie's head caused him to ask, "You aren't running this place all by yourself, are you? I mean, you don't run the house all alone." He was thinking of his own household, and he had been hoping to find the handsome Gracia here. He couldn't let go of an idea.

"No one could run a place like this alone," said Ralph. "Not by a long shot." He explained that the housekeeper stayed for a few days, left, returned as the work was gauged; a team of ex-GI's came around and did the lawn, laying black stuff on it which the rains had just now washed in, and trimmed the shrubbery. They were equipped to cut down the largest tree. When tree-roots lifted the sidewalk, it was not even Ballardi's business to do anything about it, and he would not tackle anything like roofing the garage, which the boys had gouged by playing on it, jumping from his to Dixon's. Ralph had warned his own boy off, and with Dixon in the yard at unexpected times, also, there was not much more of that trouble except with kids who seemed to be homeless.

This kind of information was evidently what Leverence was after, and Ballardi thought of how terribly insecure the man must be, to go around checking like this, and write it down.

He mentioned the black lass who had ruined the knives, and her lack of any sense of order, saying, "I had to keep hunting for things down in the basement until I thought I would blow my stack. I mean, I was working down there, because the temperature is always right, you remember; just because I worked there, she had to clean it up. I've found every damned thing behind the books in the bookcase, and I haven't got the place straightened out yet."

Billie laughed appreciatively, though it was not humor in any ordinary sense. Though the simile wasn't entirely fair, the throat-sounds were like those of a suction-cup worked rapidly on a plugged kitchen sink. Ballardi looked at his drink and wondered whether he had forgotten to put anything in it.

Feeling that he had to make it not quite so bad, he mentioned the disorder, when Billie remembered Ralph's dad using some strong persuasion about putting things back, the tools belonging in place and nowhere else. Ralph's papers were mixed up, often smudged with handling, and even the line of books on the shelves was uneven. He had simply told the maid that he was sending the boy to the country, which he intended to do, giving her proper notice in that way. But that black maid had been so good in some ways that he wondered what had gone wrong in others.

Leverence asked bluntly about the papers on the library table. Ralph defined an abstract of title, mentioned the property on the Chicago road, adjoining the Driver-Tarrant farm. The thing that flashed in Ballardi's mind was that he might sell that out, sell this house as well, and go West again to start over. He knew that he wouldn't do that. A journalist friend had studied maps from the Department of Agriculture, picked the perfect climate in a particular spot in the far West, and kept right on moving. Ballardi corresponded with him. The itch to move was something on the order of a mistake; once you start it, it keeps right on going.

And there is an argument that there is no rest where you are.

They sat in comfortable chairs, Billie with his arm on the library table, and Ralph turning his attention a little to hear a ballad being sung softly on the monster machine. A lass was singing with a kind of silvery joy, "Let him go, let him tarry." He had the temptation to turn the thing on full, but he had never run his car wide open either, or not recently around here. The same for the radio. In New York he had turned it on, and felt something on his shoulder and brushed it off, and it was a cop's hand. There were three of them, and people in the hall; the cop had said, "They can hear that all the way down on the Battery." When Gracia was out somewhere on a tantrum.

Flowers, that Billie hated. He had always kept the vases filled in New York. Next-door, Dixon, who ran three filling stations, owning one, had a hobby of horticulture, and at least to Ballardi referred to certain bulbs as his "babies." He had explained that business drove him nuts. Ballardi had made a gift of cypripedium, the yellow lady-slipper which grew in a bed in the shadow of his own garage. Dixon got a dozen out of thirty blooming plants.

These same flowers were in the picture of Gracia, where Billie returned his attention; with his direct way of thinking, from the garage, where they had tinkered with the old car, and the freedom of either's house, he asked, "Remember the clubroom down the basement?"

There was no laugh this time. The room was the room under the basement stairs. There had been no door then, only the piece of canvas tacked overhead. There was no electrical connection, and they had burned candles. Turns were taken at keeping records of meetings, in an old ledger. "Indian" drawings were made on the walls by dipping a finger in a can of screen paint. There was an arsenal of an old shotgun, two bows with the arrows, a pump-gun with which they shot matches, and a small automatic for which there was no ammunition. There were .22 caliber cartridges, which they set off by hitting them with a hammer on the sidewalk, until someone got hurt. That had been an argument ever since. There were no weapons in Ralph's house and there was no ammunition until Billie showed up with that box of cartridges, and Ralph remembered just now where he had gotten it. They had gotten toast and bacon at his aunt's, and when they were well away, Billie had that box of shells in his pocket. It had been in a cabinet drawer, and there were other boxes of shells in the drawer. There were also two guns on a rack, in view. Billie had tried to set one of the bullets off, having gotten a hammer from his house. He was the same one who had shot off his father's shotgun and knocked himself off the porch roof aiming at his own weathervane on the roof-peak. His father had whipped him, since he wasn't hurt in the fall, and sworn, "William Lev'nce, I'm goin' to wea' you out!" But in detonating the bullets, when there was no success, Ballardi had taken his turn, saying, "Let me feed it one."

He had struck it, when a little gal pushed past. The bullet exploded, sand from the walk stung her face, and she screamed. She was scared, not hurt, but a man came running across the street, grabbed up Ballardi and knocked him cold on the grass between the sidewalk and street. After all this long time, he remembered.

The clubroom in the basement was a storage room now, for winter clothing, or it was going to be one as soon as Ballardi got hold of a mason to cement the crumbled area in the range-rock. The place was insulated, and the door was in, with a light. There was a huge bag of calcium chloride, for refilling a mesh bag which dripped into a pan on a shelf.

The only fault in the cellar walls was in that chamber where the clubroom had been. The mortar everywhere else was like iron, like stone, fine and smooth and hard. The same cement was on the garage, and the men who had drilled through the three inches of it, and through the netting and wood siding, in order to blow in rock wool for insulation, hmh; he had heard them talking back and forth, as they hit unexplainable crosspieces in the studding and had to drill more holes, and when he went out, one of them asked what kind of cement that was, or whether he knew what it was. Ballardi didn't; the garage had been a barn and was pretty old, but the spools drilled out showed that the wood was as solid as the day the pine was nailed to the sides. The insulation there had been Gracia's idea, and the pipe for heating.

In that one spot under the side entrance, the mortar had sifted out in an area of five to seven stones, and was in little heaps on the flags like gray sand. If a man wished, it looked as though he could pull one of the limestone blocks right out of a row of range rock in the foundation.

There was a paved courtyard between this house and Dixon's on the corner, the pavement sloped to the center with a drain there. Ballardi thought that the drain-pipe might have rusted through, over the years, and the soaking of the subsoil downgrade had gradually eaten away the mortar of his foundation at that point. It was nothing of any seriousness, but it was one of those things on the self-continuing list of things to do because of the dimension of passing time and his preoccupation with having things in order.

"I suppose the boy uses the clubroom now," Leverence suggested, and usually as now he drew breath in three times for his nonsense laughter.

This time, though, one could suppose that there were recollections of the meetings in the clubroom. There had been a long succession of episodes, for the boys seemed to have the freedom of everywhere in those days, and every hour of the day was paradisaical in some manner, whether climbing the trees on the boulevard and eating the tiny "monkey-nuts" or walking the bright railway tracks, away from home or in the yard. In this house they had access through the grade entrance without disturbing the people upstairs. There was the time that Billie had pinched a quart of green home-brew from his own basement. The thing had exploded when uncapped, and the boy trying to stop the lavish reducement of the contents with his thumb had soaked them all with foam. Then there was the panic, and all of them cleaning up the place with wet rags. One of the mysteries which Ballardi remembered was the time the pump gun was fired, empty, and they all went running to the boy who went to his knees crying on the grass. Somehow or other a pebble the size of a BB shot had gotten into the gun, and they picked it out of the flesh over the bony structure in front of the ear. Hard little black stone like a seed. They had set the place afire with the candles, and put it out. And so on in an endless series.

The boy did not use the clubroom, of course, not now. "No," Ballardi said. ". . . Claude is down there." Then he explained immediately, because Billie looked back at him with such a blank expression, "Claude is the poltergeist we have here. You know what a poltergeist is."

"Polter," Leverence began, with bewilderment. "No," he challenged, "what is it?"

Here was a man with no sense of humor at all, and a man of poor perception. The lightness of attitude which Ballardi had felt died back in his eyes. There was no communication here. He guessed that the trouble with Billie was stubbornness. He was insensitive, and had always simply refused to learn, was hostile to anything which he didn't find out for himself. Ralph thought about how to express it, and said, "Why, it's just a folklore name for a noisy ghost. It's a way of explaining why pictures fall down from the walls, and why there are noises at night, and so on."

"You don't believe in ghosts, do you?" The laugh.

"You would have to define what you mean by ghosts," Ralph answered in a gentle attack, though he was not attacking his boyhood chum but his own wife Gracia, who had been too long away. "When we were kids, you didn't have any trouble getting scared by stories like a pair of poltergeists wheeling around in a figure-8, and wondering what noise to make in a haunted house."

Ballardi laughed, in the really pleasant and resonant way he had, his sense of humor relieving the strain of this call, for he remembered the past better with every clue. "You surely remember the time we explored a haunted house out there near Gay's Ferry. There was a noise in the attic, and we all left running. Your sister was along. You probably remember the way we got scratched up going through the bottoms of prickly ash there." He didn't say anything about the fact that Leverence had done something quite natural in the midst of the prickly ash and wild raspberry bushes, and his older sister had to wipe him.

Leverence remembered the prickly ash.

"Well, thinking of things the way kids do," Ralph said further, "I just gave a name to the thing, for the boy."

"You don't believe in that stuff, do you?" Billie asked. He was getting down to the last of his tall drink, so Ballardi didn't have to answer at

once. Billie had had his attention on the portrait of Gracia most of the
time, and of course the canvas was there to see. At the same time,
Ballardi knew that the ideas in his friend's mind concerned mostly his
wife's mouth and breasts, and her crossed legs.

Ballardi said, "You know, it's easy to make a mistake. It's like misplac-
ing the keys to the car. You said that you have had a lot of accidents
recently, for example. Or your wife can't find the can-opener. The idea
is, that instead of getting into an uproar about it you invent something
like Claude the poltergeist, the one we have here, and figure out where
Claude has put the key to the front door or hidden the can-opener."

Ballardi had different ways of finding things, mostly in the fact that he
always had a "spare" for everything, a duplicate.

"I just look for anything like that," Billie volunteered. "Let me tell
you about an experience I had in Chicago."

He recounted the experience, of losing the contents of his wallet.
After a desperate search, and on the verge of wiring for money, he had
found his travel-funds, licenses, and the like; rolled up and stuck into the
roll of toilet tissue in his hotel bathroom.

"That's what I just said," Ralph commented, and looked at his friend
with a kind of scientific interest.

"Let's take a look at the clubroom," Leverence suggested. He finished his drink, and moved his briefcase farther under the table when he
got up; no doubt it contained things valuable to him.

The lights were left on. Also, he had left a light on upstairs for the
boy. As it happened, Ballardi had installed that one himself, and in
tracing the lines had found wiring which seemed very heavy-gauge to
him, even needlessly heavy, and no doubt capable of carrying considerable power. There were two fuse boxes in the house, and two sets of
wires strung from the house to the power lines in the alley. Much of the
equipment in the house was old, and heavy; the furniture was massive.
Everything was designed to last. . . . Ballardi put his cigarette out,
leaving the radio booming softly.

At the grade-entrance they could hear the crickets, as Ralph swung
the door open for a glance to see what Dixon was doing. This doorway
was simply an entrance to the house at ground-level, at about the center
of the side elevation. There was no grade in the sense of slant.

"They're making a noise, all right," Ralph commented, referred to
the crickets. Apparently the neighbor, Dixon, was grubbing out a homely
piece of shrubbery near his garage with a mattock. He seemed to be

talking to himself, or saying a few words after grunting, or else it was a boy and girl murmuring on a level of romance as they idled along on the cross-street. Elms squared every block in the residential areas, making the streets handsome avenues of foliage, out this far from downtown and a block to the East, after the little woods of the estate across the way.

The two old friends descended the steps to the basement, Ballardi going first. The floor was paved with large flags, and the blocks of level stone had been oiled and painted, from years back. There was still a little of the color to be seen, otherwise the stone was black.

The bottom of the staircase was flush with walls left and right. At the right was the laundry-room, typical and spacious with the stand-tubs, mangle, and a gas stove for cooking in the well-known suffocating weather of summertime; the wash-machine. The windows were three-quarters below ground level, and protected by an iron grill. . . . On the left, from where they stood, was the fruit cellar. This ran back from the wall-line and was a room of good size. The shelves were filled with canned goods which had been the work of Ballardi's mother, and perhaps a grandmother. Ancient cherries had gone to mush, for example, and the place should be sorted out.

Off the center of the full basement was the heating plant; the furnace and humidifier, tanks, a maze of pipes of different kinds running all over. About half the main room was screened off and livable. Here was where Ballardi had done most of his work until the housekeeper had messed it up.

Just around from the bottom of the steep stairway was the old clubroom, now closed with a pine door, the entrance being between the stairway and the laundry room.

Hanging across their way when the reached the basement was a heavy extension cord sheathed in rubber, as thick as a finger. This was the plug-in line for the washing-machine, and had been left hanging across a couple of nails when the housekeeper had last mopped the laundry-room. The cable was so heavy, and the plug-in so peculiar, with its across-and-across points, that Billie Leverence lifted it from the nails. This cable was hooked into the wall at head-level, out of sight in the laundry-room, in a most unusual porcelain fixture no longer made. As the cable was quite old, bare copper showed at the plugs where long use had worn the insulation away.

Ballardi started to say something, trying to contain the whole idea of his existence in words which would be understandable to Leverence, and thinking of the mood of the instant.

They could hear the music from the upstairs, a famous work in a brilliant new arrangement which made the thing speed with rhythm, charged with excitement, so that if one were relaxed and simply receiving impressions it sounded like a description of a golden panther full of danger, readying the ferocity for the smooth violence of the attack. Good music, and it rang crystalline with a swift and subtle percussiveness.

The idea in the air had been that Ballardi had a pretty good thing here, a sound house, secure; home, and very fine. Yet through an act of ungoverned will the thing was wrecked, the dream, the castle.

Leverence had said something about the solidity, and how heavy everything was, just like the cable in his hand, as though everything in the place had been made to last forever. The remark which Ballardi had been trying to frame was, "Gone like a shot." And said in the hardest way, if he had said it. He never completely formed the idea.

Listening to the peculiar haste of the music, and the puzzle of the syncopation, not the writing of the score but why it had that effect, Ballardi took the last step down to the flags.

He had seen the cable, didn't know that Leverence was behind him and looking at it. He turned to take the cable from the nails and hang it in the laundry-room, and in that instant both were holding it.

Ballardi saw a jigsaw line, or rather a fat, snaky thing of blinding violet-lavender which passed between the two men and shot into the old clubroom. The whole place jumped and threw both men to the floor. The phenomenon afterward left both men with the eerie feeling that lightning had rustled in their hair. In the jolt of shock, and the confusion, neither man ever thought twice again about having seen a pair of powerful hands, not their own, as the phenomenon was easily an example of double-vision.

It was just as though there had been a pair of hands in the basement, and the boy had "actually" seen them in the panes of the grade-entrance door because of the angle of reflection. Then he had asked his father in all innocence, "Whose hands are those in the basement?" The boy was in a half-dream; sometimes during the quarrels the boy had come into the kitchen from outdoors and asked of no one in particular, "Who is it?" not recognizing his own daddy, his eyes blurred with exhaustion from play, but also as though they were all becoming strangers. Both Ralph

and Gracia were sensitive persons, and the question had stopped them cold.

That was a long time ago. Right now, Ballardi was lying on the flagstones unconscious, either from shock or cracking his head on the stone. Likewise, Billie Leverence was in effect lifted from his feet and hurled backward into the laundry room, as with the fast reactions of his type he executed an athletic jump backward, and in going down heavily he struck that broad head of his on the heavy iron underwork of the old gas mangle. Billie had lighted one of the cigars which he always carried in his handkerchief pocket. The cigar rolled away and came to rest with the ash knocked off, so that the coal glowed like a red-hot button in the darkness, all the lights in the house having gone out. Outside came a shout and the pounding of feet.

It could be put in this way: If the boy had looked down the cellar stairs, where he had been told not to go, and seen a reflection in the panes of glass in the door, a reflection which looked like a pair of human hands, a little further description was needed. If they were shaped like the strong hands of a man, with five fingers (or four and a thumb), something would have to be done about the wrist-end, as nothing was visible but the hands—no arms, no person to whom they were connected.

With this supposition, then the hands had emerged from the wall of range-rock in the space under the cellar stairs, once the clubroom in Ballardi's boyhood. In this pocket was the one place where the foundation was rotten, rather, where the mortar had decomposed. In fact, a block of limestone had been taken out and set on the floor, so that there was a hole going into the earth, and making a lazy turn if one showed a light into the opening. If one were mathematically-minded, that curve would continue an endless spiral.

As though the hands had intelligence in themselves, they had explored the whole basement. There was nothing much unusual about them, except for the wrist-end, where there was a joint or musculature, not at all with the unpleasantness of the healing from an amputation, but a normal envelopment of skin, puckered at the rear with an orbicularis. Except for this freakishness, they were just hands. It would have to be observed that the hands were matched, like anyone's right and left hand, and that they worked in concert like male and female, or with telepathic smoothness and efficiency of a couple long associated.

These "visitors" would be able to find endless interest in the realities of the working-plant which Ballardi had in the cellar. Any single object would do, like a pencil, or an empty tin can, when all is discovery, just as a child explores the things of an adult world.

There was a jacket hanging on a chair, and all the sewing on the jacket, and things in the pockets. Take the hinges of the doors, and particularly the screws. The men who worked out the principal of the screw really discovered something. The worn English pocket-knife lying on the desk was a marvel, beautifully made. The key in the old desk was very interesting. So was cloth; so was paint, so was the faucet in the laundry-tub. The most interesting thing was dust on objects in a subterranean chamber, this basement.

When Ballardi and Leverence had been talking upstairs, the hands had been grasping the top of an eight-by-eight post supporting the crossbeams. They had twisted, and the old wrought-iron nails had been drawn a little to give the sound of shuddering, as the maple flooring upstairs was caused to rub. There was so much stuff in the basement, using the furnace alone as an example, that it constituted a wilderness of the patience and labor and ingenuity of man. In this one place there was the product of colossal labor, lifetimes, in cabinetmaking, masonry, tinsmithing, and all skills . . . One might think that the hands had twisted the post to try the roots of the house.

Leverence and Ballardi had nothing to fear, even if they had seen clearly the terrible hands of the "guest." It was the stranger who was frightened, no matter what power might be there. One resting on the other, the hands whisked past the two men, and through, into the old clubroom. There they plunged into the cavity in the range-rock near the floor.

This room was going to be the storage-space for furs, woolens, and so on, as soon as the wall was cemented. The lights and racks were in. There was the debris on the floor.

. . . The hands came back out of the hole in the foundation, picked up the block of limestone, and snugged it back into place. For a moment there was a thudding sound of earth being packed into place, the sound withdrawing.

Next door on the corner, the huge and sweaty Dixon had been working in the yard. He was working with a mattock, half-turned, when the flash of light shot from his friend's basement. The light was so brilliant that he had the impression of seeing the foliage of trees in the next block. The Ballardi house had gone dark, and Dixon shouted, dropping the mattock.

He was working under a floodlight which he had rigged to his kitchen window, but also had one of those long warehouse-flashlights lying on the grass.

He came running across the paved court separating the two yards. The back door was locked. Dixon went around to the side, and without any intention of doing so, took the bolt out of the door when he put his shoulder to it. He went down the steep stairway into the cellar so fast that it took some agility to jump Ballardi at the bottom, and Dixon got up with skinned knees. He found Leverence with the powerful light, snapped the nearest switch, and it was dead. He did a piece of authentic swearing, because he could not find the fusebox, and had to follow the old cables, looking along the 2-by-8's overhead. Ballardi kept a box of fuses next to the meter; the lights went on.

Ballardi was sitting up groggily, propping himself with his arms and sitting stunned on the cold flagstones. Billie was lying there with a cut in his scalp, just some blood in his hair.

"My stars and garters," Ballardi said.

"What happened?" Dixon asked.

"So help me, I don't know what in the hell happened," Ballardi said, dazed. He started to get up, and sat down again. Dixon had seen the cable, and the spattering of bright copper around the ancient porcelain fixture. He went upstairs, found the phone, and called the neighborhood doctor.

With this phone-call to the medico, Ballardi went upstairs, and the boy was still sound asleep in the spacious grandfather's room. Up here, the light was again burning in the hall. He removed the pillow from under the boy's head and put it to one side, and went down-stairs, after rolling the handball around very thoughtfully under his foot. The weather was terribly sticky, and in the back of his mind he heard the radio forecasting, "Continued fair and hot; the temperature is expected to reach one hundred degrees." Murder. This was worse than the time he had gone deep-sea fishing off Chincoteague with Gracia. The temperature had stayed at a hundred and two degrees the whole time, and there was no relief of any kind on the low island. No sleep, an unforgettable waking nightmare, tempers snapped, as though even the weather was his fault. . . .

When they were gone, Ballardi washed the glasses in the kitchen, remembering the early days when he had hit on the tricks of washing the sieve immediately after straining the orange juice, and the same for the plates from which they had eaten eggs. Gone, gone. Gone forever. The happy days, the dance of time. He stood on the back porch thinking of the spiral swing of the stars. He wondered whether he was getting soft, as in the stifling night he framed the idea, "Don't do this to me."

Ballardi shook his head, thinking of men speeding down the narrows of the world's darknesses. Leverence had taken his bottle of wine along with him in the briefcase, and he would probably do some more writing in his journal because of his bandaged head. In his travels, he would say that the shock of the heavy current in the old house had thrown him sixteen feet under a laundry tub. Then he would bring the distance down to his own length, which was more convincing, and was pretty nearly right.

In the morning, Ballardi awakened late. The housekeeper had come, and the boy was outdoors after having had his breakfast. The housekeeper was very effective and casual in getting the boy to eat.

It was about time for the mail delivery when Ballardi got downstairs; he expected to see the housekeeper and say hello to her, but she wasn't anywhere on the ground floor—possibly over at Dixon's because she and Dixon's wife had things in common The boy was in the alley again; he had met his friend, and one could listen to that strange, elastic echo of the handball being struck between the brick walls of the garages. Occasionally there was the sharp, thin cry of "Hindrance!" as when the ball struck the downspout. The rest was the charging of feet, and the rhythmic smack of the ball, the boys being pretty evenly-matched.

The half of a cold-grapefruit was waiting for Ballardi in the refrigerator, a maraschino cherry resting in the center of the fruit. He nodded, and was aware of the stifling day stealing through the open front and rear of the house. His intention was to have strips of toast covered with melted cheese, sliced olives on top, and these sprinkled with paprika. These had been a favorite of Gracia's but first he made a trip to the front door.

The thumbnail of his left hand found the nicks in the frame of the screen door, something as though he were counting the houses on the ridge in the distance, through the trees.

There were a number of things around the house which had been put off, not really forgotten, aside from the business of making the decision on the property on the Chicago road. . . . For example, there was a piece of stripping under a bay which merely needed nailing back into place.

That item was one of the least things which bothered him, delayed because of the jungle of tools in the basement. He couldn't seem to find anything down there, and would have to put it all in order. He could not find the box of drill-points, and the nail-sets were in that box, too.

While he was looking down the block for the postman, a kid of fifteen came sailing around the corner on a popping motorbike, and he cocked the machine at the curb in front. He came up the walk in a straight line, whistling in the morning. At the stoop he ducked his head and took an envelope out of his cap, identified it and handed it through the opened screen with a greeting. It was a night-letter, though it didn't really matter what sort of communication it was, a letter or phone call. The communication was the thing.

It was from Gracia, and he didn't even have to open it. She was fed up with "being gay" and was coming back. Probably she needed money. The boy was turning down the steps, apparently lark-happy, when Ballardi woke up and said, "Wait!" He gave the boy a dollar, received a smile and thanks in return, and the motorbike went popping happily down the street.

Ballardi placed the envelope on the dining room table, where the mail had always been put in this house, and where Gracia had always put it. It was a dead certainty that she was on the way home as soon as it could be arranged.

At the telephone, he tried to think of what number it was that he was going to call, as he played with the idea of her coming home. There was a call which he had intended to make, and the stores were open now. Perhaps the hardware store, as there were items of paint and nails, and having their electrician trace the lines in the house. Also there was a call to locate a mason about calking the bricks of the stoop in front. He never thought of the crumbling mortar in that spot in the old clubroom.

The yellow envelope containing the long night-letter lay on the linen of the tablecloth like a jump of sunlight, or in a soft rectangle that was like smooth foil of gold.

The Wall

ONE EYE BLACKENING, his clothing disheveled and his necktie jerked into a permanent knot, Jasper watched the scene with amazement and incredulity. He had fought his way out of that incredible chaos inch by inch, and at last gained a point of vantage at the top steps of the public library.

This was no mere traffic stoppage. There was something else, an element of terrible surprise and the suggestion that something more was involved than the wreckage of a few fine cars. But 42nd Street was a chaos past belief, wherein men and women fought like animals in a kind of nightmare in broad daylight.

A short, dog-like man came running around the corner of the library and accosted Jasper as though he had found the man responsible for the whole business. He was breathless, and soggy with perspiration.

"Well!" he ejaculated.

"What?" said Jasper.

"They got a jam like this on Sixth, and another one, only a damn sight worse, on Broadway!"

"What are you talking about?" Jasper shrank away from the fellow, appalled and a little angry.

"You don't haff to believe me," said the stranger, "only the subways is all smashed up all across town, and all the L's is spilling off the tracks. What I seen, you wouldn't believe it. Listen! I been tryin' for more than an hour to get uptown, and there's no place you can get past 42nd Street, not even through the buildings. I simply got to see a man! What the hell is this all about, hah?" He seized Jasper's coat and began weeping.

Jasper looked down at the man as though he had not heard a word he said. A truck down there had overturned, and something in it was screaming, above the whole uproar. The pedestrian crowd, entering the spirit of the occasion, swarmed over the jam of cars and fought with each other whole-heartedly. It was not the accident itself, but this ugly aftermath of mob violence that caused so many injuries and deaths.

It was then that Jasper saw the pigeons. There was a heavy beat of wings that came from an uncommonly large flight of these birds that frequented the library courts. They wheeled in a wide, frightened arc over the street, high over the scene of the accident, where they piled up in the air in a flurried mass. They seemed to have struck an invisible wall in mid-air; their fuddled wings thrashed, and numbers of them showered down on the wreckage below with broken wings and necks.

At this same time there was another aerial disaster far worse. A scout plane cruising over the metropolitan area had taken interest in the unaccountable state of affairs below. It dropped as low as it dared, hurtling down in a fatal power dive, and met that invisible dividing line, thenceforth to be known as the "42nd Street Wall." It was actually about thirty feet from the building line toward 43rd Street. The plane exploded with the impact, and before that unlucky land crew of motorists and pedestrians knew what had occurred, the flaming ship was down on them.

Where the 42nd Street Wall crossed the North River the liner *Bergen* was to account for a badly damaged hull by having struck the wall obliquely. A number of small boats were totally wrecked, but no lives were lost on the water. Ashore and inland the damage was more serious. Commerce north and south ceased completely, and minor accidents of the most bewildering nature had an appalling frequency.

As one might expect of them, the columnists took it up as a kind of grim jest. If you read the columns you saw: "Now that the most salient feature of the New Yorker is his broken nose—" This because of those scores of persons who charged unwittingly into the Gotham Wall.

Worse, the Hudson quickly inundated the land once it was dammed by this obstacle. Aside from the incalculable property damage, numbers were marooned in the taller buildings as the waters of Flushing Bay were enormously augmented and the Hudson found a new course to the sea.

However confounding this state of affairs was, two persons knew where the trouble lay and were the entirely innocent cause of it. While picked corps of engineers were attacking thin air—the wall had no measurable thickness—with every tool at the command of science, Harold Jasper and professor Maxim Gorsch stared at each other in an experimental laboratory on Lexington Avenue in a cold sweat of fear.

Jasper arrived at the office in mid-afternoon on the 17th, looking as though he had spent the day at rough and tumble sports. He made no apology for his absence, but for that matter Professor Gorsch did not turn around when he entered the room. Gorsch kept his position in the arena of experimental crucibles, retorts, and what-not, and rocked complacently on his heels. A swivelled power-drill, of the sort using tanganim-metal bits, was mounted on the floor. It was turned on a one-sixteenth-inch sheet of steel that had just received a coat of an iridescent green lacquer. This plate was securely mounted between concrete pillars. The professor was pleased because sixty tons and a needle drill were making no headway whatever on what was little more than a tin can rolled flat.

At last he did turn around. He did not notice Jasper's battered face nor his dishevelment.

"It works. You see? It works," he said, rather smugly.

Jasper glared at him, speechless. All he could think of was the uproar in the streets. Along that wall New York was a madhouse. Upper Manhattan was like some idiotic aquarium, with men and women thrashing about in the muddy waters of the Hudson and random fish leaping between their legs. Mud and muck were suspended in sheets against the transparent wall, like some juggler's hideous trick. And simple Gorsch engrossed in his labors all this while, with no thought or knowledge of anything that might occur outside this laboratory.

"The armor plate there," the professor explained, frowning. "I haff broke three of the smaller drills on it, and still it is only one-sixteenth of an inch in thickness. My boy, no projectile in the world will pierce it. That drill hass been going since ten-thirty, and yet not a mark. My boy, we are both of us millionaires, easily. I will give you half."

He rubbed his hands with satisfaction.

Jasper thought of a number of things, both his job and the chaos in the streets calling his attention at once. The plate was about thirty feet north of the building line. That was coincidence. It was mounted perpendicularly, parallel with 42nd Street. And Gorsch had turned his trick at about the time Jasper had had his eye blackened. More coincidence.

"What have you put on that plate?" he asked suspiciously.

"Why, the lacquer," said Gorsch.

He pointed to a jar full of green stuff on the desk. It was so, then; he had already used the paint. This material was Gorsh's new development, prepared, of course, with a few of Jasper's own ideas. This particular paint was the by-product of high-power discharges which they had filtered through a "perfect occurrence" mixture of the inert gases— these gases proportioned as they occur in the atmosphere.

Both men were retained by the Greater American Products Corporation as "engineering counsels in new construction methods." They had perfected the company's synthetic wood and stone and various paints of remarkable permanence, not to speak of a superior brand of flexible glass. The power discharges through the inert gases, under a pressure of from thirteen to fifteen atmospheres, produced a brilliant green powder, for which Jasper had found a solvent. In solution the stuff made magnificent paint. In Jasper's absence the professor took unto himself, as usual, the prerogative of doing a little fiddling on his own. He had already named the product "Beetle Lacquer" and was thinking about retirement.

"When did you put it on?" barked Jasper.

The professor was startled. He looked at Jasper with considerable resentment. "Ten o'clock sharp," he said. "I painted the plate at ten this morning. What is the matter with you? Did you have an accident?"

"An accident!" Jasper ejaculated. "Have you been outside at all today, you old fool?"

"When I begin a test," said Gorsch, bristling, "I bring my lunch. I do not leave anything half-done."

Jasper strode past him, ignoring the insinuation, and hastily went over Gorsch's apparatus. The drill was turning at high speed, but making no impression whatever on the steel plate. Jasper started around it and ran into the invisible wall. He swore. There it was, coinciding exactly with the plane of green lacquer on the plate. He flattened his hands against it and followed it to the lacquer itself; he was ready to assume then that the great Gotham Wall was of the identical thickness of the coat of paint, and no more.

Gorsch watched him, dumbfounded, as he cranked the drill off to one side and turned the point into this impassable barrier. The motor snarled, and the oily tanganim point began to smoke with heat. There was no drilling through that substanceless plane.

He rightly suspected that some similar phenomenon must be connected with the original jar of lacquer itself. Turning to the desk, he tried to pass his hand over this jar and met solid resistance. He was totally flabbergasted. Once before this they had concocted a paint that would turn a drill, but this was something quite else. This paint, some disastrous allotropic form of the inert gases, so changed in hardening, a freak accountable to the vast, unlucky store of power in the laboratory, that the air around it was rendered solid and immovable.

Gorsch, of course, had smeared the edge of the jar somewhat when he painted the plate. Wet, the enamel was unremarkable save for its intense color, for Jasper had handled it carelessly enough the night before. But as a dry coat it became a singularly impenetrable substance which exhibited the further property of extending a plane of resistance outside itself, in a ratio yet to be discovered. Thus, by encircling the invisible column above the jar with his hands, Jasper found that its diameter was that of the jar, measuring from the rim of dried lacquer around the cover. How high this column extended he could only guess.

Jasper rapped the air above the jar smartly with his knuckles and caused a clear, faint, bell-like ringing. This column of air, subtly changed by the influence of lacquer, had the rigidity of metal. Outside, there were so many collisions with the wall itself, of all natures, that it sounded over Manhattan and over the sea like an everlasting gong.

Jasper turned on Gorsch and said, "Beautiful! Millionaires, eh? Gorsch, though it's no fault of yours, you'll have us on the penal island as public menaces for this. Do you know what you've done?"

Gorsch listened to Jasper's account with glassy eyes, fluttering to the windows with bird-like fright and chirping with dismay. The wall, Jasper figured, was only of the thickness of the coat of lacquer, and certainly not thicker than the steel plate. It ran across town, through all structures crossing a point about thirty feet north of the building line on 42nd Street. What its length was he did not yet know.

There was something that must be found out, and that quickly. The plane, the Gotham Wall itself, could not be moved in the slightest. Though it had the transparency of air, it had a greater inertia than any mass of stone or metal. It had stopped a plane and motor trucks driven into it at high speed. But, possibly, the plate could be taken off its supports and destroyed.

Gorsch watched him free the armor plate from the binding posts. He took a deep breath, then, with a suction cup from the toilet, he pulled the plate outward, the faintest shadow of a degree off the perpendicular. The concrete floor cracked briskly across the room. A bit of plaster fell. Jasper shuddered and screwed the plate back into position.

"Professor Gorsch," said he, his voice quavering, "you put that thing up—now you can take it down again!"

Gorsch was alarmed. He chewed at his white moustache in perplexity.

"We could bring the plate to the horizontal," he suggested timidly.

"I just tried that," said Jasper. "If you move that plate you'll shovel up half the buildings in New York and throw them into the Atlantic Ocean. For all I know," he shuddered again as he thought of this, "you'll scoop a hole in the bottom of the ocean itself. And then where will Manhattan be?"

It was the absolute inertia of the lacquer which they could not cope with. The invisible wall which extended outside the film of paint was impassable, an immoveable object. But the fact of such a wall's existence was not so disastrous, after all, as the fact that the object which had been painted *could be moved*, and moved easily. For, in motion, its extended and transparent plane moved with it; and in moving was irresistible.

On the third day of the tie-up New York was declared under martial law. These extreme measures were found necessary when the mob of rioting, bewildered citizens had caused incalculable property damage and when organized crime began to avail itself of the opportunities offered by this unprecedented confusion.

All cross streets were re-routed for policing; Governor Harris stationed a sixty-mile double-cordon of militia to the limits of the wall on the mainland. North of the wall there was a brisk trade in small boats. These carried the police and the overflow of citizens from the elevateds. The subways, of course, were flooded, with Manhattan somewhat more than a fathom under muck and water.

At the end of the second week, on the thirtieth, the city itself split in two governments. The old political machine enjoyed a brief renaissance under an emergency board on its own side of the wall, with its own mayor, and having its own special officials by appointment. Mayor Russel, casting aside the minor financial troubles of the moment, set up a "Commission for Inquiring into the Nature of the 42nd Street Wall." Mayor Byam, having preempted a fine suite in one of the marooned uptown hotels, followed suit, creating a great deal of unnecessary confusion. There seemed to be small logic in any extensive underwater inquiries when the south of the wall was not so obstructed, but a step of some kind had to be taken since the fire departments and Red Cross had already relieved most of the victims from their distress with scaling ladders.

The Russel Commission gave Jasper and Gorsch one sleepless night after another. While Gorsch stood guard, Jasper bathed the plate with every acid in the laboratory and treated the lacquer with every chemical that might have an effect on it. The solvent he had discovered for the powder would not dissolve the lacquer once it had dried. Heat altered it not at all, and there was no safe method of applying more pressure than had been used in the drill. Jasper could have knocked down the two supporting concrete pillars with comparative ease, but that was just what he was afraid of doing. If the plate moved at all, the building would have been split from top to bottom.

Like a leash of ferrets, the Russel Commission's engineers went over the wall from beginning to end. When anyone came in sight in the halls, Gorsch would make a sign to Jasper, who would slide a bureau that was innocent enough against the plate. This bureau, with two cots, made the laboratory into very satisfactory living quarters. Many had done the same, making their offices their homes when they could not conveniently get back uptown.

There was nothing extraordinary about the room, but Russel's men were a suspicious lot and looked upon every man along the wall as a potential criminal. They held powers of arrest, and would brook no interference even of the most casual nature. They were uncomfortably inquisitive.

"Where did that come from?" asked one of them narrowly, pointing at the drill.

"Why, it belongs here," said Jasper. "We're engineering counsels for the American Products Corporation."

"Counsels hell!" snapped the inquisitor. "What's it for?"

"We're trying to get through the wall ourselves," said Gorsch meekly. "I haven't seen my wife for three weeks."

"You leave that to us," said the engineer menacingly. "If there's a way of getting through, *we'll* do it!"

He passed on an order or two, and that morning the power drill was dismantled and confiscated by authority of Mayor Russel. This same engineer—he was Francis Herder, soon to become a great name in engineering—came dangerously near the jar of lacquer. Jasper's heart

Time Burial

was in his throat. If that jar had been moved, the building would have been down about their ears, knocked to pieces by the pillar of rigid air that extended above and below it. The plate would have gone down with the building, and the city of New York down with the plate, into the sea.

Both sat down weakly on the cots when the Commission had gone.

"Did you hear what they said?" asked Jasper.

"About Lexington Avenue?"

"Yes. They've measured the wall from end to end. Even the meteorologists are in on it. They've measured rainfall, and say that the wall is a hundred and twenty miles long and approximately sixty miles high. Lexington runs through the middle of it. If they're right about its going sixty miles deep into the earth, that damned plate has made a wall that's a perfect square. Gorsch, this is the end of everything. They say they'll find the reason for all this somewhere near Lexington Avenue."

"We have got to run away," said the professor.

"We have got to do nothing of the sort," Jasper retorted. "Don't you feel any responsibility for all this? If that bungling Commission starts poking around in this room, all they'll have to do is upset that damned jar of lacquer. It would be wholesale murder. Tell me how you'd feel, Maxim Gorsch, with thousands of deaths on your soul! If you've got one," he added bitterly.

"But you are unjust—I can do nothing!" the professor wailed. "I am going to the Commission and tell them what I have done. I am sorry for it!"

"You're not going to tell anyone anything!" shouted Jasper. "There'd be an investigation that would smell to high heaven. And how about the formula of that lacquer? Would you keep your mouth closed, eh? Let any unscrupulous agent get hold of it, and you know what would happen as well as I do. Absolute inertia. It's a perfect weapon for offensive or defensive war. Think, Gorsch! Think of what a long range club you could make out of—out of a pencil! Why, with a plate at your back, the size of a penny you could plow up a navy! With a pencil! I don't suppose you'd care about that, though, would you? Oh, no, Maxim Gorsch, you won't tell. We have got to destroy that stuff somehow, and no one but ourselves is every going to know what happened.

It was easily said, but time was getting terribly short. Something had to be done in a hurry, because The Russel Commission was definitely concentrating at Lexington Avenue. Buildings there were infested with them. The Lexington area became their headquarters, and you could not come or go without running into someone who was an engineer and a secret agent in one. There was a war scare that year, and there was reason enough in eyeing even the most innocent citizen twice when this thing might easily be an alien government's first surprise move.

The Commission evacuated subways and made tests below ground. They agreed that the wall extended deep into the earth and were satisfied that the distance was roughly sixty miles.

The wall would not pass anything solid. It would filter water very slowly, however, and air circulated through it to some slight extent. Electric cables that were laid north and south functioned as well as ever, but all radio broadcasting was cut with a terrific field of static. It was only the fact that all parts of the wall caused equal disturbances that had prevented the radio finders from locating the dead center of the wall.

One engineer wanted to run diagonals from corner to corner and thus find that dead center. Other engineers wanted to know what diagonals running from what corners to what corners. Jasper told professor Gorsch it was a damned lucky thing he hadn't used a two-yard plate instead of a two-foot one, or he might, if the area of the wall did answer to the area of the plate, have cut the whole country in two and very likely sunk the continent before he enjoyed the honors of discovery.

The jar of lacquer was rapidly assuming importance of the grandest kind. There was dust on the desk that neither counsel—Gorsch and Jasper were bitterly sorry they had ever heard that title—dared to disturb. The slightest tremors of the building, the merest vibration at all, filled them with anguish. Finally Gorsch opened a container of one of their own incomparable glass binders and tenderly applied it to the base of the jar. Sweat pumped out of his old frame in a steady flow. He catfooted nervously back and forth, perfectly aware of the possibility of unequal hardening, until the binder was thoroughly set. Then, and not until he tried a needle on it, he breathed a gasp of relief, and Jasper and he set about fixing the legs of the desk to the floor.

As they were so occupied, the building superintendent, a fat, harassed, but soft-footed individual of fifty-five, puffed into the room. The two counsels were completely surprised and rose shakily to their feet. The superintendent announced pathetically that the Commission was evacuating, one by one, all occupied offices on the line. No notice was to be served other than verbal. When the Commission arrived, an office was expected to be unoccupied. Apologizing tearfully, the superintendent puffed out again.

"Well," said Jasper, somewhat relieved, "at least they can't get this outfit loose without using an axe." He meant the desk and jar. Once set, the glass binder made them part of the concrete floor.

But Professor Gorsch sank back to his cot and groaned. He was a proud man, and could see nothing for himself in this affair any longer but ruin. Jasper stamped back and forth, his brow wonderfully wrinkled, and abruptly vanished through the door. He was going down to see the Commission.

Herder was in charge.

Jasper walked up to him and said: "I understand you're clearing us out."

Herder didn't answer. He simply nodded his head at Jasper and kept on nodding, as though he never tired of agreeing with someone. Underneath he was still a politician, the one-time proprietor of a cigar store in Brooklyn.

"We *can't* move. All our crucibles came through the elevator window in the north end."

"Leave them behind," said Herder, softly. There was something vicious in his manner.

"We're in the G suite on 14," said Jasper. "What's the deadline?"

"We may be up there tomorrow," said Herder, "and maybe not for six weeks. Take your pick. But don't let us find you there when we call."

Jasper hurried out, feeling outraged, as though he had been caught in the act of counterfeiting ten dollar bills. When he arrived at the test room he was panting like a dog.

"The game's up," he said. "If you can think of something, let's have it. Gorsch, I never had to come into this thing with you, and now we're both in to the neck. I'm not sorry. I've seen that louse Herder and he's got a bad eye. Think of something, Gorsch."

"I was thinking," said Gorsch, "that maybe lacquer would dissolve lacquer."

Jasper swivelled around in his chair and stared at the jar of green paint anchored to the desk.

"Maybe it would," he said, but how are you going to get at it? You can't get to the cover any more, because the column starts with the dried lacquer on the rim and the cover is inside it. There's no time to make any more of the stuff, either, because our apparatus is on the other side of the wall."

"There is acid," suggested Gorsch, "to eat the glass away."

Jasper shook his head. It was too dangerous. Paint would spill out of the jar, some of it was bound to, and they would be in a worse predicament than before. It would mean immediate discovery; at this moment someone might have run into that fourth-dimensional column that extended upward from the jar of lacquer, and downward from it also, through the floors below, through the very headquarters of the Russel Commission.

Jasper rose and examined the jar again, effectually sealed against the most determined safe-cracking by an invisible barrier. His knife slipped off this column like a pencil on glass. If only he had the time to inquire into the nature of the phenomenon, and how the paint in drying effected this absolute inertia in the air extended from it! It would have been valuable to know whether the same freak took place in a vacuum; whether this column in particular stood only as high as the Gotham Wall, or, indeed, mounted above the earth's atmosphere into open space.

The column was not a perfect cylinder, its contours following the conformation of the dried lacquer on the rim of the jar. At one point, where areas of paint touched but did not overlap, the knife blade caught in, but did not enter, a crack.

With a glass trained on that crack, Jasper called the professor and told him he thought they could get in, or at least find out whether it would do them any good to get in. Gorsch hunted up a tray of platinum filaments in graduated sizes and tendered them to Jasper as though he were handing over his soul. Jasper took them and fished with one wire after another.

Gorsch hung on his shoulder and said: "Does it go? Does it go?"

"Get away, I can't see!" exclaimed Jasper irritably.

He set himself to the brain-racking task of twisting an almost invisible corkscrew of platinum through a quite invisible crack in the air, down through the brush hole in the lid of the jar, and into the lacquer. He managed it. A few glistening green beads of paint came up on the wire and scraped off in the crack. Jasper fished again, and once more the beads scraped off. One small drop collected. The two "counsels" stood there, fidgeting and waiting.

Jasper tried his knife in the crack. It had widened; the new paint had softened the dried film on the jar.

"It works, Gorsch!" said Jasper in a hoarse whisper.

He tried a pencil. The pencil passed through the crack, and shortly he was able to reach the brush Gorsch had left in the jar. In a few moments he had applied lacquer to the circumference of the rim.

Meanwhile Gorsch had started a crucible, and by the time it had reached white heat Jasper had penetrated the whole column above the jar and wiped off the excess lacquer with waste. He threw waste, pencil, wire, and cover into the crucible, instantly. All were consumed, with a sharp, clear report like the explosion of a shell. The glass cover melted at once, and danced and blistered in the trough of the open crucible.

Jasper worked desperately, polishing the jar with waste soaked in the chemical solvent of the lacquer powder. He kept throwing these pieces of waste into the crucible while the reports diminished and finally ceased. Then he poured a quantity of the solvent into the jar to insure Gorsch's "Beetle Lacquer" against any quick drying, slid a glass cover over it, and rested, mopping his brow.

A trio from the Russel Commission's gang downstairs burst through the doorway and shouted as one man: "What was that!"

"What was what?"

The whole thing seemed very silly, now that success was on the way; Jasper eyed these intruders with irritation and contempt.

"Those explosions. What's going on here?" It was the cursed voice of authority speaking again.

"Nothing!" snapped Jasper enigmatically. "Get along, you! We're moving out of her."

That was his sole explanation, but he stood against Russel's men so belligerently that they shuffled their feet like a group of small boys. They hesitated, then moved on together, as though no one of them had a mind of his own. Gorsch returned to the crucible at once, extracting every last calory out of his machine. The glass cover had blistered out of sight. There was no time to find out whether the air above the crucible had been affected or not, but they rightly assumed that the lacquer had been broken down into its essential gases.

Gorsch worked as though he had only one purpose in life. He had rigged up a "booster" line for additional current and nursed this power supply until he came within a hair of reaching the fusing point of the crucible. There was smoke in the air. When he looked at Jasper there was impatience, but still something boyish and eager in his manner, as though he realized he had done something well.

"Ready?" asked Jasper.

"Ready!" Gorsch croaked.

Jasper painstakingly inserted a ball of waste into the jar, removed it and managed not to spill a drop. He applied this evenly to the armor plate, covering every pin point of lacquer, and tossed the waste into the crucible. There was an eruption of green flame; the vertical explosion which followed dropped a perfectly cylindrical piece of the ceiling, a disc of beryl-steel and concrete, into the crucible, where it quickly melted and puddled like a mass of hot quicksilver. Jasper and Gorsch stood on their toes and cracked their jaws, momentarily deafened.

The whole Commission would be in on them in no time at all. Jasper kept his knife blade against the plate until he could scrape through to bare metal. He waited a second or two before he hazarded everything, then clipped the screws holding the plate and tossed it, plate, knife, clippers, and screw heads, into the crucible. Another column of green flame struck up from it. Gorsch and Jasper plugged their ears and watched fragments of concrete shower down from the floors above. Another stone splashed out of the furnace and peppered them with miniature showers of sand as particles exploded in the air. There were pin-pricks of blood on Gorsch's head.

"The jar!" Jasper shouted.

Gorsch pointed to a bottle on the shelf. Jasper and Gorsch never prepared a perfect binder without a perfect solvent for it. Jasper unstoppered the bottle and poured its contents liberally around the jar of lacquer. Gorsch left the crucible and stationed himself in the doorway. The empty halls were still reverberating with a long chain of echoes, but he thought he could hear an uproar of voices below.

"There they come, Jasper!" he shouted.

Jasper pulled at the jar.

It gave.

"Ready!" he screamed, with all the power in his lungs.

Gorsch nodded and covered his face with his long, bony fingers. Jasper tossed the jar gently and carefully into the exact middle of the furnace and sprinted for the doorway. He was a fairly powerful man, and picked up Gorsch as though he were a scarecrow. He guessed right, and leaped into the air with Gorsch in his arms as the lacquer went off.

The crucible plunged down into earth like an act of God, missing, as luck would have it, every last engineer in the Russel Commission below. Jasper and Gorsch had stopped their ears and felt rather than heard that cataclysm of sound as they sprawled along the corridor. It was a fortunate thing, for a long section of the wall of the building caved in following the tremendous suction, and eardrums burst with it.

The report was heard, or so it was claimed, in Ireland and in the Isles. But what reached widespread fame was the pole of solid green fire that flagstaffed far out into space. It was an unforgettable sight, like a connecting bar between earth and the shell of stars.

The Hudson, undammed, returned to its channel at once and tossed stranded boats into wreckage. The uptown subways emptied, and for hours the whole underground system ran like a network of sewers. Uptown New York lay stinking under the sun, blanketed with muck the diverted Hudson had left behind.

There were earth temblors that year, running east and west. Out to sea the bed of the ocean boiled and a certain area in the Atlantic was unpleasantly warm.

As one consequence of the affair, a source of ever-lasting joy to Jasper and Gorsch, Francis Herder, the Russel Commission's chief engineer, came in for considerable attention. He had been working below with a machine using centrifugal explosives of a perfectly ordinary patent and had fired at about the time Jasper threw the jar of green lacquer into Gorsch's crucible.

Jasper and Gorsch, totally helpless in the matter, had managed to advance the man, as engineer in charge at the time the Gotham Wall was broken down, into being the most sought-after engineer anywhere in the world. Neither counsel cared very much about that. They were free.

Here Lies

C HAUNCEY KNOCKED THE dottle out of his corncob and briefly startled Old Shep by inquiring unemotionally, "Will you never finish that blasted stick?"

Which in Old Chauncey was tantamount to fury. Words being precious things, both old boys hoarded every syllable; Shep tightened his leathery lips and with the scalpel point of the knife flicked away a mote of pine. Each link of the chain he was whittling from that interminable stick of soft pine resembled ivory in its smooth, faultless finish. He might produce one link in a day or let it require a full week. No hurry. The current chain numbered four hundred and seventy-two links.

Under Shep's surreptitious scrutiny, Old Chauncey stood erect purposefully and stalked to the woodpile. There a fat log stood on end. With one swift, seemingly effortless stroke of the ax he cleft the log in two, spat explosively and hiked into the house wagging his jaw.

The log-built house, a jewel of conscientious carpentry, stood on the wooded elevation called St. Paul's hill, near town. On the side hill, one hundred and twenty feet below, stood another log-built affair, formerly the icehouse. Since Old Shep had become Chauncey's permanent guest, this structure had been equipped with furnishings as complete and comfortable as the house, including plumbing. So there was no reason for Shep to hang around Old Chauncey's kitchen.

The housekeeper, Celia Lilleoden, performed the chores incidental to both houses with easy efficiency that Old Chauncey was repeatedly reminded of his bachelorhood. From continually sunning themselves behind the kitchen like two old snakes the men had acquired a wrinkled black-walnut finish, but Celia still retained the firm, buxom ripeness of an apple.

As a practical communist Old Chauncey kept his latch-key out by inclination. His generosity was limitless.

Thus, Old Shep did not have to ask for anything he wanted. It was share and share alike.

For example, he charged tobacco to Old Chauncey's account at the store in town. He always had. If he preferred a grade of tobacco superior to what Old Chauncey himself used, such was his privilege. A plug is a plug.

Shep and Chauncey once had occupied the same double desk of raw cherrywood in the schoolhouse which was now a weedy hill of rubble and rotten wood a half mile away.

Besides words, Old Shep hoarded tobacco plugs in case the cause of communism ever collapsed.

In accordance with this scheme of living, Old Chauncey gradually became accustomed to being spared the nuisance of opening the occasional letter he received from another old soldier in Sackett's Harbor, New York. At first, Shep had gone to the trouble of sneaking the mail down to the icehouse and steaming it open. But currently the mail arrived slit open without any subterfuge. The knife, incidentally, was the better of Old Chauncey's two. Shep had borrowed it, knowing that in communism there can be no Indian giving.

On one occasion Chauncey accosted Old Shep behind the kitchen with a crumpled letter in his fingers.

"Shep," he suggested casually, "I wish you'd slit my letters open at the top instead of an end. It wouldn't bunch the writing up so much when you shove it back inside."

"Chauncey," Old Shep replied tremblingly, "You're not serious with me, are you? If you want to keep secrets from me, why, you just tell me seriously not to open those letters any more and I won't."

It used to give Chauncey a funny feeling when Old Shep talked like that.

On a somnolent summer morning while Chauncey was scrubbing his long yellow teeth, he glimpsed blurred movement through the starched white bathroom curtain. Tweaking the curtain somewhat aside he witnessed Old Shep scampering down the side hill to the icehouse with a load of kindling in his arms.

"I'll be dog-goned," swore Old Chauncey with toothpaste foam dribbling down his chin. "He complains he can't do his chopping on account of his rheumatism, and look at the old turkey go! I see where I chop kindling for both of us from now on."

When Old Shep showed up to get in a few licks of whittling before breakfast, Chauncey inquired, "How's that rheumatism?"

"Fierce, Chauncey. I'm getting mighty creaky."

"Well, help yourself to my kindling, Shep. Long as I *know* where it's disappearing to, I don't give a durn."

"Thanks Chauncey; thanks! I knew you'd feel that way."

The bacon, eggs, and delicately crusty fried potatoes hit the plate so ambrosially that, after breakfast, Chauncey was seduced into the disastrous error of mentioning to Shep the chances of marrying Miss Lilleoden. For it was only human nature to covet the goods which another man prized most.

Thenceforward Old Shep neglected his whittling or idled awkwardly with it in the kitchen, were a housekeeper spends most of her time. Chauncey observed blackly that Old Shep had a cunning way with him, too.

"Durn it," Chauncey ruminated dismally, "everything I want, he gets. If I tell him to stay away from her he won't take me seriously. The old hoodoo always has his way. Anyhow, his durned whittling is out of sight."

Befell a morning when Old Shep didn't appear, and Chauncey found him stretched out stiff half way down the side hill. In Shep's vulturine right fist was clenched a small crumple of bills. This pilfering had occurred with such regularity that the friend of Chauncey's childhood had accumulated just about enough to get started with Celia Lilleoden.

Chauncey asked the coroner, a glistening, round little man like a wet dumpling, "Is he dead?"

"Of course he's dead," said the coroner. "Obviously."

"He has no kin," Celia reminded Old Chauncey in her slow, soft contralto.

"I'll do him one more favor," Chauncey offered unblinkingly. "He can have my lot in the cemetery."

The lot in Dream Hill Cemetery measured eight feet long, five feet wide and ten feet deep, meaning that it had been excavated and ready for occupancy these past five years. The walls were common brick. On the floor was placed a stone bed to lie on. Old Chauncey had also installed a small table with a tobacco bag and pipe, matches, an alarm clock with an illuminated dial and an ashtray. And a thick, plumber's candle. The old pagan.

Anchored in the foot wall of this cell, ladder-like, were iron rungs which had enabled Old Chauncey on past occasions to descend and inspect his subterranean property. So, on this occasion, he made the trip to deposit Shep's unfinished wooden chain.

The stone slab sealing the cell had long been cut with the dangerous advertisement: HERE LIES CHAUNCEY D'AUTREVILLE WHOSE WORLDLY GOODS WERE ANY MAN'S FOR THE ASKING.

Naturally, a new inscription had to be chiselled. "But there ain't any room on that stone for any more cuttin' Chauncey," the stone-cutter objected. "You want 'nother slab."

"Turn it upside down and cut it in the bottom," Old Chauncey directed. "With that topside staring him in the face, he'll have something to read in the hereafter."

The underside, becoming the face, carried the inscription: HERE LIES SHEPARD FRANKENFIELD WHO FEELS NO ANXIETY FOR THE FUTURE NOR REGRET FOR THE PAST.

On the day before Old Shep's interment, Old Chauncey paid a visit to the nearest Justice of the Peace with Celia Lilleoden, and no one thought of the act as in the least peculiar. As Chauncey balanced accounts with himself, the state would otherwise inherit his property, as was right, but he wanted to insure Celia's staying on as his housekeeper, in which capacity she beggared superlatives.

While six huskies furnished by the undertaker replaced the granite sheet over the brick chamber, Old Chauncey recollected the particulars of a certain fit of Shep's, dating about five years ago, shortly before Celia. That catalepsy, or whatever, had gripped Shep as though in death for nearly three days, until Old Chauncey had thought of making a brassy rumpus next to his ear with the big dinner bell. The alarm clock in the subterranean mausoleum was set for eleven o'clock, terminating a like period of time, when Old Shep might be expected to wake up and yawn in the hereafter. Just a whim of Chauncey's, since the coroner had pronounced Old Shep indisputably defunct.

Late that night Celia surmised worriedly that Chauncey might be visiting the tomb of his lifelong crony and there he was, in the sickly forest of tombstones hunkering down on Shep's horizontal tombstone like a boy watching a game of marbles.

But he was listening, not watching. He knocked again on the slab with his bony knuckles, cocked his head. Listening for the response while the lazy breeze lifted his silken gray hair in the starry cave of night he asked, "Cele, do you hear him rapping down there?"

Celia's gentle mind recoiled from the idea that the dead might rise in answer to a human summons. The stoically restrained grief for his departed friend must have touched her husband somewhat in the head.

On the fifth night Chauncey observed, "That Old Shep's ghost must be getting tired out."

Celia decided that there was a limit to indulgence. "Chauncey," she said firmly, "you mustn't come down here any more. You'll be taking pneumonia."

He agreed without protest.

"Maybe *that*," he commented to the frankly puzzled Mrs. Old Chauncey, "will teach the old grasshopper when to take a man seriously."

Exit Willy Carney

DIM GREEN LIGHT reached the lounge from a single muffled lamp. It suggested opulence—a rich pile in the rugs, brocade in the hangings and on the walls. It revealed the deliberate gleaming curves and planes of luxurious furniture.

It showed Ben "Denver" Caldwell kissing a girl on the lounge. He kissed her slowly, artistically, supporting the back of her head in the broad palm of his hand. He had large hands, tender in spite of their strength—hands that met her body so understandingly they seemed to become part of her flesh. Madge shuddered with a slow surge of ecstasy as vagrant fingers slipped along her sides, downward. Exploring hands, fingers that found out all the delicious, soft ravines formed by the meeting of their bodies. Her hips lifted gradually, trembling. Ben took her firm, lovely buttocks so that she was seated in his hands in the sweetest embrace of all.

Their lips joined lastingly in a kiss richer than honey as Madge gave him her tongue, a tender, liquid tongue that seemed scented, determined on an alliance of its own. They swept headlong into ultimate union, and wave after wave of intoxicating shadows rolled over them as they locked in a rhythmic turmoil of rapture.

A small, dry sound at the window. *Pit.* Then deep, intoxicating silence. Without warning, Caldwell's teeth closed convulsively on the girl's tongue, drew blood. Her lithe body arched up, contorted with pain that flashed all through her, exploding in her head and chest like agony so that even the nipples of her breasts tingled. Caldwell's mouth made a wet path down her cheek. His forehead met the lounge, and his massive, shaven chin drove hard into the tender muscle of her shoulder.

Madge gasped, stirred uneasily.

"Ben." Her voice was sweet and husky. He didn't answer. Madge felt as though she were being smothered in shadows, and by the reality of his moist, limp weight.

"Ben!"

She wriggled free, all at once sickened with terror. A dark stain on the lounge, wet. A neat blue hole in his temple. Leading away from it was a narrow dark line as straight as though it had been ruled. Blood.

She sprang up. Down in the street someone whistled. The tune was "The House Is Haunted." At the window Madge caught the incisive smell of used powder.

The young man whistling the tune was now about thirty feet from the bottom of the fire escape, walking leisurely. In his shoulder holster was a gun with one exploded shell. Willy Carney was a good shot.

The girl returned to the circle of green light, beautiful, frightened into a moment of immobility. She was good to look at, standing with her knees slightly bent, listening. Her hair was a tumble of glinting bronze, shoulder length, soft. Ears small, exquisite. Good, smooth throat, shoulders right—high, firm breasts tipped with small coral. Narrow, capable hips. Her armpits were bare, but a shadow of gold-bronze showed at the delta. Good long legs. She brushed a hand through her hair and it came away with blood on it. A thin smear of blood on her cheek. She inhaled sharply. Quick work in the bathroom and she was back, the blood gone, her appearance again calm.

It doesn't take a woman long to dress when she's scared.

Madge knew of no one having a motive for killing her lover. In New York she had found that such things just happen. No solution would appear until the murderer got himself in another jam, had a lot of facts pried out of him when they twisted the ears off the sides of his head. Ears. Twist them until they come off in the hand. They come off.

Madge Powell had come to New York looking for work as a model. When she walked through Grand Central Station she carried just a small bag and a purse with less than three dollars in it, a letter scribbled with a name, address, and telephone number. Letter of introduction from a Chicago agent.

She called the number in a Terminal booth, the private phone of Caldwell.

"I have a letter of introduction to you from Jimmy Hoyt."

"Read it," said Caldwell.

Madge tore the note open.

"Dear Ben; This gal is good, a damnsight too good for Chicago. Her name is Madge Powell, and I told her you'd give her a break. Yours ever, Jimmy."

"Come up to the office," said Caldwell. "I'm not in that game any more, but I can probably help you. Come on up."

Denver made a number of phone calls in the office then and there, numbers she couldn't have gotten in ten years any other way. Will Gowan plastered her face through the back pages of a few national magazines, and then Lewis Webb got hold of her. He had a rip-snorting studio on Park Avenue, full of deep seats and carpets like mattresses. He wanted her for a Diana. A rich broker had ordered the painting for his private gallery.

He had black eyes. He came over and sat on the stand where she was resting and dropped his hand on her thigh. She wore a Chinese wrap between poses which she now pulled together at the throat.

"I'm giving you ten, baby," said Webb. "It's twenty from now on, h'm?" He slid the wrap up her leg, and she let him do it because of Caldwell. Then he tried to embrace her, but Madge slapped his face a good one.

"I'm getting out of this rat trap!" She was pretty mad. Webb grabbed her and the wrap fell. He breathed hard and fought with her a little; he was the kind of man who loses strength fighting with a woman and he was rotten with drink, but he managed to cop her square on the mouth. Madge braced her hips against his, trying to get away. He had an arm around her waist, the other around her shoulders. He tried to force his tongue between her teeth. Madge gave him the knee, bit through his lower lip so that he couldn't get away if he wanted to.

"Wait till Caldwell hears about this," she said, stepping back.

The blood dribbled down Webb's chin.

"For God's sake, how would I know you were Caldwell's girl?" He apologized all over the place—offered her money, anything she wanted. She finally promised not to tell.

Max Nagian had been the next one, and a little worse. Like most modern artists, he couldn't forget for any length of time that models, if good, are naked human beings. Nagian took full advantage of his sculptor's rights. He had the damnedest way of using his hands without seeming to mean anything by it.

"Won't you move a little this way, please." He would say something like that, cup her breast in one hand and rest the other on her thigh till the new pose was assumed. He'd stand looking at the delicate blue veinings in her breasts, in the hip hollows. Bring her hips forward by taking firm hold of her bottom. Madge was never sure about him because his hands were very steady and impersonal. It was the glint in his eyes. She passed all these preliminaries; near the end Nagian persuaded her to raise one knee slightly by encompassing the base of her thigh with both hands.

Madge went to Caldwell. She told him that not all artists could afford to pay her price. If they met it they got the idea that something went with it besides posing.

"You want to ride along with me?" asked Caldwell, a little surprised.

"Why not? You look good to me."

He gave her an amused up and down appraisal.

"Why not, indeed?" He liked her frank way and the clothes Madge wore fitted like skin. Ben liked the way her nipples stood up through the snug cloth; he found the smooth, frankly inviting knees of her crossed legs irresistible.

"Eight sharp Friday, my apartment." He accepted her.

Madge kissed him full, long, and cool on the mouth. She slipped her hand under his shirt, laughed to feel his heart thumping. She got by the asking what other women had fought for. From Caldwell.

Caldwell hailed from Colorado originally, had tried just about everything in New York. Politics first. He had bootlegged, directed a symphony orchestra, an advertising agency; he wound up in the slot machine racket. He was manager of the Barnard Machine works when Madge met him, and was having a lot of trouble with a rival company in Brooklyn. The take of these slot machines was so vast that the business necessarily ran to occasional open gunning, but the murder of Caldwell himself was the rival outfit's first open bid for Barnard's supremacy. Heinie Gross, an ambitious Brooklyn mobster, was chief of the Brooklyn gang.

"I got a job for you, Willy," said Gross. "Business is slack, ain't it? You tell Denver I got ambitions, and I give you ten G's."

"Nuts," said Willy Carney. "Wherever he goes, his lads go along with. I'd never collect even if it was a million."

"For twenty G's, you should be able to use your head," Heinie cajoled him. "It's more as you ever got before in your life. He ain't got only two lads usually, and there's one time he ain't got any. Twenty G's."

"Whaddya mean, no lads?"

"How about his dame, Willy? Tell me that. Baby! When the hot-shops close up for the night he wants to go home to his trundle bed. He don't want nobody around when he is with that doll, does he? Smart, ain't it? Next time he signs his lads off I give you a buzz. Ten G's. Easy money."

"You said twenty."

"Sure, twenty G's. That's what I said."

No one saw Carney shoot Denver. Everything was clear, as though Caldwell expected a common truce in gangfare to be observed whenever Madge came. Willy enjoyed the sardonic thought that any minute now Madge Powell was going to get the surprise of her life. Things were going pretty well in there. Denver's technique was expert; it was the real McCoy. Willy watched the two entangled figures with vicarious pleasure while they reached consummate union. Madge's knees rose. Willy squinted at Denver's gray temple.

Pit.

Down the iron escape like a sailor. Bottom. Caldwell was dead weight by this time, and Madge would be wondering what he meant by passing out on her. For good. Willy pricked up his ears, expecting a scream. He whistled.

Enter detectives Alton Fess and "Quiet" Moran, of the homicide squad.

"He was shot from the window over there," suggested Fess.

"Wonderful," said Moran. Moran was looking at a spot on the rug where Madge had scruffed powder into the pile before leaving. All rugs smell musty, but Moran got a woman's scent in this.

"A woman, hah?" Fess asked. "Do I get a knife?"

"Quiet. Yeah, we'll cut up the rug and get the powder out of it. So what? If we put the finger on every doll that uses that kind of powder, pretty soon we'd have a harem."

"He had a model named Madge Powell. All evening." Fess consulted a notebook.

"Who has skipped." Moran gave Fess a fishy look. "Breezed. They were stuck on each other. She don't know anything about it anyhow."

"Yeah? Maybe she saw this sharpshooter."

"Phooey. She got the surprise of her life and just don't want to get mixed up in anything. She'd be too scared to identify her aunt's wig."

It was eighteen hours since the shooting. Moran tried the green light. Effect now was the same as then, probably. Dim light. Took an eye and a half to make the shot that killed Denver Caldwell. Moran went through the window and squatted on the escape platform. He peered through under the curtain. Fess was dummy and lay on the lounge in Caldwell's position.

"Bang. You're dead," said Moran.

"Rats," said Fess. "What other ideas you got?"

"It's a nosegay," Moran chortled. "My, my! What carelessness!" He flashed a light on the window pane.

"Whaddya mean, nosegay?"

"Quiet, quiet. Call headquarters and say we've got the prints and to send somebody before they blow off. Handful, so help me. Get it, Al. Heinie Gross was putting the squeeze on Caldwell, and if he didn't pay Willy Carney for this job my name is Iggie Miggie. Carney could do it."

There they were. Squatting on the platform, Carney had rested his fingertips on the window to steady his aim. Four clear prints at the bottom of the glass. It didn't take the papers long to hint broadly that Caldwell's killer was very well known indeed and that the chief of police would like to have a little *téte-à-téte* with him. Willy tried to hold up Heinie Gross for fifty G's, but Heinie was smart enough to keep only twenty in the safe—no more, no less. Willy finally hid out with Violet Hale on Horatio Street. Carney's girl.

"Why don't you grab a handful of boats and learn to speak Frog for a year? Money gone already, Willy darling? I have some."

"They'd *like* that," Willy retorted. "Moran and Fess are hopping around the piers like it was a checkerboard. Twice I try jumping a boat."

"This is the last night anyhow," Violet insisted. "You're poison, Willy, and tomorrow you've got to scram."

"Forget it, honey," Willy pleaded. "We're in church. I did it at the point of a gun, see?"

"The point of a gun is right," Violet mocked him.

She had long hair like running honey, and the bright red lips blonds wear. She was pleasantly soft, and Willy appreciated all the little things about her—her delicate, clean smell, the curving hollows of her creamy face, her really pleasant voice. It was hot and she wore only shorts.

Willy was fully dressed. Violet stared up at a moth on the ceiling, resting in Willy's embrace. Her crossed thighs were well-fleshed and inviting. Only thing he didn't like about her was the broad nipples of her breasts. Big as dollars, like most blonds. All beautiful women have a very definite flaw in them somewhere. Hair wrong color, bad walk, uneven shoulders, something like that. Willy reflected, very brightly, that the flaw only emphasized her beauty; he allowed one hand to stray along her smooth skin, leisurely exploring. He traced the arousing curves under her breasts, pinched the nipples and watched them stand up. Violet's breathing accelerated.

Willy sat up, turning to face her. He drew his hands down her sides, found that her shorts were held with elastic. She raised her hips, then her legs so that he stripped the flimsy shorts from her with a single gesture. He grinned peacefully, remembering a joke—about the woman who went to the masquerade in black gloves and slippers as the five of spades. Very pleasant here . . .

The bell sounded with two sharp rings. Violet sat bolt upright, and Willy stopped unbuttoning his shirt.

"That's Marge O'Brien's ring," she said.

"So you've been giving out rings." Willy gripped her wrist till his fingers felt like knotted ropes. "What ring did you give that bastard Mike Welsh?"

"Willy!" It was a desperate whisper edged with pain. "Marge is visiting her mom in Albany. I had a letter from her this morning!"

The bell rang again, sharp and short.

Willy stared fiercely at Violet in the dark, freed her wrist.

"Sorry, baby," said the killer. "You know how it is. Which way?"

"Garden. Hurry, for God's sake!"

It was Fess and Moran.

"Where's Carney?"

"Carney who?" Violet blinked innocently at the two plainclothesmen.

"Ah, can it, sugar. Willy Carney's been here. I smell him."

"A'right, copper. I haven't seen him for three weeks and I don't know where he is. I wouldn't tell you if I did." Violet let her silk wrap slip a little so that a V of naked skin like living white satin showed down to the navel. When she shrugged, the wrap slipped off the shoulder, exposing a round, silken breast copped with a flushed nipple. Her mouth was a juicy scarlet, and in her somnolent condition she looked as though she were anyone's for the asking. Good acting.

"I suppose not," snapped Moran. He picked up an ashtray. "You smoke like hell, don't you?"

"That's my business. What's the matter with your boy friend. Dumb?" Her voice was insultingly casual. Moran had the idea she was wide awake.

"Say something, Fess."

"Them butts haven't any lipstick on 'm. Only one or two 'm 're smeared."

"Wonderful," said Moran. "That's all that keeps the chief from shifting you to Brooklyn."

"Yeah; why don't you count yourself one time, Sherlock? I get the same answer every time. One." Fess held up one finger.

"Quiet. We're going out into the court." Moran looked hard at Violet.

The swell blond shrugged, put her hands on her hips so that the robe opened. Moran gulped, glancing downward automatically. Her legs were apart and her hips sidelong in an easy position. Some doll. By this time Willy was miles away; Violet laughed a little.

"I'm not stopping you," she murmured. "Shall I leave my door open?. . . Or may I go back to sleep now?"

The court was fairly large, the common yard of half a dozen houses. Rock garden in center, ratty goldfish, a few bedraggled shrubs. Fire escapes. Maybe Willy went up one of them, and maybe he didn't. The blond had them fooled.

Moran jumped for the bottom rung of an escape, Fess after him. Willy watched them from the opposite roof ledge; the roof was a trap. Light from a single shaded window illuminated the court; Willy took no chances on an angle shot, waited till Moran was almost on his level before he fired at the shoulder. *Pit.*

At that instant the light went out; whoever burned it had decided to go to bed. Willy listened anxiously, didn't fire again. He couldn't see. Moran didn't make a sound, though the bullet had trimmed the big muscle under his arm and caused him to drop his gun. But Fess swore loudly and shot wild. The flash gave Willy a perfect target.

Pit. Pit, he fired again at a shadow higher up that he thought was Moran. No luck. Fess slumped outward and free, spreadeagled on the concrete below with a loud thump. Willy's bullet had entered the inside corner of his eye.

Willy was worried now; no one showed a light; this district was in the heart of the trucking belt, where backfiring went on all night. Fess's single shot had attracted no particular attention.

Moran swarmed over the roof ledge opposite Carney where he crouched, heard the dead body of Fess smack the pavement so hard it split his head open. Tough. Fess was a damn' fool to shoot. Moran took a deep breath, removed his shoes and started around the roof. *Pit. Pit.* Moran kept going. *Pit. Pit. Pit.* Bullets from Willy's gun smacked the bricks behind the fire escape from top to bottom.

Sockfooted, Moran dived on Carney from behind. Willy dropped his gun, cracking his chin a good one on the tiled ledge. He cursed murderously under his breath, but neither made any further sound as they grappled. Moran tried to deliver a rabbit punch, but merely scraped Willy's ear in the dark.

Afoot one minute, sprawling the next. No mercy on either side. Moran bruised Willy's mouth with a glancing blow, clipped him solidly under the ear. Not hard enough. Willy retaliated with a wild kick that caught Moran in the groin, followed up by sinking his fist deep in the pit of Moran's stomach. A long groan like the mooing of a cow escaped the detective. He vomited copiously as he sprawled forward on his face, out cold.

Gasping, Carney found his gun, scrambled back into the courtyard. He ran two blocks, came on a cab waiting with a call.

"I got a call, buddy. Sorry." The driver shook his head.

"I'll say you have." Willy rammed something stiff into his back. He started uptown. The driver slowed up on a red light.

"Skip it, skip it!" Willy swore, licking his bruised lips. A cruising patrol car turned down Eighth after the cab, forced it to the curb. Willy crouched on the floor of the car, mentally counting the shells left in his gun. When the rider in the police car got out to take down the cabbie, Carney shot him through the temple with unerring precision. The bullet ricocheted from the windshield of the patrol car, cracking it into a burst like a frost flower.

"Hey, what—" the police driver showed his startled face; Willy lined a bullet hole through the exact middle of his forehead.

"Wheel!" Willy rapped out to the cab driver.

"For Chris' sake, what you doin'?" The cabbie was shaking with terror.

"*Wheel!*" Willy jammed his gun into the driver's left shoulder. He got out on Eighth and Thirty-Fourth, thinking fast.

"I don't want to get a swell girl into a jam," he said. "What does it take to keep your mouth shut?"

"Maybe I lose that call. Maybe not. Gimme a hundred."

"Hundred she is." Willy snorted and paid him. "I've got your name and number off your card. Don't forget it." He dove into the BMT station, caught a train after three or four minutes of fidgeting. He had an idea, a pretty good one.

It was Dr. Eugene Bannister, long known to the eastern underworld as a friend in need. Bannister was a ranking brain specialist with several inches of small type in the medical Who's Who. Office and living quarters on West Seventy-Second.

"I don't know why all you rats come in here heeled. I don't do anything I don't want to do, and absolutely nothing at the point of a gun." Bannister tapped his desk with a letter opener. "What is it you want?"

"I hear you gave Sol Schiller a new nose and did wonders with his chin." Willy didn't like Bannister's lingo, but he took his hand off his gun.

"So what?"

"And know how to change the color of eyes. And hair. Permanent."

"I fit lenses, if that's what you mean. They can be of any color. Frankly, I don't think it would help you much. Your build doesn't change. You're Willy Carney, aren't you?"

"What of it?"

Bannister gave Carney a somber, calculating stare, thoughtfully took the letter opener between his teeth. Bannister had an idea, starting where Carney left off. He saw a chance of making a lot of money if Carney had what rumor said Gross had given him.

"Take you, Carney," he decided. Life is very precious, near the short end. If Willy hadn't been certain that the law was next to snagging him, that Bannister was easily the cleverest surgeon in the game, he wouldn't have listened to Bannister's plan. He'd have walked out in disgust. He asked Bannister how much.

"Ten thousand, and cheap at the price. A thousand dollars now. I may have to keep you a month and during that time I'll get the shakedown at least once. There's a secret room in the basement. If the room bell rings once, get out as fast as you can. Scram. If it rings twice, short, come up here; I'll be ready for you."

"It's a crazy idea, doc." Carney shook his head. "Nothing doing. I guess it's too chancy."

"So long, Carney. Your funeral. They don't come back."

Carney thought about being chased bowlegged for the murder of four men, three of them police, and the fact that he would probably be beaten to jelly before he ever got to trial. He was caught.

"Show me that room." Carney fished a thousand dollars from his fat wallet and laid it on the desk. If Willy Carney had stopped to think about it, he was just one sneeze from cracking with desperation.

Late the following afternoon Quiet Moran cruised into West Seventy-Second, stopped across the street from Bannister's brass plate. Fess had been replaced with a heavy-set man named Stielen, newly transferred. Stielen had ideas.

"You thinking of nabbing the doc?" queried Stielen. "Right now we should be in Brooklyn putting the screws on Gross. Wasting time."

"Quiet. Gross doesn't know anything. He'd pay us to keep Carney away from him. Carney's bushed. Nobody knows where Carney is but I'll bet he shot those two cops on Eighth last night after he got Fess. Fess was all right. This Bannister has some funny connections."

"'Quiet'? You're Quiet Moran, aren't you? You talk too much."

Moran was watching a whopping Cadillac full of swanky gypsies. Two men in the rear seat turned black, menacing eyes on him. A girl minced down the steps, stiffly, and joined them. The doorman assisted her. The girl was greensick with anesthesia, her complexion rich olive.

"Cripes," Moran muttered. "I wonder where them Romanies get all the shekels. That gal just paid in two hundred flat anyhow." The Roms in the rear seat gave Moran a last vicious glare and the Cadillac swept up the street with its horn going. The moment it started, Madge Powell alighted from a cab in front of the door.

"Well, I'll be a—. Get that, Stielen." Moran grinned.

"Bonehead luck," Stielen sneered. They waited five minutes to make sure there was no slip up.

Madge entered the reception room, which led off the building's foyer.

"I'm pregnant. My husband died, and I can't afford to have a child now. I want an operation at once."

"How do you know you're pregnant?" Miss Nigace was the nurse-receptionist.

"The usual signs, of course. Morning nausea—it's simply impossible for me to eat breakfast. I'm late a month, softening, those things . . ."

"Your husband," said Miss Nigace. "How did he die?"

"His heart stopped beating."

"A common ailment," Nigace observed drily. "It will be two hundred dollars, in advance."

Madge paid her in new bills.

"And twenty for the anesthetizer." Nigace thought that Madge looked like clear profit.

"Ten." Madge corrected her coolly, gave her ten dollars more.

Bannister barely greeted her, but his eyes sharpened. When he had Madge on the table he decided that she was about the healthiest specimen that had ever walked in. He tapped a button in the wall behind his sterilizing cabinet. Twice. Willy heard it in the basement room and had a fit of shuddering. Bannister didn't wait long when he had work to do. Good thing. Willy went upstairs shakily whistling "The House is Haunted."

He recognized Madge as he stripped. The irony of the situation struck him; he emitted a single short laugh that sounded like a snort. Madge was under the anesthetic and her head was already shaved; Nigace was swabbing her naked scalp with alcohol. Carney stretched out on a tilt-table alongside hers, and as he was strapped into place released a long groan.

"Shut up," Bannister suggested. "You've got nothing to lose. Want to back out?"

"No."

They shaved his head. He took the anesthetic thoroughly stunned with fear; he went chicken-hearted at the mere smell of antiseptic. He was in it now, in as deep as death—rising and falling endlessly on a bed of profound, reverberating shadows that were freaked with needles of unbearable light. He dreamed that tall, enshrouded figures took turns sucking the breath of life out of his body.

Bannister worked like mad, wasting no time. His impersonal voice uttered commands in low staccato. Nigace left to answer the bell.

"Thread. Scalpel and clips. Swab, quick! Shoot both of them in the arm again, Stevens." Sweat stood on Bannister's face; a bloody foam of looped gray stuff oozed out on the plates above Madge and Carney's heads. A keen blade severed vital cords—plates deftly reversed. The glittering knives leaped in Bannister's mad fingers, were replaced with other knives, other tools from a frightening cabinet of implements. Sweat trickled down his hawk's-nose, soaked into his mask.

Bannister quailed before no mechanical problem. Both Madge and Carney were perfect physical specimens. No fear there. The rest of it was in his own gifted hands and eyes, in the surgical genius of Eugene Bannister.

Hurry. The double operation proceeded with ghoulish speed, like some abomination tried by crazy surgeons in remote Soviet Russia. One eye and the blackhead-sprinkled nose of Quiet Moran appeared at the door. All Moran saw at first was a bloody horror at Madge's head. Her eyes were sunken purple. Stevens, the young anesthetizer, was sitting in the corner with his head out the window, bushed.

"What you doing to that girl, doc?" snapped Moran.

Bannister jerked, gave him a quick glance of cold, blasting fury.

"Brain tumor. *GET OUT!*" His voice was low, but his words exploded with command. Then he was back at work with his rapid hands and fierce eyes. He had lost a second or two.

When Carney returned to consciousness his head hammered with staggering pain. He felt like a balloon stuffed with barbed wire. Nigace stood over him. He raised a white arm and felt a turban of bandages.

"Don't move," said Nigace, smiling. It was an important fact to report—that Carney had at least partial control of his body, could raise his arms. She gave him the needle for the last in a score of times. Carney's arm was a sheath of needle pricks, hard as board. Back into the aching hell of shadows . . .

Willy Carney the killer stayed in Bannister's hospital quarters for five months recuperating in easy stages—a way of saying that the law would never trouble him again. His hair had grown back in, had been cut twice. He was not disfigured. The trephine left no mark save an insignificant thread-like white line around the scalp. His hair concealed most of it.

Early October.

"You're leaving us," said Bannister. He tossed two parcels on the bed. One contained freshly laundered clothes. In the other was the rest of Willy's money, the personal trinkets of Madge Powell—rings, rouge, lipstick, a bunch of keys, bank and checkbook. Willy opened both bundles and sighed. A question in the back of his mind had been troubling him for a long time.

"What happened to her?"

"Transferred direct to police hospital," said Bannister indifferently. He gave Willy a hard look. "When she got well she did the one thing in the world that saved your skin."

"Well?"

"She's been confined in the state insane asylum for four months. Incurable. She said she wasn't Carney, had fits of screaming and tearing her clothes off. Crazy. So that's that."

Bannister watched Willy dress, noted with satisfaction that his patient had built up full muscular co-ordination. There was something humorously feminine, already, in the way Willy patted his glinting bronze mass of hair into place. Bannister grinned with pride. No mean achievement, grafting the killer's brain in Madge Powell's body.

"God damn it, I don't like it!" Willy shouted suddenly. "What the hell have you done to me?"

"Shut up. I saved you from the chair," Bannister reminded him. "You can't do anything about it now. I can't either. Miracles happen only once."

Bannister had installed a cheval glass; Willy looked at himself contemptuously, legs astride and arms akimbo. His body was lovely, but he couldn't appreciate it. Good smooth throat, shoulders right—high, firm breasts tipped with small coral. Good long legs. Sure, dainty feet with pink toes. Willy's own toes had been crippled things, the result of a car accident years ago.

There was scarcely any hair on his white body, and that was what got Willy most of all. Just his corona of flowing bronze, a shadow under the arms, the *tache-d'encre*. There was something wrong about this; he felt supremely naked, as though he lacked part of himself. He was not a man any more, never would be. The prominence of his magnificent breasts still surprised him. He supported them in his two hands, studied their subtle blue veinings and dainty rosebud nipples, small as a man's.

Willy gave Bannister a stricken look, passed his slim hands down the exquisite contours of his hips, across the tender hollows between. Not a man. Muttering disconsolately, he slowly snapped a ribbon of brassière, donned flowered shorts. He fumbled a little with the garter belt, hitched net stockings to it. He eyed his high-heeled kid slippers suspiciously, but they fitted to perfection.

Madge had always been careful about that, about shoes. She took no chances on ruining feet that the photographers paid money to see. Slip. Over his head went a printed crêpe frock. He put his breath-taking, graceful arms through the sleeves of a light coat trimmed with fur.

He scowled prettily at Bannister, trembling uncertainly on his high heels. The arch straps didn't give him much support.

"You'll get used to it," Bannister mocked. "All if it—dressing, and the other things. Good-bye, *Miss Powell*, and good luck. Come up and have a cocktail with me some time when my wife isn't home."

Willy swung gracefully out the front door. The doorman wondered what had been the matter with the girl all this time. She had been a material witness in the Caldwell murder, had never been called to testify because the killer had been located and gone nuts. Been found in Bannister's office. Brain tumor. Bannister had furnished Madge Powell's evidence by proxy in what had become a cut-and-dried case. Bannister himself had beat the charge of harboring, on the grounds of the instant necessity of operating.

Willy walked a little farther along Seventy-Second; his long skirts fluttered softly and he experienced the novelty of a cool little breeze stirring between his swell legs. His tiny pointed slippers clicked confidently on the stone as his heels came down. He touched a delicate pink tongue to well-rouged lips, rather liked the way his silk garments stroked his skin as he walked, walked with a consummate grace that was entirely natural.

His step was truer, his gait more decided as he went on. He felt his confidence mounting by the minute. Intoxicating, a little. Too bad someone had shot Caldwell, he thought sardonically. A man named Carney, they said, who had later gone insane and been sent to an asylum. Suddenly Willy was seized with a fit of trembling. He leaned against a light-post for support. Headache. A violent shaft of pain.

"Hello, Madge!" Someone recognized her, someone she had once posed for, probably. It looked like Lewis Webb, if Bannister's three months of coaching was accurate. There was a terrifying moment of amnesia. Powell, Carney, Powell. The names twisted and flickered in her mind as she fought valiantly to fix her attention on just one of them. Webb passed by, shrugging indifferently at the snub. Exit Willy Carney.

Madge Powell! The name exploded in her mind and she was back to reality, suddenly weak with relief. She was Madge Powell, of course. She hailed a cab.

"Where to, miss?"

She gave the number of a commercial photographer downtown that had used her before. As she sank back luxuriously into the cab she indulged in a deeply personal memory of Caldwell's final embrace, of the magnificent, generous way he had of doing things like that. A pleasant memory save for its shocking termination. Well, she could find another man just as satisfactory, could probably renew her old connections without much difficulty. Good models are always in demand. The cab jolted.

Now and then Madge touched a thread of scar running around her scalp, and couldn't recall how in the world she had come by it. It perplexed her a great deal. It was something she did not have before....

The God Box

"**B**UT I AM not a locksmith," said Thorn impatiently. "I have never made a key in my life. Why don't you take this Chinese cabinet, or whatever it is, to one of these fellows in the street who does that sort of thing for his business?"

"It's too heavy to carry," Pence smiled.

"A box no larger than a camera?" said Thorn.

"I told you," said Pence, "that it was extremely heavy, though I didn't say *how* heavy. The exact dimensions are four and three-quarters by five and one-half by seven inches. It weighs, I should judge, somewhat more than a ton."

Graham Thorn, who was a pretty good engineer and no fool, stared at the young man incredulously.

"What I am getting at is this:" said Pence. "This job has me stopped. I can't make head or tail of it, and I know a great deal about such things. The box is heavily carved but has no moveable parts. Nothing like a lid, no keyholes. It reacts like gold, except for hardness, and sounds hollow. I can't imagine why such a container should weigh so much unless there is something remarkable inside. I heard about you as an engineer with an unusual imagination, and thought I could afford to pay you for opening it by some means of your own."

"What do you think this container is?" the engineer asked.

"A battery."

"A battery!" Thorn's feet came off the desk and banged on the floor. He pulled his chin thoughtfully, weighing possibilities more remote than a dream. Suddenly he rose.

"Come," he said, taking his coat and hat, and the two men left the laboratory.

Like many wonderful curiosities of the goldsmith's art, Pence's box had no history. No one could say anything more about it than Pence himself, and that was little. The earliest Egyptians certainly did not discover America, nor did they live in an ugly old residence on thirtieth street. Nevertheless, a locksmith plied his trade there in what was little more than a hole in the wall, and there Pence had discovered the box. What attracted him were the fine carved figures. Figures of an Egyptian character.

Finding a thing so precious in this rubbish was odd enough, but there was something besides. The place was infested with cats. Huge cats like small panthers. He watched the beasts while his key was being filed. One of them sniffed in the corner, at this box, a lovely thing without counterpart. All that the locksmith could say of it was that it was there, crated to the floor, when he moved in a dozen years ago. He seemed to be a little afraid of it. He had never succeeded in opening it, and thought it was welded shut.

Such an object, so richly smithed, could not be a mere arbitrary form. Somewhere, in whatever crypt or antique vale, it must have been worked for one particular purpose. Which was probably contained in the book of Thoth.

"I know considerable about such things," said Pence, "on the side of archeology. Beyond any doubt, aside from its arbitrary form, this work is earliest Egyptian. There's no trace of conflict.

"These knobs on top are royal heads, each different in one small particular which would probably not be apparent to you. These two on the side represent the head of Thoth—one is an ibis and the other a dog. There is no good reason for their being placed where they are—you can see they aren't part of the design. I got to thinking of terminals—a battery. . . ."

Young Pence cocked his head in an odd way he had.

"Listen!" he said sharply. "Do you hear anything?"

Thorn squinted around the room, puzzled.

"That humming?" he asked. "What is it?"

"The cats are coming," said Pence. "I heard it in that shop. I think the sound comes from the box."

He walked to the window.

"Look," he said.

Thorn joined him, and looked into the courtyard. A number of uncommonly large cats were prowling about down there, and glancing up at the window with yellow eyes. More were coming, one by one, over the wall. Thorn looked up. It was a grey day in spring, with clouds overcasting the sky like a sheet of slate.

He turned into the room again, and without a word picked up a few tools Pence had been working with, knife, pliers, file. The gold box was tempered enormously and the file dulled.

Thorn looked at young Pence, then cut a lamp cord. He looked closely at the two heads of Thoth and saw that the pupil of the right eye of each head was in reality a small hole. He inserted a bared wire in each hole and plugged the cord into the wall. There was a flash.

He bent over the box.

"There's a connection here," he said. Pence nodded. This thing was operated by an electrical force. A thing out of oldest time, engraved with forgotten characters, and it was controlled by the most powerful tool of modern science. A cat screamed outside.

It was Pence who discovered the next step. He had been trying the heads on top of the box, and one of them gave, turning to the left. There was a smart click. Both looked, and saw that a square carved plate had been withdrawn from the front of the box. They peered in through the aperture, at what was apparently a flat crystal. In this crystal were imprisoned myriads of phosphorescent particles which seemed to have a motion of their own, endless and slow. Beyond the crystal was an impression of wheels and queerly shaped ratchets. Miniature drums mounted eccentrically on their axles. The entire mechanism, what they could see of it, was foreign to their knowledge, but beautifully machined for some baroque purpose.

The knob Pence had turned unlocked all the others. The royal Egyptian heads that encrusted the top of the box were engraved with perplexing symbols, but though Pence could not hope to decipher them in their connection here, he guessed there was a definite purpose in the pattern of the heads, at least. A second knob yielded.

Suddenly Thorn flapped his arms grotesquely and cried out, "My boy!" as though Pence had struck him.

Darkness descended on them like a blow, and was so oppressive that old Thorn uttered a groan. The humming sound increased in volume till the room seemed to be spinning around them. Pence staggered to the window, and opened it. *At once, the darkness which filled the room spilled through the window and fell into the courtyard in a well of shadow.* The host of cats were drowned in it and their fighting and crying ceased.

There was light behind him. He turned and saw the engineer regarding a cube of light, some ten or twelve feet in dimensions, in the middle of the room. Thorn seemed to have recovered.

"Mr. Pence! Mr. Pence!" he called. "I cannot believe this!"

"What is it?" Paul asked. A chair and table had been there where the light was, but now even the rug on the floor ended where the cube of light touched it.

"It is solid!" shouted Thorn. "You can feel it with your hands!"

Paul was frightened. Solid darkness and solid light. This cube of light stopped Thorn's hands as though it were made of glass. In it was nothing but its own thin brilliance. It was the abyss, and he backed away from it.

It came from the box, though there was no visible connection between the two. If that was its source, it could be controlled. He had a crazy memory of having read somewhere that in the great book of Thoth were powers that controlled light. Was it so, indeed? He warned the engineer of what he was going to do.

"There are seventeen heads," he said recklessly, "and we have tried only two."

Graham Thorn smiled.

"I believe I can account for the weight of that box," he said. "Did you observe the row of cylinders in the bottom of the box? Each connected in some way to the crystal or to the gears? I don't know whether they are hollow or not, but I believe they contain power in some form, and a great deal of it. That light is a manifestation, and it is certainly not the kind of energy we are familiar with. What do you suppose might happen if that force were released all at once?"

"I think we'd be blown to smithereens," Paul grinned.

"Very likely I am an imaginative old jackass," said the engineer, "but I think it would be something worse."

Thorn did not specify what he meant. But the two men soon discovered they were tinkering blindly with a force of a peculiarly awful nature. At the same time there was a prankishness in their experimenting, as in the encounter that followed with Swane, the archaeologist, or "digger", as he fondly called himself.

Russell Swane, who could speak several languages fluently and had seen practically everything on earth worth seeing, was crossing the African desert by motor. The sand in this section had a fair crust, but he had been travelling slowly, as itinerant diggers do. The right rear wheel broke through.

"I *will* be a dirty so and so," he said, by way of beginning. It would be a long, nervous job getting out, and a worse one getting up enough momentum to travel again. Whereupon he commenced swearing easily and rapidly, which is the best thing to do in such cases, and got out of the car. He cast a profound glance into the distance ahead, mentally calculating kilometers yet to go, then stiffened with amazement under the blazing sun.

About fifty paces ahead, a twelve foot cube of sand rose in the air, drifted sidewise, and dropped with a thump that fissured the entire stretch of pie-crust he intended to travel across.

"I say!" he shouted. "Damn it!"

He dropped his shovel and board and strode angrily toward the pile of sand. Another perfect cube issued from the ground at his feet, and he scrambled away from it. It rose high in the air without dropping a single grain, and moved directly over his head. He heard a droning sound like a single monstrous bee, and knew this was some damned new kind of machinery, American-made, for excavating.

"Ahoy!" he yelled, shaking his fist at the block of sand. "Ahoy! Ahoy! Heads up!"

The cake of sand moved about uncertainly in the air, approached the hole it had occupied, and sank deliberately back into the ground. Swane passed a hand over his forehead, and confessed to himself that his eyes ached. He had resigned himself to the fact of being an authority on mirages, when his ears commenced playing tricks on him.

"Ahoy!" said a clear voice. "Where are you?"

Swane whirled about. A solid block of intense light stood on the ground nearby.

"Here!" he said. "What is this?"

"Sorry, old man," said the voice apologetically, "didn't know you were about. Can we help you?"

"You can," said Swane belligerently, as the light enveloped him. "You busted my crust, and you can tell me how I'm going to get my car out of here."

"Where is the car?"

"Down there." Even as Swane pointed he felt himself lifted in the air and deposited easily by the side of the car. He heard the voice say:

"Does it fit?"

"Just," a new voice added.

The car shifted in the sand.

"Get in," Swane was commanded. "Where do you want to go?"

"Cape Town. I forgot my watch."

There was a moment of silence.

"Really?" the voice asked.

"No!" said Swane angrily. "My digging is thirty kilometers ahead, and now I'm not going to make it."

The car left the ground and was rapidly carried forward.

"When you see the digging, let us know," said the voice.

As the rippled dunes passed below him, Swane heard several incomprehensible remarks. One of the voices said:

"Gift horses, and all that, but this thing ought to have a bigger focus."

The other voice agreed. Then:

"What puzzles me, now that we have tried all heads, is the fact that we have no finder. Why, a Kodak has a finder, of a sort! Do you suppose two heads work together—say nine and eleven?"

"Possibly."

"So, they do! In that case, thirteen and eleven would give this digger a look at us?"

"It may be. That must be his destination, by the way."

"Is that your digging?" asked the younger voice.

"Yes," gasped Swane, and was unceremoniously dumped on the desert with an experience he never fully believed himself.

"When I think of what we have in this god-box . . ." said Paul Pence. "Why, there is no privacy on earth any more!"

"Never do that which needs to be concealed," said Thorn smiling.

"We've looked into the bowels of the earth, and seen the ruined fanes off the Dolphin Ridge. Here we are in New York, and yet we can step into that cube of light—hard at first, wasn't it?—and find ourselves in Yucatan, if we're focussed there. What's to prevent us from looking around the moon?"

"Nothing," said Thorn.

"Mars, Jupiter, the Milky Way?"

"Nothing."

"Beyond that? The stars we can't see? The worlds out there in the black?"

"Nothing."

"What," said Pence, "do you suppose we'd find, in the end, if we went far enough?"

"I don't think you would find anything out there," said Thorn quickly. "You would not find God."

That was the trouble with old Thorn. He was forever expressing some thought like that when life was at its highest. Anyhow, what was the good of Graham Thorn now? He had served his purpose, accidental as it was. Pence could have had the machine entirely to himself. Thorn knew too much, and he might possibly speak of the machine to strangers. Graham Thorn was a menace.

In the early days of experimenting, it was Paul who discovered the various powers of the machine, which he affectionately called his "long-legged camera," or "the Eye of Thoth." He found what heads served a simple three-dimensional function or controlled motion. "King 17" was a deadly weapon of vengeance. When there was a self-reciprocal action between two or more heads, both Paul and the subject he was shooting were visible to each other as solid, living objects. He could enter the cube of focus himself, and the subject could leave it, and enter the room from, say, the streets of Bombay. But when "King 17" was turned, that subject—camel, deep sea fish, or man—was "crushed with darkness." Paul had thus "blacked out" a giant squid and part of the whale it was fighting with. When he released this blackness the squid and the snout of the whale exploded in a smother of foam. This was after he found how to increase the focus two and three times over. Outside the original cube, however, no object had any reality nor substance beyond visibility. He could follow an eagle in the sky, and throw a stone through the eagle. But as soon as the bird passed through the twelve foot cube, it became a solid object.

Murder by proxy, wholesale theft, every crime on the calendar was within the reach of the long arm of Thoth, and divine justice as well. Pence became a little arrogant with his increasing mastery of the camera, as was only natural. But Thorn frowned a little when Pence met him at the door dressed in the robes of Egyptian priesthood and holding the tau; and he frowned more at the stink of some antique temple incense filched from deep in the African sand. Worst of all, Pence had saved a huge "European black" from the hands of tribal enemies in the north African jungle, and this oily colossus, of royal black lineage, was Pence's slave.

The prankishness increased.

A liquor ship in the north Atlantic was nearing the American coast. The skipper was standing at the rail of his vessel, smoking. This man's name was Ganning, and he was a hard-headed, blonde-whiskered individual who was not himself given to drinking. The sea was so quiet that his own vessel seemed to be sliding through dirty green glass. A small, chunky sailing vessel stood offside without a ripple, and two men in ducks sat in her stern yawning or coiling a small rope.

Ganning swore vehemently that he had seen a man dressed in a long white skirt appear in mid-air above the bow of this vessel, and holding a funny kind of gold-headed cane. Pence in his robes, with the tau. The next thing he knew, the sailboat creaked from stem to stern, and leaped straight up into the air as though a whale had boosted it from underneath. The two men in ducks sprawled on their small deck, and one of them yelled, rather pointlessly, "Man overboard!"

This boat disappeared. An instant later, before Ganning realized he had lost a good pipe in the water, another boat appeared in mid-air and floated down to the water like a big feather. It was a freaky little hull, not like the first in any particular, and full of gibbering little men talking something like Dago.

Ganning was quite right. The harbor authorities wanted to know how a fishing boat from the bay of Naples could have arrived at the port of New York without being seen in transit, let alone weathering the ocean. Ganning never read a paper himself, or he would have found point in a simultaneous report of two Americans, both apparently insane, who had showed up in their sailboat, on a perfectly calm day, in the Bay of Naples. Unhappily, the times were against them. Otherwise their apotheosis would have been automatic, their having dropped from the sky.

This "wingless angel in a white skirt," with or without the long cane, appeared in three reports. A certain actress, foreign-born and thus subject to the folk-tale beliefs of her people, was awakened one night in a suburb of Los Angeles by a brilliant light all around her. Into this light stepped a very handsome incubus clad in a white dress ornamented with gold thread and jewels.

Her mother, whose English vocabulary consisted of "Yes," "No," and "How much?" slept in an adjoining room and awakened also. She was a very agile old woman, and immediately skipped through the hall in her night-dress when she heard a rumpus in her daughter's bed. A cloud of black stuff was rolling out of the bedroom, and billowed around her naked ankles, imprisoning her. She heard a calm, arrogant voice say these mysterious English words:

"Pride goeth before a fall. What's more, all is vanity."

Then she was released; she found the room empty of Americans when she turned on the lights. Her daughter, almost unrecognizable, was sitting up in bed with an expression of surprise and disappointment on her face. Her head, which one could now see was shaped something like a cue-ball, was cropped to the scalp, and her extravagant platinum tresses were strewn all over the room.

Shortly after this, an unpublished and profane account of James Grogan Torres, a soldier of fortune, described this angel in greater detail. Torres, who had found that the most profitable insurrections were those under already satisfactory governments, was leading his expedition for gain down on a certain South American city when he saw a solid block of what he thought was white hot metal leave the city and advance along the road toward him. He concealed himself at once. His army of three hundred, deployed along the hills, stopped their advance and commenced chattering with excitement at this phenomenon.

There came into view, behind this cube, a white angel with a wand, who pointed at the army from a point not ten feet from Torres, said "Death!" and disappeared. This shining cube then began to plow the men into the earth amidst agonized screams. Three besides Torres escaped death or mangling. The hill was very fertile that year.

Paul Pence never fully understood the working of the camera. Thorn could have given a great deal of information if he were asked for it, but Paul was increasingly independent. Even Thorn had no knowledge of the nature of the force which some time-forgotten wizard had harnessed; but it showed a singularity of nature which was referred to in at least three ancient literatures as "god," and the learned deities of fable, and others, most certainly had traffic with it.

In its various forms it explained, if it did not excuse, certain well-known miracles. Barring accidents, there was no reason why Paul Pence, a mere archeologist interested in the origins of Egyptian culture, could not have acquired considerable power, and, in fact, come near making himself a god, if he had any such purpose in mind.

But he was as much interested in what people contrived the camera as in using it, and his attention, by his training, was diverted to that end. He dimly guessed at a people long vanished, ingenious beyond belief, but found it difficult to account for their unrecorded passing, and, indeed, for the existence of the camera itself. The seventeen gold heads, he thought, perhaps represented a highly organized priesthood with divided powers. It was difficult to conceive of such an almighty and yet so ephemeral a government on earth. In the end you ran into the blank wall of being unable to explain anything, when, in the last, nothing would really be explained.

There were more cats than ever. M'Gwallah, the African servant, closed every hole in the old house that might admit a rat, but as fast as Pence got rid of them he would appear, spread his black arms with imperial magnificence, and say apologetically, "Cats."

There was something in the droning, snoring sound of the camera that attracted them, and that was puzzling. It seemed ridiculous to suppose that the cat family had a generic memory of that sound... The cat once held the distinction of being a venerated beast, but so had other animals.

Pence took the simplest method of disposing of them. M'Gwallah would throw chicken, freshly roasted, into the cube, and Pence would transport them abroad when the cube was full. Load after load. The captain of a transatlantic liner was considerably disconcerted when several dozen nondescript cats suddenly appeared in his cabin in mid ocean, eating chicken. Paul estimated that he had transported more than five thousand of the beasts altogether. A shoal of them swam ashore in Ireland, and yowled for several nights along the beach.

Nevertheless, they found ways of entering, and removing them was a daily nuisance. When the machine droned they would appear, and the worst of it was, it would occasionally sound when the camera was not in use. It was affected by mild electrical disturbances of the atmosphere.

One night, Paul decided that Thorn must be done away with. He approached Thorn's room with the dark focus and found him asleep. This room was fitted up like a power plant, and the old man lay sound asleep on a studio couch in the midst of apparatus. To Paul's surprise, for he thought the engineer might have appreciated dying in his sleep, Thorn said, "I have been waiting for you."

Paul brightened the focus at once.

"You knew I was coming?" he asked.

"Not at all," said Thorn, sitting up. "It was a trick. I have been saying that at intervals for at least a month. I thought we were getting pretty close to the end. Are you—going to kill me?"

Paul felt disconcerted and very much ashamed.

"You must have lost a lot of sleep," he said stupidly. "You must be terribly tired."

"Yes," Thorn admitted.

Hesitating a moment, Pence turned a head on the god-box and stepped into the focus himself. As he did so, both he and Thorn were aware again of the mysterious attraction they felt toward the camera. A subtle pull existed between the shining circle they were in and the box.

"I'm sorry," Paul said, holding out his hand.

"That's quite all right," said Thorn. "You see, I don't think your camera will work in this room, and I want to live out my normal span of years anyhow."

"It won't work? Why not?" Pence's flesh tingled, as did Thorn's. There was an unusual tension in the air. Ghostly fires chased over their bodies in phosphorescent ripples, and the hair of their arms and heads bristled.

"I've had the idea," Thorn explained, "that whatever force is imprisoned in that box is only related to electricity as we know it. That's obvious. But a common house current sets the camera working. I repeat, I am just an old fool, but I have a few ideas. Do you see all this apparatus? Well, this bed is in the middle of a field of resistance that ought to prove very troublesome for your god-box. I have a supply of current here large enough to create a sizable lightning bolt, and the more force you used the more current it would meet. I think the camera mechanism would weld. By the by, haven't you found any way of keeping those monsters of yours outdoors?"

"The cats, you mean?" asked Paul humbly.

"Yes. Every batch seems larger than the last."

Pence turned to watch the animals. They filed through the open door of which they could see beyond the camera from Thorn's laboratory room and slunk around the camera stand as though they were in search of prey. Momentarily the two men heard the rumble of M'Gwallah's bass, and the great black appeared in the doorway. He glowered at the cats, which now numbered more than a dozen, and began to stalk them. One of the beats leaped up on the table, glared into the crystal, and leisurely assumed a position on top of the royal Egyptian heads.

"M'Gwallah!" Pence shouted. The surprised black looked up.

"For the love of god, Pence!" Thorn said, "don't move!"

Thorn was sitting where he looked into the camera's eye, and he could see something Pence could not. It was the first time either man had looked into the lens when the camera was working. The crystal, curiously, seemed to be increasing in size, and behind it was not the mere jumble of wheels there should have been.

The cat had leaped off the camera, meanwhile, which was what Thorn had hoped to prevent. It was too late now. For the cat had disturbed the position of the heads.

"Pence! Pence!" whispered Thorn. "Come down here and look!"

The sound of the camera increased to a great booming drone. The camera, on its stand, approached the cube of light which was its focus, met the cube with a shivering sound of metal, and vanished. They could still see M'Gwallah off in the shadows, a cat screaming under each arm—great fighting cats that were raking his glistening black hide with their steel claws.

The cube of light was so charged with cross currents of force that their flesh stung. Paul Pence and Thorn looked around the room amazed. Graham Thorn gasped with realization, then screamed, "God help us! PENCE! WE ARE INSIDE THE CAMERA!"

Their surroundings changed. They were on a sandy beach, and saw to the left a mighty building fronted by countless steps in terraces. It was of red stone, and of unrecognizable architecture. They saw a scintillating blue sea, and at perhaps a thousand yards distance a towering, brightly-painted galley at anchor. Red-skinned men and women, clad in a kind of shimmering, easily draping cotton when they were clad at all, stood about them, and eyed them incuriously, smiling. Large cats, or beasts of that family, wandered about freely and seemed to be held in high esteem.

"Egypt?" whispered Thorn.

Paul shook his head.

"Don't you see?" he said. "There are two suns in that sky. That's a western ocean."

Meanwhile a small boat was nearing shore, in which stood erect a negro holding a plate covered with a red cloth. On it was a golden box, having the general appearance of the camera Paul had found at the locksmith's. And behind them, behind Pence and Thorn, a black shadow had been moving up across that plane of the cube of focus. It was the shutter.

Paul stood up, terribly afraid and glaring sightlessly. The camera was nowhere to be seen.

"M'Gwallah!" he screamed. He could still see the negro. The red people frowned at him and uttered blurred, musical words of protest in their own language. "M'Gwallah! M'Gwallah!" He made twisting motions with his hands, as though he were turning the royal Egyptian heads.

The African giant, totally dumfounded, stood there like a black shadow. The cats shrieked and fought against his fixed arms, unheeded. He muttered anxious sounds, shifted his bare feet uncertainly.

The small boat they had seen touched the shore of the blue sea, and the negro carrying the box stepped pompously on the sand. Paul pointed violently at the spot where his camera should have been, and made gestures as though he were pushing the camera over. M'Gwallah still did not understand. Pence hurled himself forward, and his body met the shining wall of the cube with a thud. M'Gwallah strode forward and seemed to be busy with some invisible object. His mighty back arched and cracked as he strove to move a ton or more of metal, the camera they could no longer see. Suddenly he sprawled into the cube of light himself. The black shadow crossed the cube behind them with a crash like cataclysm.

At the same instant, the walls of the Manhattan residence of an archeologist named Paul Pence collapsed inward as the result of a vertical explosion of unknown nature. This man Pence could not be found, nor could his friend Graham Thorn who disappeared at the same time, and who had been well liked in local scientific circles. Another phenomenon occurred at about this time, also, no one having heard the explosion.

Quite a number of persons, considering the average New Yorker as a rather unobservant individual, saw the rocket go off. This rocket was of a singular shape, being that of a box-kite, or cube, of about twelve feet in dimensions. It was reported by several loose-witted persons, too, that though this rocket was blinding in its brilliance, there still could be seen in it the figures of three men, one of them a negro. A statement wholly untenable, since the authorities had no knowledge of any persons working on passenger rockets at this time, and particularly not of this shape. Nevertheless, the cube had a meteoric course—brilliant, instant, and free; and if any astronomer were observing it, he would have said it was pursing a mathematically direct line for a point a fraction of a degree off the north star Vega. Toward that certain planet, in fact, which the imaginative tribe of astronomers count as one able to support life as on earth.

The Missing Ocean

SINCE THAT DAY when he was fifteen years old—a husky kid with broad shoulders and an insane determination to sail all of the seas, to box the compass, to get to know so much about navigation, by easy stages, as would relieve him of the obligation to take his hat off to any man—Captain Amandus Rudolf had not spent as long as two weeks at a stretch on dry land. In port he kept to his vessel mostly. Nowhere was there a black, brown, red, yellow, white, or pink girl waiting for him. The sex was not essential to steering a straight course. Captain Rudolf liked his water deep, and the dirtier the weather the better.

It was three days now in the lodgings on Bethune Street in Manhattan, and it would be five days more before the *James A. Waltham* sailed—some governmental curiosity about her cargo. More than that, his cabin still stank from the spray used to kill the big tiger roaches which had eaten his fingernails down to the quick one night. So he thought he would take a stroll down Bethune to West and take a look at the Hudson, which he once thought was a big river. The *James A.'s* mate was to meet him in a joint in one hour, and probably he would have breakfast with the slob. There were some things to talk over.

The morning was bright and serene. For a moment Rudolf stood at the top of the steps with his legs wide apart, his old hat jammed on his head as though in a high wind, his horny thumbs hooked under his suspenders. He turned an ugly look toward Greenwich on the left, then scowled west. He started down the steps.

As yet there was no sunlight in the street. Two kids were trying to open up a hydrant at the corner. Three pedestrians were in sight, and a couple of trucks—then a resplendent sedan rolled by. At first Rudolf thought it was a reflection from a polished windshield. At any rate it was light.

It was as quick as a wink of sunlight on water, seen blindingly, and then gone forever. It had the electrical hue of violet, and was an instantaneous flicker that serpentined down from the sky. Captain Rudolf ducked involuntarily, and fell.

It was as though the earth had been snatched from under his feet. He clapped his hand on his head to save his hat, as the feeling grew on him that he was rocketing in a descent of howling velocity. At the same time he felt suspended, as though the law of gravity had ceased operating, like the time in Liverpool when he had gotten himself nauseatingly swilled-drunk; or, the seeming interruption in gravitational pull might have been the deception of the wind tornadoing out of the cosmic abyss and tearing at him, knocking another law out of kilter—the rate of acceleration of his particular falling body.

His feet hit bottom gently, but he went to all fours on general principles until he could reconnoiter. Brushing his knees off automatically as he rose, he looked back at the steps to see what he had slipped on. There weren't any steps. Aghast, he took a hurried look at the street. He was in a spacious vaulted corridor, or arcade, which was paved, walled, and domed with bricks giving off a luminous glow like daylight. Since the reverberations of this light were so complex, a man didn't cast a shadow. More than that, the silly-looking citizens inhabiting the place each had his nimbus shining like a visible aura. Amandus stuck his arms akimbo and growled: "Now, what the hell?"

At a respectful distance of ten or twelve feet a ring of citizens formed and inspected him with solemn intentness, from his big bulldog shoes on up through his baggy pants, his shirt, candy-stripe suspenders, flowered neck-tie, to the limp, leathery felt hat on his head.

Amandus took a few steps, knotting his powerful fists and using marked elbow action. The ring of rubbernecks stayed intact, moving with him. Amandus stopped, skinned his hat off and mopped his forehead. A man in the imprisoning ring ejaculated: "My word, they've done it!"

All around Amandus sounded a rush of spontaneous laughter, because every man in sight was as bald as a frog, whereas Amandus boasted a head of thick reddish-brown hair. Besides, he only shaved his upper lip—and it only to keep soup and the reek of rum out of it—so his long equine countenance was framed in a spade of coppery beard.

There were only two types of garment in the crowd—one for the women and one for the men—as though they all belonged to a cult. The hair of the females was an identical medium blond, just as all the bald skulls looked as though they had been cast from the same mold.

The girls wore shorts and a snug, sleeveless tunic belted at the waist. Their legs were bare, and the shoes on their feet differed from those of the men only in size. In form they were all nymphean, superlatively curvate in the modeling of their breasts, hips, and straight long legs. Amandus reflected that the orbs of the *James A.'s* mate, Mr. Kendall, would have bugged out of his head.

The men wore shorts of the same lusterless material, a shade grayer and not draped, and wore their tunics inside their pants instead of outside. Legs bare again. If you didn't count the baldness, they were all of princely stature. It was as though ugliness, skinniness, disease, obesity or any departure from standard measurement—the fixed average—was against the law.

"Well, what the hell are you laughing at?" roared Amandus. With the way time was passing he would have to proceed directly to the joint on West for the confabulation with Mr. Kendall.

"What do you expect?" a bald young man inquired pleasantly. "After all, your appearance is ridiculous."

"It is, is it?" snarled Amandus. "What do you think you look like to me, with your damned-fool clothes, your bald knobs and all of you alike as sardines? Who are you, anyhow?"

All around the circle the men and women eyed each other with wonderment. A young man cut a radius to Captain Rudolf, sat on his heels and asked: "Do you mind?"

He scrutinized the blobs of shoes, which Amandus had shined by hand, with smiling offensiveness. But he neglected to ask Amandus' permission to tweak the trousers leg and raise it in order to inspect the woolen socks purchased in London. It was too much. Aggravated, Amandus made a paddle out of his right hand and cut at the air with it. There was a *whop* of iron-hard calluses meeting the side of a head with bullet speed; the young man rose a few inches, changed direction and assumed a horizontal position in which he slid on the glassy pavement all the way into the crowd.

"Anyone else?" Amandus inquired briskly, and the circle expanded somewhat. There was a commotion to his right. A gap formed in the circumference, and through the passageway hiked two men in military

step with each other. They were distinguished from the other men t
the broad leather belts they wore around their waists. They hiked up to
Amandus, and when they observed his bunchy fists they drew an article
from their belts in unison. The instruments resembled satin-finished
steel cigars, fitted the hand snugly, and were aimed at Amandus. He
asked: "What do *you* want?" His voice was inflected downward by
belligerence.

"Where is your license?" he was asked.

Amandus decided that he had tarried too long and that he had business elsewhere. Time to get under way and out of the building, if he had
to knock these slobs down one by one. He had heard the click of the
instrument held by one of the men—they were policemen—but didn't
connect the sound with the fact that his feet were stuck to the floor; he
tried to look down to see what was the matter, and found that he
couldn't. His heart was beating like big gulps in his throat, but he was
petrified. He couldn't move.

With one of the streamlined cops holding the innocent handle of
metal, the other advanced smartly and searched Amandus from stem to
stern. Under all eyes it was very embarrassing, and he strained to his
utmost. The cop scanned the sheaf of papers in his breast pocket, spent
an infuriatingly long time examining the collection of coins, keys, heavy
gold watch—the odds and ends Amandus carried.

"Come along quietly," he was ordered.

Whatever nightmare force held him was released suddenly, and he
almost fell down. The two policemen grabbed an arm apiece. They were
strong boys, single-minded. They warned him that they would use the
ray on him again if he didn't behave, and Amandus' shoulders jerked
with humiliation as they escorted him to an elevator.

"That was very convincing," said a man in the crowd they had left.

"Oh, I don't know," a girl replied. "He was an ugly brute, that's the
only thing. I suppose there were such specimens, but I don't believe
they wore clothes like that all the time."

On the way up in the elevator Amandus asked his captors: "What's
the idea of this? Where are we going?"

"To police headquarters. Where do you suppose?"

"Am I under arrest? What for?"

"You can't go around like that. You know the law."

"I must be going nuts. Listen, boys, I'm captain of the *James A.
Waltham*, and I've got to get aboard my ship."

"Just keep your shirt on," he was advised courteously.

"What part of town have I got to? I never saw this place before."

"That isn't surprising. This is the main tower."

Amandus glanced at his watch and said anxiously: "Look, boys, I haven't done anything, and it's getting later and later."

"Everything will be taken care of, old man."

Amandus cursed under his breath and waited for developments with grim impatience. It was uncommonly warm. He decided that he had gone momentarily nuts with the heat and wandered into a private building where his mere presence was a violation of law recognized by the city police, unless, in fact, a practical joke was being played on him. If it was a joke it was a serious matter to him, and he would start some fireworks before he left.

It was his feeling that the car's speed of ascent was luxuriously slow, since the motion was smooth and the car was completely inclosed; but when it stopped, he had the vertiginous feeling of having had his weight abruptly reduced to two ounces.

The arrest was no joke, and he was in the hands of the law. His captors escorted him to an office and left him with an elderly man whose eyes were the brightest and most dangerous that Amandus had ever seen. In spite of his effeminate, brief costume there was no doubt that this was a person of authority. Amandus' belongings were distributed on a desk and subjected to the most detailed scrutiny by the chief, John Cutten.

"Where did you acquire those articles?" Cutten asked. "These coins in particular."

"Why, they're mine. I got the money in change last night at Joe's Bar down on—"

"Oh, no, you didn't. Tell the truth, now. Either you're a collector or you stole them from the Metropolitan."

"Neither!" Amandus exploded angrily. "I never stole a cent in my life!"

"Then where did you acquire a handful of valuable coins, every specimen of which is three thousand years old?"

"Three th— You're crazy!"

"Perhaps one of us is," Cutten rejoined significantly. "What is your story about these old manuscripts?"

"Them's nothing but my private papers. Nothing but letters and stuff."

"All of them dated between 1931"—that was a promissory note from a man he had been chasing around the seven seas for as many years— "and 1939." Cutten opened a letter with the reverent fingers of an Egyptologist unrolling a papyrus inscribed with the complete works of Sappho. "1939, and this is 4939; exactly three thousand years."

"This is what?"

"4939," Cutten answered absently, reading the captain's letter.

Amandus stared, so thunderstruck that he wasn't worried about the letter being read. The letter contained full instructions for assembling a cargo of guns, ammunition, airplane and light tank parts, and other war materials for Loyalist Spain. He hiked around Cutten's desk to the window, and looked out, aghast.

He was, at least, a mile in the air, in a room in the column of an unimaginable tower. In lower levels the giant skyscraper eased away in flowing terraces. In the distance gleamed other towers in the morning sunlight. Amandus screwed his head around to look up fearfully, leaning out, and the mighty shaft of the tower continued right on up into the blue. There was no sign of the Hudson or East rivers. No doubt they flowed somewhere beneath the sprawl of masonry down there. There was no indication that the Bay existed any more. In the most distant east were mysterious, half-seen pencilings of metal against the haze.

Cutten's hands pulled him back into the room.

"What is your address, Mr. Rudolf?"

"I've been staying at a place on Bethune Street, but my address is the *James A. Waltham.*"

Cutten's remarkable bright eyes got a little narrow. "There is no such place as Bethune Street. What do you mean by this other name?"

"My ship." Amandus' alarm was slowing developing into the beginnings of horror.

"Your ship?" Cutten prompted.

"Sure. The *James A.* You know what a ship is. A vessel. It has engines in it that burn coal or oil, and screws that push it through the water. It's the way you cross oceans."

"Yes, indeed. The way you cross oceans." Cutten touched a button on his desk, and in came a pair of men wearing the broad leather belts. The chief said merely: "Dr. Davency."

Dazed, Amandus was escorted to another elevator, and they went higher up in the tower. Their destination was a suite of offices filled with laboratory equipment, masses of glass and metal apparatus. Shelves filled with labeled bottles went up to the ceiling all around. The two cops delivered Amandus to Dr. Davency and departed.

Davency wore spectacles whose lenses were a half inch thick, giving him the goggling, inhuman expression of something fished out of the deep. He asked Amandus a few preliminary questions, which Amandus answered automatically in a low voice, then indicated a chair. Amandus sat down. Davency pushed up a mass of apparatus mounted on wheels and adjusted a shell of metal, the business-end of a jointed metal arm, until it was touching his hair without making contact with his skull. A switch clicked, and a thin whine filled the air, a penetrating needle-slim whine that became hypnotic as the seconds passed. Something touched the base of his skull and traveled up and over to his forehead—latitudinally the same. Unerring metal fingers that measured him. Click of another switch. The air was warm, but Amandus had the feeling that his brain was turning to ice.

Davency dabbed at Amandus' forehead with a wet swab. In his other hand he held a four-inch darning needle, from whose head a cable ran to the humming machinery. He centered the point against Amandus' forehead, aimed, then slowly drove the bodkin into his skull up to the butt. Amandus didn't realize what he was doing because there was no pain; he raised his fingers to feel, and after that he was afraid to move.

"Hm-m-m," Davency grunted, commenting on a discovery. He went to an instrument set on his desk, pressed a button and reported: "There's nothing wrong with this man, Cutten."

Just as clear in the room was Cutten's answering: "How about his hair, Davency? And his costume? And the specimens of his pockets? The old coins and manuscripts? Where did he get them?"

"Inexplicable," said Davency. "The only worry I have is whether this man's brain is normal, and it is, except for the time quotient. It's the same phenomenon we observed in the others, and they were readjusted easily enough. Do you want me to go ahead, or shall I send him back to you?"

"Go ahead. But this is the seventeenth time one of these birds has turned up. What's the secret?"

"You've got me. We're working on it."

Davency came back, pulled the bodkin out of Amandus' head. He asked: "Where did you tell Cutten you were staying?"

"On Bethune Street," Amandus answered, feeling the hole in his forehead. It was already no larger than a pore.

"Don't worry about that," Davency recommended. "It will close up completely. Come along."

They passed through several rooms where men were working too intently to notice them, into a library where there were only maps—in books on the shelves, done in brilliant coloring and detail on the walls, large ones backed with cloth and hanging from racks.

"Bethune Street, Manhattan, the nineteen hundreds," Davency told the librarian. While the young fellow was searching among the racks, Davency asked Amandus detailed questions about the exact spot where he had found himself a mile or so below. So many feet from the elevator to Cutten's office, so many feet out from the wall of the corridor, approximately the distance below the uptown turn in the corridor.

They looked at the map of ancient Manhattan, and the librarian retired.

"Taking into account the drift in latitude and longitude," Davency reflected aloud, "you turned up in the spot which corresponds approximately to the address you gave. It is quite, quite baffling. With seventeen such occurrences known, there must be some force at work indeed."

Amandus was staring at the map covering the whole wall to his left, and asked: "What's that?"

"The map of New York," Davency responded, "of course." He went on talking to himself, and the librarian glanced up with a smile now and then. The doctor mentioned stray "fissures in time," which might catapult a man, when he walked into one as had Amandus, for varying distances into the future or the past. There was the queer, slow, soft, drifting lightning bolt through which Amandus had passed on his way down the steps from the door of his rooming house on Bethune Street. In the police records were dozens and dozens of cases of disappearances, of people who never were seen again. In the newspaper files these disappearances were vastly multiplied in a world-wide survey. More to the point, there were documented cases of appearances which could not be explained by the most ingenious scientific tools. A man steps up to a mailbox on the corner to drop a letter into the slot; the letter flutters to the sidewalk, and with suddenness too brief to be registered by any instrument—least of all the human eye—the man isn't there any more. Gone—completely, irrevocably. And all through recorded time people like Captain Rudolf turned up, phenomenal, since long before the phenomenon of Christ. The unknown force which whisked individuals out of their own times into distant ones, at random, was not a thing that could be harnessed like electricity and directed and controlled through wires. Davency thought it had a connection with telepathy. One fact was certain, inescapable in the law of averages. Disappearing meant never showing up again. Conversely, appearing was settled; there wasn't a chance in billions, in a legion of lifetimes, of a man like Rudolf ever returning. He could never go back.

Davency turned him over to a couple of assistants, and the assistants made him strip. They ordered his garments sent to the museum, and after a compulsory shower he dressed in the regulation soft shorts and jerkin. He had hairy legs, and a tuft of hair peeked out from the opening of the shirt near his throat. It was just as silly as wearing a bathing suit.

They escorted him into a three-room apartment near the top of the tower, allowing him to keep his watch. The watch had been made in France and it was a good one, varying only a couple of seconds a year at the most; it had been his grandfather's, then his father's. He had taken it apart and put it together again several times on the high seas, and it was still good for years.

He looked out into the corridor, and the men waiting for the elevator motioned him to get back inside. He closed the door and went all through the apartment systematically. There were many conveniences, several whose purpose he couldn't imagine at all. He was living in a tower of Babel, and he looked out the window at the immeasurable reaches of it stretching away.

It was inconceivable. He was remembering the map of Manhattan he had looked at in the library, and the other mural maps. There was the one of the ocean. The Atlantic Ocean wasn't there any more; it was nothing but a twisting lake running from Greenland down to the Antarctic. What was more, all of the geography of both poles was drawn in, green with vegetation, crawling with rivers and dotted with cities of strange names. The climatic cycle had swung around and this was the Golden Age again. There wasn't any winter, any more than there was before Ragnarok, before the Edens and the Isles of the Blessed of legend were destroyed. That was why it was so warm in New York, and around the world for that matter.

What was worse, there weren't any ships. No liners. The oceans were all crossed with bridges from shore to shore, and otherwise radiating like the spokes of a wheel from a cluster of new islands in mid-Atlan-

tic where Atlantis was supposed to have been. There was a new continent in the Pacific south of the Equator.

All the water was bridged. There were no ships any more, no boats
but the small ones used along the shores for amusement—for fishing
and the like. All cargoes went by truck and train over the bridges.

There weren't any ships. This was the year 4939, and there wasn't
any need for the kind of ship which Rudolf understood. He kept staring
until the sound of the door opening behind him made him turn.

A handsome girl entered the apartment, closed the door and looked
at him, waiting. She took a step forward, looked puzzled and backed up
to the door again.

"What do you want?" Amandus growled.

"Dr. Davency sent me," she explained in a soft voice.

"Get out," Amandus ordered.

The girl put her hand on the knob and turned, then faced him again.
Her eyes dropped to the floor. She said: "Please don't send me away, Mr.
Rudolf . . . Captain Rudolf, I mean. If I'm not satisfactory, I'll be disci-
plined."

Amandus turned scarlet. He thought of the seaman whom he had had
to hang in irons on the last voyage, wondering what she meant by
"disciplined", and by "satisfactory". He grumbled: "All right. Sit down
there in that chair and don't bother me." He turned to the window and
looked out again. He knew she was staring at his back, and after a few
minutes she began to sing a song seductively, a persuasive little song
that was compelling in its melody alone.

"4939," Amandus muttered, trying to shut the song out of his ears.
"I'll be damned."

Long Island wasn't an island any more; it was grafted onto the
continent by the upward shouldering of earth. And the continental shelf
and beyond were now coastline. There were cities and rich farm land.
Between New York and the greater city of eastern New York at the new
mouth of the Hudson, several hundred miles away, twisted the greatest
of all river beds, the Grand Canyon of the Hudson.

Amandus turned around suddenly and asked the girl: "Is this 4939?"

"Yes, captain," she whispered.

"There ain't no ships any more?"

"Only by air—the planes, and the rockets."

"What happened to the Atlantic Ocean? It ain't there any more. It's
gone."

"You don't have to yell at me," she said. "The Atlantic has been that way for the last thousand years or more. In a few thousand years from now—I don't know how many; you'll have to ask Dr. Davency—the continents will sink and be the way they were. We'll never see it."

"Hm-m-m-m," said Captain Rudolf. "There ain't any ships?"

"There aren't any ships. The oceans are bridged."

"You mean there ain't any oceans," Amandus said morosely. He gave a sour look out the window. "I've got to find out about my ship, the *James A. Waltham*. Where is it? Eh? Who do I ask about it?"

She said, hesitantly: "You . . . you might call the Bureau of Public Record. I'll call them for you." She rose from the chair with practiced grace and pressed a button on an instrument near the door, on the wall. She said: "Yes, the newspaper records of 1939. Yes, that's right."

"It might take a little while," answered someone from somewhere in the great labyrinth below.

"I'll wait," said the girl. Lovely as she was, she smiled at Amandus as though he were the most-sought-after creature on earth. He looked out the window, trying to see the ocean. He took hold of his left shoulder with his right hand, and tweaked the cluster of hairs there.

From the instrument on the wall came the masculine voice, saying, "All right, Honey Child. What do you want to know?"

"There was a ship called the *James A. Waltham*, here in 1939. . . . That's right. There was civil war in Spain, with the Germans and the Italians helping the Rebels, and this ship was loaded with material for the Loyalists. What happened?"

"Wait a minute." Far down below in the greater tower of inland New York, a man held a box which he had taken from a cabinet. The box was labeled "1939." The box contained films, micro-photographs of the newspapers of that year. One by one the man stuck the films into a projection machine. He said at last, "The *James A. Waltham* slipped out at night when her captain disappeared, in the spring of 1939. The mate survived, having stayed ashore, waiting to locate the captain, who was believed kidnaped by persons not in sympathy with what I read as Communists—whoever they were."

Amandus turned around.

"The *James A. Waltham* blew up in the bay which used to exist below the district of Manhattan. The ship was loaded with explosive material; someone dropped a burning cigarette in the hold; an assistant engineer discovered the fire while he was looking for a place to take a nap; he reported, and there was time to radio. The S O S calls were answered by the government and the private concerns existing then, but the ship must have blown up. The *James A.* was an oil-burner, and nothing was found but a patch of oil where the *James A.* was going to head out to sea, with or without the blessing of the U.S.A. The old lady's plates had been scattered across the water every which way; no survivors. Want any more?"

"Ask him what time she blew up—the exact time," Amandus ordered hoarsely.

"The explosion was seen at two minutes past midnight," came the prompt answer, "and was followed by a noise like an arsenal going up. Anything else? O. K."

Three thousand years ago at two minutes past midnight, tonight, the ship had gone to smithereens with all on board. If it hadn't been for the millionth chance, Amandus would have been on deck. He said to the girl: "You must have something to do. Go away. I want to think."

"I'm to say with you."

"Go into one of the other rooms, then."

She left reluctantly and sat down on the edge of the bed, watching him. Amandus paced the living room gloomily, cursing his luck. Back there in 1939 he would have been a dead man, but this was practically as bad. He was a prisoner; he could not go and come as he pleased, nor had he any use for this girl who had been assigned to him. They were going to "readjust" him, make him conform to their confounded lousy average.

Amandus was too old a dog to learn new tricks. Independence was his god. He was ocean-going, and at sea he was the law, the supreme authority on his own ship. But now he was a nonentity, merely a guinea pig for Davency to work on. According to his specifications there was no longer such a thing as a ship, and the very ocean was missing from the maps. Bridges connecting the continents! Hideous!

The afternoon sun was hitting the tower broadside now. At dinner time a tray was brought in, just as food is brought to a prisoner in a cell for his first few days in prison. The young man who carried the tray inquired: "Are you the new one? What year?"

"1939, squirt," Amandus growled.

"That so? I'm a 2937er, myself. Been here two years now. Got whisked right off the campus of Midwestern University the day of graduation."

"What's that to me?"

"Don't get huffy, pop," the kid recommended. "They'll hammer you down to the right size and make you like it. Take me, for instance. I had six years of law, a job waiting for me in the biggest firm in Chicago, and a promise of getting my name lettered on the door inside of two years. I was bright, see? Hell, I'm still bright, but what am I doing? I'm a waiter. The lawyers in this tower have a guild, and they won't let any more in. They've got a long waiting list, and I'm at the bottom of it. Isn't that a kick in the pants?"

"It is. Say, didn't they have any hair in 2937?"

"Sure. I had curly hair, and the girls were nuts about it. There's something wormy about the climate now; no winters or anything. Bet you that you'll be bald as a football inside of six months."

"No."

"Yes; absolutely."

"I mean I'm not betting. Beat it, youngster; this food is getting cold."

"O. K., pop. If you get hungry or thirsty later on, just buzz the kitchen. See you at breakfast."

The waiter lingered in the doorway, eyeing Rudolf's girl. He remarked, "Hm-m-m— Nice pair of legs there, sister."

At about ten thirty the girl went to bed with all the assurance of her being Amandus' legal wife. He gave her one horrified glance because he was taken by surprise, and after that kept his back turned. He was so embarrassed he could have died. She called to him: "Come to bed, Amandus. It's late."

"Do I have to?"

"I have to report in the morning. If I lie about it, they'll know. If you don't come to bed, it will mean that I'm not satisfactory and I'll lose my rating."

"They ought to be ashamed of themselves!" he exclaimed. "Damned if I will!"

She began to cry, and he growled: "All right, all right. But wait a while; I'm still doing some thinking."

She went to sleep with tears beading her eyelashes, as inviting a morsel as his eyes gazed upon in all his travels. There would be no more traveling.

He looked out the window, and even the stars didn't look right. In three thousand years, of course, there might be a little distortion in the constellations. Orion's belt was slipping.

Midnight. If this were 1939, the *James A. Waltham* was due to go up in thunder in two minutes. If it hadn't been for the stink of disinfectant in his cabin, he would have been aboard. He was as much a part of that ship as her engines. He loved the old tub with a deep and true masculine love.

On second thought, he *was* aboard.

The girl awakened with a start and cried: "Amandus!"

Then she sprang from the bed wide-awake and sprinted to the window. She leaned out and screamed with all her might, "Amandus!" as though a call sent after him, with whatever speed of terror, could ever catch him and bring him back.

For he had swung his hairy legs over the window sill and given himself a strong push into space. He was now going down like a shot and picking up speed all the time. Some of the windows in the tower were lighted, and some were not, but in a couple of seconds the line of windows melted together to form a continuous streak of illumination. The breeze got stiff. In a jiffy, practically, it became a hurricane, a wind of a velocity that never existed on earth. From a whoop its voice turned into a witch's scream, scouring his flesh like sandpaper.

He had his watch in his hand, and by squinting mightily he was able to read the time. He glanced below, and the first terrace jutting out from the tower was going to receive him, as well as he could gauge it, at just about the split second of the *James A.'s* blowing up in the lower Bay. The tradition was as natural to him as the beat of his heart—the master going down with his ship, with no regrets and without any longing.

The Hand of the O'Mecca

IT WAS Elof Bocak, large and unmistakable. Like the two figures which waited for him in the lane, he most nearly resembled an erect shadow. His formidable stature alone identified him. Unlike those two shadow-figures, which were still, his body gyrated remarkably above his feet. Elof had that in him tonight which was stronger than himself. In John Colander's kitchen behind him the whiskey ran. They had filled him with drink tonight, for was he not questing after the hand of Kate O'Mecca? A hazardous quest, perhaps, on this night. Fog trapped the land; and murky skeins of it crept stealthily southwest over the Colander farm, over the rolling Minnesota hills as though they needed to be concealed. While Elof profoundly calculated through which of the thirty-two points of the compass lay the O'Mecca farm, he plucked a quip of felt from his head as one would skin a grape and wrung the whisky out of it. Naive Elof! There were more shadows in his head tonight than walked abroad, and a brace of still phantoms awaited the mighty, befuddled Bocak in the lane. In back of him the drinking Finns made the Colander Kitchen re-echo like a giant's hall.

"On the head of himself!" the Colander had roared, upon which six farmers had lifted their brimming tumblers to the O'Mecca. The seventh, who was John Colander himself, crowned Elof's pate with a full glass. This, the farmers agreed, was an efficacious, Finnic means of expediting Kate and Elof's troth.

White, inland fog brimmed the hollows with ghostly pools and phantom lakes as Elof reeled across Colander's acres. The spirit of the corn hummed in his veins; there seemed to be a bumblebee locked in his

skull, a bee that droned and strove to escape as he mounted the lane
through the east hill pasture, singing. Elof had a short throat, but he
could send up the staggering notes of his love song high enough with it.
It was a fool's defiance, and a fool's lusty passion. Diminutive owls
hooted at him and fled through the woods. When Elof sang, the night
was only big enough for himself.

On the far side of the hill a long slough sprawled in ambush, drowned
in a pool of darkness and fog, fog too heavy to breathe. It was the
thickest fog that any man had ever seen, but it would take more than a
slough to mire the feet of him. His headlong gait steered down into the
slough, and then the two figures which had been standing and waiting for
him disengaged themselves from the fog. They joined him so that they
were three abreast, with Elof between. The hill rose behind them and
blinked out the rollicking lights of John Colander's kitchen. Hereupon
Elof halted, puzzled. He thought he heard someone chuckling in the fog.
Either that or the fog itself had taken a voice. Summer insects clicked
and chattered in the wet grass, and the silences were flooded with
strange low sobbings and stilly whispers. Elof moved on warily. Suddenly he found himself set upon.

Sometimes, belike when you have the cosmic night and the foggy
silences to yourself, it becomes fatal to advertise. Highwaymen
amongst the Minnesota hills are few, to be sure, but down that dingle
lurks the hobo and his kind, and other creatures not so easy to lay your
hands on.

The two strangers had a damned familiar way about themselves.
When Elof realized that these shapes were solid and not figments of fog,
he stopped short with his legs astraddle. He looked first at one and then
at the other; he hunched his shoulders ominously; he raised his hands
and turned his hat completely around once. The two shapes took hold of
his arms at the biceps. Thereupon Elof growled, as beast speaks unto
beast, for the scruff bristles at the tail of the scalp when things accost
one in the dark with their own silence.

The grips on his arms strengthened. Bocak answered by spreading
his hands. He spread them flat with his thumb ends resting lightly
against his thighs. While he peered into the eyes of these alien shapes,
thunderstruck, his churning wits plunged back and down into the murky
lore of his people.

Werewolves loped over Kalevala's moors, indeed, in Finland. His
own grandfather, with a long and lucky shot, had brought down a thing in

the vale of Woinemoinen. The thing his grandfather slew left black blood and drowned itself in running water before it could be captured. In the morning they dragged the naked body of a handsome farm girl from the stream, a human being with a bullet through her breast. No one doubted that this girl was a werewolf. Elof's grandfather swore he had shot a hairy thing running on all fours. The fact that the girl was pregnant had nothing to do with it.

But the shadows which had taken the Bocak prisoner were standing erect. It was difficult to see one's own feet in this fog; nevertheless Elof perceived the things were not wolves. True, they might be vested with a hide of short black hair, and he could truly see the gleam of a pointed tooth, but they were never wolves. Then he saw, indeed, that each freaked a short, broad tail like that of the fallow deer, but shorter. The things had tails that flicked and frolicked in the fog in a rhythmic dance of their own. When Elof saw the tails frisking, he howled like a wild dog that has newly discovered the moon.

They heard him howl down there in Colander's ribald kitchen. They laughed in their rural way and they drank high, tumbling flat-footed jokes across the Colander board.

"Ha!" said John Colander. "Himself has run into himself in the fog!"

A brief, terrible conflict began at the edge of the slough. A savage conflict in spite of the fact that it was one-sided from the first. Confronted with sinews like his own, Elof turned literally berserk. He methodically set about tearing the fog to shreds. A suddenly born army of shapes in the fog nibbled mischievously at his flanks. He lifted a young poplar out of the ground and whirled with it, snapping the tree short to wield it like a club. The ball of earth at its roots described a meteoric arc over his head, showered sand on the streaming grass. It thumped on something with the sound a football makes when it hits one's stomach. Armor might have cracked under that mace. Elof's legs became entangled in solid shadow, which he seized forthwith. This mass he lifted on high; he sent it rioting round and round his head in endless, giddy revolutions while he twisted off a troublesome skein of fog that had clutched his windpipe.

"Elof! Elof!" The thing barked softly at him with a sound like palms clapping. "Elof! Elof! Oh, Elof!" it whimpered.

Elof didn't hear it. He brought the soaring, twisting shape to earth with a crash of finality.

He planned to dispatch the first shape in like manner, but when he searched for it on the ground on hands and knees it had vanished. Continuing his search, at the same time getting earth stains on his fresh trousers, he came to the conclusion that the shape he had just felled had managed to absent itself from his ken also. Wherewith he assumed his feet, marvelously unsteady. With the easy transit of intoxication from one mood to another, once more he conjured up thoughts of the O'Mecca and this night's mission. As victor, he could not determine just whom he had beaten. He saw mocking lights in the distance and stumbled through the slough toward the O'Mecca farm.

The history of events leading up to those of this foggy night was of a singular order. Three farms, the Bocak's, the Colander's, and the O'Mecca's, lay in a direct line southwest of Mankato in the Minnesota hills. Two Fridays preceding this, Elof had rested on his plow at dusk. He narrowly considered the fact that he lacked a wife. The old fogies having gone their way, he had a rich farm of his own with a red, hip-roofed barn filled with cattle. Elof's brother Frankel, in reality the elder son, had forfeited his birthright two years past. This deed Frankel executed easily by capping a wheatstack, tobogganing down its golden side and spitting himself on seventeen inches of pitchfork. Careful farmers stand the fork up against the stack to keep the tines from rusting. Two years Elof and his sister Edna had turned the earth, sowed and harvested alone. Intolerably alone with Edna—that valkyrie of a woman was dumb. The Bocak house was silent. Elof had abandoned the plow, tossing the reins to Edna, and stamped across the furrows to the kitchen of John Colander. Was not that the shortest way to the O'Mecca?

"Ho, John, I am in need of a wife," said Elof.

"Then sit you down and eat," said John, his mouth crammed with bread and potatoes. "A woman can always wait until afterwards."

The Colanders were pillaging their evening board—John himself, his slaved rag of a wife that he was plowing into the ground to join the first one, and his two stalwart sons. Elof set to with no delay. He sacked his frame tight with fried potatoes drowned in sorghum, three tender chops from the carcass of a freshly slaughtered pig, and fat pie made from the pregnant purple berry that grows on the hillsides. Colander tossed his knife and fork into his plate.

"Kate O'Mecca has no kin but her old mother," said John, "and this year she plows but one field. Her cattle are dry, her land chokes with weeds. The O'Mecca man is dead."

HOWARD
WANDREI

It was Severin O'Mecca whom John spoke of—Kate's brother. Elof had known him well, had matched speed and strength with him hoeing down the long rows of young corn. The O'Mecca windmill was old, and Severin had set about repairing it. It was in the spring. Severin had disconnected the shaft of the windmill from the pump and climbed the tower to repair the vanes. From that height he had fallen; the metal shaft pierced his stomach, spitted him down to the lock nut on the pump before he could stop himself. Kate and her husk of a mother could never hope to till the broad O'Mecca acres alone.

"We are ripe for each other," said Elof, tremendously pleased within himself. It was the wife he wanted. The Colander had named the one who walked in the distance like thistledown, with her fleet grace and yellow hair. Elof cultivated a hill that rose against the Colander's northwest acreage. Twice it had been seeded in clover, and not long since he had plowed the hill in for wheat. Elof never grudged the time required to plow-in that stony hill, for it had a far view of the O'Mecca farm and the road she used. It had a nearer view of the brook that fed the slough, where Kate bathed like a blonde angel in the sight of God. She bathed at the exact start of dawn. Elof wondered what the red stains were which she washed from her naked body. "When I am an old fogy," said Elof to the Colander, "I must have sons like yours after the plow."

"She will never refuse you," said the Colander, eyeing his neighbor up and down with a show of envy. "You will sell me some of your land. . . and I will let some of mine so that all your fields, yours and Kate's, will lie together."

They clapped each other on the back, as though by the turn of a phrase the marriage had been consummated. They drank clear corn liquor that was three summers old. When Elof traversed the O'Mecca farmyard an hour later he found it difficult not to trample on the flight of bats that skirmished next to the ground around the weather-torn farmhouse. Leather shadows flirting next to the ground. A phenomenon to consider well, whether one is drunk or sober.

Kate and her mother, a hawk-eyed wisp who reminded one of a cornstalk with her twist of scant dry hair, received him with considerable but guarded interest.

"The bats are aground tonight," said Elof, grinning. "In Finland, then, the werewolves are running. It is the sign." Kate and her mother nodded. They looked at each other, making some sign with their eyes. They did not speak. With this introduction Elof went on easily into the talk of earth and cattle. For forty minutes Elof spoke confidently and with that specious eloquence furnished by corn. There is a rural method of making a point sidewise. By treading on its skirts, by firing a word or two nigh it but not at it, by speaking of himself in terms of someone else, Elof gave the mummied ancient and the corn-maiden to understand precisely what he wanted. It was the courtship oblique. He departed with the sole reason for his call not once mentioned, yet stated in classic restraint with unmistakable clarity.

Outside the rotting farmhouse the eccentric shadows still moved in darts and flurries over the ground. The sidelong statement of his argument for Kate's hand had gone far toward untangling Elof's wits. A cool hand played across his shoulders. His skin roughened. Untilled, the O'Mecca farm was yielding a fine harvest of burdock and rank grass which had become speedily populated with mice. There was a kind of squeaking, quasi-cannibalism going on here. The bats flew next to the ground at their nocturnal feasting. It was time indeed that the sinews of the Bocak furrowed this wretched crop into the ground. So he delivered a lordly, proprietary kick at the leather wings that frisked in the moonlight. Very likely he sundered a shadow or two.

Next Friday, Elof had perched on the high stone steps of his woodshed and fretted with impatience. The engine he balanced on one extended forefinger was the rifle he had been shooting rats with. It was a heavy repeating weapon which he wielded with terrible efficiency. The last clean shot, indeed, had not only parted the rat's vital thread, it had ricocheted off the boulder supporting the corn crib and, save for a negligible string of feathered hide, decapitated a prize black Minorca. The cock still sprang into the air in its bewildered, mortal dance; Elof continued to sit on the stoop of the woodshed, bent on solving the casuistries of courtship. His elbows rested on a blurred crease in his trouser legs. A crease, nevertheless. He was freshened for the chase, against his will. Clean trousers—the distant smell of raw gasoline was still among them. A black cloud of hair on his bared forearms, the reward of wonderful toil with boiled yellow soap. Edna looked up at him regularly from the doorway of the summerhouse as she whisked the handle of the separator. She was a kind of female clockwork. She knew well enough what ailed him. She was a woman.

Through the woods beyond Bocak's stock yard came sounds from the busy kitchen of the Colander. The two farmhouses were only the long cast of a stone separated. The voices of field men who had toiled and were now in their cups—the sounds stormed Bocak's simple imagination with illimitable promise. He thought of his neat, clean, cold bed of down, cursed once in Finnish. The rhythmically rising and falling whine of the separator was intolerable. He stood the gun in a corner. He made off for the Colander kitchen with Edna, the dumb one, standing in the doorway looking after him. She would stand there with her eyes on nothing for a time. Edna dreamed. Edna, having no tongue, held converse with nature alone, and knew hidden things by one of those common caprices of providence. She knew, for example, that Kate O'Mecca would never sleep in her brother's bed. She herself could not say how she knew this. Presently she would make a slow shrug, lug the can of cream into the cool depths of the root cellar. The cream was uncommonly heavy this year.

Colander and his men welcomed Elof with a tumbler brimming with the clear fire of the corn. Afterward, when the Bocak mounted the lane that lifted over the east pasture, he was well fortified against the hell's-play of low-flying bats that came half-way down to meet him. Bats earthbound, perilous to walk among. It had been his sober intention to give the O'Mecca two full weeks of grace. If this was haste, the guilt would lie with John Colander and his corn whisky in the morning. They had made him drunk. Well, one week was sufficient. Now that his wits had been given a stiff prodding, he knew that he would have hung fire only one week anyhow. Was he not his father's son, and was he not master of his father's acres? Having addressed himself at length and aloud, Elof swore that he was. He swooped low with a hand outspread like a flail and whooped as he sent the bat-like shadows tumbling. Bats. He thought again of the werewolves of Finland, whose appearance must be announced by these grounded bats. Werewolves and vampire-wolves. Last week a young man was buried, a handsome boy who had his throat torn open one night by a wild dog. It was an odd thing that no blood was found on the ground. The dog must have been a ranger, since all known dogs in the community were chained at night. The bats flicked somberly among Elof's feet like Satan's own hellish skirts as he traversed the O'Mecca farmyard and clubbed his knuckles on the door. It was a moderate sound, comparatively. There was elephantine elegance in his love.

If Kate and her mother had received him with guarded interest on one occasion, on this it was a covert eagerness before which he stood abashed, even with his head spinning at this pace. Elof sat his frame amongst Kate's fine cushions with immense precision; the two women rested delicately before him on straight walnut chairs, their heads cocked at precisely the same angle. There was something gracefully winglike in their white hands as they folded them in their laps. These were no ordinary farm women. They did not look as though they toiled. On this second visit Elof dared to look upon his woman directly. It was a thirsty appraisal, as though he would take her down at one draught. Elof scarcely knew whether he were safe to have her within reach of his hands. He could stand his team on the hill and covet her puff of yellow hair at a distance of a hundred rods, with no immediate consequences.

Kate was a smooth white filly with narrow hips like a panther, like a woman who had never labored and never would. Elof frowned somewhat at that. She was as slender as a city woman. But he remembered that his own mother had such hips. Her three children had come easily and unharmed save for Edna, whose voice, when it sounded at all, had a unique kinship with the owl's. The tiny nipples of Kate's breasts stood up through the fine woolen cloth of her dress. That was a good sign. She knew well enough what he was after. The O'Mecca had sidelong, subtle gray eyes that forced one into speech.

"John Colander," said Elof, "has land against mine which he will bargain for with me."

The O'Mecca smiled, whether with amusement or agreement he could not determine. But it was a neat, correct speech, compact and well phrased. When you considered it, you knew there was a plan afoot to stagger the acres of the three farms. This plan could be realized best by marriage. You knew that John Colander was going to slip to the southwest over O'Mecca ground and get somewhat the better of the bargain in the end. You knew that Kate O'Mecca was going to sidle back around him so that her land would meet that of the Bocak's.

The third Friday came with the fog. It was presupposed by those testing the wind that it was to be a courtship in three tries. On the third Friday Edna trimmed Elof's duster of black hair with the long, sharp shears in her sewing kit. Edna wanted to say to Elof, "You want Kate O'Mecca's long white body in your bed. Much good may it do you." She wanted to say, "Where is Kate tonight? Do you think a woman like that rests in her parlor after nightfall? Have you never looked into those long gray eyes of hers?" She wanted to tell Elof that marrying Kate was fatal, but Edna was dumb.

The fertile black soil of the fields that had stained Elof's nails a full summer disappeared under the carving knife, after prodigious scraping. Edna watched the futile toil with a curious smile. When the door closed after Elof, Edna made her singular slow shrug again, but her face was uneasy.

When Elof announced to the assembly of farmers in John Colander's kitchen that he was inquiring after the O'Mecca's hand tonight, his ears rattled and his back ached with their approval. In two weeks' time! They had to drink to this Finn who could not contain himself. They had to drink to his lucky woman, too. And they drank again. They envied him in the only way they knew about. By saturating him with liquor, and themselves with him, they conferred their own kind of regard on him. Corn whisky flowed like a treacherous brook. They poured it into Elof's gullet up to his throat level.

Elof sat in their midst with the thick glaze stealing into his eyes. He was not joking this night, nor smiling at the jokes of others. Nor would he ever do so afterward. He was thinking of Kate's straight, pale yellow hair that rested in a knot on her shoulder. It was the hair that should flood across his pillow at night like sunlight. He thought of her high breasts and the sound color in her cheeks, her scarlet mouth. She looked strong. Their children would be the sturdiest that ever sat on a peg stool to take a lesson in milking. He would show them how to knuckle the udder, the knack that shot milk into the pail so that it filled with foam. Yet neither of the O'Mecca women had every spoken a word to him. Like Edna, the dumb one. Elof thought of that, but never thought it was singular. Well, then, he had never asked a question that needed to be answered. Tonight was the third Friday and the night of troth. He would ask his question and take his answer at last. Yet here he stalled in the Colander kitchen while the corn went round in uproarious draughts. A stronger thirst brought him to his feet. Elof used a particular Finnish curse and shouldered his way through the door into the creeping festoons of fog. Two shapes on the hill looked down at him, and then looked at each other.

The most tremendous fog within memory was on him, the thickest that had ever moved over the land. He mopped his narrow forehead with a yard of red kerchief when he reached the hill's base. They had saluted his queer hat with a full glass of whisky back there. It stank. He took the round, sopping skim of felt from his head and crushed it in one hand. The night was against him. All the way up the lane he quarreled with his feet.

Farther on, shadows set upon him, and though Colander's whisky had nearly mastered him he defeated those scavenging shadows with certainty and dispatch. In his drunkenness the Minnesota hills and the Finnish moors were one. He thought the bats had grounded and the wolves were abroad. He thought they had tried to take advantage of him, and that he, in the full lustihead of his prowess, had torn a forepaw from one of them. It may have been a dream. The fog was magically embodying itself; when he tripped in it he purposefully dismembered it as though he were matched against human antagonists. It was impossible for him to distinguish between the true and the false. His wits felt heavy as a grindstone, a stone that was shooting off sparks in all directions as he bore down heavily on it. Bore down on it with *something*. What was it? He shook his head. He had done something important on the hill, something to tell Kate about. Someone on the hill had called him by name. He could hear the thin echoes mocking him. Elof. Elof!

He thrashed through the slough with a million muck-demons sucking and snapping after his heels, and raised the O'Mecca farmhouse, vaguely and gingerly patting himself as though he had been beaten on the way or had forgotten something. It was probably the thing he was bringing to bear against the metaphorical grindstone. There was a thing in his pocket. The lights in the O'Mecca parlor still welcomed him dimly in the fog, thought it was past twelve, just past twelve by the clock. Love waits on time when it goes spinning in drink.

It was that *thing* he had picked up on the way, the trophy that would prove his prowess and his fearlessness to Kate O'Mecca. Had not two werewolves leaped on him and been defeated? That was it. For he was not in the least damaged by his encounter at the edge of the slough. He had neither scratch nor bruise, nothing but the fresh earth stains on his knees, a spattering of muck from the slough. Something pressed against his thigh in the pocket that confined his handkerchief. When he brought his knuckles down on the door he was remembering what it was. He had fought with a pair of werewolves across the slough. That was it.

Kate was looking down at him long before he knew she was there. Drunken and bewildered, the Bocak had taken a terrible object from his pocket and was glaring at it. It was the prize he had won in the epic battle at the hill-bottom. When the fog in the slough turned solid, an erect beast with a frisking tail had tried to throttle him. He had twisted off its offending claw as he would behead a chicken—by whipping its body around his head like a limp club. Without giving it much thought, as is the way with mighty men, he had deposited the claw in his pocket for safe-keeping along with his kerchief. At the time, he had been vaguely aware that it was a fairly large claw as claws go, one with a stiff scrub of black hair and short toes mounted with panther-like nails. He remembered that the claw was singularly naked between the toes. But now, as he stupidly regarded it with supreme and swiftly mounting horror, he saw that it was a claw no longer. It was smooth and slim and white, a human hand. It was, in fact, Kate O'Mecca's hand—he had plucked the O'Mecca's hand out of the fog.

Kate stood in the doorway. Her arm was outstretched toward the hand, a graceful, perfect arm that ended at the wrist. Her scarlet mouth was fixed in a smile. Elof knew now why neither Kate nor her mother had ever spoken to him. It was because they were afraid of showing their teeth. Kate's teeth were pointed like slim, curved ivory needles. Only the two dainty front incisors met squarely. The gums were not the moist pink color of a human being's. They were scarlet, the glistening jeweled red of the wolf's. And though he could not see it, he knew she had a long shiny red tongue like a ribbon. He knew it now. Kate O'Mecca was a werewolf. He had killed her mother and Kate had drowned the skinny carcass in the slough. Elof stepped back, dropping the hand on the ground. Kate's long, sleepy eyes slanted into Elof's with an expression of profound scorn and pity, as though she were imparting secret knowledge. He was hearing her cool, husky voice for the first time:

"Then you have asked-," she began. It was a lie. The night, the fog, and the corn whisky had played a ghoulish prank on him. It never happened. Yet Kate O'Mecca once had two hands like anyone else, for he had seen them, when he courted her the last two Fridays. And now her right hand was limp on the ground at his feet.

She was a werewolf.

The werewolf had a voice and spoke to him. It was the same voice that had wept "Elof! Elof!" at the edge of slough, whimpered when he had torn off her hand. The cool, inexorable voice went on to haunt him forever: "Then you have asked for my hand, Elof!" said Kate.

Master-the-Third

COMPLETELY BAFFLED, Lieutenant Stan Rawls fixed his scowling blue eyes on Karen's warmly-fashioned slenderness and exploded, "But something must have happened, Miss Gwynn!"

"Yes," she agreed with the inhuman composure of a hard-boiled egg, "something did. Alan killed himself."

That was as much as he had been able to wring out of her—the naked, single-track admission that wealthy Alan MacCord had committed suicide. There seemed to be no more feeling in Karen, who had kept her stage name after marrying MacCord, than there was in her reflection in the splendid crystal pier glass before which she stood. Rawls expostulated, "But surely you remember where you were that night. You must remember!"

"I'm sorry, but I don't. I really don't."

Rawls swallowed hard on a four-day diet of exasperation. But he couldn't bear down on the girl any harder because he was here at the Mitchell Arms in the swanky MacCord apartment on the scantiest sufferance. Karen's first, because he was exceeding his authority and acting in the capacity of a private citizen. Next, the inspector's, and ordinarily the inspector was not a man given to playing long shots. The MacCord death was listed as suicide, it was suicide beyond the shadow of a doubt; it was such a clear thing, indeed, that there was something indigestibly peculiar about it. There was something in the air. Something crawlingly sinister.

Rawls tried once more, because the MacCords' whereabouts on the fatal night would supply him with the key to this mystery that was nagging him. Apparently shock had ripped all memory of that night's doings out of Karen's mind. "Please, Miss Gwynn: where were you? At a night spot? The theater; with friends somewhere?"

No soap. Karen shrugged her boyish shoulders expressively. "I'm terribly sorry, but I just don't remember where we were. I don't remember!"

Her gray eyes were large and luminous with tears desperately held back. So getting over that hurdle, for the present at least, was an impossibility. This thing had been keeping Rawls cudgeling his stubborn brains for long hours. Muscles bulged in his lean jaws as he camouflaged a yawn.

What he had to get out of this open-and-shut case of suicide was evidence of murder, because there was murder here. Murder just as sure as his nose had never betrayed him. But not a single blasted particular in the dirty crime could be proven false by so much as an eyelash.

Succeeding his father, the suicide had been president of MacCord's, the fashionable old store on Fifth Avenue. His wife, Karen Gwynn, would have gone on to become the most highly paid stripper in burlesque if handsome Alan hadn't persuaded her that he was on the up and up and yanked her out of the business. Nature had given Karen a monopoly on a torso and legs and things. What she did in a blue spotlight that gradually, gradually dimmed was crazy-making.

Long before the blackout, when she postured tantalizingly and toyed with her last ornament in the last blue dimness of the spot, the customers would be running a temperature with their eyes sticking out of their heads. One glimpse of her was enough to plant a permanent ache in Alan MacCord. She nearly killed her manager with anguish when she quit, and married MacCord for his two and a half millions, because he was good looking, because she loved him anyhow.

They had been back only a few weeks following a round the world honeymoon, had established themselves in the most sumptuous suite of the Mitchell Arms, just off the foyer. One dangerous thing about Mac-Cord was the fat worm of jealousy in him. But Karen knew about the green worm gnawing on him and walked on a tight wire. They loved each other; nothing short of earthquake, pestilence or murder could have disrupted that alliance. Not suicide. A hard-headed, healthy young businessman like MacCord would have dug in, identified any snide intriguing with his wife and taken him apart with his bare hands.

"Here," gloomed Rawls to himself, "is a young, healthy guy with barrels of scratch, a wife with a knockout figure, everything to live for, and what does he do?

"He comes home with her from somewhere one night. After a while he looks at the clock and says, 'It's time to do it.' Just like that. So he hikes into the bathroom and comes back with that razor set. It's Tuesday. So he chooses the 'Tuesday' blade from this set of hollow-ground Danish razors, and— Like hell he does!"

But he had. He had lain on the bed, stuck his chin up out of the way, and with one powerful swipe laid his throat open in a silent, bloody, Rabelaisian laugh. He had still held that wicked wedge of steel in cramped fingers when Rawls got there. In recalling that gory horror he shuddered.

"And she looked on while he did it, too. She phoned headquarters right there while he was doing it and didn't try to stop him. And look at her now; no more feeling in her than there is in my great-great-grandmother."

Her composure was in truth eerily tranquil now, with her wide, striking, deepest-gray eyes agleam as though she were hypnotized by something in the immeasurable distance. Thinking of jolting her out of that subtly disturbing trance, he said casually, "Karen, we know that your husband did not commit suicide. Who murdered him?"

Slowly her strange gray eyes found him. In the late afternoon shadows she was a work of art, her hair a fluid sculpture in jet, her whole body a sorcery in marble. Her prolonged, stony quiet sent a trickle of ghostly fingers playing down the detective's spine. She was listening so intently that Rawls listened, too. Her luscious, moist carnelian mouth was slightly opened as though to accept a kiss; her lungs were held inflated, so that the rich, pussy-willow gray crepe of her dress detailed the amazingly firm symmetry of her breasts. Profound despair, and terror, touched her expression momentarily like a breathless trace of breeze fingering still water. *What was she listening to?*

Abruptly, but methodically unhurried, she fitted a piquant, small gray felt hat on her head, picked up her handbag and gloves, and started for the foyer entrance.

Rawls sprang to his feet. "Miss Gwynn!"

Her hand grasped the knob as Rawls thoughtlessly slipped an arm around her supple waist, brushing the resiliency of her breast. He got a sharp whiff of ozone, pungent and stinging, that stopped his breath in his throat. Something hit him. Something like a gigantic fist, slamming him headlong on the thick carpet.

It was the first time he had ever been knocked out, and it was nasty. When Karen closed the door, he hadn't heard it, didn't know how long he had lain unconscious. In thickening twilight he goggled up at the ceiling, breathless. Whatever had hit him, and it was something violent and tremendous, had paralyzed his diaphragm. With an effort that took all his strength he gulped a thimbleful of air, and a convulsion of paralysis squeezed it out of him again in a groan. A band of cold elastic steel seemed to be closing on his skull.

He scrambled to his feet feeling like a dead man, hauled the door open and lurched into the foyer. A uniformed employee bustled across the lobby to him as he closed the door and blinked in the light.

"Something wrong, sir?"

Rawls shook his head. Something was most hellishly wrong, but it was none of this blond college boy's business. He got his next puff of air at the front portals, and after that his wind came back in steadily longer and easier drafts. He could not imagine what had given him that terrible wallop. It was as though the wrath of God had materialized out of thin air, with Rawls on the business end of it.

In a constricted voice he asked the doorman, "Which way did Miss Gwynn go?"

The doorman looked at Rawls' savage blue eyes, then craned his neck and indicated a yellow hack dawdling in traffic. The hack was waiting for the change of lights to make a horseshoe turn. Rawls nodded; there was another hack prowling along the curb, the hackman eyeing him expectantly; Rawls took it, whipping the door shut when he got inside. His breathing apparatus had just about returned to normal. "Make a U turn after that hack," he directed. "Don't lose it and don't get too close."

"No dice," the driver regretted, "unless it's police business."

Rawls fished something from his pocket; the driver cocked an eye at the bright gleam of a shield in the rear-vision mirror and got going as the lights changed.

The hack in which Karen was riding proceeded up Fifth Avenue to Fourteenth Street at average speed, turned west, eventually hit down to swing into one-way Horatio Street from behind. With a name like Horatio the street could be practically anything, and for most of its short length it was: A commingling of modern apartment house, labyrinthine tenement, warehouse, stable, el, pavement gone scummy with silken mist now falling, and shelving sidewalks interrupted with slanting, cobbled driveways to make the footing treacherous. The light was niggardly and there were smells.

It was not a new street to Rawls, but like any other street it was a street on which anything could happen. Murder, suicide, daylight hijacking at the warehouses, crimes of passion, burglary, highway robbery, and just about anything else except barratry within Rawls' own experience made this street, like any other street, something to think about from end to end.

Hereupon Rawls' heart gave a bound. For as he squinted through the side window he saw a phantom horse sticking its head out of a third-story window. Then he grunted, for the thing was just a stable's wooden figurehead, painted a scabrous white and nailed to the bricks high up. Karen's hack closed in to the curb in front of a three-story warehouse which had been converted into an apartment building.

She paid off her driver from the inside and quit the cab without once bothering to see whether she was being followed.

As his hack drifted by, Rawls saw her standing in the tiled vestibule, in the act of pressing a bell with a gloved forefinger. He waited; at length took his turn in the vestibule to obtain the name in the slot over the bell. The name, "Wiley Lamphier," meant precisely nothing at the moment. Rawls returned to the hack and gave instructions.

"Park in front of the entry," he directed, "and wait. If you get a fare from that house, tell 'em you're waiting but you guess you'll take a chance, then come back here after the haul and report to me in that store if you don't see me around."

"Okay with me." The driver was agreeable.

An El train went by with a roar like an avalanche of scrap-iron. Rawls hiked down the street, into a small grocery store where he enclosed himself in the single booth and called headquarters.

"Lieutenant Rawls," he reported. "A guy named Wiley Lamphier,"— he spelled it—"in connection with the MacCord business. What about him?" He gave the number listed on the store phone. Sitting there in the booth on a little seat the size of his thumb, he smoked cigarettes with the door open while he waited. And he thought, and he couldn't think of anything save that, although he had smelled ozone, the shock he had received was not electrical. From head to foot, in front, he would have bruises tomorrow. The telephone rang; he shut the folding door and lifted the receiver.

"Rawls?" It was the inspector himself. "Okay. That's Dr. Wiley Lamphier. He's Master-the-Third of the Great White Lodge of the Himalayas, if that means anything to you."

Some kind of monastery, Rawls guessed. He said, "Shoot."

"We've got a cable in the files from Scotland Yard, and that's what it says. Reports him as Lamphier, M.D., Ph.D., M.A., K.C.A., D.P.M., Ch.B., F.R.G.S., F.R.S.M."

"Sounds like a brainy guy."

"He's been married twice, and both wives committed suicide. A lot of his friends have committed suicide. One of them is known to have willed everything to this doctor. There is nothing questionable about any of the suicides; all of them have been thoroughly investigated."

"Now we're getting somewhere. Anything else?"

"There's some stuff in a clipping here. Says this Lamphier is an Englishman, the only European ever admitted to the Lodge; 'The Great White Lodge is believed to be a survival of a great university in Atlantis.'" Rawls grunted. "Ever since he turned up, Lamphier has been on the move. Showed up in Stockholm first; three suicides there, some money unaccounted for. He went down to Mexico City, backtracked to Paris, where this count he had just met blew his brains out and left Lamphier a few barrels of francs. He got married in Dublin and his wife drowned herself in a bathtub. After he collected all the potatoes, he went to London and got married again. She jumped out a window, and he had an alibi you couldn't split with an ax. Happy landings, Lieutenant."

Motive, money. Rawls left the store and his breath fumed in the mist. The hack was still parked where he had left it. The address of the building's owner, which he had noticed framed in glass in the vestibule, had been given on Jane Street. Rawls tramped down there under the El. It was quite dark now, and lousy damp.

The owner was a pleasant, plump little man. After a look at Rawls' credentials he removed his after-dinner pipe from his teeth and asked, "What can I do for you?"

"I want the keys for that house," Rawls requested, adding confidentially, "there's a cat burglar working this district. Any skylights in the house?"

"Why, yes. A Mr. Lamphier has leased the studio; that's the whole top floor."

"How about the roof? Could a man, say about my size, prowl across the roof without being heard by anyone inside?"

"Well, that building used to be a warehouse, and the roof is supported by steel I-beams. It would be just like walking on Fifth Avenue asphalt."

The night was getting inky by the time Rawls reached Horatio again with the keys. The hack driver was still there, burning his second or third cigarette in the gloom.

Without giving him a glance Rawls opened the vestibule door, went through the lower hall into the garden. In the soupy blackness out there he located the fire-escape with a lipstick-size flashlight which he wore in his key-case. No acrobatics required; an iron ladder ran down to the ground. He went aloft with athletic silence. A closed third-floor window was lighted but curtained and another passing train found him making the roof and slipping over the parapet.

As the owner had said, walking on the roof was like walking on soft, creak-proof and sound-absorbing asphalt pavement. Nevertheless, Rawls kept off his heels and drifted to a tremendous lighted skylight with the stealth of a breeze. His knees kissed the curbing of the sky-light; he bent over.

More than forty feet long and the full width of the building, the studio below him was sumptuously furnished with thick, overlapping oriental rugs loomed in smouldering colors; a great lounge in soft white leather hugged the wall on his right; other furniture, much of it in that same opulent leather, made a prince's chamber of the studio.

Karen Gwynn stood before the white studio lounge in an attitude of resignation, head tilted up. What Rawls saw then was difficult to believe. While she stood there as though fashioned in the quiet of marble, her slate-gray outfit slipped piecemeal from her. She did not disrobe herself. Her dress simply rippled to the floor of itself, like woven liquid flowing from her. Her tailored satin slip followed. Rawls' jaw almost hit the skylight.

In the alluring gossamer of her panties, sheer hose and high-heeled slippers she was a miracle to behold. With her gorgeous breasts, the enchantment of her torso, her long legs and all of her, she was a dream that a proper man would never want to wake from. This was not nature, it was witchcraft. Rawls swallowed, nearly groaned; he was a goner; like MacCord and Lamphier, he in turn fell for that peerless beauty, had to have it whether it was fatal or not.

Then he glimpsed the partial reflection of Wiley Lamphier in a great pier glass and ducked back. Without knowing whether he had been seen or not, he was irresistibly tempted to crane forward again. If this was not sorcery below, it was the most baffling stage stuff he had ever witnessed. For with lazy, dreadful languour, like a body drowned deep in mingling currents, Karen's body floated to the massive white lounge and lay upon it. Invisibly, it was borne there. Teleportation . . . Her lips were moistly parted as though to receive a kiss and the twin treasures of her breasts, each of just the prominence to brim a man's cupped hand, were lifted as though to be kissed in turn.

Paralyzed with fascination, Rawls gandered until his nose brushed the glass of the skylight. His dry lips burned, and he gargled inaudibly. For as surely as he was not a Chinaman the girl was being kissed. She was alone, but . . . The weight of some damned thing was on the sensuous leather surface of the lounge with her. Some invisible agency gently parted her satiny thighs. Bracing herself with her arms flat and fingers fanned out on the leather, she arched her body upward and writhed with her hips clear of the lounge.

Rawls' lips moved. What he watched was astounding, a rapturous pantomime more tantalizing than any given ton of strip routines on the stage. It was as though an incubus were . . . It did things to Rawls; the rhythmic, sinuous dance developed, culminated in a series of straining upward lunges. For a long moment she postured rigidly, save for the deep, impassioned abdominal breathing; then it left her, whatever it was that had been tormenting her, and she fell back in complete exhaustion. Her lips trembled; her head rolled to the side.

Rawls waited, but she lay as though dead. Straightening up to let his fever cool off, he ghosted to one of the smaller skylights, looked down into a princely, unoccupied bedroom. The other skylight gave him a view of a kind of anteroom or foyer somberly draped in black, with a thick black broadloom covering the floor. Lamphier was just quitting the small room. Rawls hastened back to the studio skylight, where he was amazed to see Karen departing with Lamphier, both being fully dressed. The doctor carried a slender cane. The dispatch, Rawls philosophized, with which a woman can disrobe and dress again was one more miracle.

On soundless feet he skimmed to the front parapet of the house, looked down, and told himself that the whole thing was a crazy nightmare. They couldn't have reached the street so fast, but already Lamphier was helping Karen into the hack.

Anything that Rawls couldn't understand put him into a dire humor, besides giving him insomnia. Festering in his brain was the suspicion that someone was making a monkey out of him. Lamphier. Rawls abominated practical jokes, like the sorcery of Karen's exhibition on the lounge. Smouldering with mixed passions, he descended the fire-escape. Inside the house, he sped up to Lamphier's door, opened it and entered without compunction.

This was off the record, without warrant, so he had to hurry. A biting whiff of ozone stalled him temporarily in the anteroom. He growled with impatience.

His glance fell on a solid ebony desk standing out from the wall on the left of the small room. On the desk stood a three-gallon, cylindrical hood of black glass, an object which might be used to protect a microscope from dust.

Gingerly he snared and lifted the fragile shell; after a while, as he stared, his flesh crawled.

It was no microscope. It was a hollow cylinder, a container, of carved brownish-lavender quartz. Aside from the hieroglyphs, or ideographs, the strange object was fashioned with such mathematical nicety that no line could be discerned anywhere the cap joined the body of the container. The ideographs girdled the cylindrical jar in parallel bands spaced regularly from top to bottom. Thirteen of them.

Each girdle consisted of units done in masterly, wonderful detail. Rawls' scrutiny skipped from the delicately-conceived relief of a multiple-breasted woman—normal human breasts with another pair placed directly below, and below them two pairs of vestigial pectoral markings—to that of a man whose arms two serpents had swallowed to the shoulders.

Next to this glyph was a youth holding a massive length of chain with his arms stretched high over his head, about to cast it; probably an athlete making his try in some ancient and forgotten game. One, the majestic figure of a king wearing a high, elaborate crown. In all, perhaps three hundred individual carvings.

The crystal vessel was filled with liquid to absolute capacity, leaving not even the most minute air-bubble. And in this liquid was suspended an eye—a human eye which had been removed from its owner with surgical exactitude—with the nerve and delicate, emptied blood vessels hanging from it in worming threads of translucence. The iris was a ring of startling, hard, deep green. Live jade expanding and contracting under Rawls' horrified gaze.

From somewhere the eye caught light which it condensed into a brilliant blue-white beam piercing the crystal jar with the solidity of a fine long needle. A strong reek of ozone spilled from the black glass hood. This was no common laboratory specimen.

In perfect suspension, the eye turned indefatigably with a ceaseless, slow, repulsive motion as though scanning the narrow confines of its prison for a means of escape. Rawls extended his hand, but before they reached the crystal, his fingertips stung violently as though they had been dipped in concentrated acid. The shock made his heart pound with hammer blows. Breathing hard and covered with gooseflesh he replaced the hood.

In the bedroom he found a promising piece of furniture. The two top drawers of a high burled-elm chest were false, the fronts opening down to make a desk with cubbyholes crammed with papers. He bent over . . .

There had been no sound. A slim, naked arm crooked around his throat and cut off his wind, and a knee was rammed into his back. Rawls was compactly muscular and an intelligent scrapper, but he had been surprised with violence from behind.

Momentarily he broke free by lunging to his knees and hurling his assailant over his head. It was a girl, barefoot, and she came back like a tigress. Her sole outer garment was a form-moulding dress in a coarse brown material. Her skin was tawny, her features Mongoloid; in a feline, savage way she was comely. Very.

Neither of them made any attempt at conversation. Smiling, she had ripped into him and for a moment they were locked together. Her breasts, firmly ripe, were flattened hard against his chest. Repeatedly she tried to smash a knee into his groin, but he had snaked his arms around her and welded their torsoes together, breast and hip. She was disconcertingly strong.

It took all Rawls' strength, but gradually he bent her backward to a point where she had to fall if she didn't want a broken back. What he expected to do was fall on her and beat it from the apartment while her wind was knocked out.

As he tried to throw her, a blinding pain stabbed through his shoulder. He felt the shock of it in his heels, cursed agonizedly and let go. She didn't. Her sharp white teeth pierced through flesh and muscle, grated on bone.

Rawls delivered a short, explosive jab toward her solar plexus but she wasn't there any more. Staggered by pain, he reached out with a powerful snaking right, but she was turning with the blow. His fingers hooked the neck of her dress and ripped it down to the waist, abruptly baring the trembling golden roundness of one breast. At the same time she kicked out with lithe vitality and caught him squarely in the groin with her bare heel.

Rawls whooped with agony and doubled over, completely out of commission. It was the sickening kind of hurt that robs a man of all defense. White-faced, with the worst of it over, he was the silent, tawny girl's prisoner. His hands were twisted behind his back in a curious, baffling finger grip. The girl was breathing hard. Rawls measured his changes, got ready to free himself with a violent wrench. Whereupon he was subjected to torture that just about tore his heart out.

Her slim, steely fingers worked and she systematically dislocated two fingers of his left hand, kept grinding the bones together until he fell in a half faint to his knees. Even then she didn't relax that maiming, inescapable grip.

"You see, you can't escape," she remarked in fluid, meticulous English. "Do not try again."

"Rawls, Rawls, you fool!" he groaned. It wasn't so much the fact that he was caught in a plain case of trespassing as it was that he had underestimated his slender opponent. Fatal error.

The girl gave him the knee from behind, directing him through the apartment to the somber foyer. In a modernistic black-leather lounge, opposite the desk where the sardonic Lamphier sat, Karen reclined broodingly. Eyes dizzy with pain, Rawls looked from her to the hypnotist.

"Good evening." Lamphier's voice was clipped. "How did you like tonight's performance from the angle you had through the skylight?"

So the doctor had left the house deliberately to lure Rawls inside. Lamphier was one of those sinewy Englishmen who look overly lean in build, but who apparently eat a couple of Mexicans for breakfast regularly. His face was tanned and tough, immobile as the shell of a walnut, he wore his tweeds with casual elegance, and Rawls didn't like the tool-steel gleam in his narrowed eyes.

Advancing, Lamphier frisked him expertly, sneered when he found the badge; to show what he thought of American detectives, he slashed Rawls across the face with an open hand, the fingers of which felt like whip handles. Rawls shook his head with helpless fury and tasted blood in his mouth. His face was numb.

"Tell this—" he choked, indicated the tawny girl close behind him, "to let go of my hands, will you? I think she's broken a couple of my fingers."

Lamphier shrugged, smiling. "Let go, Lilitha."

Releasing Rawls she stepped back, casually drew her dress up again to cover the ripe, golden breast. Rawls eyed his twisted left hand, gritted his teeth, jerked and returned the dislocated fingers to their sockets. "Go head," he said bitterly. "Call headquarters and turn me in. You can get me discharged."

Behind the desk Lamphier clipped, "It was stupid of you to leave your fingerprints on this glass dome."

Rawls longingly eyed the point of Lamphier's jaw.

"Because now I know you were looking at—this."

"Sure, I was looking at it. What about it?"

"Curiosity is sometimes fatal, as in this case."

"What do I do?" Rawls asked sarcastically. "Get hypnotized and walk into the Hudson?"

"Something similar," Lamphier promised. "But wouldn't you prefer a method more original than MacCord's?"

The man was in deadly earnest. Deliberately baiting him, Rawls indicated the carved crystal vessel and asked, "Just what is that damned thing?"

After staring fixedly at Rawls for an interval, Lamphier said slowly, "It is the oldest living thing. The eye, as I am sure you observed, is alive." A kind of ghoulish relish entered his tone. "The Masters of the Great White Lodge say that it is, and I believe that it is, the right eye of Uranus."

The thin, diamond-bright beam of light from the obscenely restless eye glanced ceaselessly about the room.

"Uranus," Lamphier elucidated, as to a backward child, "was the first king of Atlantis. He hated Gaea's children and was dethroned by his own son, Kronos. That's Greek mythology, which is a garbled history of Atlantis, passed down from father to son after Atlantis went to the bottom of the sea by the surviving Atlantides who sailed through the Mediterranean and colonized Greece."

In its unending motion the beam of the eye reached Karen, lingered over her. Stiffening, she drew her breath in sharply. Whether it was her cringing or not, Rawls saw her skirt curl back from her knees, exposing morsels of her fever-kindling thighs. The beam flickered there, resting on the naked thick of her thigh in a fluid drop of brilliance.

Rawls was getting restless under Lamphier's merciless, metallic stare and decided on ridicule. He snapped, "Gibberish!"

Lamphier responded with the soft, fluid syllables of a language unknown to Rawls, and Rawls looked down at his feet with a grunt of surprise. Something had taken hold of his shoelaces and untied them with a jerk.

Lamphier chuckled; Rawls glared at him and commented, "That was cute. I've been wondering about that stink of ozone. You've got a big electromagnet in here somewhere; you pull a switch and the magnet gets the metal tips of my shoe-laces."

"Ozone from a magnet? My dear lieutenant!" Lamphier scoffed. "Could a magnet knock you down the way you were knocked down at the Mitchell Arms? Come, come! Can a magnet do this?"

Something happened at Rawls' ankles; the shoelaces were tied again. He didn't look down, but forced himself to look back at Lamphier and compliment, "Pretty good."

Because Lamphier was mad, with the colossal vanity of a madman; Rawls was at his mercy, and the only thing he could do was play for time. Some intervention had to occur, before Lamphier got tired of him just as a cat tires of playing with a mouse and delivers the *coup de grace.*

"Very good indeed," he admitted with a rigid grin. "How do you work it?"

"It will do no harm to tell you," Lamphier considered, gloating. "The language of Atlantis, to learn which I went to the Great White Lodge of the Himalayas, was ideographic. The ideographs carved on this crystal vessel are Atlantic. Each ideograph symbolizes an idea or conception which can be put into effect. The expression of such a symbol in syllables, in Atlantic, awakens the sleeping titans, as it were." Sardonically, "Do you follow me, lieutenant?"

Rawls squinted, hoping to high heaven that the inspector might have worked up a curiosity and started hunting for him. He regretted politely, "Sorry, doctor, but you're ahead of me."

"The scientists of Atlantis solved the mystery, the principle, of the human will and isolated it in their laboratories. This force occurs in diffused form in cosmic rays."

"Something in the air, eh?"

"Indeed. This force or agency, stepped up billions of times just as electricity can be stepped up, is generated and stored in this crystal container. The force is actuated by the various sound combinations symbolized in these bands of ideographs."

A sort of glorified Aladdin's lamp, was it? A titanic force controlled not by levers and switches but by certain sequences of sound vibrations in a forgotten tongue. The chemical composition of the liquid in which the eye was suspended was the real secret, of course. However the diabolical contraption worked, Rawls was going to take care of it while there was still time. Just a matter of snaking his gun out. Just one bullet socked through the belly of that cylinder would shatter it, spill the liquid it contained, and kill that damned gandering green eye at last.

Even as the determination occurred to him, Lamphier spoke again almost inaudibly in the eerie, dulcet language of the Atlantides. Rawls didn't move, because he couldn't. He couldn't even clench his fists. The eye had turned abruptly when Lamphier spoke and Rawls was transfixed by the blinding thread of light originating from it. Lamphier had anticipated him; now it was too late.

Rawls' eyes bulged with the effort to move, and all the while the green iris seemed to expand, spinning, around a core of blackness, a roaring tunnel sucking him in. His brain numbed; all desire to struggle drained from him until he stood waiting in blind obedience to Lamphier's commands.

Lamphier's sardonic lips didn't move; the communication with Rawls was telepathic, as it had been with Karen, MacCord, and the previous victims. "Did you think you could outwit me, imbecile? Understand me. You will proceed to headquarters from here and kill your inspector. Following which, you will fire indiscriminately on others, killing as many as possible. You must kill at least one man, so that you will be sentenced to die in the electric chair. . . ."

A small, wiry man oozed into the foyer from the studio, behind Lamphier. He was garbed in brown, the cloth being a heavy, soft weave of natural fiber, like a silken burlap. Tibetan, his somewhat slanting brown eyes were large and somber, and his skin was an extraordinary, molten, tanned copper in color. According to legend, the Atlantides were red-skinned, just as in Christian myth Adam's skin was red. The Tibetan stood behind Lamphier. Quicker than the eye, he had struck, snatched the lavender crystal vessel out of Lamphier's hands and reached the door with a bound.

"Renegade!" His voice crackled with abomination. With an oath of fury Lamphier had snatched at the precious crystal in an effort to retrieve it. Having lost, he stood with folded arms behind the desk. Eyes alert. His own eyes molten with vengeance, the Atlantean spoke a few syllables in his ancient, golden language. Rawl's trance was broken even as he was on his way to carry out Lamphier's murderous orders. The nervous shock staggered him. Likewise, Karen gasped and began whimpering on the lounge. The Atlantean priest glanced at Rawls. "You want her, don't you? Then take her!"

Rawls stumbled groggily to the lounge, took Karen's yielding body in his arms. The Mongolian girl, Lilitha, had prostrated herself at the red priest's feet, groveling, praying hysterically for forgiveness. Her torn costume slipped again from her shoulders exposing her smoothly flawless back, writhing now, and trembling breasts like swells of golden fruit. The priest set his foot on her neck. She tried to kiss his foot but he kicked her aside and spat on her. Addressing Lamphier, "I have followed you through the capitals of the world. Now that I have obeyed the Masters, found you and recovered our treasure, what punishment is great enough for you?"

Lamphier maintained his calculating silence.

"Because of your learning, you were admitted to the Lodge, even initiated into the priesthood; you were in our midst as one of us. You learned the language, the lore and secrets of Atlantis from the few of us who survive. How did you repay us? By laying hands on the holiest of holies, the very symbol of our religion," —he clutched the crystal vessel more tightly—"stealing it and fleeing with that wench in the night!"

Lamphier smiled imperturbably. These were just words.

The red priest seemed to grow in stature with his rage and his voice became sonorous. "You wanted to play at being a sorcerer, and get rich, did you? A wretched stage magician! Using the sacred instrument with which we communicate with our dead!"

Lamphier, looked startled fleetingly, then said with his same iron calm, "Tell the Masters that a good gambler is a good loser."

"Yes, you are a good gambler, and the saying is better. Master-the-Third." The Atlantean said with slow emphasis. "Some sayings which ignorant wretches think were manufactured yesterday were told in Atlantis in the remotest antiquity." He spoke as though he himself had walked the streets of the drowned Atlantic cities. "One of these bywords was made for a greedy alien like you who sows the wind and reaps the whirlwind."

Lamphier's condescending smile became a sneer. The priest pronounced a rippling phrase in Atlantean. Not a trace of fear showed on Lamphier's face. Out of the unimaginable depths of time and space grew a sullen, cataclysmic roar. The first fingers of the whirlwind slashed through the room, tearing at Rawls' clothing like steel claws. He yelled. Then the whirlwind struck deafeningly like the crack of doom.

Entwined with Karen, Rawls found himself sprawled in the gutter across the street from Lamphier's. Neither of them had any broken bones, but their clothing was in shreds. Karen's dress was rent to the waist, and her creamy breasts shook with fright. Rawls removed the remains of his coat and wrapped it about her shoulders. To distract her from the concussion he kept saying, "It's all right. It's okay now, Karen. It's all over."

She took a deep breath, and he drew her to her feet, kept her in the close embrace.

The whole top floor of the building across the street had been demolished; it was gone completely, it alone; debris lay scattered about on the street, some still coming down. People were sticking their heads out of lighted windows; the street was full of running people. A girl clad only in a flimsy robe and slippers stepped out of a doorway. A hack came boiling along up to Rawls, and Rawls recognized his driver. He helped Karen in, followed, and told the driver to get going as he slammed the door.

"Cripes, what happened here, mister?" the driver gasped.

"Gas explosion," Rawls answered shortly. "Where were you?" He took Karen's slim, willing loveliness in his arms again; now that he had her he was never going to let her go. As she snuggled closer, he caressed her and her eyes were ashine. She might never remember what had happened during the hypnotic trance in which she had moved since her husband died, but she acted as though she had always belonged to Rawls and liked it.

"I did just what you said," the hack driver swore. "A man and a woman came out of that house, and he told me to drive up through Central Park. I got onto the express highway and started hitting it up. Now, you can believe it or not, mister, but when I got off the highway there was nobody in the cab! They just vanished! That's the first time I ever lost a fare."

Wearily Rawls sat down in Inspector McFarlane's office. The thing on Horatio Street had been called a gas explosion. It was presumed that the pilot lights on the range and refrigerator had gone out and let the closed apartment fill with gas. When Lamphier returned to the place, he must have crossed the room and turned a light switch to investigate. Walking on the rug had charged his body with static, and the spark that had jumped from his fingers to the switch had ignited the gas. At any rate, human flesh and blood had been found smeared on pieces of wreckage. Not enough to bury.

"She wouldn't go back to the Mitchell Arms," Rawls explained. "She's still asleep at my place." This was a full day later, and Rawls' pulses hummed when he thought of that breathtaking beauty waiting him at home. More of her . . .

"All right," Inspector McFarlane began quizzically. "This Lamphier was going to marry her and get all the money she inherited from MacCord. That's what he was doing all along. How did he work it?"

"He was a hypnotist, and he was living high, wide, and handsome. He traveled around the world making the acquaintance of rich people, hypnotized them, got their money away from them and made them commit suicide. He'd offer to give them a demonstration, I guess, and that would be the end of them."

"Funny; I never believed in this hypnotism stuff, much," McFarlane growled. "But if it works, what Lamphier was doing was murder. How'd you get the idea this was murder, Rawls?"

"Why, I didn't say it was murder, inspector," Rawls hedged.

"Alan MacCord cut his throat on purpose, so it was no accident," McFarlane reminded. "If it wasn't suicide or murder, what the devil was it?"

"I didn't commit myself," Rawls said cannily.

"You didn't," McFarlane reprimanded. He plucked a cigar from his pocket, snapped off the cellophane and spiked the terrible black weed between his teeth. "You didn't commit yourself. And all I did was trust you to hell and gone and spend the taxpayers' money on you while you bungled an investigation. What evidence did you have?"

"I didn't have any evidence," Rawls mourned. "It was just something in the air. What I had was not evidence, and if I told you you'd laugh at me."

"Are you keeping it a secret, man?" McFarlane roared indignantly.

Rawls sighed with fatigue. "Inspector, you may not know it," he said sadly, "but my full name is Stanley MacCord Rawls. My mother was Ellen MacCord herself. Now, when I used to sit on my old grandfather's knee, Gramp would always tell me that the MacCords had the strength of the strong. Not a MacCord ever committed suicide. When Alan MacCord opened up his throat with his 'Tuesday' razor blade, why, inspector, I just knew it wasn't so. D'y' see?"

Without the guidance of a finger, Inspector McFarlane gazed squarely ahead at nothing like the understanding Scotchman he was, and rolled his poisonous black cigar from one end of his lean mouth to the other.

Over Time's Threshold

A CLOCK TICKING IN an empty house.

What might that bode? Finch turned to the girl and said, "The agent told me this place has been closed up for four years."

Connie nodded. It was an undeniable ticking, the heavy, clipped chucking sound of a large timepiece. The sound came from the one unexplored room on the ground floor and Finch walked with the girl toward the door of the room with some curiosity.

The uncovered furnishings of the old house were gray with dust. There had been no caretaker for these four years, and its present condition gave it a cheap place in the market, even among prevailing low prices. The dusty furnishings were of a rather respectable nature, some of them rich enough to give the girl's eyes an incipient sparkle. And those of the room in the left wing which they were approaching were especially interesting. Subconsciously, Finch noted that the door of this room, of the several they had tried on the ground floor, was the only one standing open. The two paused on the threshold of the room and looked in, harking to the ticking of the clock.

A heavy work table in the mathematical center of the room supported a large retort filled with a liquid coloured a pale apple green. The glass arm of the retort appeared to deposit this fluid by slow drops into a fair-sized graduated glass whose capacity must have been about the same as that of the retort. A drop now hung from the extended retort arm, minute accumulation gradually inviting its fall. Finch looked at the litter of test tubes and other apparatus on the table and glanced at the book lined walls.

"Capal's laboratory," he said. Connie looked at him inquiringly.

"Professor Capal," he said again. "He used to live in this house and it looks as though he worked in this room."

"Oh, he used to teach at the University."

"Yes. He sort of disappeared four years ago, and the house has been vacant since."

Loud ticking filled the room, and now the two watching the clock noted its peculiar character with some astonishment. It was of unusually heavy construction, and had a broad, engraved face set with antique numerals. Around this face the two hands were describing arcs with furious irregularity. The minute hand passed with appreciable movement past the numeral 3, stopped dead and retreated almost to the top of the face. Then both minute and hour hands disappeared in a blurred whirl. The heavy ticking became confused; the sound was full of unaccountable interruptions and double strikings and displayed as many irregularities as the movement of the hands. The weights in the case changed position uncertainly, and the motion of the pendulum could not be followed; it seemed to appear ubiquitously in its arc. The whir of the machinery behind the face suddenly stopped. Finch automatically took out his watch and looked at it. Both pieces gave the same time, 3:10.

At this moment Connie stepped into the room to examine the clock more closely. As she crossed the threshold and Finch was about to step after her, the retort deposited a drop of the green stuff in the fractionally filled beaker on the table. The hesitating hands of the clock leaped and the girl vanished.

Finch looked about blankly.

"Connie . . ." he called questioningly.

The ticking sounded rhythmically, now clear, now confused, as with the sound of another escapement striking somewhat faster. The hands hesitated, whirled, stopped, swung back and forth like the steadying needle of a compass.

"Connie!" Finch ran into the room and looked about him, breathless with fear. And now the clock ticked with precision. But terrifying things were occurring about the house. Finch turned to the room's long windows and looked at the sky. It had blackened in less than a minute. It was night. He looked amazed at the stars, and then turned his shocked eyes from immediately succeeding daylight. The sun had burst like thunder through the belt of Orion. What was happening?

Night again succeeded. The sun became a mere arc of fire across the sky—a yellow golden rainbow, and night was an instant's blur of darkness. The hands of the ticking clock followed precisely the progress of the sun. The alternation of night and day fell swifter and swifter, and for Finch, at the window, it was like looking out of the rapidly shuttering eye of a camera. A time camera. The succession of light and darkness merged into a tone of twilight under a gray sky sliced lower and lower by the arc of the sun, as cold crept in the room, and snow fell abroad over the land. Then the arching sun mounted the sky so rapidly that its many appearances seemed one broad band of fire in the sky.

Now it was midsummer, and the hands of the clock ceased their crazy whirl and hesitated, performing aimless arcs back and forth across the circled numbers of the face. This happening had almost the appearance of malice, as if to allow the man to take account of his disaster.

Finch looked about him. The room seemed the same; there was a thickening of the dust if anything. He wrote "Finch" in the dust on a free end of the apparatus-littered table, and noticed the new accumulation of green stuff at the end of the retort arm.

Capal had been a physicist, and this arrangement of liquid and glass looked like one of his remote experiments in chemistry. Finch thrust his forefinger into the liquid the beaker had collected, and withdrew it hastily. The stuff was so cold it burned, and pain rushed up his arm like a train of exploding needles. In the summer sky the sun marked the month as June, but Finch and the girl had entered the room in early August. He believed nothing, but accepted everything under the name of phenomena.

At the university Capal had propagated a number of scientifically malodorous ideas, and was accounted a trifle mad; Finch pleasantly conjectured that the professor had been tricked by his own queer notions, and wondered what his disappearance had to do with his laboratory.

The retort was mounted upon legs that separated it from the table by almost an inch. To one side was a clockwork mechanism screwed firmly to the table. Projecting from the side was a free metal arm, to the end of which was fastened a small plate of some reddish composition that glinted with metal filings. This plate would swing under the base of the retort, but a test-tube rack had fallen and blocked its progress. Copper wires led from binding-posts on the clockwork to a series of jars of colorless liquid ranged along the side of the apparatus.

The girl had vanished before his eyes and he himself had vanished from his own time. Where was she? Where Capal was. And Capal? Finch had good nerves, and knew the uselessness of dashing about looking for the girl aimlessly. He was caught in a trap, and the spring was set by Capal. The phenomena that played in this room were incident to the professor's clutter of glass and clockwork, and it was by means of these that he would find normality. He was ready to follow any adventure through to its completion, and now ascertained that the clockwork was in order by pushing out the metal arm to the limit of its swing. The composition plate was carried forward by clicking little wheels until it met the test-tube rack again.

As he was about to remove the rack he noticed the arm of the retort, and decided to start evenly by cleaning off the small quantity of liquid that had collected at its mouth. His finger tip wiped the glass, and at the contact his arm jerked convulsively with electric shock as he caught sight of the girl standing opposite him, looking about wildly.

Finch retreated from the table confusedly and called the girl's name. The clock's ticking blurred into one continuous sound of speaking metal, and the hands spun hazily. The room rocked and reeled. Again the world was in twilight, and in the speeding seasons Finch alternatively shook with cold and perspired in summer heat. He was aware of a dim, avalanchian roar which that clarified and approached portentively. The old house crashed about his ears, having run into complete decay in a matter of minutes, and he choked in a chaos of dust and falling, rotten timbers.

He found himself prostrated among ruins that dwindled and supported vegetation even before his eyes. As he scrambled to his feet on a pile of crumbled wood and mortar, howling chaos dinned in his ears and then the world was calm and he was looking out over a late autumn wilderness.

There was no house; there was no city about him, and an ancient cottonwood sank its wrinkled trunk in the ground where the table had stood. A terrific shock tumbled him to the ground and when he arose the world was cold and the sun directly overhead was a great, dim, glowing red ball.

Far off on the horizon was the glow of flame. A creeping blanket of smoke marked some great fire. About a hundred yards off, standing beneath another cottonwood, was the figure of a man anxiously examining the ground about him.

He wore tattered clothes, and spectacles reflected light as he turned his head. A great beast of some odd canine species tightened a leash he gripped in one hand. The animal saw Finch and growled. The man looked up and shouted. Whereupon the beast jumped against the leash, and man and dog beat their way up the knoll toward Finch. All his skin prickled and his throat stiffened in fright.

"Stop!" he screamed.

"I'm Capal!" shouted the other. "Don't move! You *can't* move!"

Finch shuddered and turned white. He heard a confusion of syllables, something about "clockwork," and looked around dazed at the suddenly present room of the old house. A drop was hanging from the arm of the retort. It fell, sparkled globularly on the table of liquid in the glass, and then became a part of it. As he hastily ran through the door and sprawled on the floor outside he thought he heard the girl call his name. At which he raised his abraded cheek from the floor and looked back, but the room was empty. He lay there for long and long, sleeping heavily through the early hours of the morning.

He awakened with the sun pouring through the doorway, shafting the spot his body occupied. His face lay closely against the floor. His cheek hurt with raw soreness.

"God. God. God," he said, and turned stiffly to look into the room, sitting up. A drop of green fell from the retort and Connie's body appeared on the floor, twisted angularly.

"Connie!" He started to his feet and she disappeared. He stopped at the threshold, muttering to himself. The dust in which he had written his name, he noted grimly, was undisturbed. Then, burying his face in his arms, and leaning against the wall, he listened to the aimless, staccato chucking of the clock.

The sportive changes in the room mocked reason and Finch was hungry. After walking around the empty house for a time, absently combing his disordered hair with his fingers, he left the place, slowly and took his way to a nearby restaurant. The reality of food made Capal's curious laboratory seem exceedingly remote. But the girl was gone. *Where?*

Was that really Capal he had seen running up that confounded knoll? What cursed beast was that with him?

This time Finch circled the house and stood on the ledge that footed the window of the laboratory. He could hear the ticking through the panes, like a mechanical heart. Otherwise, everything was quiet. The windows were curious in themselves. They didn't open, and the panes were of quartz-glass. The place was built solidly and would last a long time. He glued his ear to the glass and listened to Capal's strange clock for a few minutes, and then peered closely at the only other significant object visible—the retort. There was a glimmer of green at the end of the arm.

He dropped from the window and walked across the unkept lawn to the front steps. Here he looked at his watch and noted that the girl had been absent for nearly sixteen hours. He had awakened at about six o'clock, just as a drop had fallen. Last night one fell at five, when they entered the room, and again at about ten, because of the modicum he removed with his finger. It took about four hours for one drop to accumulate, granting one had fallen while he had been asleep. So. His worried face suddenly straightened. He had seen the girl when he touched the retort, and when the drop fell as he awakened this morning; and heard her voice as he was leaving the room. Coincidences.

Hurriedly jumping the front steps, he snatched open the door, dashed down the hall, and cut through the living room into the left wing. About ten feet from the door he caught sight of Connie lying in the same position in which he had seen her last. He shouted and dived headlong through the yawning door as another green drop fell into the beaker.

His body sprawled into the table and he stood up dazed to find himself once more in the room alone. Thereupon he stumbled toward the door. The capricious clock again forecast the unknown with its spinning hands and syncopated ticking.

The hill on which Capal's house was built flattened, and suffocating, humid masses of foliage crowded the spongy earth. Finch, lying prone, looked on the blanketed peaty leaves and vegetation covering the ground, and saw near his face black beetles and spiders crawling horribly. A train of soft red insects about the size of peas mounted his arm on their clinging, tentacle-like legs, and licked his shuddering flesh with little red tongues like small flames. He shook them off, and rising to his feet, stamped on the lot, and dispatched the beetles and spiders within the area the room would enclose. Then he fearfully returned to the spot his body had occupied when he first recognized this new change. Here he stood waiting patiently, resolved that these things were so. First, two objects cannot occupy the same space at the same time. Second, every four hours the retort introduced a magical green drop into the receptacle under the arm, and time momentarily identified itself with the fall of the drop. It was either Capal's scientific necromancy or coincidence, and Finch didn't care to dispute existence with the table or bookcase; and leaving the room's area might mean never returning.

For four hours he would be lost in time, and therein he was prey to everything about him. He closed his eyes in a savage agony of nostalgia. A curious sensation about his feet attracted his attention. Looking down, he saw the peat-blanketed ground mounting his legs graspingly. All around were palisades of trees, and the surface of the land was jungled with brush and vines. A huge creeper the size of his wrist commenced life at the base of a smooth-boled tree nearby and careened through the air with dizzy life, whipping and cracking as it grew. The peat-level mounted to his knees. He stood stupefied. A shaggy beast hurtled past him, pursued by a barking uproar of wild dogs. He listened to the snarling tragedy dully. The level of earth withdrew suddenly, and whole stands of trees disappeared.

Time in retrograde? Cursing Capal's genius he sat weakly on the ground as he thought of going back and back and back. But there was little time after all to wonder whether the influence of the lost professor's apparatus were limited or not. There was just time to see a stagnant expanse of water, soupy and green and crawling with life. The damp, heavy atmosphere was unbearable. Upward rushes of moisture-laden air choked his lungs and spun his brain. The sun flamed whitely, and the forest reeked and shimmered with wisps of steam. Then the rushing vegetation swept in and buffeted him so that he stood on his feet against the billowing foliage. A lithe, active vine whirled through the air and burst through the fleshy part of his arm. Finch clutched futilely at it, crying out at the pain; the vine had already disappeared in the shuttling years.

Another period was running to its close. Finch looked at his watch, and stooped purposefully in one of time's hesitating moments to pick up from the ground a handy water-rotted root. He heard the ticking of the clock, and the laboratory of Capal's house formed instantly.

He stood anxiously eyeing the clock and retort, gripping the root. The arm gleamed greenly and a drop of liquid hung trembling as the hands of the clock ceased their spasmatic whirling and swung back and forth over the twenty-first hour since the phenomena had begun. Finch gripped the root, poised to throw, while the skipping noise of the clock resolved itself into regular heavy ticking. He looked eagerly for the girl, and now the hands were almost at a dead stop. The ticking became a slow hammering.

Finch trembled; with nervous accuracy he flung the root at the glass works on the table as the body of the girl appeared at his feet.

Quickly he stooped to lift the girl from the floor, although speed was no longer necessary. The root struck the retort squarely and smashed it into a green soup of liquid and shattered glass. The beaker was raked from the table along with the wired jars, and a tinkle of dropping and breaking test tubes and glass rods accompanied him as he left the room.

Where the green stuff touched the table the varnish fumed and blackened.

The clock stopped.

Time Burial

THE DOG WAS mad; it was a huge, wolfish fellow, a German police. The engineer Markel sprang up the stairs nearest him to wrench at the knob of the door. It was locked. He was cornered now, for he dared not try leaping the spiked ironwork of the railings. Backed against the door, he waited the attack. The animal stopped at the bottom step and scrabbled with its paws for a moment, twisting its head sidewise curiously for an ugly snarling howl. Markel was pounding on the door with clubbed fists, and bystanders across the street were edging nearer fearfully; a woman screamed.

The dog crouched itself into a tense, pointed threat, breathing convulsively through its teeth; foam dropped from the slopping jaws and splattered on the stone walk. Someone in the street shouted something about a gun as the dog sprang up the five steps, onto the landing of which Markel stood. The engineer accepted the attack by delivering a mighty kick under the animal's jaws, sending the infuriated creature scrambling. It returned at once; silently.

Markel's thundering fists elicited no response from the house behind him. An old woman peered, frightened, through the curtains of the bay window at his right. An old gentleman in the group in the street saw her, and shouted to her to open the door. But she merely looked back with the piteous appeal of fear and age.

In the meantime Markel was defending himself as well as he could. The dog had scored on his leg, ripping the trouser and tearing the flesh. Now the keen, gray old gentleman stepped forward from the increasing crowd and mounted the steps. He was carrying a hickory stick that had a heavy crook for the handle. Having adopted a convenient position near the quarrel, he brought the cane over his head, making the handle the bludgeon end, and allowed it to rest on his shoulder momentarily while he leaned against the iron railing waiting for a point of vantage.

Markel kicked; the dog eluding him brought its head directly before the old man, who lifted the cane by its point and brought it down in a crushing arc on the mad animal's skull. The crack of the impact sounded like a violent handslap, and the beast tumbled dead down the steps, quivering.

At once the now sizeable crowed surged forward, offering all manner of aid; someone suggested an ambulance, which the engineer grimly refused. But he requested his saviour's company home, whereupon the two walked off slowly, Markel commending the old man for the strength in his arms, and he in turn making remarks about leverage. The noise of the milling crowd, busy looking at the dead dog from every possible angle, was soon lost behind them.

"Hadn't you better call a doctor for that?" The old man nodded at Markel's leg in interrogation, but the engineer shook his head.

"It was a mad dog . . ." pursued the old man.

"That doesn't matter," said Markel; "we're home now. Will you come in?" They had entered the gate of a fenced yard, neatly kept, and mounted the steps of a rather quiet-looking, unremarkable house. The engineer held the door open, and the old man stepped in with a kind of casual smartness, as if this were his own home, or as if all places were alike to him. There had been no introductions as yet, each understanding the other sensitively without names. Anyhow Markel now found point in some show of haste, preceding his saviour through a door to the right of the entry. This room turned out to be a chemical and physical laboratory, the center of which was occupied by a tremendous worktable covered with a fume hood and hung generously with drop lights. It was crowded with retorts, filters, racks, with apparatus of all descriptions, and paraded loose collocations of bottles and other containers, a large one of which Markel set about opening. It held a colorless liquid, apparently water, which the engineer poured measuredly into a graduated beaker and drank off.

"That's that," he said, with a short sigh of relief. The old man shrugged, perplexed, and found himself a comfortable chair, while Markel, having offered no explanation, excused himself to wash his wounds and change his clothes. He returned momentarily. Upon which, having offered his guest wine and tobacco, he perched himself on an acid-eaten corner of the worktable while they discussed the merits of the liquor and cigarettes in silence. Markel swung his legs idly in deepest thought; the old man meanwhile took in his appearance with great interest.

The engineer was compactly built, falling an inch or less short of six feet in height. He was muscular and active, as proved by his unexcited encounter with the mad dog. His hair was fine and black, and he had straight, slanting black brows which, with his smooth white features, gave his countenance a sculptured or chiselled appearance, while his black eyes enlivened it with the alert intelligence discernible in his clear white forehead. His hands were shapely, moulded by little convexities of muscle that flexed handsomely as he absently screwed his cigarette into his thin red lips. Consistently enough, he was very neatly and tastefully clothed, this time in gray. Markel's visitor, having taken in these things, was about to compliment his host once more on the wine when Markel anticipated him. He seemed to have arrived at some decision.

"Would you like to take a journey with me?" he asked.

"Journey?" The old man raised his white eyebrows in inquiry.

"In time." Markel looked at him fixedly.

"I'm afraid I do not quite understand," he said, smiling and puzzled.

"Perhaps I should have said, 'would you like to live forever? . . . be immortal?'"

The old man stared at the engineer perplexed and shifted uneasily in his seat, wondering just how much danger there was for him in his host's madness. He tapped his cane firmly against the floor and closed his hands over the crook, clearing his throat and looking intently at the points of his polished shoes. The engineer, feeling that he had made himself out somewhat ridiculous, changed his approach abruptly and said,

"How old would you say I am?"

His visitor raised his head and looked at the engineer with an oddish smile.

"I was once so young," he said, to which Markel returned—

"I have no doubt you were," with an oddish smile of his own. "But my age?" he insisted.

"Well, you have a sort of old youngness. You are not thirty?"

"When I took my first drink of that stuff," said Markel, pointing behind him to the container from which he had drunk the colorless liquid a few moments ago, "I lacked a month or so of thirty years. You have good eyes. Nevertheless," he said rather violently, leaving his perch and standing tensely, "that was almost fifteen years ago!"

His visitor waggled his head slowly in smiling incredulity.

"Very well," said Markel. "You have showed no sign of recognizing me, though I am called a well-known, and shall I say remarkable, character. At present those facts constitute my chief difficulties. My name is Markel. I am chief engineer of the telephone company. And you are?"

"I am an Anonymous Person," said the old man, capitalizing by inflection.

"As you please. May I remark further, that in the past fifteen years I have had not an hour, not a moment, of sleep."

The old man nodded pleasantly; the maniac seemed to be harmless. Markel looked at him sharply, saying,

"I can hardly criticize you for disbelief. You did me a good turn, though, and in return I should like to account for what you very likely think is some harmless insanity. Will you listen, or am I imposing on you?"

"Please tell me," said the Anonymous Person. The engineer had only threatened his credulity, and not himself, so he prepared to hear some whim of mad logic that might compare in degree with the madness itself. The whim, however, was to assume definitely grand proportions. The engineer lit another cigarette, in which the old man gravely accompanied him, established himself once more on the worktable and told his curious story. During the recitation the brisk old man betrayed no lack of attention and did not interrupt nor comment till the engineer had finished. Markel had a mighty strange accident to recount, and began abruptly.

"You know, I suffered from violent colds. That accounts chiefly for all this apparatus." He gestured toward the elaborate grotesquerie of glass all around him. "After my graduation I took a job as one of the assistant engineers at the telephone company. There was work to be had then for us fellows, but believe me, we weren't paid very much. This place was cheap, so I moved in to be near the offices. When I had saved enough from the contemptible pittance they rewarded my services with, I took another room here, this one, and installed the equipment I had on my hands at the time of graduation. I planned to work in the evenings. There were a few textbooks left, so I sold them all and bought all the cold cures and headache cures on the market."

He looked at his guest narrowly. The old man had his ears cocked at this fishy turn of affairs, and there was an odd expression of wonder on his delicately modelled pink face. As the engineer continued he smiled in appreciation.

"The object was to analyze the lot. As a general rule none of them work, you know, but I wanted a few formulas to start on. If I could cure my variety of cold I could cure anyone's, and there's money in patent medicines. I wanted money, because I knew what it was like to be without. When I was at school I lived with Uncle Ben—Ben Druse, you know—and he made me work my way through the university. He had a notion that learning which came under difficulties was most valuable. He was my sole relative, and I suppose he quite reasonably urged that the wealth which would someday be mine as a matter of course would be of more use and more appreciated as a final reward of effort than as an obstacle to it. Anyhow his plan gave me 'distinction' with my diploma.

"He was a tough old man and lived a long time. I couldn't wait for him to die, and after God knows how many concoctions I brewed, and I mixed powders enough to sink a ship, I had a drug that I patented and sold. There were slight increases in the way of salary at the office, which with this new wealth gave me a sizeable working capital. I got another room, enriched the place with a few comforts, and bought more supplies and more equipment."

The old man listened with never a word, stroking his chin, nodding, smiling, as the narrative of achievement progressed. He looked up understandingly as Markel passed remarks about Uncle Ben's sustained longevity, who had long passed his grand climacteric, and nodded again at the resultant commercial flavor of the engineer's long index of experiments. The list of patents in his name lengthened, the laboratory suffered new elaborations in the way of equipment; Uncle Ben was still alive at seventy-three, and might live indefinitely. By this time, when Markel was approaching his thirtieth year, he was supporting himself comfortably, and regarded the mirage of wealth with no great anxiety. He was first assistant engineer now, and still continued his experiments in his spare time. Then, in that hard winter of the year following the great war, occurred the ridiculous business which was to very nearly turn his brain.

"I told you I suffered chronically from violent colds," he said, "and several times I had to return from work. The patent medicines I compounded didn't work any better than the market variety, and I was all for moving to a warm climate. But it would only be a matter of suffering from hay-fever instead." The engineer regarded the expectant old man sardonically.

"On this particular occasion Fonce, our company physician, sent me home over the weekend to keep warm and eat a cupful or so of his pills. He didn't know I can mix up more bitter doses than he ever heard of. My supplies were running low, so on the way home I stopped at the drug supply house down the street and got a batch of chemicals for a new formula I had in mind."

Markel casually selected a new cigarette and lit it carefully, now contemplating the glowing end, unhurried. He turned his gleaming black eyes on the old man, and smiled humorlessly. The old man waited, fidgeting with his feet.

"You know," continued the engineer, "wine enables you to smoke with some degree of pleasure when you have a cold, so I downed a tumblerful as soon as I got home, took a cigarette, and unpacked the new powders. I set up a beaker of distilled water there on the tripod over the big burner. When it had reached the proper temperature I introduced about a thimbleful of common salt first, which I keep in that large jar. While I was watching it dissolve I reached aside for a pinch of one of the new powders, largely a chalk compound, and dropped it in the beaker before I discovered that my fingers had gotten into the wrong box. I was annoyed, but you can imagine how startled my face looked when I saw that beaker effervescing generously. I had taken the wrong powder, but there should have been no effervescence anyhow.

"I examined that box with considerable interest, you may believe, and tried the powder pretty gingerly on the tip of my tongue. Tasteless, just as it should have been. Whereupon I repeated the experiment in another beaker of distilled water, cold this time, and the concoction effervesced more violently than before. What was still more interesting, the beaker got so hot I couldn't hold it, but when the ebullition subsided moisture collected on the outside of the glass. I touched the glass and it was cold. As a matter of fact I found with a thermometer that the temperature of the liquid was slightly over a degree and a half below the freezing temperature of water. I performed the same experiment five times successively with varying quantities of materials, always with the same result. You know what inclination my experiments had—in the meantime I was using that unaccountable brew I had made for all manner of baroque purposes.

"The stuff was cold. In addition to that it was colorless, tasteless, and odorless. Now, for one thing, about beverages . . . There was a squat bottle of strawberry flavoring among a lot of trash in that cabinet behind you, and I introduced several sirupy drops of the stuff into the last beaker. Having mixed it up with a stirring rod, I sipped it, and then drank it down. It was delicious, ambrosial. What was more, my head cleared at once—the cold was gone. All in one, then, I had made a smooth, clear drink that cost almost nothing to manufacture and needed no refrigeration—it was always cold, you may feel the jar there if you like—and a cure for violent colds as well. You know, old man, I could have made millions in the soft drink business."

The old man nodded, his face bright with interest.

"You can imagine how excited I felt," Markel proceeded. "I paced up and down this floor like a madman, and stopped at the telephone a dozen times or more to call up my employer at his home and resign my position. I'm glad I didn't now, because more was to come.

"That evening I climbed into bed later than the usual hour, but I was too excited to sleep. Once I went out into the cold for a long walk, and I believe, too, that I read a new book which I found rather amusing. I've forgotten the name of the author now, and what the story was. I felt in extraordinarily good health, broad awake, and was not a little amazed when I looked at the clock and found that it was turning five in the morning. I tried to sleep again, but it was impossible. When I prepared a scant breakfast some time later, I felt as refreshed as though I had slept for hours.

"It puzzled me not a little that I had so poor an appetite, because I loved food. At any rate, as soon as the shops opened in the morning I returned to the supply house and called for the entire shipment of that particular powder I had purchased the day before. The clerk just looked at me, and I suppose I must have spoken to him rather sharply, because he disappeared and came back in a hurry with two men lugging the whole crate of powder, about two hundred pounds of it. It took nearly all my ready money.

"I carried the box home myself; my muscles are quite strong,"—Markel extended his arms demonstratively—"and I was quite equal to it. The distance is not great from here, and I felt in peculiarly good condition anyhow. There's the box over there in the corner, where I established it fifteen years ago. I continued experimenting through that day, trying to break down that unparalleled chalk compound, but it seemed to be very enduring, and would not react save with the other salt ingredient. The stuff can't decompose, and the supply in the crate is as efficacious now as it was when I bought it."

Here Markel frowned a little. There was a fly in the ointment, and his voice lost some of its exultation.

"When I say I was not hungry, I mean that I practically did not eat—scarcely an ounce of food in two weeks. But there was no sleep for me at all. You know," he exclaimed pettishly, "I used to occupy myself just before going to sleep with the most magnificent half-waking dreams; I can't do that any more. Two weeks later, though, or thereabouts, I began to feel very tired quite suddenly, at high noon. It was the most unaccountable thing, and I was badly frightened, though it was logical enough after so long a time without sleep. Why, I hardly managed to get from the doorway there to the jar here on the table. I was dead on my feet with exhaustion, and experienced the most terrific delusion of complete starvation. Believe me, the tumblerful I drank was a boon. It was a feast and a long, dreamless, refreshing sleep altogether. I call it simply Ambro, by the way, for ambrosia, since that was the liquor of the gods."

The incredulity which the old man had shown at first had slowly disappeared, and the expression on his face by now had developed into a certain grimness as the engineer neared the end of his account.

"Do you remember how the pest swept the country several years back? People breaking out with the black smallpox in a miniature plague. Well, I found the symptoms in myself. I can't imagine how it happened now, unless it was that I was exposed to the disease when the efficacy of the last draught of Ambro was wearing off, because I proved a number of times later that the liquor was a preventative as well as a cure. Anyhow, I took another draught of the stuff, and all symptoms of the smallpox vanished, well—like a handful of dust in the wind. They never developed.

"Now . . . in the course of time, you see, I discovered these things about my impossible beverage: It renders sleep unnecessary, perhaps impossible; it is a cure of disease, exactly how general I can't say, but I believe absolute, and it is very probably a proof against disease, if exposure doesn't take place after the working time of a dose of the Ambro has expired. It is surpassingly pleasant to drink, and insures perfect physical, and consequently mental, condition. Precisely what the mysterious workings of the stuff might be, I couldn't venture to say, save that they are tonic and seem to compensate almost completely for oxidation in the body. I shall not age one year in a million.

"The Ambro is peculiar, too, in that the period of effect of successive draughts varies. Sometimes a glass keeps me only till the following night, and then I have carried on without food or sleep for a few days over three months. Usually a drink lasts about three weeks.

"Now," said Markel, "I am a thorough worker, and am not one to jump at conclusions. I have tried this Ambro for about fifteen years,"—here he spoke with staccato impressiveness—"and I am ready to say that I have found a panacea, even for old age, which may be called a disease. I show no evidences of decay, and never shall. Do you still disbelieve, or will you find my birth certificate at the court house?"

"I believe you," said the old man quietly, polishing the handle of his cane with his palm.

"I number myself among the gods," said the engineer, and then, taking fire from his words, said with a kind of grand intensity—"I shall live forever. I am immortal!"

"I believe that, too," said the old man again. "May I ask, though, why you have not used your discovery beneficially? Think of the crowded hospitals. Think of all the poor, suffering people in this world."

"I am no altruist," said Markel contemptuously. "Once medicine discovered a single curative property of this liquor there never would be any satisfaction. To find that it was truly a panacea, that it insured immortality, would only be a matter of time."

"What of that?"

"What of that! Would you perpetuate ignorance, vice, crime, stupidity, hatred, the whole catalogue of human meannesses?" He spoke sarcastically. "The world is not ready for such a gift as mine, and may never be."

"But you are not invulnerable, are you," queried the old man, smiling a little. "Not quite a god?"

"Well, no," said Markel thoughtfully. "In addition to that, as I hinted some time ago, I am a marked man. I am chief engineer now, as I told you. Two years ago Uncle Ben died and fulfilled his promise. With wealth and a sound, respectable position behind me, I am much sought after, and have entree to the best homes of the city. I am marked, because I have valuable experience, a huge bank account, and because people see that I am young, strong, and attractive, for all my forty-odd years. My youth, old man, is attracting too much attention."

"Someday you will be known as the oldest man in the world," said the sardonic old man with some grimness. "You will have to be careful."

Markel shook his head slowly, worried. Then he said abruptly,

"But to the point. You helped me. Will you take a trip in time with me? I can't promise you a return."

The old man got to his feet and planted his cane firmly on the floor before him. Leaning on the cane easily he said,

"Thank you, no."

"It's a rare chance," Markel persisted.

"Engineer Markel," said the old man, "when I first met you, you seemed to be defending yourself well. The dog might have been dangerous if it had knocked you down, but at the time there seemed to be nothing to worry about beyond the poison in its jaws. I know now that even that did not matter. Now, mark you," he enunciated very distinctly with a deadly monotony in his voice, "if I had known then what I know now, and that mad beast had been at your throat, I don't know whether I should have interfered in the encounter." He turned to go.

"Just a moment," said Markel sharply, a dangerous gleam in his black eyes, "how do I know that you . . . that you won't . . ."

"You may rest assured," the old man interrupted, "I shall forget everything you have told me immediately upon stepping outside your door."

The engineer stood there discomfited while his remarkable visitor left the house, closing the door behind him, and stepped briskly down the street to pursue whatever business the encounter with the mad dog had interrupted. But at least the long, one-sided conversation had clarified enormously Markel's own position. It was so; he was too well known, and now a definite attitude toward the future was absolutely necessary. He was much too marriageable, too conspicuously young, and had kept his position with the telephone company, unnecessary during these two years since Uncle Ben Druse's death, much too long.

He had been staring blankly at the door with his feet planted wide while it got darker and darker as the afternoon waned. Now he turned slowly and walked through the laboratory to the long disused bedroom, where there was a stocky old desk. After scratching his chin once or twice he composed a rather careful note of resignation. He decided that he was taking a trip around the world.

What a crowd of difficult problems were coming upon him all at once! This situation must necessarily happen again and again. He leaned back in the chair in deepest thought, sealing his note absently. Never one locality for any length of time. He would be a kind of civilized nomad, transient, always moving, and all places would be alike to him. This was the first step into the future, the first of many, and already he was an outcast from familiarity. The Wandering Jew. He must learn to be inconspicuous. The old man had said, "I am an Anonymous Person," and that was precisely the new role that Markel had to adopt as a matter of necessity, of being absolutely average, completely anonymous. He must practice an everlasting alias, and now was the time to start, for the consequences of his discovery were already running at his heels.

The process of concealment was purely mechanical; within three months the thing had been effected, and rather thoroughly. He had sold Uncle Ben's estate, sent in his resignation, much to the regret of president Harriss, and packed the few belongings he intended to keep. These consisted of the crate of the chalk compound, a few other chemicals, but none of the apparatus, and a few items such as socks, shirts, and handkerchiefs, the latter uninitialled. He was destroying his identity, and even disposed of his expensive suits in favor of new, unassuming garb that he found at a strange tailor's.

Parting with the apparatus, though, was like losing a dear friend. Finally he had taken the complete laboratory furnishings into the back yard and smashed them against the stone incinerator piecemeal. Test-tubes erupted over the bricks and tinkled musically when they shattered. The retorts and other glass works crashed more effusively; the metal work he twisted shapeless. All this was a sacrifice to memory, because, after all, he was not invulnerable, and remembered vividly an explosion or two in his past experimenting that had come near costing him his eyes.

Then he had shipped his belongings west, and shortly followed them, leaving quietly for the other side of the continent. A seat in the smoking car carried him all the way, insured by a flask of Ambro in his hip pocket. His sleepless ride caused him to be eyed curiously several times, much to his annoyance, so he destroyed his fresh, immaculate person partially by rumpling his hair and rubbing his eyes. He was satisfied as to his arriving in California as an anonymous person. Thereupon he took a room in a San Francisco hotel under an assumed name. On the day following his arrival he filled out a check to his new name for a third of his account in the New York bank, depositing it in a bank near the hotel.

This business he repeated until the New York account was closed, and the engineer Markel had vanished into the unknown.

II

Smith, Jones, or Robinson? Contemplating himself before the closet mirror, behind which he kept the box of Ambro, he marked his striking reflection and considered that Plumes was a good name after all. He had registered himself so on impulse, but it might be as odd as he pleased, since every ten years or so he would have to change it anyhow. So Plumes he remained while he kept the apartments at the Emerald.

The anonymity progressed, and in a year's time the engineer had become a model of irregularity. Variety became a habit with him, and repetition seldom or never occurred in his habits. He would extend his stay as long as possible, and this was the only method. So sometimes he dined at the hotel, sometimes not. The switchboard girl could never be sure he was familiar, but imagined she had seen him before. If he spent an entire night reading in the lounge, he invited no confidences from idlers there, or made his conversation so uninteresting that he was readily forgotten. In the meantime new quandaries presented themselves, and he found himself exerting his will with more and more effort to live the life he had planned. But it was just the infinitely subtle part he had to play that kept him always on the alert and ever skirting a suicidal monotony. He became a master chessman, mentally protecting himself, the king, from any injury by walls of triple steel.

He fully intended to drink life to the lees, through the years, and the centuries, and the thousands of years, and already he could see himself exposed to terrible temptations. There were things forbidden to him, consequences of which would be fatal. One of these was ambition, other than that to live indefinitely. He had a terrific weapon of power in his hands—money, through which he could eventually become—why, become master of the earth. Why not? One merely invested his money and waited. A hundred years, two hundred years, a thousand years; buying property, more property, interests, corporations, till he had his fingers on every enterprise of government. He would have enough money to buy all the souls in the world. With the exercise of ingenuity it might be managed, but even the slightest possibility of error forbade it. Even the existence of the word was a warning of discovery. No, however the stupendous responsibilities involved intrigued him.

Another denial was faith, the warning against which was *violation of trust*. *No one* was to be trusted, and Markel marvelled at his mad readiness to empty his secret into the ears of the old man who had killed the dog. However, if that old fool preferred to let nature take its course and complete the cycle of his particular life without opposition, he was probably dead in these seven years of summer sunshine, in his grave, buried like a potato. *Requiescat in pace!* "I am an Anonymous Person," the old man had said rather insultingly. Good. Let him stay so.

Then he denied himself the pleasure of owning his own house. Breaking it up would be too hard to bear after another ten years of possession, and anyhow, nothing could be more inquiring than a neighbor. He could move every other year or so, but then the joys of owning his own place would hardly compensate for all the bother involved. There could be no free indulgence, then, in a taste in rugs, furnishings, and all the other luxurious impedimenta of the household. He did, however, enrich the apartment at the Emerald to a wonder of unspectacular luxury. The maids never suspected the breadth of the stream of clinking gold that went into this furniture, the cabinet, that grand mockery the bed, the brocade, and his careless apparel.

Since he trusted no one, friends were impossible, and they would be made only to be parted with, anyhow. Then, who knows what deceit lies in them? Markel had found cause to question the existence of honor in friends before this, and knew that there were mighty few things more pretentious than the name of friendship. The many concessions of friendship that tell of the gradual and subtle breaking down of reserve would be very difficult to deny—the casual appearance of the old man was heavy witness to the weak guards of his immortal secret. The temptation to tell was very strong, and some happy night he would find himself telling his story on impulse to eager ears, and that would be the end.

Markel would have to be sufficient unto himself, then, dependent on no one for his well being. His sole desire was to live, and he must not be encumbered with attachments. To accomplish his end a certain behavior was compulsory, but he was goaded constantly by the black beast of idleness. How to pass the time? Being primarily an active man he looked for a physical outlet, but now had to avoid any occupation which might cripple or endanger him. He was not invulnerable. But he took long walks, and three bathers got the scare of their lives one afternoon when a man appeared from nowhere and passed them at a furious, incredible run along the beach. The engineer could do things like that, because he could not hurt himself if he fell. Running, though, made him feel curiously, unpleasantly, like a machine. He did not get warm nor perspire, and could not tire himself. Once he ran crazily for more than thirty miles along a country road. He learned how grotesquely he was doomed; he was not properly a human being any more. For his slow, light heartbeat could not be detected save by expert fingers, and his lungs functioned so imperceptibly he might have been dead.

"At least I bleed," he muttered broodingly as he returned slowly from that wild run. Yes, he bled—the dog had proved that—but his blood was cold, as his flesh was cold, and his heart and brain were cold.

Books were a variety of escape from himself, and he read habitually, spending as many as sixteen hours a day reading books of every nature, glutting himself with knowledge. Several times he himself tried writing, and dispatched a number of grim, cryptic tales that editors sometimes dared to publish, sometimes not. One magazine published an inquiry after the author.

At the city library one could turn troglodyte, and there he ransacked shelf after shelf for books and more books, but even that pleasure eventually turned out to be a kind of boomerang, when one book's reading became a matter of minutes. He had a photographic eye, and developed his skill in reading so highly that his quick fingers were troubled to keep pace with his brain. The girl at the desk, having seen him exhaust several books within an hour, walked over to his seat, and bending over him asked pleasantly whether she could help him in what he was searching for. She was the new assistant librarian, a handsome young person of twenty-three or -four, and the bright, fatal youth of Markel was reflected often in her eyes as he spent hour upon hour flipping over those endless pages.

Her name was Irene Coines, and she was one of those women who so successfully translate themselves from pursuers into the pursued. Though even the acute Markel did not know it, he had encountered the first strand of the web when he had replied to her greeting one morning several days before. And for all his safeguards, lost as he was in the other worlds of those books, that same web was now being spun thick and fast, unseen, before his eyes. He saved time by inquiring for a certain book (as though he needed to save time!), and came upon her entangling smile. She brushed his shoulder in passing. He left the library when her work had ended one evening, and escorting her to the car was inevitable. She had deliberately made herself desirable, and again Markel found himself exposed to the most irresistible temptations.

Rather guardedly, then, he improved their acquaintance, and for the time being gave it a strong literary flavor, in the way of comment on books and writing. But he was unconsciously thorough, and Irene Coines early began to bank on the new asset that was Markel, in his cool charm, his youth, and the sparkling brilliance he displayed in the most casual conversation. This was early in the year 1942, just about ten years after he had come to California. As yet he could see no reason whatever for moving on again.

By the time the May of that year came around they had reached a point of half-intimate understanding. He leaned over the desk one morning confidentially, and invited her to his apartments for dinner. She accepted with that same inviting smile. In the afternoon of that same day she came to the table where he was reading and perched herself youthfully on the edge. She was excused from work for the time, having obtained permission to attend a lecture in the auditorium upstairs, and asked Markel whether he would like to go along. Refusal would be unspeakably rude. So he hastily skipped through the last few pages of the book he was reading and joined her.

Dr. Matthew Garden, the educator, was lecturing on immortality. Markel stopped before the placard posted outside the hall and his face brightened with interest. Irene tugged at his arm; the little auditorium was rapidly filling. But they found seats well in front, and spent the few minutes before the program started in passing rapid, satirical remarks about the mortal white heads ranged all around them. Then, when the white-haired educator himself advanced across the stage, he stiffened in surprise and dismay. It was the old man, who commenced his bitter lecture at once, without preliminary.

"For the purposes of this lecture, regard me as an Anonymous Person," he said. Then followed a calmly contemptuous, slashing attack on the longevity which the common man seemed to worship as a god. The point of the lecture struck Markel with terrible effectiveness, and he hung on Garden's every word so anxiously that the girl beside him finally gave up her whispered commentary.

It was Markel himself that the educator was speaking of. Every remark was an insult, and every allusion brightened the picture of his inglorious encounter with the old man many long years ago. He had not forgotten Markel's godly ambition, but he seemed to be dangerously near forgetting his promise. He was still the brisk, active old man, with the same quiet force of manner, and the same sardonic gray eyes. And he possessed Markel's fatal secret. Now, glancing through his audience, he sighted Markel, who half rose from his seat. The girl caught his arm, pulling him down, embarrassedly whispering to him. Without hesitation Garden carried on his talk, concluding with dispatch.

"We live so long, and no longer. The immortality of the gods, the artificial longevity of today, the blind, foolish worship of youth, are a snare, a delusion, and a dream. Any sound philosophy of life must partake of fatalism, and I, who may die tonight—who knows?"—here he looked steadily at the engineer—"consider alike the pleasures of living one day more, and the narrowness of my grave. Thank you." He bowed and left the stage.

"Come, Irene," said Markel, "let's get out of this." But at the door he hesitated, and on impulse asked the attendant for Dr. Garden's address. Garden, apparently, was also a guest at the Emerald for the time being. Markel walked with the girl to the door of the reading room rather absently, but he was always a trifle strange in his manner and there was little point in asking him to account for his behavior. At the door he did remind her of her dinner engagement with him, though, and left her then, descending the easily terraced steps of the library in a highly disturbed state of mind. It took him about an hour to walk back to the hotel. He stood idly before its tranquil entrance for a moment, but he could not tolerate the doorman's stare and entered, stopping at the desk to find Garden's room. The clerk gave him the number mechanically. Top story. Markel wondered whether the doctor chose the heights because he liked to look down on common humanity, or whether he liked to be remote. It amounted to the same thing.

Engineer Markel was again at the parting of the ways. The girl, after all, was occupying too much of his mind, if not his time. The two saw each other often enough at the library, but the evening or two they had spent together forced him to exercise the most unbearable restraint. He was falling in love with the way her hands selected a book from the shelves, the voluptuous swing of her skirt, her red lips, and herself. And her whole manner proved that she wanted him. He could not contain the terrible secret that feasted on his brain much longer, and she was the person to share it. His desire for companionship had expanded mightily in these years, and stepped measuredly toward madness. He loved that girl, however little his restraint and coldness might indicate it, and was now experiencing the gnawing temptation of taking her along in time with him. He would have to move again shortly after all; the mere fact of Garden's death was hounding him out already. It was to happen this evening, then. He struck the arm of the lounge with decision, stood, and proceeded to knock the apartment into some show of order.

He had ordered the dinner trays for seven o'clock, which would give the girl ample time to arrive in the cab he sent for her. This was a concession to form and to hospitality, for he never ate a full meal, having learned the tremendous building effect food had on him. He would gain in weight by as much nourishment as the food contained, pounds at a time. A full meal would signalize his departure this time.

Next to the bathroom was the mirror-doored, roomy linen closest, and as he paced the floor waiting the girl's arrival he stopped at it and tapped it idly with his foot. He opened it then, and contemplated his crate of powder, now somewhat increased in content through the admixture of the salt. This was the Ambro compound ready for solution. Still as effective as ever. It would never depreciate, for there was nothing in the compound to break down save by highly artificial means. He kicked at the crate, smiling thoughtfully. As if in echo, there was a knock at the door. The girl had come.

Markel accepted her young loveliness with a pleasant greeting, taking her hands. Irene stepped to the center of the room and looked around at the apartment with full appreciation: at the quietly rich, comfortable furnishings, their thoughtful arrangement, and through the door at the fresh, massive bed in the spacious bedroom, the engineer following her every motion with possessive eyes that brightly gleamed.

"Do you like it?" he asked.

"You know I do!" she answered, and taking his hands, pulled him down on the lounge beside her. He cocked one knee up on the cushions in awkward comfort, and they chatted animatedly till a knock at the door announced the arrival of the dinner trays.

Both ate keenly, and perhaps the handsome tip Markel gave the waiter increased her appetite a little. The food was excellent, and what few silences there were could be accounted for by sheer enjoyment. There was a lot of ridiculous conversation, which sped both toward understanding and affection. By the time the champagne came around the engineer was courting her beauty with generous flattery. Afterward they had music, and though Markel felt horribly stuffed he sent out for more champagne, the dinner bottle proving to be a mere invitation. There were kingly tips again when their clutter was cleared away and the liquor arrived. Thereafter they drank and smoked in dim lights, the girl all enwrapped in ecstatic contemplation of the future. Markel was making special point of his departure; the secret was ripe for the telling. No woman was ever to receive a proposal like this one.

Irene rolled her fair head on the back of the lounge, tipsily eyeing Markel as he took an unsteady turn about the room and returned to her. Now sitting on the lounge, he gripped the girl's arms below the armpits with his mighty hands and forced her, squinting with delight and pain, into the massed cushions that filled the crook of the couch. The majestic secret still faltered on his lips, and he mumbled incoherently, fingering the stuff of her dress in hesitation. But there was novel fire in the champagne after his long abstinence, and the stored passion of his cloistered white years suddenly burst. The two entwining there in the couch's deep bosom to the rustle of silk and the whispering sound of flesh crossing flesh, he kissed her receptive mouth and cushioned his thin, cold lips on her eyes. All this while he endured the most horrible feeling as though he were a robot mechanically directed through the antics of love. The passion was a delusion. For all the display he was no more aroused physically than a fine watch. He drove his fingers into Irene's white flesh, closing his teeth through the warm, firm roundness of her cheek. She writhed convulsively, stroking his face in turn, saying, "You're cold, you're cold . . ."

His foot overturned the glass of champagne she had set on the floor; under the dim lamp the spilled liquor picked out a patch on the rug in the form of a long dark spade. There was blood on her face. At the sight of it Markel straightened up, aghast at his handiwork. And one bare side was conspicuous in her dishevelment; red furrows crossed the beautiful skin, made by his nails. Quite abruptly he spoke of marriage. Upon which, and most unaccountably, the girl opened her eyes wide and laughed long and musically. Markel frowned and played his fingers across the crimson furrows he had made in her shuddering flesh. Then, with as little preliminary as Garden had exercised, he poured forth stumblingly the secret which he could not contain, as an irresistible persuasion, promising her immortality with him. It was a poetic way of making love, but too palpably absurd for such a moment, a kind of grand anticlimax. Irene laughed hysterically, her head cocked back into the pillows and her round, firm breasts shaking with merriment when he told her he was more than fifty years old.

Appalled at his madness now, he clutched her soft white throat violently and flung her tumbling off the lounge. Her long, shapely legs sailed ridiculously over her head in a human V, and the girl struck the floor flatly sprawling. Markel picked a large bill from his fold, crumpled it, and flung it at her. At once he left the room to change his clothes, which he effected rapidly, also packing what belongings seemed necessary to him, and returned to move the crate of Ambro out to the center of the floor. When he lifted the phone to call the porter he saw the girl standing neat and passably freshened at the door. She had removed the blood from her cheek and skillfully repaired a large rent in her dress.

"What are you waiting for?" he asked irritably. "Why don't you go?"

She walked up to him a little unsteadily, her hips swinging gracefully, and crowded the bill he had flung at her back into his hand.

"I didn't earn this," she said with tremulous insolence. "Take your filthy money. If I see you at the library again I'll have you arrested." At the door she turned for a parting shot. "You'd better go somewhere where there aren't any asylums, Mr. Carl Plumes. You're crazy."

She stood framed in the open doorway, looking at him with her face completely expressionless. Markel advanced a step toward her, his lips thinning viciously and his hands knuckling into murder, but the memory of Garden dead in the little room above him warned him against any folly. The handsome, intelligent girl regarding him closed the door very slowly and quietly. It vibrated soundlessly as she leaned against it heavily outside before departing at last.

On the train east the engineer recast that last hideous business with the educator and found it as unsavory as at first blush. He had entered Garden's room without ceremony, unarmed of course, and found the old doctor sitting at a desk near the door writing. Garden had laid down his pen quietly, and looked understandingly at the engineer's powerful fingers before looking at his face. There was a glass of greenish liquid before him, which he brought closer and played with thoughtfully.

"Come in, Engineer Markel," he said, his voice edged with delicate irony. And as Markel moved closer, "No, please stay there where you are."

"I should not have made you that offer," said Markel. "It was a mistake. And after your lecture this afternoon, don't you think you have broken your promise?"

Garden shrugged, eyeing the engineer's approaching violence unconcerned.

"I don't want to hurt you," Markel continued, "but, well, you are dangerous to me while you are alive."

"You mean to kill me?" asked Garden, looking at his hands. "I had rather you wouldn't . . . that way. Stop, just a moment," he commanded as Markel advanced on him. "Markel, you function just as blindly as a piece of machinery, and eventually you will as surely wear out. Whatever damage you do on this earth, you are only destroying yourself. I warn you that you are already damned forever." He had been slowly turning the glass, and now raised it to his lips, stopping Markel with a gesture.

"I am an old man, and prefer to die my own way. This liquor takes my life, as you prolong yours, but you have murdered me." He drank, looked at Markel with dumb perplexity, and fell forward on the desk, saying, "May you live forever."

The consequences of the cursed discovery were heaping on him with a vengeance. The thing was two-edged; he was hoist with his own petard. So around the earth and around the earth, girdling the globe innumerable times, Markel sought vainly to flee from himself, losing himself in the variety that would make life endurable. He haunted crowds, and spent year after year crossing and recrossing the ocean because it gave him a sense of movement. He confused his eyes with the color of the world's market places and frequented the dives from San Francisco around to Shanghai and back again because they were always inhabited, with whatever scum.

In the fall of the year 2114 occurred one of those great reversals of fortune which made the walls of his cursed solitude manifold. He was a passenger in one of the luxurious coaches running from Paris to the Orient, and as night drew on was engaging the attention of a corruptly beautiful yellow girl who had a compartment at the far end of the car. She was immediately affected—there was that little vein in the neck that changed pulse and gave even her slant-eyed reserve away. Markel cast an indifferent, oblique glance down the aisle and stepped inside. She spoke French well and furthered the conversation he was building up with some intelligence. She was modestly warm, and he was as icy cold as ever that afternoon, cold unchangeably. The attraction of the opposite. However blinding the sun, his clammy heart would never thaw again. He thought back along that gallery of women that had occupied him in the past, and how he had cast his wintry fear into every last soul of them. That little tigress in Mexico had called him a devil, a ghoul, a human cockroach, and shivered with fear and cold when his deathly flesh touched hers. He looked at the palm of his hand where a parenthesis of scars was a reminder of her strong little teeth. She had been dead now for thirty years. Now he extended his fingers fanwise toward the Chinese girl's unblinking face, and one by one smeared his stiff fingers through her heavily rouged lips. The train screamed to a disordered halt. Green-uniformed officers of the world-league police entered the cars and pronounced the word that is death. "War." The horrible nine years' war of 2114 had begun.

The engineer's desperation during the first few weeks of panic was his salvation, and at his suggestion the governments of the four-power alliance selected the vaults of the Bank of Northern Italy as their headquarters. Here, as secretary to the Italian minister, he chafed impatiently while the nations of the earth struggled furiously and futilely with one another for God knew what, certainly not honor. The vaults were a dream of impregnability as far as ordinary engines of war were concerned, but the chief weapons of offense seemed now to consist of projectiles carrying bacteria, so hurled that their bursting meant universal defilement. It was for this reason that no one knew when the war had ended properly, though activities ceased in 2123.

A curious crimson plague had developed during the war, which could only be accounted for by the hybridization of bacteria. No one had succeeded in effecting a cure for it, and though it burned itself out, having exhausted the human soil like all great plagues, it was never completely understood nor controlled. Markel, though, twice protected in the vaults, had ample opportunity to watch its incredibly quick and thorough ravages among his companions, and held his peace.

The engineer pursued his course through the cycling centuries, preserving himself with the coldest passion, but noted a curious recklessness gradually possessing him. When he looked back on that great red war he found himself wishing that he had deserted his post and joined those who had gone to be mowed down in the fields. The endless variety which he was seeking had no genuine interest, and had turned inevitably into the most fatal kind of monotony. He could sincerely call his life absolutely flavorless, and the toiling years more certainly assured his cosmic ennui. His ambitious love of living was being menaced by a boiling impatience, an impatience irritated by the constantly receding dream of the world's end.

One thing that would have spiced existence was the alternation of sleep, for which the Ambro could not entirely compensate. His invention was becoming more and more unmanageable, and looking back down the dim avenues of the centuries he could compare his own development with the world's cycles of petty warfare and the revolutions of empire. Periodically he suffered from attacks of scourging horror, periods of extreme mental disturbance that brought him dangerously near the black gulf of insanity. At such times, when his mental and physical life seemed held in abeyance, when he had almost irresistible impulses to commit outrages on himself, when his soul was black with fear, he drank glass after glass of his precious compound, fighting blindly against the unknown.

There was a caprice in the workings of the compound that could not be gauged, and what horror he was perpetrating on himself by his determined indulgence was beyond all conjecture. This was some subtle flaw in the Ambro, whose direction no one could map but himself, and he was all at sea. He wanted terribly to sleep, and sleep was disobedience to himself. The weariness which advanced on him chronically like a palpable, warning fog could be measured in exact degrees, and he always kept a solution of Ambro at hand. Once he had tempted himself by allowing one of the massy fatigues to carry him to the brink of a swimming unconsciousness with intoxicating celerity, and he had finally reached for the liquor nauseated with terror, scarcely able to lift his arm. . . .

"I shall never sleep again. I shall never sleep again," he cried through his hands, and wept with deep masculine shudderings, tearlessly.

The adventures of his solitary immortality were more than any man could prophecy, and as soon as the end of the twenty-fifth century his hope of the world's end went glimmering, and his horizon receded beyond imagination. In the University of Central America two associates in physics discovered a counter-gravitational influence, which was put to use commercially as a force in elevators and certain types of machine. Mastery of the force depended only on time, which Markel lived through with increasing dread. The projectile was erected which was to lose twelve daring men in outer space. But ingenuity contrived new cars whose elaborate apparatus made them subject to the most exquisite control.

Columbuses of the sky returned with incomparable tales of the deeps of the heavens, and in the course of the seven centuries before 3200 the universe was mapped into inhabited globes. There was no end. What did it matter when the world was dead? There were other worlds, and more, and more to visit when he had seen one serve out its usefulness. The people of the earth now assumed a character of mastery over the worlds of space, being first in exploration, and having proved their superiority in the peculiar twist of intelligence which enabled them to master great distances. Lovely and horrible creatures returned to earth with the sky voyagers, creatures from the far-flung worlds of the Milky Way, but Markel himself never went abroad through the sky. He was not afraid to, however many of the sky-liners had cracked up in space. He simply had no desire to. He had suffered no physical injury on earth, aside from a minor abrasion or two, since the affair with the dog, and doubted now whether he ever would. The inertia of his great age enwrapped him, and then again he had always before him the prospect of this at least being new. Once he had gone into the sky the monotony would by so much increase.

But there was really nothing new in life. What folly made him believe there was? And even if there was, what significance had it? The Ambro was a curse. It was teaching him the forbidden arcana of existence and the knowledge of God, the familiarity with which is suicide. Live forever? It was unthinkable, and the vast distances before him still found him plumbing all manner of distraction. The image of Dr. Matthew Garden crossed his thoughts repeatedly, and that last curse of his was never so bitterly appreciated as now—"May you live forever. . . ."

The voyaging never materialized, but he at least made the acquaintance of one of the voyagers. Walking along one of the upper deserted ways of one of the great half-abandoned cities of the eastern coast, he encountered princess Moya, who had been brought back from the little green paradise near Aldebaran. Once famous, she was now as obscure as Markel, having been eclipsed many times by greater prizes. She had been making arrangements to return, and Markel, looking back on his acquaintance with her, half regretted that he had not gone back with her, as she most feelingly desired. But at least she was remembered in the son he had by their union.

By this time the concealment of the engineer's mighty stature was as important as the secret itself. For the food he had taken, however little it was comparatively, had increased his height to over seven feet, and his girth proportionately. The limit of his variation in size in the future was a thing not to be contemplated, for now he was an impressive giant. Moya herself was of Junoesque proportions, which probably accounted for their mutual attraction to each other among the earth's pigmies. It was a pleasant memory. They had talked about travelling, and she had told him of the fools who considered plummeting the lightless abysses of outer space. And Markel, remembering Garden, had shocked her a little by saying he should like to join them in that long, deliberate plunge into darkness. It was a variety of escape, which had been proved in two hundred years to be certain death. Markel had followed the chronicles of the voyagers himself, and knew that none of the seventeen plummeting fools in that time had returned. But one had succeeded in flashing back his famous word when several years lost in the abyss, to the effect that in the remote, unreachable distance was a needle-point of light. His machine had reached a point where the force which drove it seemed to have nothing to work against, so it turned idly in the dark till the food pellets were exhausted and time entered upon its slow scavenging.

To look ahead to traversing the incalculable distance to that remote gleam . . . Yet it would be done. There was no end. The resentment Markel felt against his fate was gradually turning into hatred, and the hatred took in first, logically or not, the ingenuity of man which had given him those worlds without end. An ugly thought entered his head as he was passing the steps of the great government library of central Washington. He turned up the steps, the idea materializing into a last recklessness, a subtle revenge.

All these books. Markel could write a book of his own, on himself, and the liquor of the gods. Let man suffer as he had suffered. But as he idly ran through a shelf of books here, flipping over the pages with his quick thoroughness, an equation in a chemical index caught his eye, that obliterated for the moment all thought of revenge. It was the equation for the Ambro compound. It had been known for hundreds of years, and was good for sore throats. Impossible. He left the place at once and proceeded to a nearby drugstore, where he purchased the ingredients and mixed them at once on the counter, having asked for a glass of distilled water. There was no effervescence, but he downed the mixture anyhow. It was bitter and unfamiliar; the clerk smiled at the expression of distaste on the countenance of his giant customer.

A suspicion that had lurked in his mind since the dim days with the telephone company was now realized. The efficacy of the Ambro was due to an impurity in the chalk compound. Well, he would have discovered that shortly anyhow, without the chance find in the library, for the supply of powder, having lasted him for over two thousand years, was at last running low. There was enough left for only a year or two.

The next day he took a small paper of the compound to the university laboratory for analysis. There wasn't enough left for him to experiment with himself, and the analysis was a thing about which no embarrassing questions would be asked. It was all done while he waited. The chemist handed him his sheet, took his fee, and vanished without a word. Markel returned home before examining the sheet, but when he did he laughed softly. So common . . . And this chance combination of elements made you immortal. He was safe again now, and shortly set about finding materials for his revenge; he was going to write the story of the catholicon, and this long labor proved to be an eminent diversion, as well as the cruelest possible expression of his misanthropy. The people who read his book might laugh at him, but some fool would be sure to try the formula after seeing his mass of data, and then . . . It would be the simplest matter in the world to taint the drinking water—a few pounds would pollute the oceans—and then man would know what it was like to be deathless.

Somewhat more than a year later, Sosia, who lived nearby and was his son by the princess Moya, called at his rooms. He had just returned from seeing the long-tailed horses of Australia and was afire with accounts of their grace and beauty. Furthermore, he had *ridden* one, at a fabulous price, but the ecstasy of the experience was invaluable.

"Come with me sometime," he urged.

Markel was working at the table on a manuscript, looking up at intervals to carry on his end of the conversation.

"Perhaps I shall," he said with a smile.

"What's that you're working at, dad?"

"Oh . . . a book." Markel took a paper from his wallet, and after numbering the last chapter, simply pasted the slip to the page instead of writing. It was the formula for making Ambro. "There, it's done," he said.

"May I see it?" asked the young man.

"Perhaps. Some other time. But hadn't you better get along? It's almost midnight."

"You *never* sleep, do you dad?" said Sosia. At the door he stopped to remind Markel of the horses. "They say there won't be any in ten years," he said.

"We'll arrange it tomorrow," said Markel, who had seen millions of horses, long-tailed and otherwise. "Good night."

"Good night, dad."

Markel looked at the door by which Sosia had gone and reflected that it was two weeks since he had taken the last of the Ambro. New materials would have to be purchased very shortly. He had better do it in the morning. The narrative he had just completed had taken up an unexpected length of time. Well, he would read the stack of paper now for errors, and by the time he finished the shops would be open. As he knocked the manuscript into a neat pile on the table something happened. The familiar long fangs of fatigue were closing into his arms, legs, heart, body and brain, suddenly. The engineer leaped to his feet with dreadful anticipation, and ran clumsily to a small closet, where he kept a little box that had contained the last of the Ambro. A grain left, two grains? He licked the interior of the box with a dry, trembling tongue, sobbing.

His weariness was cut into at once by a slight, saving sense of freshness that enabled him to walk back to the table. But he walked as though he were mired in glue, and his stiff eyelids would apparently neither open nor close. He stood at the table listening while a grandeur of sound roared up out of the vast silences of time and shook his brain. He would have lived forever, and now there was only a throbbing in his thighs, and a tuneless and intoxicating singing in his ears . . . Markel roused himself from the morass of sweet weariness that was engulfing him, fighting sleep with magnificent willfulness. His scalp prickled slowly with terror, and a painful shiver attacked him violently, beginning at the shoulders. Obscure mists piled thickly and more thickly into the corners of the room, and out of the depths of these stepped the brisk figure of white-haired, sardonic Garden, who said:

"We live so long, and no longer. The immortality of the gods, the artificial longevity of today, the blind, foolish worship of youth, are a snare. . . ."

Markel lifted inchmeal one tired arm toward the phone.

Sosia, just entering his bedroom, heard a tinkle, and pressed the receiver button to hear his father's thick, weary voice, curiously touched with fear, asking him to return at once. He released the button and, in a matter of seconds, was mounting the steps of his father's house. He called his father's name, bursting through the doorway. The house was awake with light, but no one answered him. There in the library, though, where Sosia had left him, sat the engineer at the long table, glaring at his manuscript.

"What's the matter, dad?" he asked with some relief.

Markel didn't move. The large signet ring on the hand lying on the table gleamed steadily.

"Dad . . ." said the boy, stepping forward impulsively. The old man had had an attack; he had an ugly expression on his face. Why was he looking at the manuscript like that? Now standing by the engineer, Sosia clasped his father's hand affectionately. Whatever he was about to say was lost in horror as an unutterable stench breathed up suffocatingly into his lungs. He stepped back aghast, for Markel's hand had broken chalkily in his own, a piece or two falling to the floor weighted by the ring. The forearm broke at the elbow and hung swinging massively, suspended in the shirt arm. That colossal wreck, that giant of a man, was dead, and from out of the porous fractures of finger, palm, and wrist, there crept and dripped a pale orange ichor that announced itself unspeakably.

Several weeks later, Sosia, trying to forget the horror of that last scene, arrived at his hotel in London, thereby completing the first leg of a long journey. When he was unpacking his belongings he came upon the manuscript Markel had spent his last days working on. It was one of the few effects he had claimed at the time of his father's death. The irony of the title was still arresting—*Catholicon*. He had come to London to arrange for passage on the year's liner to Aldebaran. He had not seen his mother for several years, and on the long journey to her reading Markel's manuscript would practically make him live again. In no better way could he honor his father's memory.

O Little Nightmare

WHEN THE BUILDING next door was being remodeled a few months ago, Rodney Quist had awakened one night. He had listened to a stealthy succession of sounds for a full minute, then swiftly and silently slipped from bed, turned on the lights and looked.

They had twin beds, he and Ursula. Between them had run a streak of some compact, powerful creature in motion. The glance he had of it wasn't sufficient; a streak of something traveling lightning fast, and it was gone. He thought it might have been an unusually large and damned speedy rat forced into the open during the demolition of the neighboring building. With his heart pumping and his throat too dry to swallow, he stared into the darkness between the French doors, open for ventilation, where the nocturnal thing had disappeared.

The impression he had of the animal was incredible, the product of a lunatic imagination rather than any thing which could be alive. If it was alive, it was a solid, scampering figment of nightmare.

For a while he stood staring, arguing with himself that it was uncertain whether he had really seen it or whether his eyes had projected something from a vivid dream into ugly actuality.

Shaken, with his heart still hammering, Rodney had called softly to Ursula. His wife was lying supine, exquisite as the day he married her, in the deep sleep of drunkenness. She slept with her slim arms bent above her head, the position drawing the lace yoke of her nightgown taut over her firmly rounded breasts. He gazed at her speculatively, called again, "Ursula!"

Then he closed the rear doors, and after smoking a cigarette, turned the lights off.

While they struggled with mutual hangovers in the morning, he related the episode of the huge "rodent," and was laughed at. Rats never attained such a size.

It was several weeks since the superintendent had caught a rat in his traps. The more he thought of it, the more Quist doubted whether the thing he had seen was a rat; he couldn't forget the eerie, puzzling sound that had awakened him, nor the violent, primitive fear that struck him with such electrical suddenness, at the imagined strangeness of the animal. It wasn't anything common. The sound he had been hearing at odd times for two or three days, now, most often in broad daylight, was much the same as what had shocked him with that stab of horror. The sound didn't stay in one place. It prowled. It would come from an open closet, from the seat of a chair, from a far corner of the studio, or frisk in the walls or along the walls, along the baseboards.

He couldn't locate it. He had sneaked out of bed twice at night to search for it, and by day he had left his work many times to go hunting for it. Either there were rats in the walls, he decided, or the foundations of this building were sinking with remarkable rapidity, or the house was haunted by a ghost which had appreciable weight besides being invisible. Or else there was a creature which could move too fast for the human eye to see it. Or else he was drinking too much, and only imagining that he saw movement out of the corner of his eye, when there couldn't possibly be a moving thing.

There was a group of the sounds. There was the dry, delicately popping one, as of a cat sharpening its claws on woolen upholstery. Then the sound of eggshells being slowly crunched in a fist, an eating sound. Then an empty shoe being pushed across bare floor. Then a long-legged, barefoot man walking; the space impacts of bare heels against the floor. Quist developed the habit of sitting frozen, listening. And swallowing, Quist the artist, high-strung, alert to details, whether of sound, or color and time.

He was listening now on this bright afternoon, thumb hooked through the palette, paintbrush sticking out from his hand as though he intended stabbing a fly on the canvas with it. From the bedroom came a gentle *thud*. His head jerked. Of course, there was nothing to see through the archway between studio and bedroom. Irritably he stuck the brush into a jar of turpentine and commenced scraping the palette.

"Through already?" asked the girl on the model-stand.

"All through. Guess I'm not in the mood today."

"Something wrong? Anything I can do to help?" Her voice was lazy and suggestive.

She was Betty Orson, slim, young, lovely, an excellent model, though not a better model than his wife. He inspected her figure in silence, slowly and sensuously cleaning his hands as though he had her slenderness in them, remembering her remarkably firm round breast, the litheness of her waist, the conformation of her narrow boyish hips and the breathless curves of her thighs. His hands moving, counting the exquisite details of her anatomy like a hoarder fingering gold-pieces.

"Ursula thought she might go to a movie if she finished shopping early enough," he remarked. "She might come back any minute now."

"Oh," said Betty disappointedly. She left the stand and walked to a chair on which her clothes were draped. There was a screen, but she didn't observe the propriety of getting behind it. She stepped balancingly into very brief, snug panties of elastic satin only a note of color darker than her rosepetal skin. The brassière was just as snug; she moved her shoulders, raised her chest, adjusting the bra with the nicest exactitude. When she had her shoes on she returned unconcernedly to Quist with her dress and slip over her arm. There was a pair of scotch and sodas on the table next to him, and she took one.

"Them's some lingerie you've got, Betty," he commented. "Recent purchase? I haven't seen them before."

"It's about time you noticed." She smiled, her lips wet from the drink. Indicating, she asked, "Isn't this cute?"

"There's nothing quite like the female anatomy," he assured her. They were only a step apart, and she took it. With the most gentlemanly acquiescence he bent and kissed her once, twice, as though picking up sweet wild raspberries with his lips; he kissed her parted lips with their bodies joined tightly. Betty set her drink down, feeling for the table; her hand returned to him and was quick with its straying pressures.

He felt as though he were being watched, as though someone hidden in the apartment were watching him with active dislike. Hatred.

"What's the matter?" Betty asked, in a rapid, eager whisper.

"I've got a funny hunch," he said slowly; he frowned, looking about the apartment. For something strange. Someone observing. She breathed deeply, making him fully aware of her breathing. His arm was still around her waist. With their drinks in hand they gravitated toward the studio couch.

They *were* being watched, and by his wife Ursula, who had once been a model for him. The tall front windows of the studio were hung with Venetian blinds, the slats being turned up so that no one could look in from the street, and to let in sunlight. The street was broad. No one in the upper apartments across the street could look into the studio, either, unless he had a telescope.

Ursula's friend Cicely Bourne had an apartment across the way, unknown to Rodney; further, she owned high-powered binoculars which she had bought in Germany; and Ursula was sitting at the window holding the heavy field-glasses to her eyes, her elbows on her knees. As she watched Rod and Betty embrace, her attitude was almost that of mere scientific curiosity; no emotion changed her pulse-rate nor made her hands tremble.

Cicely, a hard-headed, athletic English girl, paced the apartment smoking strong cigarettes of pure Virginia leaf. She smoked like a man, inhaling with pleasure. Her hands were thrust into the pockets of her heavy silk robe, which was unbelted. The opening revealed that she was wearing tailored panties, no brassière; if she wasn't going anywhere she didn't dress. Occasionally she glanced at the back of Ursula's pretty head sardonically. Ursula watched Betty and her husband end the embrace and go to the studio seat with their drinks. A few minutes later she laid the binoculars down on the window-seat where she knelt.

"Well?" Cicely demanded.

Ursula nodded and said, "Damn it, men are rotten."

"They're—?"

"Oh, yes, of course!" Ursula said angrily.

"And you still don't want a divorce?"

"Get me a drink, Cicely," Ursula requested. "No, I don't think I want a divorce. Not on New York grounds. Cicely, I'm not homely, am I? Have I got bad breath or something?"

"Darling, you're a beauty. Don't be idiotic. That girl Betty what's-her-name has a good figure, but yours is better."

"Do you really think so?" Her voice was hard.

"You ought to know it yourself; you can see yourself in the mirror, can't you? Your legs are better, and your breasts are definitely superior."

"Then what does he do it for?" Ursula complained. "If I had an affair with a man and he found out, he'd hit the ceiling."

"Of course he would; it's a man's privilege."

"He can do it and I can't. Why?"

"Because men are that way. You're certainly not in love with him any more, are you?"

"I certainly am not," said Ursula with conviction. "It's worse than that. I'm afraid of him."

"You're afraid of him! Why?"

Ursula sipped her drink. "Mostly because of his eyes," she said finally in decision. Her lips were darkly rouged and as ripe as cherries. Offset by her soft dark hair and creamy unrouged cheeks, the color smoldered. "Lately it's been worse. When he thinks I'm not watching him, he does things that insane people do."

"All artists and writers are a little nuts," Cicely pointed out. "The good ones are the nuttiest."

"He stands in one spot for fifteen minutes at a time, just moving his eyes in the craziest way, as though he's listening for something," Ursula reported. "Like this." She rose and held her drink in an exaggerated position, demonstrating. "It's his eyes. Very bright and very pale. I don't mind his being a little bit cracked, but I wouldn't want to be around if he goes completely off his nut sometime."

"Be a lucky thing for you if he did."

"How do you mean?"

"You know what I mean, darling. He's a damned good painter. Some of those pictures he's refused to sell will go into museums. He's got a lot of money in the bank, which would be yours. You could have him locked up in a private hospital and keep him there till hell burns out. There wouldn't be any stigma; the newspapers could be fixed to call it a 'nervous breakdown.' Isn't that about right?"

"Cicely," Ursula said sweetly, "your insight is miraculous. But things never come out so easily. I'll still be hoping a truck runs him down, or he commits suicide, when I'm an old woman."

"You ought to get a divorce, Ursula. There're both Bill and Mulford, and you could have either one when you got back from Reno. They've told me, and I'd bet on it," said the English girl. "I know them."

"Really?" Ursula asked. "I mean, interested?"

"Of course, my sweet. Look—how about a careful, genteel, foolproof murder at moderate rates?"

Ursula laughed and said, "Uh-uh! The police are awfully good at murders, and I'm not gutsy enough to play the role of bereaved wife. Uh-uh."

"I killed two men on that last hunting expedition in Africa," Cicely stated reminiscently. "There was no sign of a trail but they went through the motions of following one. When they had lured me far enough from my party, believe it or not they turned on me just like wild animals. One of them— Well, anyhow, they were listed as hunting accidents by the authorities."

"But that was in Africa."

"By the way, did you live with Rod before you married him?"

Ursula turned her glass reflectively, took a sip from it and said, "I wouldn't marry again."

When Betty Orson left the studio it was late afternoon. Rod mixed himself a new drink and broodingly paced the apartment with the drink in his hand. The idea of divorce occurred to him and he nodded his head.

He figured, "I'm an artist, and people think artists are nuts, so I can do just about what I please. But there's Bill Wicker and that rat Mulford; they'd grab Ursula if I let her go. She dances with them just as though she's in a bathing suit, just as close together as strawberries and cream. I've watched them. Just the same, I've got to have a free hand with Betty Orson. She won't start getting wrinkled for maybe twenty years yet, and I'll be figuring how to get rid of Ursula in five, six or seven at the outside if she goes to the right beauty experts. Around the eyes."

There was a picture he had in mind, of a fantastic and violent nature. Not a salable subject in the open market, but worth enough in private commerce. Ready purchaser for it, that broker; paid good prices for that genre if it was first-class. This would be. There was a hop-skip-jump to Rod's imaginings. He thought of strange things which had the reality of common-places. Sounds which he translated into shapes.

From the bedroom came the whirring ring of the phone.

What he could do to Ursula in a painting, for example. He could recite the details of her from memory, and that was a job he was going to do when she was gone. Need perspective. He entered the bedroom.

When he saw it he stood in his tracks, and goggled at it in stunned disbelief for a minute before the gooseflesh crawled on his back. It was a horrible little beast about the size of his clenched right fist, and was sitting on the floor next to the leg of an enameled modernistic chair of Ursula's. The phone stopped ringing after the fifth buzz.

It was the beast he had seen that night between the twin beds.

Quist took a slow step forward, tried to smash the strange animal with a sudden stamp of his foot, trying to keep away from it at the same time. His shoe bashed the chair leg and chipped the enamel.

For a moment of hard breathing he thought his overwrought imagination had created the thing, and the fantasy had flown to smithereens. But he rediscovered it clinging to the spread hanging over the foot of Ursula's bed. It had arrived there in a leap too quick for the eye to follow. Quist retreated, swallowing, taking quick glances aside in search of something to throw, afraid he would lose sight of it. This was the thing that had made the curious, unidentifiable sounds he had been hearing. It was there. It was absolutely alive and incredible.

Abruptly the animal opened its muzzle and addressed him with a squealing, rapid liquid chattering. Hysterical gibberish. The thing had a voice, and command of a wide range of vocal effects. It might have been a language, if he had been able to understand the angrily telescoped words.

With his bulging eyes fixed on it he reached for a crockery ashtray, picked it up in a good grip. He slipped his left foot forward along the rug, got a good stance, and with a madman's patience cocked his arm. Twelve feet from the target, he couldn't miss; he let fly with a peg that shattered the ashtray against the foot of the bed. Six feet away, the pygmy nightmare came to rest on the floor in front of his own bed, unharmed. It scolded him again, with tufts of the broadloom pile sticking up between its tiny, perfectly formed fingers, ready to move with equal facility and speed in any direction. On the blunt, neckless muzzle of its dough-naked body, its chatoyant green eyes watched him unwinkingly. Quist stalked it, again stamped wildly. When his foot struck the floor the hideous animal was a yard away out of danger, as though it had been there all the time.

He tore into the aisle between the beds, stamping and kicking, but it anticipated every movement he made as though it was thinking in unison with him.

In the flurry of violence it sprang aloft once and fastened on his thigh, and he touched it for the first time. Nearly gibbering, he batted it loose with a downward swipe of his hand and heard the bump of its muscular rebound from the floor. He hunted for it, trembling.

This time it had gone farther, getting behind him and perching on the saddle of the French doors to the studio. Its red tentacle of tongue dripped from its jaws like a trickle of blood, was withdrawn when he moved. At first he sneaked, then charged insanely with his breath sounding in animal whimpers. In a couple of winks of movement it was gone, and the most exhaustive search failed to give him another glimpse of it.

In the bathroom he unbelted his trousers and painted the claw marks on his thigh with iodine. Reflected in the mirror, his eyes were enormously expanded, mad.

He tried to figure it out. There was no insanity in his family that he knew of, but he was a candidate for the honor of being first. He couldn't tell Ursula about the unspeakable vermin that had chosen their apartment as its new home; she would have to see it herself. And the thing had to be caught and destroyed. Somehow.

In a nightmare he had the capacity of telling himself, "This is a nightmare. Wake up, Quist. Wake up! Wake up!"

But he couldn't wake up from this. Evidence of the nimble horror's existence was his clawed thigh. But it wouldn't be evidence to a girl of Ursula's unsympathetic, hardheaded skepticism.

Once he had awakened in terror and gone to bed with her, to dream again, this time that she was dead in his arms, to leap drunkenly from sleep and find her in his bed.

He wondered how the disgusting tailless rodent had gotten into the apartment, where it had come from. Something that had crawled from a sewer into that long-boarded-up building next door? Its body was a ball of muscle, its flesh as firm as a girl's breast. It had four legs, and the head was closely articulated with the torso. The teeth were curved needles. Its extremities were human in miniature, the hands having four fingers and a long thumb. Its hide was tough human skin, and there were ridges of veins which he could see pulsing. The legs were sturdy, sinewy, and could propel the body with the spring-steel action of a claspknife.

Quist had just cleaned up the mess of the broken ashtray when Ursula returned. She looked at him speculatively, and commented, "There's lipstick on your face, darling."

"What? Oh," he answered absently. "Apparently the model expected to be kissed, and so I sort of kissed her."

Ursula laughed throatily. "You sort of kissed her! Why do you call her 'the model'? Isn't Betty Orson the only one you're using?"

"Of course; I told you Betty was coming to pose. Where have you been? Did you see a show?"

"No, I just shopped. Then I had a couple of drinks with Cicely Bourne."

"Who's she?"

"A girl I knew in England. She was in one of the Olympics; she hunts big game in Africa and things like that, now; once in a while her name gets into the newspapers."

"I never read newspapers. Is she in Manhattan?"

"She has a very nice apartment down here in The Village. She was showing me some trophies. She has some dried pygmy heads, and fossilized shark-teeth, and a whole trunkful of remarkable primitive carving. Stone and ivory and wood—she has some gold figurines and an emerald scarab and a section of carved bamboo with a roll of papyrus inside, all Egyptian. It must be ten thousand years old; a man from the Metropolitan is coming down to see her."

"Why haven't you told me about her before? She sounds interesting."

"She isn't good-looking," Ursula said quietly. "She's leggy and muscular, and has one of those horsey English faces. But I must say she has good breasts."

"What are you getting at?" Rod asked.

"She's awfully strong," said Ursula. "If you made any passes at her, she could give you the beating of your life if she felt like it."

"Do you think I make passes at every girl I'm alone with?" Rod demanded.

"What makes you think you'd be alone with Cicely?" Ursula asked sweetly. "People are dropping in on her all day long. There must have been a dozen around when I was there this afternoon. But I'll give you her address if you want it. It's practically across the street."

"Never mind, never mind," Rod refused sourly. "I can get along without Egyptology. What is she—a reincarnated priestess?"

"I'm very fond of her; we used to go to concerts together in London," Ursula said. "What's the matter with you? You look as though you haven't had any sleep for a week."

"There's nothing wrong," Rod groused, "except that I can't get going on the new picture Betty was posing for."

"It must be more than that; you look terrible," Ursula criticized. She went to the easel, backstepped for perspective and reported professionally, "It's first-class as far as you've gone, and you know it. Rod, what's wrong?"

His eyes were funny. He kept looking around the place, at the stacks of canvasses in the corners, through the archway into the bedroom, nervously alert for any evidence of the nightmare he had experienced earlier. He asked, "What do you mean? There's nothing wrong."

"Then don't keep on looking around as though you've eaten a goblin," she said. "It gives me the meemies."

"You keep on asking questions," he complained. He shouted, "Don't I answer them right? I'm going nuts!"

"I wouldn't be surprised."

He expressed a great contempt for motion pictures, but she liked them, and she was going to Loew's Sheridan, down on Seventh Avenue.

After dinner she went into the bedroom to get ready. She was wearing a dark gray skirt of thin, pleated wool, and a tight-fitting jacket with a fly-front and a baby-lingerie blouse peeking out from the open neck. She always did this. She made a complete change, striping down to the buff to take a shower, draping her things neatly over the end of her bed. He sat in the bedroom watching her, because the little nightmare of legs and toadstool-body was perched on the satin slip she had taken off. It sat there with the nonchalance of an inanimate object, like a purse or anything, just still.

Ursula's body quivered and she turned suddenly, stared at him. The night was chilly, and goose-flesh tightened and lifted her breasts. Her hands were close against her hips and she was beautiful. She was healthy and slim, and her lips smiled invitingly. Her legs were more than shapely. Extraordinary.

He said, "Ursula, you've got a couple of legs."

She stared at him, and he said, "When you get back from the show, I want to talk to you about something."

"All right," she agreed noncommittally. He looked at her uptilted breasts, down her hips and long delicious legs. She went in and took a shower; Quist's cane was hung from a hook in the wardrobe, and he came out with it. The diminutive monster was still resting on the bed; it gathered its legs under itself as though it liked the feel of silk. It crouched there. Quist swung at it with all his might, glaring.

He was playing with the cane when Ursula emerged from the shower, powdered and fragrant. His head jerked around to watch her, how she put on her brassière, the girdle and panties and slip, her new dress.

The little nightmare was ten feet away on the floor, and she didn't see it. Quist kept his eyes on Ursula's face, watching. She smiled at him and asked, "Remember how you used to like to watch me dress?" She put her hands to her breasts, adjusting the bra.

"Maybe you'd better hurry back from the show," he said.

They kissed on the lips, and his arms crushed the breath out of her momentarily, holding her as though he needed her, and she responded. He slapped her gently.

When she left, the little monster was directly in her path and she had to see it. She glanced down, but the thing darted aside too quickly for the eye to follow. He couldn't see where it had gone, and she remarked, "I thought my shoelace was untied."

When she was gone, there was no sign of the beast. Promptly Quist began a systematic search of the apartment, beginning with the bathroom and closing the door, searching closets and shutting them, making sure that the creature had escaped from the apartment when Ursula left. When he had finished with the bedroom he felt in need of a drink and went to the kitchen.

First he saw the giant cockroach traveling across the linoleum in a brown streak toward the safety of a crack under the sink. Its flight terminated in the wink of an eye when, with a whipcrack of motion, the four-legged bugaboo shot out from beneath the refrigerator in a pounce. The roach kicked frantically in its captor's front paws. Standing up on its hind legs to eat squirrel-wise, the green-eyed thing chuckled and chattered triumphantly in its goblin language. The roach almost exploded with its desire for liberty; then speedily, except for wing-cases, wings, and legs, it was devoured with a sound like crackling celluloid. With a convulsive stab of his arm, Quist slammed the kitchen door.

The squatty little abomination was trapped with him in the kitchen now. He laughed raggedly, because it couldn't escape unless it was able to pour itself through keyholes. Prickling with goose-flesh from head to foot he stared at it. The bloated loathsomeness of it; its obscene nudity; its utter, incredible wrongness. It was as wrong as the warped imaginings of a madman. The most violent disgust, fear, murderous antagonism nauseated him and held him for a moment, and his eyes brightened from a headache as staggering in intensity as though resulting from a concussion. He jumped forward and brought his foot down.

The beast moved like a volleyed tennis ball; it caromed from corner to corner as he pursued, hop-frogged the garbage can and took refuge again under the refrigerator. It gobbled and chattered and squeaked its fear under there. Quist whipped up an empty bottle and slung it with accuracy and power under the box.

Out of the explosion of glass erupted the wickedly agile obscenity, unhurt. It made a blind try for the crack under the door, but the crack was far too narrow. Quist pitched another bottle, another miss. There was a folded card table; he opened one leg and wrenched it off, and now he had a club. He rained blows, and the ruin in the kitchen increased with his frenzy.

He had the little horror screaming continuously with fear, shrieking like rusty steel turning against steel. He ticked the flying animal with his bat, grazed it once more and then met it squarely with a home-run swing. But it was too tough to kill with a single blow and kept up its magic speed, jump, sidestep, all-direction velocity. He shouted curses at it, and the people upstairs started pounding on the floor.

There had to be a way of killing the thing. It was alive, so it could be cut with a knife, drowned in water, smashed and broken with a heavy object. Let it bite and claw him, once he got his hands on it he knew what to do with this thing from nowhere, from the border-lands of the mind. There was one fitting way to kill it in particular on his mind, gone completely animal in the desperate chase. Once . . . he . . . got . . . his . . . hands . . . on . . . it. Sobbing with effort and mouthing unintelligibly he kept swinging at the noisy wild thing.

Ursula arrived home breathless, with color in her cool cheeks; she shut the door and called, "Rodney!"

There was no answer, and the anticipation faded out of her sparkling dark eyes and red lips. There wasn't a sound in the house; he had gone out and left the place unlocked. Angrily she jerked off her hat and snapped it into a chair. She was bitterly disappointed as she disrobed in the bedroom, and she swore, "He's just a damned man. He's no good. Out hunting, looking for legs and breasts and things all the time."

She slipped her feet into sandals, stood naked in hesitation for a moment. She decided she would have a drink and wait up for him, give him all her scorn. She would sit in the big chair facing the door, without a stitch on and with a drink in her hand, and furiously she hoped that he would return home with a guest and be shamed. She went to the kitchen and opened the door.

He was using the three-step ladder as a chair, with his heels on the bottom step, in the midst of destruction. His eyes were huge, bulging. If there was anything that ever got his immediate and industrious attention it was a bare girl, but he didn't see her at all. He was gone;

profoundly, irrevocably. He had both hands clapped over his jaws as though to lock in a shriek, and his breathing snuffled.

Though she was rid of him forever, the shock of it made Ursula gasp, then scream with all the strength in her lungs. What appeared to be a miniature human arm escaped between Quist's fingers and reached. The tiny, perfectly formed hand clutched feebly, moistly glistening. He was eating something alive, and from his crammed mouth issued a hideous, choked, broken mewling. He recaptured the miniature arm and tucked it back in, masticating.

In the Triangle

HE LISTENED.

In the familiar woods surrounding the house was some exotic beast, making its presence known in a most puzzling manner. Arnold closed the book he had been reading and walked over to the open window. The August afternoon was at its pitch, and the heavy, moist, hazy air had suffocated all other living things into silence. The man looked through the woods in the direction of the sound, and then cocked his head, listening intently, trying to identify the sound. It was a broken succession of growlings, a gobbling curiously interrupted so as to sound like a mechanical and humorless chuckling.

He was disturbed. There could be no beast on earth that could make a sound like that. Its utterly mechanical nature seemed all exact repetition. He thought of a phonograph, whose arm soullessly and maddeningly played the same groove of a record over and over and over again. His house was remotely situated, and no one from town would be here on such a stifling afternoon. The empty lightness of children was not in the noise, and it could hardly be made with implements. It was a throaty evidence of life, and now it cut regularly through the air like a vocal saw.

Arnold knew the woods very well, having lived there many years; the origin of the disturbance was not difficult to locate. Having listened intently at the window for some minutes, he dropped his book on the window-seat and crossed the room to the door. Here he stopped for a moment, but decided not to lock it. The small animals of the woods might take a bright object or two, so he returned to close the window. Then he closed the door, and after looking up at the dead blue sky and around at his greening acres, made off through the trees. No human being was likely to visit, especially on a day like this. Only one white-haired old man had come by in the last two weeks. Curious old fellow. He had eyed Arnold as though he were taking pictures of his ways, his body, and his brain; and he had taken his own time in leaving.

No air stirred. The birds were silent, and the trees stood so still they seemed waiting for life. Arnold walked rapidly and softly, peering through the trees ahead and to either side. The ground was not entirely free of brush, nor was it level. But the loose collocations of elms, oaks, and cottonwoods which were commonest in this country admitted a fairly unobstructed view for some distance ahead. As he walked he looked familiarly on his property, identifying a stump, touching a tree where he had carved his initials a year or two ago. Now he was ascending a broad, low knoll, the first site he had chosen for his house, and decided against because of the magnificent trees growing here. From the continued noise of the beast he knew that discovery was close at hand. The sound was even more puzzling than before, and it would be difficult to say whether it was caused by throat or machine. There would be enlightenment on the other side of the knoll.

As he walked, the exotic growling had assumed the character of a struggle, and now, as he advanced more carefully, a thin, plaintive human voice, oddly familiar, augmented the sound of eccentric senseless chuckling. So it was a struggle, and one of the contenders was a man calling weakly for help.

Arnold quickly crested the knoll, shouting, "Hold on! I'm with you in a moment!"

The struggle, instead of ceasing at his now noisy approach, increased, and the chuckle became magnified to a broken, staccato barking. Arnold shouted again encouragingly, and, breaking through a clinging screen of creepers and clutching brush, stopped dead as he sighted the struggling figures before him.

In this spot three venerable cottonwoods formed an almost perfect triangle, within which the ground was almost free of all growth. In this triangle was lying prone an old man with long white hair. It was the old fellow who had dropped in two weeks ago. He was plainly and neatly dressed in coarse grey cloth, and he was striving fearfully to protect his throat and abdomen from the teeth and disemboweling claws of a strange beast.

The beast was of human size, and seemed to have something of the characteristics each of ape, pig, and dog. Its fangs were of extraordinary length, however, and it made such a violent caricature of life that Arnold looked on it with disgust and horror. Coarse black hair covered the body and a short tail jerked convulsively as the beast made its barking noises and its arching fangs worried the old man's throat. A hybrid? Odd animals have appeared most unaccountably at the strangest times in the most unexpected places. There was the dog-boar monstrosity that was found in France. This might not be the worst nor the least of nature's baroque experiments.

Completely revolted by the appearance of the queer animal, Arnold hastily looked for a convenient weapon, answering the piteous appeal in the old man's eyes. If he had taken fuller account of the situation, he might have hesitated, and thought the struggle even stranger than at first glance.

In the first place, aside from the affair in the triangle, the woods were uncommonly still, so still that the air seemed charged with waiting and expectancy. There was so marked a contrast between the apparent violence in the triangle and the deadly summer stillness of the air and brush and trees that the whole affair was denied both purpose and reality. The background of silence, suggesting a toleration that approached human understanding, gave the struggle the character of highest artificiality.

Arnold missed the significance in the attacking fangs of the beast. The teeth were terribly sharp, and, though repeatedly closing on the old man's throat, never dented the skin. The disemboweling claws, full of raking death, exerted convulsive pressure and nothing more. The claws themselves scarcely caught in the old man's neat gray cloth. Arnold had heard the ugly, ghoulish barking aright, but didn't see its meaning. The barks were unfinished growlings, animal sounds continually started and never completed. The old man exhibited no evidences of physical harm; his plain garments were unsullied, and were disposed in careful folds. The waiting woods and the struggling forms insidiously represented a composite threat and nothing more.

But Arnold, unable to find either stick or stone in the enclosed triangle, and daring to take no time looking through the brush encroaching on this particular spot, flung himself bodily on the assaulting beast. The impact of his body liberated the old man, who took his feet at once, and circled the two on the ground gingerly.

"Kill him! Kill him!" he squeaked querulously.

"Get a stick!" said Arnold, furiously struggling. But the old man stood by, watching the two interestedly.

The beast emitted magnified, full-throated barkings now, and a long violence of growlings. Its rank, intolerable animal odor was suffocating and charnel in the stagnant air, and Arnold fought to finish the thing as soon as possible. Oddly enough, he thought at this moment of his pleasant room and the book he had been reading. The time-spread initials he had carved in the tree seemed stamped on the beast's rugose, leonine forehead. The hateful feeling of the moist, swine-like skin was a difficulty in itself, but more important was the fact that the animal's body afforded no firm grasp. He was holding the creature desperately by its wrists, and his superior position prevented it from using its deadly legs. Neither of them was free to use his hands.

"For God's sake, hit it! Kick its head!" he said, and looked up at the old man, his eyes full of violent entreaty. But the old man only skipped about tensely, eyeing the beast and looking at Arnold nervously. Arnold cursed his luck in hearing the beast from his untroubled house. Better the old man had died. Or would he have died anyhow? The animal might have been the old devil's pet, to all appearances. At any rate the old fellow didn't seem to have a scratch on his body from the curious encounter.

As Arnold looked into the beast's flaming eyes his brain flushed with desperation, purpose, and horror. The creature's wide, fixed stare seemed an attempt to take possession of his will, and he felt himself drowning in the engulfing shadows of the beast's mindlessness. He shook his head dizzily, freeing himself from the hypnotizing stare, and, as his one resort, sickly forced his jaws to the beast's throat. He found his face wet and warm, and the taste of blood on his lips. The reek of the thing's skin checked his breath. Convinced now that the situation demanded the beast's life or his own, he worked with distasteful hurry: there was the sanctuary afterward of his room and his books, nor would he ever bury this vileness on his loved property. The old man would hear a word or two, moreover. He had offered no help in the least, only dancing about like a gray-headed, delighted monkey.

During this time the creature had made no effort to use its own powerful jaws, only barking and growling savagely. And at Arnold's sudden determination to take its life, it closed its jaws for his convenience and merely continued the sound through its nose and throat. Its body lurched about with all the appearances of deadly intent, but it made no effort at definite harm. Arnold missed this singularity, and his revolted jaws clipped the beast's jugular.

The mingled incidents of the situation resolved themselves into coincidences. Arnold found himself lying prone, looking dimly at the sky. His throat hurt terribly, and he raised his arm to find his neck mangled, the large veins severed, and his life ebbing away in warm spurts. The arm was bare and swarthy, like pigskin, as was his whole unfamiliar body. The leathery tongue with which he tried to lick his straining lips encountered strange, curving fangs. Above him stood the beast, and his dying brain burned with shame as he recognized his own garments, his own watchful attitude, and himself, looking down eagerly with his own now weirdly glittering eyes.

Now the quiet summer afternoon afforded the scene of a hairy beast lying on the ground in the center of triangulated cottonwoods, clawing horribly at its breast. A young man and an old man with long white hair were walking off through the woods to Arnold's house, and, as the strange beast's head rolled sidewise, the eyes filming in death glimpsed finally the brisk figure of the old man looking back gleefully.

The Other

BASIL SASH WAS a feature writer and a damned good one. He knew that he was on the trail of something hot. As he skipped up the steps of Captain Bjoern Ingvaldssen's Manhattan residence that morning he had no doubt that he was going to cash in on a feature second to none. That's saying a great deal. He jabbed the bell. He gave the knocker a boost for good measure, was pretty cocky about it. Then he yawned and blinked his eyes dopily, for it was morning and Basil Sash's nights generally reeled. Sash was dead sober and wide awake all the same.

The door opened like a shutter. The man who confronted him was just exactly the man Sash was looking for, but Sash was sleepily nonplused. It was the explorer and scientist himself. He eyed the reporter with such fishy, icy fury that Sash was speechless. Ingvaldssen stood six foot two and carried the brawn that goes with it; he had something decidedly beefy about his appearance. Heavy in the face to the point of stupidity, he had eyes of a cool dark gray that seemed bottomless. Something appeared to be the matter with him. Somehow that fact pleased the reporter.

"Captain Ingvaldssen?" inquired Sash finally. He was uncommonly polite, and even removed his hat.

"What the devil do you want, mister?" barked the captain.

Sash took a deep breath, the most salient characteristic of the famous people he had met, he reflected, was the fact that no two of them performed alike. He fumbled in his pocket, gracefully offered his press card as though it burned him.

"Let's have the story on that stiff, captain," he suggested. He adopted his easiest, most persuasive and placating manner. Sash had a lot of English on the ball. He had handled some pretty knotty customers. "You know, captain, that swell little cadaver you've got in the icebox."

Ingvaldssen slammed the door violently with volcanic dispatch. This door was massive. The architect had used up four hundred and fifty pounds of logwood when he hung it, but it clapped very briskly indeed. Sash had scarcely time enough to blink and open his mouth. Then the door banged in again just as quickly as it had shut. A hand shot out, grasped him fiercely by the throat, yanked him inside. He swung his feet helplessly in the air. He plucked at an enormous hand, which he found collaring his throat. Ingvaldssen had him off the floor and pinned to the door like one of his damned trophies. Sash's eyes bulged, became prominent and bloodshot. His tongue purpled and swelled. He rolled it painfully. It popped out between his teeth of its own accord. He saw a fabulous galaxy of exploding suns and heard the roaring of the sea.

All at once the elephantine Ingvaldssen changed his mind. He gave the reporter a violent shake that came near disarticulating his vertebrae and dropped him. Sash sat down hard. He felt of his bruised throat. For a time he made cooing sounds while he fought desperately to get his wind.

"For a minute," Sash choked out, "I thought you were going to throttle me. Was that nice?"

"I was," said the captain. He rocked on his heels, keeping his hands behind his back. "That's just what I planned to do, but I felt perhaps someone might know you had come here, had seen you enter. Murder is a serious thing when there are witnesses."

The reporter shivered. The "Norski Cow", the name by which Ingvaldssen was known back at the city desk, had changed a lot since his last expedition. Whence this ferocity?

"Let's skip it, captain." Sash essayed a sickly grin. "All I want is the feature. The story about that lady corpse you've been keeping on ice. Give it to Basil Sash and we'll be buddies all over again."

The big Swede's eyes narrowed. He seemed to be thinking about something.

"Maybe," he said finally. He jerked his head at Sash, indicating that the reporter should follow him. Sash trailed the big fellow into a long work chamber opening off the hall, a room packed with an explorer's impedimenta and trophies. A great deal of stuff was still crated as it had come from the ship. The two men went through into a spacious back room, a laboratory in the proper sense. Here Ingvaldssen folded hairy, bear's arms on his chest and stared at the reporter without speaking. The reporter's eyes flickered from the captain's ominous face to an object near the back wall. He got a full view of that which he had only peeked at as it was trucked off from the pier. That peek had been enough, enough to tell him that the captain had been up to something. While Ingvaldssen turned off the reporters with a few short, indifferent words and a stock, technical report, Sash found a rent in a tarpaulin-wrapped block which a crane was planting on a waiting motor van. Something that had come on the *Petrel* from the high latitudes, via Stockholm! Here it was.

"Good lord!" the reporter gasped.

The thing really was a body, and it was a queer one. It was the body of a woman, sealed in some kind of refrigerator. It was sheathed in ice.

Bjöern Ingvaldssen, Sc. D. and well up in the services of the American Technological Survey, went to the Arctic with a machine fabricated by his sponsors. He had explored polar territories previously under his own government and was acquainted with the field. The machinery he took along was one of seven outfits being tested in various quarters of the globe by other men, all field workers in the Survey. The problem confronting these men was to set up the apparatus entrusted to them in certain strategic places, notably mountain peaks and other high altitudes, in order to check the mysterious and elusive cosmic ray drift at various latitudes. It was a mechanical problem with vast implications. The field workers, however, had merely to operate their sensitive instruments a given length of time, seal them, return them intact to the Survey. Ingvaldssen drew the polar territory. He was the most reliable man available for what was considered the most hazardous piece of work. The polar ray vortex, too, was of the utmost importance in the Survey's calculations. The captain had gotten some queer facts of ray distortion—cosmic bends, as it were—down on his recorders. He did his job thoroughly with characteristic precision and shipped all his instruments to his sponsors. But he had brought something else back with him from the arctic wastes. Distance and seasonal hazards alone were not what made him the last man in. He took the Petrel to Stockholm first, ostensibly for repairs. There was nothing in his reports about the real reason for delay, this precious cake of ice. When the Petrel finally nosed into the North River, the only newsy information the taciturn Swede had to give out was the fact that he had picked up the frozen rear quarters of what was supposed to be a mastodon, preserved in an arctic glacier. His men had eaten some of it.

Sash crossed to the refrigerator. This was a plate glass box, especially constructed so as to accommodate the body within to best advantage. A drain at the lower side of the case conducted melted ice into a small reservoir. The case stood on a pedestal or dais, and could be viewed from four sides. Refrigerating machinery was enclosed in the pedestal, and more of it spilled out, connected by cables to a mass of apparatus at one side. Dials and gauges were piped up from the pedestal alongside the glass, and more of them stood in nests on the control machinery. Nothing else in the laboratory really mattered, the usual stock of jars and retorts, a few electrical devices. Sash had seen many shops like it. But the refrigerator! He had a story here worth a whole front page, and it would have his name on it. Boy, what a feature! By Basil Sash.

He circled the refrigerator. The girl inside was five feet nine or ten in height, and not a type he had ever seen before. She was of no known race. Her hair was molten bronze, her skin reddish, coppery. Her eyes were open. They were sidelong, but not mongoloid, and sooty green in color. Her lips, a natural scarlet, were parted in derision, and on her face was an expression of the most ferocious cruelty. She stood at half turn, her right arm partly raised. In her hand was a thing like a steel cigar, a metal plug with fluted sides and a button on the end. She wore a fabulously wrought ring with a white stone on her left middle finger. Her fingernails, winking as though they had life, had dirt under the tips. That intrigued Sash. No, she was not a statue, and what a three-column still she would take! With the photograph heading his feature, the sculptural fineness of her figure would take like a fine drawing. Basil Sash dreamed of fame inside 24 hours. But what filled him with consternation was the insolence and arrogance that went with her beauty. Even when dead she had the assurance of some immeasurable power. This was no garden variety of beauty he was looking at. She was better than any earth species he could imagine, any race ancient or modern. She was a thing exalted, a creation of unimaginable splendor. And she was frozen stiff.

Sash was crouching, candidly gloating on the contours of her naked thighs, when Ingvaldssen jerked him to his feet by the coat collar. Sash faced the explorer and scientist, surprised. The man's eyes glowed like two miniature hells. He seized the reporter by the lapels and began shaking him helpless, shook him until his teeth clattered and his sight blurred.

"You don't have to look at her like that!" shouted the captain. He bared his teeth. "She does not concern you! Who found her, eh? Answer me that! I did! She belongs to me!"

Sash was afraid the man was going mad. In the opinion of the reporter, a stiff was a stiff, even if it was a woman, and even if the woman was as remarkably beautiful as this one. Captain Ingvaldssen brought his face close to Sash's. He commenced to rage. Sash thought he would choke on the explorer's heavy breath. He snarled in self defense, and struck out hard at Ingvaldssen's massive face. He kicked. Sash was no coward, but he wasn't strong enough. Ingvaldssen's jaws bulged till they looked like ripe apples. His lips flattened, hardened. He shook Sash harder.

"You know where I found her, eh? I'll tell you, you land rat! An old eskimo showed me the place. I gave him three boxes of cigars. I bought that girl for three boxes of cigars!"

He gave a bellow of satisfaction and jammed the reporter into a chair. Ingvaldssen stood back, still threatening. He was calmer, but his eyes glittered as though they had been crystallized.

"She was ten feet deep in the side of a glacier, an ice pack that had slipped all the way down to the sea from the pole, maybe. Who knows? We took three kaiaks, and Waller and I chopped her out with hatchets."

James Waller, thought Sash. And where was James Waller now? Waller had been Ingvaldssen's chief assistant, the man who had been lost overboard in a North Atlantic storm on the return trip from Stockholm. Ingvaldssen's voice deepened to a rasping whisper. The somber, brutal passion in it shocked Sash.

"Have you ever seen anything so beautiful?" muttered the explorer. He glared.

"She's clever looking, all right," admitted Sash shakily, "for an Eskimo."

"Eskimo!" yelled Ingvaldssen. "Do you think I would trouble with a damn Eskimo? No! My friend," he went on in a low, intense voice, "she is not an Eskimo. She is not Asiatic, not Mongolian at all. Let me tell you something. Waller was a geologist, and he was much better at it than I am. He was a very clever man, but meddlesome. That girl is not a hundred years old, nor three hundred. My friend, Waller told me that this girl whom we found encased in ice in that terrible polar desert was

thirty or forty thousand years old. That is a fact. There were no such regal types on earth then. There aren't any now, for that matter. Don't you know anything at all about anthropology, you blind fool? Look at the shape of her head!"

"Guff! You're nuts, Ingvaldssen!" Sash felt like arguing. One found things out that way. "How would Waller know?"

"I will not give you a technical lecture," snorted Ingvaldssen. "Even I could tell that after examining the terrain. That glacier came down from the roof of the world, the immemorial icecaps. Even I could tell that. If she is not as old as Waller said, then all the scientific teachings in the world are poppycock. They are nuts, as you say. Good God, man! Look at her closely—do you sit there and tell me a thing like that was every born on earth?"

Sash got out of the chair sidewise. He backed cagily to the refrigerator. The old duffer meant well, apparently, but Sash didn't want his neck wrung again. He looked furtively. Not of earth? That was hard to believe.

The girl was dressed in leather shorts sustained with a needlessly broad, sturdy belt, the buckle of which was jewelled. He noticed small items, the socket or holster in the belt, the loose jacket of a scaled leather, the like of which he had never seen before. He noticed that her forefingers were as long as the middle finger, and that the thumbs were twice average length. Shapely hands, though some might call them deformed. Her leather garb was blown hard against her as though by wind, revealing the intimate and provocative contours of her body. Her inescapable perfection disturbed Sash enormously, and he could see how Ingvaldssen had been affected to the point of insanity. It would take a rare thing like this to wreck the great Swede's equilibrium. That granite faced, frozen misogynist!

"Maybe you would like to know something," Ingvaldssen rumbled. "I said she is not earth-born, and that must be so. That means I believe, of course, that other planets are inhabited. It is possible. Maybe you can do a feature on it later, Mr. Sash, on this: if men are going to explore outer space personally, in some kind of ship, they have to take into account the cosmic rays which we have been measuring. The drift. Later I will give you specifications of the machine which must be built. The ray drift is a constant and is also a source of the necessary power. I will tell you about sensitized plates which absorb ray particles, a battery which no one has dreamed of. Ha! Ha! Sash, no one can get off the earth in a 'rocket' without bursting himself open. I know a good man who is going to kill himself trying, and I am going to let him do it because he would not listen to me. Yesterday I told you boys that the ray drift bends to the pole. The region above the pole is a funnel, a vortex of power, and I can tap it. That is where the rockets will start. There will be airports at the pole some day. It is the only possible place to take off from the earth, and the only place to land. That girl's people used cosmic ray power to get here, and she *had* to land at the pole."

True, she was not of earth, save only in form. She was an exotic, not mundane in the slightest. Sash lost himself for a moment in hypnotised speculation. She had traveled out of some crypt of antiquity, come to earth when men were perhaps nomadic savages. Possibly she did not even see an anthropoid in the short time she lived here. Come from where, and how? Maybe Ingvaldssen had found the answer. Sash wished he could hear this girl's voice and what she had to say. A voice from time's dawn.

Her pose indicated something. It interested Sash profoundly. She had been raising her arm when something attracted her scorn. What was it? He gave it up and looked at Ingvaldssen.

"Okay, captain," he grinned. "She doesn't belong on this little old green apple at all. Well? What are you going to do with this—this Other?"

"I am going to bring her back to life." Ingvaldssen's eyes glinted. "I am going to marry her. If you laugh, my friend, I will kill you now with my hands."

Sash had been thinking about ways of buzzing Jennings, the staff photographer. Photographs! He had to get to a phone. And he wanted to get at his own end of this grand feature. By Basil Sash. He swallowed Ingvaldssen's bait. He did not laugh, but blinked incredulously.

"Why, she's dead, captain—dead as a cold storage egg! What kind of guff are you handing me?"

Ingvaldssen walked over to his refrigerating machinery and moved the pointer of a dial a fraction of a degree with his thumbnail. Sash was aware that the ice sheath was gradually diminishing, melting away from the corpse. Certainly it was a corpse—forty thousand years dead.

Ingvaldssen turned slowly and said with enormous precision, "I swore Waller to secrecy, and we got this Other aboard the Petrel by ourselves. No one suspected. I told Waller what I was going to do. My friend, after I had gotten my apparatus assembled, he was convinced that I was going to be successful, and he wanted to steal her. He was a very meddlesome man, and a passionate one. He wanted to buy her—anything that I would listen to. Then he tried to kill me, so I murdered him. I took the knife away from him and strangled him with my bare hands. It was at night, on the bridge. Then I threw him overboard. Do you see? Nothing is going to stand in my way. People do not necessarily die from cold. I am going to prove it. Maybe you would like to stay and see it. . . ."

"Ing, old boy," grinned Sash, "you couldn't throw me out now."

"If I do not succeed," Ingvaldssen promised, "you will get a picture. Maybe you get one anyhow, and the story. But hands off of her! You had better keep your lips shut about Waller. It was his fault. I am going to succeed. What I set out to do, I do. Once I thought no woman was good enough for me. Isn't it a crazy thing? Now I want this Other."

The Other. Sash remained in his chair and examined her at a respectable distance while Ingvaldssen did business in an adjoining room. There were sounds of kitchen utensils, the crackle of frying. Ingvaldssen came back in with a piece of leather which he dropped in Sash's lap. It was a yard square and close to an inch in thickness. Like a rug. Very heavy, but soft and pliable at the same time. Sash fingered it.

"From the mastodon's rump," said Ingvaldssen with a frosty smile. "That story was true. Very shortly we are going to have lunch—rump steak from the same animal. It is still good to eat." He scratched his head ruminatively. "I cannot understand what happened to the front quarters of that animal. He was cut in two, literally broken in half."

The two men ate generous portions of the meat. It was well cooked, but remained somewhat tough. What it lacked in texture, however, it made up for in a succulent, gamey flavor. Ingvaldssen talked about his refrigerating plant while he picked shreds of meat fiber from his teeth with one fingernail after another. The scientist was an ox of a man, with long blunt fingers, but he was as high strung as a hummingbird all the same. Having had a sample of Ingvaldssen's anger, Sash wondered just what he'd be like if he chanced to run amok. The explorer was as much beast as man, a drinker of blood and addicted to a meat diet. A dog with a hungry, restless brain. The refrigerator, it seemed, was no inconsiderable achievement.

"Chiefly I am an engineer," said Ingvaldssen modestly. "I stood in at Stockholm because I knew this Other would not keep on the ocean voyage. She would spoil the way some of the mastodon did. Sweden is my country. I have friends there who furnish me with materials. Every day, I poured water on the cake of ice the girl was in to keep up the size of the block. Because no matter how cold it is, ice evaporates. In the meantime I was inventing a refrigerator.

"Sash, my boy, you would not realize how difficult it was, that icebox. Do you see why? The ice would still melt. I didn't dare expose an inch of that girl's skin. How do I know what the world was like when she came to it? Maybe there are other factors than evolution which created present animal forms. I put it badly. Perhaps it is something in the air, which would be part of evolution. If she was constituted to endure conditions then, maybe conditions are worse for her today, however we may think. Exposure to the air might definitely kill her before I had my way."

"But she didn't survive, Ing," Sash pointed out. "She's frozen. I say she's dead. All I want to see is the proof of it, and get my feature. I've got to hold down a job, you know."

Ingvaldssen paid no attention.

"Things were going on, things we would not dream of when she came. Anyhow, I was not taking chances. This icebox not only had to have elaborate temperature control, but a system of sprayers to keep the size of the ice cake constant. I had to ensure the formation of ice on all sides of the block. Look at them. Those crossbars at the bottom of the case move up the sides. They contain a solution of water and a volatile salt at two degrees below zero. Centigrade. When the sprayers are working, the salt volatilizes, passes off through the ventilator, and only the water strikes the ice cake. It freezes at once. It would be a simple matter to fill the refrigerator with ice and burst it in three minutes."

"But there's scarcely any ice on the girl's body at all."

"I don't need ice any more. I am trying to revive her, this Other. The derefrigerating element has been working at slow speed since yesterday morning when I landed, and the temperature inside the case is now close to one degree above zero. Pretty soon we shall see."

A chip of ice fell from the girl's body now and then. Sash could hear the small sounds issuing through the ventilator of the case. It was rather eerie. He had no faith whatever in Ingvaldssen's experiment. He was ready to go down on record believing explorers and scientists, as well as artists, sculptors, writers—even including Basil Sash—were dotty. A curved shell of ice slipped from the Other's shoulder and shattered delicately at her feet. The reservoir on the side of the case was full of water. There was no longer any ice in the case save on the girl's leather garments, and in the fist that held the metal instrument.

The shadowed green eyes were clear now, the face moist. The girl's expression was intensified. She must have been a person of naive intelligence. She had seen something that filled her with contempt. Her expression was scornful. Sash wondered what she had been looking at, and what she was holding in her hand. He noticed that her gaze centered on the back of Ingvaldssen's head. So suddenly that Sash jumped a little, Ingvaldssen rose and returned the dial on the case to zero. His circulation motor whined under the pedestal. He stood facing the Other. The ice had melted down evenly, planting the girl on her feet on an even balance. That was lucky, thought Sash. If she had fallen she might have crashed through the glass wall.

"Lose your nerve?" he asked.

"Of course not!" snapped Ingvaldssen. "Remember, she is still all ice. The temperature of her skin is zero. She is colder than that inside. Being a newspaper fellow, you should have some odd bits of information. Do you know what happens to flesh that has been frozen and then is warmed?"

"I know that it is fatal."

"But you surely know what is done to bring back circulation to a frozen member? For example, If you were to freeze a hand or an ear?"

"Oh, yes. Rub it with snow. Warm it gradually, in other words."

"That is correct. You suggest that ice flays the fine system of blood vessels in the body, literally. Capillaries burst. It does something like that. You know, water expands when it freezes. It is one of the few substances that does. The water in a man's body wrecks him accordingly as his temperature is raised or lowered. Water is a great catalytic agent in the life chemistry.

"I have not lost my nerve. I am waiting until the temperature is equalized throughout the refrigerator, till the temperature of the girl's flesh is zero. Then you will see something. She has to be brought just to the verge of melting, do you see? I think I have been given what you would call a lucky break. I will oxygenize her with my outfit here, otherwise. Do you notice anything especially peculiar about this Other?"

"She is a damned lovely kid, and then she has a gadget in her hand that she was going to do something with."

"You don't see the point at all. Look at her breast. It is expanded fully. You can see the conformation of her ribs. How beautifully muscular she is! She is as handsome as a wild cat."

Sash thought that was a queer remark. "What difference does her breast make, its expansion, I mean?"

"You will see," said Ingvaldssen irritably. "But you should have some imagination. I want your opinion. What is she so scornful about?"

"She saw something, naturally. If you really want the opinion of a city columnist, I should say it was something big, but where she comes from they aren't afraid of size alone. Maybe she saw that mastodon, or weren't they running around at that time? Maybe she did hop in from another planet, and she got the notion the earth wasn't worth a barrel of apples.

"Look here, Ingvaldssen, don't you think it's mighty odd that a corpse should have any expression on its face at all? They don't, do they, unless they've been drugged?"

"You're smarter than I thought, Sash," grunted Ingvaldssen. "I've been thinking. She was frozen just like that!" He snapped his fingers briskly. "It was quick, and it kept the expression on her face. The cold must have fallen instantly. That's my lucky break number two. It gives me a chance, a much better chance than if it had happened slowly."

Basil Sash had scarcely removed his eyes from the Other in the glass case all this while. There was something magical in the mere appearance of the girl, something that got you a swift one in the ribs. He did not know what chasm this divine girl had bridged by accident, but he was getting the creeps. He had a terrible feeling that something disastrous was about to happen.

Ingvaldssen spoke, consulting a watch. "I should say the temperature of her flesh was at zero all through. Now!" He pulled a small double switch that regulated an electric timing device. This device advanced the needle of the temperature gauge by infinitely slow degrees, not a degree an hour. "You are going to see something happen, my friend."

"Listen, captain!" said Sash hurriedly. "Did you ever read a magazine called *Astounding Stories*? No? Jeez, I wish you had! Listen! I'm afraid of that gadget she has in her paw-paw!"

"Paw-paw?"

"Hand. Listen, I read a story in this magazine about a gun that uses a ray, a gadget just like that one she has. What if it should go off when she melts and blow us both to hell? I wouldn't like that!"

"A gun? How could it be a gun when this Other has been in the ice 40,000 years? Are you crazy? It looks solid, doesn't it? More likely it is some kind of tool which she keeps in that socket in her belt."

"Ing, I tell you I'm scared! I don't like this a little bit! This gun I read about in the magazine used atoms instead of bullets and powder. Atomic disintegration. It cut a hole in three inch steel, like paper, and the gun wasn't any bigger than that. Anyhow, I don't like the look on her face. She's up to something, even if she is a stiff! Remember now, I warned you. If you get hurt, I'll swear on a million bibles that you kept me here against my will, and you can't back out of it. You kidnapped me."

"Can that be possible?" wondered Ingvaldssen reluctantly. "I never saw a gun shaped like that!" He frowned stolidly and closed another switch. The temperature needle swung to forty degrees, a few degrees above human bloodheat, and stayed there. This action of the scientist's was quite deliberate, and it solved a number of problems with one stroke.

Against what followed, Sash recollected several major points. Chief among these was the fact that the Other had been arrested in some mysterious action. One day forty thousand years ago the temperature had fallen deep and suddenly, stopping her hand half raised. Then, in his heart, Sash knew that the Other had really come from some place outside the earth, some alien planet in the old sky, by some unknown means. This explanation offered itself most readily, since no other logic would serve. Also, and this was something he had not dared to mention to Ingvaldssen, the Other was a mighty superior being, taken at face value alone. Sash had one brief moment to wonder about her antecedents, some age-old tradition of beauty and culture from which she had sprung. A superior race on another world. It was not impossible. He had read stories of such things and half believed them. If all this were true, that she had indeed come from far abroad in space—if the singing beauty, the thrilling and somewhat terrible intelligence apparent in her face were to live again, then Ingvaldssen was something like a stupid ox for supposing he could marry her. Marry the earth to the stars! Basil Sash wanted to get out of there in a hurry. The fact that Ingvaldssen had brought back any creature at all in the ice was a feature in itself. It had gobs of human interest. He jumped up.

The Other's hand trembled. Sash hesitated, thunderstruck. He saw her abnormally long thumb tighten on the metal tool she held. Her lungs collapsed with an audible gust; she folded forward, caught her balance again. Then she looked at both men glancingly, with a kind of bitter amusement.

Perhaps her flesh was more resistant than ours, resistant to the fate of death by freezing. At any rate, Ingvaldssen's hope was clear. In collapsing, the lungs stimulated the heart, which beat heavily once with such force as to raise purple veins in her broad, coppery forehead. Her little breasts rose and feel with her quick breathing. If she had seen something that she was derisive of when the world was much younger, what she saw of earth now deepened her expression tenfold. A small line appeared between her brows, and her fine lips curled. Her hand rose and something came from it, a blinding cone.

"Ah!" roared Ingvaldssen and spread his arms. "Ah, my love! Come to me! Co—"

Ingvaldssen disappeared. That is, nothing was left of his heroic body from the thighs upward. His spouting stumps banged on the floor and fingertips dropped from mid air. Once the Other had started to do something. Shocked terrifically by the irony of the thing, Sash realized that the Other had simply completed the movement she had begun forty thousand years ago, this time with a new target.

Suddenly, Sash knew what had happened to the mastodonic remains of the beast Ingvaldssen found. The girl had shot it.

A hole had appeared in the glass in front of the girl's hand. Sash turned mechanically and saw that Ingvaldssen had vanished save for the terrible relics on the floor. The cone projected from the girl's gun had knocked out a piece of the front chamber big enough to walk through. Sash caught a glimpse of traffic on Fifth Avenue, and the start of a colossal uproar across the street, where that gun had wrought vast and incomprehensible destruction. He saw a slashing, curved swath cut into the earth for the distance of a mile and a quarter and saw the boiling waters of the Hudson leap into the end of it.

Then Sash turned and shrieked, his face contorted beyond human likeness. He clawed himself, gouged his eyes, as though he could not bear to look quietly into the girl's time forgotten, fresh face. He heard an agonizing sound. It was the fluid tinkle of the Other's disdainful silver laughter.

After You, Montagu*

(and after getting the-hell out of certain eating places)

*John, 4th Earl of Sandwich.

THIS SALESMAN NAMED Harold Swampfellow pulled off U.S. 61 on the dirtiest and thickest night in nine years. You couldn't see whether trees had been planted on the road, whether you were roaming through the woods and ponds, nor determine whether it was the dankness which had awakened you at home on your settee where you had napped too late into the darkness to keep an engagement, or whether something had happened and this wasn't the same world any more.

Swampfellow rolled in on crushed granite beyond the gas pumps, because he could see the fuzzy eyes of lights in the diner through the dense fog. He walked in. There was no more fog inside than there was in London, if the windows are kept closed.

It was a diner. A sort of pair of counters, with leather stools of the swivel kind running along the whole length. Swampfellow knew every type of human being, was a master psychologist and he knew it, because salesmen get to know that and will pity you if you think otherwise. He sized up the counterman, the same sort as all countermen, and looked up at the menu of enamelled letters stuck into the black frame. One of them caught his eye. It read: FRIED BONE S'WICH.

"What in the hell is that?" Harold asked.

"Fried bone sandwich," said the counterman.

"How do you prepare those?" Swampfellow asked.

"Just fry them," said the bored counterman. He had his sleeves rolled up and he had hairy arms. Nice looking lad. "Sometimes," he said, "with cheese. We have them cold, too."

"I'll try one," Swampfellow decided. It was so thick and filthy outside that he expected to try several other items on the menu before he left, for he was one of those stringbeans able to pack away either a section of pie and ice cream or the same size of juicy steak for dessert and never weigh more than a hundred and forty-two pounds. It was his standard weight, never changed.

The counterman complied, turning up the gas. The sandwich was a hot one with cheese.

"Why, it *is* fried bone!" Swampfellow exclaimed in astonishment, after trying his teeth gently on the rigid spread inside the slices of toast. He cast his thoughts about for the calcium content of bone.

"Well, just eat the cheese and bread if you don't like the bone," the counterman suggested. "We really have only one customer for that sandwich. He comes in here all the time, just around now."

He drew coffee and set it down, and placed another sandwich on the counter. Swampfellow hadn't heard anyone come in, but he was aware of company, particularly because he heard snapping and crackling sounds only a foot or two from his right ear. He turned his head slowly to regard the newcomer sitting on the stool next to him. Harold had already left a half-dollar on the black-composition counter. He got up cautiously, involuntarily making a sound of "nnng-nnng," wavering up and down. He circled wide around the thing on the stool, and it seemed that no sooner had he exploded through the doorway than his car spat its wheels on the crushed granite; Swampfellow jumped from raving low gear into high and went roaring down the highway into the night.

"What's the matter with *him*?" The Thing asked.

"Oh, one of those smart-aleck salesmen," said the counterman. "I guess he didn't believe it was a fried bone sandwich."

"Well, it *is*, isn't it?" asked The Thing that came down from the hills on rotten nights, like this one.

"Are you kidding me?" the counterman demanded, leaning forward. "Of course not! You know damned well we haven't got any saw here for slicing bone that thin. These sandwiches that you've been eating for the last four years are window-glass."

"Hoo-oo!" chortled The Thing; it crunched the sandwich with a sound like clamshells going through an old-fashioned meat-grinder, with relish. "I *thought* it was kinda funny I could see through those slices of bone. Sure was a good joke on *him*!" . . . .

The Monocle

L OGICALLY THERE WAS no one in the small room with her, simply because the door had not opened and closed. She was looking out the window, preoccupied, and at the moment thought nothing of the stir of air against the back of her neck. The subtle little breath of breeze was what might be caused by a human shape displacing its dimensions in atmosphere, close to her. Nor, contrary to the ABC's of telepathy, did she feel the speculative stare of the remarkable dark-green eyes.

It was the middle of the afternoon, and warm, and August. The afternoon was a quiet, nunnish gray, and through the casement window she watched the light rain fall in successive sheets of veiling. The south lawn sloped away more and more steeply toward the river, and the isolated big trees looked bigger as they smoked with fugitive mist. The deepening of the downward-feathering gray curtained the south bank of Willow River altogether. On the flats over there, the city of Thurston's airport, Monroe Field, was as good as locked behind the barrier of a mountain. In the private cubicle assigned to her in the Sherwood University Library, Constance Ydes, twenty-three, stopped indulging in the vague nostalgia which the rain produced and returned to the open book.

She had a cork-topped desk and a straight mahogany chair in a cubicle whose length, width, and height were about the same as those of a cell in a modern prison. The floor was cork. Besides the open book, there were more than twenty books piled up on the desk neatly in the shape of a fortification. She was using typewriter paper for scribbling, and had a sheaf of notes. Though she didn't need to, and she was bored, she was brushing up on her Latin.

She was brainy, and could read Latin with facility and familiarity as though it were a memorized quatrain from the "Rubaiyat." But the examiners at Sherwood U were notoriously tough; since she was majoring in languages, they would give her an ancient Icelandic idiom, possibly, a rune derived from the Spanish somehow, and require her to trace it back to hell-and-gone through Europe to its roots somewhere in the Mediterranean. She had passed the written examination handsomely, and she was going to pass the oral in the same fashion. She knew more than any other one member of the Sherwood faculty. By the end of the year she would be Dr. Ydes. Beyond the least peradventure of a doubt she was a very brainy girl.

The open book was one of an armful which she had collected in The Pit, a room in the bindery where library gifts and purchases were received. Three girls classified the volumes from pulp junk to collectors' items, down there. Connie had prowled, and taken this one among others and borne the lot up through the stacks to her cubicle.

The book was a slim volume bound in vellum. All the corners of the covers were worn and had an eggshell curl besides, and the parchment signatures were buckled, crackling with every turn of a page. The work was in early Latin and probably was valuable; it had to do with transactions concerning corn and animals and farm products in farmlands outlying the district of Cebes, wherever that was. Connie knew her geography but had never heard of the place.

The thin volume was generously ornamented with rubrics, initial letters elaborately and sometimes fantastically inscribed in red. In reading through the book she had noted subconsciously that the rubrics taken in order formed words. Going through the book rapidly, she wrote them down, and when she reached the end she had a sentence which puzzled her. It was Latin, but untranslatable. The construction was one which she hadn't encountered before, nor was she familiar with a single word. She had spoken it aloud for the sound of it, and did so again now.

"I heard you the first time," said the man standing immobile behind her.

She turned her head in annoyance at having her privacy invaded; then her eyes grew round and shocked, and she rose to her feet galvanically with a quick inhalation. She opened her mouth to scream, and he ordered, "Don't scream," in a particularly calm voice.

Three quick steps, and she was pounding him on the chest with her clenched fists. "Get out of here!" she said furiously. "Get out! Get out!"

He grabbed her wrists, gave her a gentle shove and said very slowly and imperturbably: "Don't get excited, please. Keep your head on."

She backed away from him until the window ledge touched her; he watched her with curiosity, looking her over and observing her compressed lips and frightened breathing. The fact that he was stark naked didn't bother him at all, and the manner in which she was garbed obviously intrigued him.

Barefoot, his height was six feet two. His feet were well shaped, looking as though he had never worn shoes. His posture was negligent in the graceful way he stood erect, and he was non-chalantly tossing a circular piece of green glass which landed with a little slap like a half dollar striking flatwise every time he caught it in his palm.

"Well?" he asked. "You're not afraid any more now, are you? What were you afraid of in the first place?"

"I don't know." She corrected herself and asked: "Don't you think it's very unusual for you to be walking around all bare? Where are your clothes?"

"My clothes," he said reminiscently. "When I drowned, I wasn't wearing any. So you see—"

"When you . . . drowned?" she asked incredulously. "Don't talk like a fool!"

"I drowned," he declared flatly, "swimming at night with a friend in the sacred lake behind the temple of Uranus, in Cebes."

She looked at her book, back to him and asked: "Oh, have you read that book?"

He glanced at it. "I wrote that book," he said casually. "Originally it was in Ceban, of course. What you have there is a somewhat bungled translation in Latin, from the Greek."

"Really?" she asked, giving him enough rope to hang himself. She decided that she wasn't afraid of him, and could always scream if developments required her doing so. At the moment, her visitor was standing too close to the door for her to make a run for it, but he was keeping his distance and absently juggling the piece of green glass. She heard herself asking, in a self-possessed voice: "What's your name?"

"Ardanth."

"The name of the author of that book is Publius Nato."

"Nato was a notorious liar."

"Is Ardanth your last name?"

"My last name?" He looked puzzled. "I didn't have any name before that; it's the only name I ever had."

Recovering from her shock at first, she felt more and more secure, and sarcastic. She said: "Well, let's get down to brass tacks. Is this a practical joke or something? Or just what do you think you are?"

"I," said Ardanth humbly, in contrast with the good-humored arrogance of his bearing, "am a sorcerer."

"Oh, you're a sorcerer," said Connie, unsurprised.

"Yes. My father was something of a sorcerer himself, but if I say so myself I would have been able to outsmart him four ways from the Jack if I'd lived longer. He was a religious old toper, an he told me that if I kept on swimming in the sacred lake, I was going to die young. For once the old codger was right." He told her about Cebes and its people and customs, including details not in the book, details which did not sound invented and were not. Ardanth made simple statements of fact, and she could take them or leave them, and all the while his sardonic green eyes were laughing at her.

His eyes were the color of deep emerald resulting from the addition of a trace of brown. He was remarkably handsome in build with his broad shoulders, deep chest, lean and muscular hips. He had height, and he wasn't any hairy ape. The most remarkable thing about him was the color of his skin. It was red, not like sunburn; it was a ruddy bronze, and she commented on it, asking him whether it was his natural color. It was, and typical of his race. Also, she received the impression he intended—that he was not particularly handsome according to Ceban standards; the men and women of Cebes were all fashioned like angels without wings. They worshiped beauty, and when they started growing old they killed themselves.

Ardanth didn't want to die particularly, because living was so much fun, so, being an accomplished sorcerer, he took the precaution at an early age, during his apprenticeship, of devising means of perpetuating himself. One of these means was through the book which Publius Nato claimed to have written.

"How could you know that the book wouldn't be lost?" Connie asked skeptically.

"Part of the sorcery was in knowing that the book would not be lost," Ardanth said condescendingly.

He explained that the book would fall into someone's hands eventually, that the rubrics would be joined into words, then the sentence, when uttered, would be the incantation which he had planted for the purpose of materializing himself. There was no possibility of any slip-up. If there did happen to be a slip-up somewhere along the line, he pointed out, there wouldn't have been any sorcery in his labors whatsoever. And the evidence of his ability could not be denied. He was in the cubicle with her, and he hadn't used the door to get inside.

Nor had he put all his eggs in one basket. The work in Latin was one guarantee of his popping back into existence, no matter whether it took only ten days, two hundred years, or millenniums. It was a long jump from Cebes to the city of Thurston, and he admitted that the technical method wasn't perfect; but, no matter how erratically it might work, it worked. Another device he employed, which would work sometime in the future, was a musical composition which an archæologist was going to find; when the music was played through, there suddenly would be Ardanth. He also buried sealed bottles containing batches of a brew he invented. It was immaterial whether a bottle broke in an earthquake or was opened by scientists in the year 10,000. Ardanth of Cebes had fixed things so that he would crop up in repeated lifetimes; he was a young man who was going to go a long way.

His age was twenty-four. When he reached that age he decided that it was old enough, and performed the required acts of sorcery which guaranteed that he would never grow an hour older physically. He had been twenty-four for several years, and the natives of Cebes were beginning to look on him with suspicion, when he drowned that night in the lake.

"Sorcerer or no sorcerer," said Connie, "you can't go around the way you are. You can't stay here. You've got to get some clothes on."

Ardanth looked shocked, antagonistic. "Do you mean to say I've got to wear things like what you have on?"

"Oh, heavens, no! Men wear much different clothes."

"They do?" He was even more incredulous; then he said resignedly: "All right. Do you mind going out and getting an outfit for me?"

She hesitated. "Clothes cost money, and I haven't got enough."

Ardanth shrugged. "I'll take care of that."

He stepped the distance to her desk, opened his left hand and spilled out a pile of gold pieces, and in a very gentlemanly fashion backed away.

Connie eyed him warily, then advanced to examine the pile of two or three dozen coins. They were the size of U.S. fives which used to be in circulation, but were crude, stamped pieces with rough edges, not even circular. They were mere nuggets of twenty-four-carat gold smacked out flat with a hammer between the jaws of dies. The inscriptions on the hunky coins were in lettering which Connie couldn't read. The language was Ceban, and the head on the coin was bearded and bewildered, representing Adam, the Ceban kingdom's legendary first king.

"Adam," she reflected. "Is it the same Adam?"

"The same Adam as what?" Ardanth inquired. "I'm a lineal descendant of his, if that's what you mean."

"Let it go," Connie said. She flicked the pile of coins and scattered a few with her fingers. "This money might have been legal tender in Cebes, but it's no good now. It's not even coinage; it's buttons. It's not even worth anything numismatically, because there isn't any Ceban coinage on record. All I can do is turn it in as old gold at a discount, and that involves a lot of red tape besides. They might ask me where I got all that gold, and I'd have to tell them I found it in my grandfather's trunk or something."

Ardanth's stare was idiotic with surprise. "Do you mean to tell me that gold is no good in this country?"

"It doesn't make sense to me, either," Connie admitted, "but that's the way it is in the United States of America. If you get caught with a few pounds of gold pieces of the realm in your possession, you have to do a lot of explaining."

"Then what do you use?"

"Paper, engraved." She showed him a dollar bill.

"Hm-m-m," Ardanth commented contemptuously. He collected his Ceban gold, stared awhile at the bank note, then slapped his hand down and left a pile of greenbacks on the desk. He asked: "How's this?"

Connie picked up the wad and sidled around Ardanth, backing to the door. She said: "All right, I guess. I'll be back as soon as I can."

She got out and closed the door hurriedly, before anyone browsing in the stacks of the library could see into her cubicle. She ran to the stairs at the head of the stack, near the archway connecting with the main circulation room, with her high heels striking the marble flooring like someone tapping tacks home rapidly into wood with a mallet.

For a moment she stood at the head of the stairs, wondering whether she would be fool enough to return to her cubicle, where Ardanth, the sorcerer, was waiting in all his handsome nakedness. She opened her purse, and in it was the wad of bank notes, more than she had ever seen at one time before. If this was a practical joke contrived by fraternity men, it was a damned expensive joke. Breathing rapidly again, she snapped the purse shut and descended the stairs to the landing which led to the side entrance and the misty gray outdoors.

She proceeded directly to the campus haberdashery, Millikin's, a high-priced establishment in which she had never been before. A campus big shot, the president of the Student Council, was having himself measured for a garment. He had his arms extended on both sides like turkey wings, and the spindly little tailor was crouching in front deferentially, jabbing the big customer with the end of a tape measure in order to decide on the length of a trousers leg. The large customer was a football player; he made touchdowns; he stared at Connie, because girls never entered Millikin's, and because he had never seen her before, and she was something of a feast to the eye.

Beginning with jockey shorts, she ordered a complete outfit for Ardanth—Dan for short. She knew what sizes of things men wore, more or less, and with Dan's image in mind she ordered socks, gabardine slacks, a gabardine sport shirt, a jacket with patch pockets, and tan oxfords at twenty bucks whose leather was as soft as a baby's cheek. The woolen sport socks didn't need any garters. She bought a belt of ostrich leather, a neckerchief-size linen handkerchief for his pants pocket and another for his jacket. There was plenty of money left, so she bought a wrist watch, a penknife, a wallet, and a clouty-looking stick, a fountain pen and pencil.

"Put everything in one box," said Connie, "and tie a string around it."

"Maybe," the clerk hazarded, "the gentleman had better come in and have the trousers fitted."

"Maybe," said Connie with a dead pan, "I'm going to wear the garments myself. How do you know?"

"I see," said the clerk ambiguously.

Connie put the remainder of the money in the wallet, the wallet into the box, and the box under her arm. She walked back across the campus to the library and used the rear entrance to the stacks, went up to her cubicle and entered. She sighed, let her shoulders sag and leaned back against the door for a moment. The room was empty. Ardanth had gotten tired of waiting, or else it had only been some kind of unique practical joke, after all. At any rate, Dan was gone.

She shrugged, moved slowly over to the desk and dropped her package on it. Looking out the window at the foggy river, she puzzled over what his purpose had been. If it was some kind of fraternity prank, she didn't understand why she had been picked on. She felt a little bit crazy in a daydreaming sort of way. But throughout the episode she had maintained her poise, except for the initial jolt of Dan's arrival. She hadn't screamed or acted foolish to any extent, and there was the inexplicable fact that the prank was fairly costly.

Behind her the door opened abruptly. She turned, and Dan ducked in furtively; he put his eye to an inch of crack and stared out into the stacks for a moment, then closed the door soundlessly. He was still as ruddily bare as an Easter egg, and he carried a large flat tome under his arm. An atlas.

"Wh-h-h-h!" he said, whispering a sigh. "Was that ever a close call! Someone came up the stairs and nearly cut me off from the alley running this way."

"You're a fool to take chances like that," she said critically. "You could get thrown into jail, or anything."

"Well, I guess I can get out of jails," he said. "I was only thinking of how embarrassing it might have been for you. No harm done, anyhow."

He opened the book on the desk, explaining that he had gotten curious about his home town. He had a hard time locating the atlases and would have waited for her, he said, but he had no idea how far she had to go and how long it would take to do her shopping. He riffled through the pages of maps and opened the atlas at Africa. He prowled around Egypt with his forefinger, and located an unmarked point in the Libyan Desert. Disbelief showed in his face.

"There isn't anything there," said Connie, "but sand. It's all desert."

Dan muttered unintelligible words, then commented, "I wonder what happened to my people."

"If their skin coloring was like yours, there aren't any, any more, or at least I never heard of any. Very likely they were absorbed by the blacks."

"And what a beautiful place Cebes was!" he mourned. "Well, there's no point in visiting it if it's gone."

"When did you leave it?"

"Rocks were falling in the water of the lake all around me that night," he remembered. "A hail of hot stones from the sky, and I wasn't able to dodge one of them. The tail of a comet, possibly, and it must have wiped the city out. That was a long while ago, evidently."

"After the pyramids?"

"What pyramids?"

"The Egyptians built some pyramids. Stone monuments."

"No," he said absently, moving his finger. "There were cities here, and here, and there was a lake that would surely show on a map of this scale. They're all gone." He shrugged, let his shoulders drop and closed the atlas with a slam.

Connie had untied the box. She said: "You've got brains enough to figure out how to put these clothes on without my showing you. I'll wait outside; rap when you're ready."

When she re-entered after his rap she stared at him for a long time from head to foot; her having a hand in getting him up in his resplendency gave her at least a half of one percent ownership. She took a long slow breath with a slow smile.

"I know how ridiculous I look," he said curtly. "You needn't laugh. But I didn't think you'd play a trick on me."

"I didn't play any trick on you," she protested. "You look all right, Dan. Turn around."

He turned around, looking over his shoulder at her suspiciously. He said: "I never felt sillier nor more uncomfortable in my life. If men wear clothes like these and like them, there is something wrong with their minds. Or else they haven't any more fight in them than rabbits, and women are responsible. However, when in Cebes, do as Cebans do."

"There isn't anything wrong with the way you look. Really there isn't."

"And this thing." He picked up the watch, and listened to it tick, curious. "Is there an insect inside? It is trying hard to get out."

She explained what the watch was for, and the pen and pencil, and showed him how to open the knife. With the articles distributed in his pockets, she took one of the handkerchiefs and tucked it expertly into the breast pocket of his jacket with the four corners of crisp white linen showing. He rested on the cane negligently with the lazy convincingness of a man who has always carried a stick, and scrutinized her expectantly. The steady regard of his green eyes made her nervous, and then she became a little frightened.

"What's the matter?" she asked.

"To coin an understatement," he said thoughtfully, "you've done me a good turn, regardless of whether you acted knowingly. I'm under an obligation to you." He juggled the piece of circular green glass in his right hand, making it spin and glitter with winks of hard, bright light.

"Oh, no," she refused quickly. "I would have done the same for anyone. You don't owe me anything."

"You'll have to be repaid whether you like it or not," said Ardanth. "You're a bright girl and you know what you want. You plan things ahead, far ahead. If it's something material that you want, tell me what it is, and it's yours. You certainly have ambitions. Tell me what's more important to you than anything else, and I'll take care of it immediately."

Connie swallowed, shook her head. She suggested: "Take me to dinner sometime."

Dan looked annoyed and refused, saying: "Out of proportion entirely. Don't hesitate because you think something is impossible. Out with it, Connie."

His voice was slow, liquid with the Ceban accent; he could probably sing; his use of her nickname gave her heart a twinge. She still refused, smiling and shaking her head.

"Because I'm going," Dan said. "I have places to go, and a lot of things to do, and you're delaying me."

"Then go," she said, looking aside through the window at the wet campus.

"Stubborn little fool," Ardanth commented unemotionally. "Here."

She turned her head to look at him, looked down at his extended arm. She put her hand out, and he dropped the green glass into her palm. She asked: "What is it?"

"A piece of emerald," he said. "A lens; a monocle, I think you call it."

"Emerald?" she asked.

"Emerald; I said it was emerald." His voice didn't sharpen, but his impatience made her confused. "Something I picked up along the way; it's yours."

It was of monocle size; if it was stone it was flawless, and it was flawlessly ground. The edges were beveled, and caught light with the splintered glitter of precious stone. In color it was true smaragdine of a lighter shade than Ardanth's eyes. The glass was thick, not even shallow at the rim, and fattening at the center to an axis considerably greater than that of the run of solitaires on display in a jeweler's window. The stone from which the lens had been cut must have been a stone of royal dimensions, and she said as much.

"It was," Dan said succinctly. "I pried it out of the royal scepter in the palace treasure room one night myself."

"What's it for?"

"To look through."

"But why emerald?"

"Because," said Dan, with exaggerated politeness, "it happened to be best suited for the purpose."

"I'm sorry I'm so stupid," Connie said defensively, "but I don't understand. My eyes are all right; I don't need a monocle." At the moderately baleful look he gave her she said hastily: "I'm awfully sorry. Thank you very much. I'll keep it as a memento."

"The monocle has a particular and peculiar property," he said, "which is its raison d'être. It is not like any other monocle. It has the property of revealing to the person who wears it the manner in which he is going to die. The circumstances surrounding his final moments alive."

"Then you must have known that you were going to drown," she pointed out.

"Naturally," he agreed. "And incredible as the event seemed to me, because I was the best swimmer in Cebes, the details of those last few minutes didn't vary in the most trifling particular from what I had observed through the monocle long before. I was inclined to discredit the evidence of my own eyes, but fortunately took the precautions which were responsible for my being here now."

"You'd better keep it," she said, offering it back.

Ignoring her hand, he said: "I also looked through it while you were stringing the rubrics together and wondering what the words meant. So I know what is going to happen to me this time."

"What's going to happen?"

"I am going to die in a way more horrible than I like to contemplate," he said. "You're better off not knowing. There's no way of knowing just when it's going to happen, either, and that's why I'm in such a hurry. I've got a lot of ground to cover. Will you excuse me?"

He started for the door.

"Wait a minute!" she called. "I want to know what's going to happen. I've got a right to. And, anyhow, if you know what's going to happen, can't you do anything about it? You can stay away from it, can't you?"

"You can't do a thing about it," he said with finality. "If it's going to happen, it's going to happen." He opened the door and started out.

"But I don't want this!" she cried. "It's yours!"

"I don't want it, either," he retorted. "This time is bad enough. I'm going to die in a much nastier way than last time, and next time I'd rather not know anything about it and just let it take place. Good-by."

"Ardanth! Wait! Don't go yet!"

"You don't need me now. If you get into any kind of trouble, all you have to do is call me."

"Please!" she entreated, and in answer she heard his footsteps descending the marble stairs rapidly, as though he hadn't a second to waste. She ran after him and called down, "Is your name really Ardanth?"

"My name is really Ardanth," came the voice from below.

"How can I get in touch with you?"

There was no reply, only silence punctuated finally by the thud of the steel door to the yard swinging shut. A girl entered the stacks from the circulation room and stared curiously; Connie straightened and returned to her cubicle. Now he was gone. If she got into any kind of trouble she could call him, but beyond that she concerned him nothing. She interested him not at all, except through her agency in materializing him out of the unknown. She had a high regard for herself, and thinking about his attitude and manners made her scowl. She sat down at her desk. She never had seen, never would see, a more handsome animal in her life than the vanished sorcerer of Cebes.

After a long while in thought she remembered the monocle clenched in her moist palm; she opened her fingers and inspected it, polished it with a handkerchief which she took from her handbag. She held it against the print of an open book, and it magnified the letters enormously. The green hue of the stone didn't interfere with its transparency; the magnifying power was high. It was cool to the touch, cooler than what she thought the temperature of the room was.

She brought the monocle to her eye gingerly. She blinked, closed her left eye. Nothing. The field was black and she saw nothing, in spite of the fact that print showed plainly through the lens when it was laid on the page of an open book. She put the thick concave-convex miracle of emerald in her purse, and for a while just sat.

Constance Ydes was a very fastidious girl. She was skeptical of the motives of men, and had learned in her twenty-odd years to abhor the time-wasting of the common, or garden, variety of fun in the precincts of Sherwood U. She didn't think drinking beer in Stiffy's with a man across the table was pleasurable. For an hour or so dancing was all right, except that a man insisted on murmuring idiocies while he hitched around to the music with his feet. She had come to the conclusion that most men didn't bathe more than twice a week, or that they liked the smell of themselves, or exerted themselves too much during the day, or used a secret brand of obnoxious scent.

She was a desirable girl and had a rounded shapeliness. Her bearing as she walked was an advertisement for physical culture. Besides which, she had an eye for choosing flattering, right clothes from the crazy *mêlée* of the fashion dictators' current bellyache in hats, dresses, shoes, and accessories. She was independent; her name was listed in various handwritings in many notebooks as "100%, but nix," "Ydes; nope," and so on. She had a successively knocked-down opinion of men and hadn't considered their importance very much because she was brighter than any of those whom she had run into. Callow, rough material, all of them. Boys.

Rising abruptly, she returned the books on her desk to the stacks in three armloads, and sallied forth. She crossed the campus and hied herself down University Avenue to the Green Lantern, which was what Stiffy called his place. There she had four daiquiris all by her lonely. There was a telephone booth and a directory, a search through which yielded no information. There wasn't any Mr. Ardanth. She transliterated the name, spelled it backward, but it wouldn't work. She dialed information, and was informed that no Ardanth was listed under a new or private number, either. How was she going to call him, then, if she wanted him? She paid for her drinks and quit the bar in disgust.

Studying any more today was out of the question. She lighted a cigarette and betook herself down University Avenue into the city of Thurston. On impulse, as she was passing a jewelry shop where diamonds and old gold were purchased, she decided to have the monocle looked at.

Behind the counter in the long, narrow shop was a gnome of a man with sorrowful round poodle eyes separated by a long caricature of nose. He was bald, and his cheeks would look black and unscrubbed no matter how often he shaved. Mr. Paulson. The proprietor was being conversed with by a young man in jaunty snap-brim hat, lushly knotted necktie, and a pup tent of camel's-hair coat. Dick Hermann. When Connie entered he uncrossed his legs, took his elbow off the counter and retreated politely to give her room and the once over.

"How do you do?" said Connie.

"How do you do?" said the colorless leathery lips under the nose in a surprisingly sweet voice.

"I'd like to know if this is worth anything." She produced the monocle and laid it on the little red velvet prayer rug atop the counter.

"You want to sell it?" he asked disinterestedly, ready with a shake of the head.

"Has it any value?" she countered.

The glance of his bright, round brown eyes descended, more interested in her figure than the green object. The monocle was a circle of cold-green fire on the velvet. His gaze reached it, and for a moment he was carven in immobility. Clocks, and repaired watches hanging on a board, were all ticking together in a somehow sinister, frustrated hurry. Paulson's delicate, womanish hand, the fingernails grimy, picked up the monocle with leisurely reverence. His calm, muscular, shiny fingers turned the lens, and his narrow chest slowly inflated. He put the lens to his eye, and he stared ahead with a kind of bughouse intentness. His features stiffened into an expression of astonished horror. He expelled a weird snort through his nose; the monocle escaped from his fingers and landed on the velvet, and was recaptured skillfully on the first bounce.

"Sorry," he mumbled apologetically. He chuckled with a kind of horrible beguilement and said: "As the horse who died said, 'I never did that before.' No harm done though."

"I asked you whether it has any value," she prompted, aware that young Hermann was inspecting the fashioning of her legs as though she were merchandise for sale.

Paulson cleared his throat and hazarded: "Sure, I guess it might be worth something. It's a nice job of grinding; no nicks on it or anything. Where'd you get it? If you don't mind me asking."

"In my grandfather's trunk. What is it worth?"

Paulson went into a trance; suddenly he smiled as though afflicted with generosity this afternoon, and in his mellow little voice offered: "Give you a dollar."

"A dollar!" she exclaimed with sarcasm.

Patronizingly he inquired: "What did you think you could get for it? It's only a magnifying glass, a reading glass, and it's green. You can see how green it is. But I tell you, just because I got a use for a glass like this personally, I'll give you two dollars."

"On second thought, I don't want to sell it." She took possession of the object from his reluctant fingers.

"Tell you what I'm going to offer you," he urged. "On account of that's such a fine piece of glass even if it is green, I'm going to give you ten dollars. That's a lot."

"No, thank you."

"I'm giving you twenty. That's the limit."

"Good afternoon."

"Wait!" His voice lost some of its charm, and his bright eyes looked dangerous. "You can't offer an object for sale and then change your mind, miss. That's the law, and I got to use it." He shook his head regretfully. "I offer you a fair price and you don't take it, then I have to charge you a fee for appraising. The fee is ten dollars."

"Do you mean to tell me that I have to pay you ten dollars if I don't sell you the monocle?" she asked incredulously.

"I'm sorry I got to do it, that's all. I give you twenty or you give me ten, that's the way it is. Otherwise I got to hold you and call a policeman. You make up your mind now, or I can't let you leave the shop."

Connie came back to the counter, nearly squirming with revulsion, and blazed at him: "You contemptible little monkey, do you know what I could do to you for threatening me if I wanted to go to the trouble? Just try to prevent me from leaving this dirty little crooked place." A swift, sharp slap of her hand made him blink his eyes and back up against his shelves. She departed unmolested, walking stiff-legged.

Hermann came up along the counter grinning, and asked: "What was that all about, pop?"

Paulson groaned, chanting: "My God, my God! Oh-h-h! She had an emerald and she don't know it, maybe. And the color; suffering snakes!"

"Get hold of yourself, pop."

"You saw me look through it, Dick. I couldn't believe it, but— Listen; I got to have that stone."

"Pretty good piece of rock, eh?"

"Of all the crazy things, cut like an eyeglass. But thick as red caviar even at the edges. I got to have it; I got to see it again, what I saw."

"You sound a little bit screwloose," Dick remarked. "Well, a pair of legs like that would be hard to lose sight of. So long, pop." Dick strolled out of the shop and sighted the legs again without any delay. He kept them in range, window shopping and otherwise loitering along.

Connie felt a little sick from her encounter with the jeweler, and for a moment considered speaking to the cop on the corner. But she had the average person's wariness of the police, and also the resilience to recover quickly from her indignation. Besides, she had come out ahead on the deal; there was no trace of doubt now about the monocle being emerald.

Certainly there were some things which couldn't be foreseen. Like that. Like Ardanth's materializing in her cubicle at the library in the first place. Up to now, everything in her life had been planned well in advance. She was alone, and eminently personable, but had made no major mistakes which would have been so easy for a girl like herself. She had a little money from a trust fund; she had brains; when she wanted to talk intelligently with someone she would have dinner with one of the faculty, or someone who had been closely associated with her father.

At the U she graduated with highest honors, because she had studied indefatigably, because she intended to teach and perhaps do a little writing whenever she got around to finding out whether she had a style. There was no question about her getting her doctorate. There was a job waiting for her in the Thurston schools, teaching English, but she wanted the language post at Sherwood, and she knew she was going to get it eventually if not even in the near future. Eventually, too, she was going to get married, because she believed in the institution, to someone older than herself, to the proper person when he came along. That would take care of itself in time, though she would take steps to make sure that it happened before she was thirty.

She knew exactly what lay ahead—the mountain of books she would read yet, the hats and dresses and shoes she would buy, classroom routine, faculty teas, strolling on the river road in the evening, symphonies at the memorial auditorium on the knoll, quiet dinners excellently prepared, the regular sabbatical which would mean travel. She didn't know when she would have time for children, the arrival of which would, of course, depend upon the man.

Her purse was under her right arm, and she hugged it to her side, thinking about the monocle. If one could see his future through it, it would be an advantage, of course. But that was a fantasy; she had looked through it, and it was as blank as holding a poker chip to her eye. On the other hand, Papa Paulson had dropped the monocle convulsively; his face had gone flabby and his eyes had bugged with a look that couldn't have startled her more than if he had howled.

Annoyance made her walk rapidly, and she kept up the pace through Thurston's shopping area until she ran into a girl whom she knew. The friend was a Sherwood postgraduate and was already teaching, now on her summer vacation.

They had cocktails together while Connie pumped her about the circumstances, salary, good and bad of her job, and had dinner in the same restaurant. At a table near them was a young fellow having a sandwich and beer. Connie thought she had seen him before, but since he showed no sign of recognizing her, dismissed him as a Sherwood undergraduate.

She walked home, since the business district was sharply defined by Cathedral Hill on the west and the distance to her house wasn't far.

There was a little fog but no rain, and there was no wind in the twilight. At the downtown mouth of the trolley tunnel began the terraced crawl of granite steps leading to the top of the hill. After fifty or sixty steps she became aware of masculine feet ascending unhurriedly behind her. Her curiosity wasn't aroused. She was independent, more or less; she could take care of herself; she wasn't the kind of girl to look behind even casually. Anyhow, the big globes of the lamp-posts were abloom with milky light.

Her address was two blocks beyond the cathedral. It was a squat and square stone mansion, shabby between its neighbors, whose wealthy owner had left it to his faithful housekeeper, Mrs. Geraldine Horrigan. In the yellow stone fortress lived Mrs. Horrigan, Connie, and two bony, aristocratic old gentlemen who snored all day and were gone all night on their mysterious labors, with the consequence that she never saw them except coming and going, exhausted or only half awake.

The bell did not ring, because Mrs. Horrigan was nearly as deaf as the golden-oak newel at the bottom of the broad staircase curving majestically to the upper hall. Mrs. Horrigan spent all her days reading newspapers in the kitchen, and a thumb pressed to the button of the doorbell only turned on an electric light over the refrigerator. Sometimes this didn't work either, since the old lady's vision was deteriorating, so she wasn't bothered very much by panhandlers, salesmen, or prospective boarders. She thought Connie was somewhat more attractive than she wanted any girl in the house to be, but gave her a key to the front door before the end of the month.

Connie used her key, found that it was unnecessary because the door was unlocked. She called hello to Mrs. Horrigan in the lighted kitchen and received no answer, as usual, and ascended the leisurely sweep of the stairs to her room.

She washed off her make-up in the bathroom; her lips looked pale, so she applied some of the ripely colored lipstick she used, grimaced at herself in the mirror and washed it off again. She stripped, then showered, soaping herself briskly all over, rinsed with care as though she

were covered with dye, and dried herself with the unhurried sleepy
raptness of a cat.

Her bed was a four-poster. She stuck her arms and head through the
soft lace and ripples of a crêpe gown, and indulged in her regular
backward leap onto the bed. For a while she lay looking at the yellowing
wallpaper of the ceiling. One of the two wide windows creaked and came
down shut with a whispering bump as the house settled. She stuck her
legs in the air, came erect and sat on the edge of the bed. She dipped her
feet into her slippers and went to the window, raising it wide with a jam
so that it couldn't fall again, and walked back to her dresser.

Her purse lay on the dresser; she opened it and took the monocle
out, stared at it, fingered it like a coin and polished it with a handkerchief. She was a great hand at resisting temptation and didn't look
through it, beyond seeing the embroidered figures of the dresser scarf.
She pulled the top drawer open and slipped the slab of emerald into a
slip which she folded up in the middle of the pile. She returned to bed,
lay tense in thought for a long while after she turned the light off. Every
time she stirred she relaxed a little more, until complete muscular
repose invited her into the pool of sleep.

A metallic click awakened her. She blinked drowsily, looking toward
the windows over the plump curve of the pillow; then her eyes stayed
open and awake, and what oppressed her in a smothering embrace was
fear. The room was entirely dark and silent, completely dark except for
two accents of light. One was the keyhole; the other was the dial of her
radio on the shelf. While she stared at the radio, which she had not
turned on, she was sure, the illuminated dial was blotted out. It reappeared as the prowler passed in front. The click she had heard was that
of the radio being turned on.

There was a hum as the tubes warmed, and dance music from Frisco
gushed from silence suddenly into a flood of rhythmic sound in the room.
Connie turned her head with a jerk when the yellow eye of light at the
keyhole went blank. The wall switch was snapped, and the chandelier
overhead jumped the room into light. At the door stood a young man in a
polo coat. She had seen him before, at Paulson's and at the restaurant
where she had had dinner. Hermann. He had a handkerchief across his
nose as a mask, and his eyes gleamed under the brim of his hat.

"I wouldn't make any noise," he said calmly.

She wouldn't. A glance at the alarm clock showed her that it was past
midnight. Mrs. Horrigan would be sound asleep, and a bomb wouldn't

awaken her. On the dresser her purse was opened and the contents dumped out. The drawers had been rummaged through. Connie said with calm that surprised herself: "There isn't anything here worth stealing. Take what you can find and go away."

"I couldn't find it," he explained over the swing and volume of the radio. "Where's the emerald?"

"What emerald?"

Hermann advanced step by step toward the bed and observed: "I'm going to like this. Nobody's going to hear you over that radio, and they'll think it's part of the broadcast even if they do."

He reached for her, and Connie jumped out on the other side of the big four-poster with a convulsive effort. He circled the foot of the bed deliberately, and she threw herself on the bed and bounced off on the side toward the door. Hermann really got his legs working this time and shagged her, cutting off escape to the hall. She fled to the open windows and he snagged onto her before she made them.

Struggling, she attempted to claw him, but only tore the mask loose. Twisting and wrenching, however, she did break free from his embrace, whereupon Hermann walloped her one across the head with the flat of his hand. Trembling, she waited for him to hit her again. He marched upon her to do just that thing if she didn't talk. She had never called for help in her life and wasn't sure of the procedure, so her cry was the merest wail, without any volume, as though she were whimpering to herself.

"Ardanth!" she cried, simply because all this was his fault, and there wasn't anyone else within conceivable earshot.

A cyclone entered the room. In the violent air, paper on the desk went flying; her flying hair stung her cheeks, and Hermann staggered as the square yardage of his coat got caught in a buffet of the wind. The door to the hall opened, closed with a thundering slam. Hermann jumped like a cat in a bathtub, and Connie opened her eyes just in time to see Ardanth reach the prowler with a spring of headlong ferocity. Seizing him by the necktie, he batted Hermann's head back and forth while he warmed up.

"Oh, you want to make something of it, do you?" Hermann asked in an ugly manner, and he clawed murderously for the faithful rodney which he wore in a shoulder sling on occasions such as this. He just got the butt of the revolver into view when the man took a homerun swing at his jaw with a baseball bat. Hermann's feet left the floor and, as gravity almost ceased to operate, he floated down to the rug in a horizontal position as gently as thistledown.

"I think you broke his jaw," said Connie.

"I wouldn't be surprised," said Ardanth. "That's what I was trying to do. Why didn't you call sooner?"

"It never entered my head that you'd be in the neighborhood and would hear me," she said.

"I'd hear you if I was a hundred miles away or a hundred years," he said. "I told you that. Remember." He picked up the sodden form of Hermann and started for the door with him.

"What are you going to do with him?" Connie asked anxiously.

"I'll think of something."

"I wish you wouldn't go to the police."

"I don't intend to. Some method of persuading him not to come back will occur to me."

"Will you come back?"

"Well, for a little while. I was busy on something when you called."

It wasn't long before he returned; in fact, she was pacing the floor and only finishing her second cigarette when he opened the door. She had shut off the radio. The fact that she was wearing only the diaphanous robe didn't occur to her, nor interest him particularly.

She asked: "What did you do with him?"

Ardanth regarded her somberly with his strange green eyes. He assured her, "He won't bother you again."

But she had to know, being female.

"First, I filled his pockets with gold."

"You did what?" she asked, startled.

Ardanth shrugged his broad shoulders and explained naively: "His object in coming here was personal gain, with the idea of making a little love besides. I filled his pockets to bulging with American gold pieces; his pants pockets, his jacket pockets, and his top-coat pockets. I would have given him a gunny sack full of gold besides, but he was already staggering with his load, and when I asked him he said he was satisfied, and he promised not to come back. A little quickly, I thought; without any doubt he was scheming to come back to the place where money was so easily acquired. Then I asked him whether he was thirsty. He said he was a little bit, and that he hadn't met anyone like me in quite a while. So I gave him a drink and sent him on his way."

"Dan, you're absolutely incredible," she said. "You didn't have to treat him to that extent. After all, he broke the law coming in here, and he hit me besides."

"Forget about him," Dan recommended. "He's gone; and I think I hit him harder than he hit you." That was true enough. "Where's the monocle?"

"It's still in the drawer where I hid it." She got it out, unrolling the slip. "He would have found it if he'd hunted very carefully."

The emerald lay on the soft silk in a circle of glittering, exciting frozen green, a miracle in the skill with which it had been cut. It had the quality of stealth, of a blind eye with a great brain behind it; and in it was concentrated the mysteriousness of a provocative sound heard briefly and only once, and never again no matter with what patience of listening.

Dan's tone was respectful. He said: "I've been thinking. I underestimated you at first, because it isn't pleasant to die even when you know that you'll be born again. You're very unusual, and I like you."

"I like you, too," she confessed softly, and batted her long eyelashes. If she let herself go she could have cried, she liked him so much.

His manner was still elegant and arrogant, and he stared as though her response didn't entertain him very much. He cleared his throat and asked suspiciously: "Of course, you've used the monocle? Looked through it, I mean."

"No," she said. "I mean yes, but it didn't do any good. I looked through it and it was blank, all dark."

"Extremely odd," said Ardanth. "Excuse me."

He picked up the monocle and screwed it into his eye, and for a moment watched critically something in the remote distance. He pried the monocle out of his eye and returned it to the pile of silk underthings.

"There's nothing wrong with it," he announced.

"It doesn't work for me."

"It must," he told her flatly. "The lens is transparent; you can see that it's transparent. Obviously, if you put it to your eye and you can't see through it, it's working."

"It doesn't make sense to me."

"When you walk from bright sunlight into a dark room it takes a while for the rhodopsin to function. Visual purple. For your eyes to become adjusted. What is going to happen to you will occur in a dark place, and you didn't wait long enough. You didn't look through the lens long enough."

"All right, I didn't. And perhaps I don't want to."

"That's up to you. The monocle is yours to do with as you please. You can sell it for its carats in emerald, or throw it away, or what you like."

"That's what I almost did. Sell it."

"I know it. Didn't you believe me?"

"No. Obviously I didn't."

"I thought you wanted to sell it for another reason," he reflected. "So you're an ordinary little opinionated and faithless girl, after all."

"Suppose I tell you what I think of you."

"Suppose you do."

"Big as you are, you're the most conceited little boy in seven States and the District of Columbia."

Ardanth grinned, and the humor stole into his eyes. He said: "You'll get along."

He turned his back and started for the door.

"Why don't you vanish in thin air?" she asked bitterly.

He turned around in surprise and asked: "Why?"

"Just to show off."

"Hm-m-m," he decided, eyeing her. "Women have a habit of blaming men for everything wrong and convincing them, and you're no exception. It wasn't my fault that Hermann tried to rob you. You brought it on yourself by taking the emerald to that jeweler. You didn't believe me, and you never asked yourself what reason I might have for lying to you. When I told you that I was a sorcerer in Cebes, I meant that I was a sorcerer."

"This is 1939," said Connie.

"You've had that emerald for several hours," said Ardanth, "and you haven't taken advantage of it. You're not so secure as you think. You have your future planned in a cast-iron outline of Roman numerals and capital letters, and you allow nothing to chance. You don't allow for a broken leg, or falling in love and making a fool of yourself, or even a cheap episode like Hermann's trying to rob you. Or war."

His hand was on the doorknob.

"Ardanth," she said, delaying him, and he was annoyed.

"What?" He stared at her, and those cold green eyes of his were merciless. "Hurry up. I was busy, and I've stayed too long already."

She lighted a cigarette, turned her back on him and took a few steps, turned around again and expelled a deep breath in a sigh. She asked: "Can't you stay a little while?"

The sorcerer shook his head. "Lock your door. You won't be in any danger for a while. And I have work to do."

"I wish you wouldn't go."

He waited, looking at her, and when she didn't say anything after a moment he shook his head. "Good-by," he said. "If you need me, call me, but don't ever call unless you're in trouble."

She ran to the door and threw her arms around him. "I don't want you to go," she said. "Please stay. I'm frightened."

"No, you're not. You're lying your little head off."

"I suppose it would be asking too much of you to kiss me good-by."

In the instantaneous encirclement of his arms she melted against him, and the kiss of their lips was as heady as the Song of Solomon. Afterward she leaned against the door with a stilly smile on her red mouth, and couldn't remember how long he had been gone. By some means of the most ingenious science she got to bed, because that was where she awakened in the morning.

Since the fall quarter at the U hadn't started yet, she had no work to do, and slept till eleven thirty. Connie had only two meals a day, anyhow—bruncheon and dinner—and the deaf Mrs. Horrigan prepared a sumptuous omelette in spite of Connie's protestations.

Mrs. Horrigan muttered darkly when she served it: "You'll find this is better than you think."

"You shouldn't have bothered," said Connie. She shook her head, still numb with sleep.

"I love you, too," said Mrs. Horrigan, irrelevantly. "You're a nice girl." She stalked back to the kitchen, stoop-shouldered.

The old men were snoring upstairs, having completed their strange nocturnal transactions, so Connie had the breakfast table to herself. She had a trifling hangover from the daiquiris, and considered going back to sleep until two or three o'clock before she took the trolley to the U and the library. Her eye fell on the folded morning newspaper, the Thurston *Citizen*, which was no longer fresh because Mrs. Horrigan had read it from end to end, and which was crimped between the heavy restaurant-crockery sugar bowl and a weighty, chipped, cut-glass decanter of soy sauce; Mrs. Horrigan liked chow mein and served it often along with egg foo yung dan and chop suey and other remote triumphs of Asiatic vegetables. Connie opened the newspaper.

On the front page was a remarkable item of news, and Connie stopped eating. She licked a crumb of egg off her lips, and laughed without meaning to laugh. She got up and lit a cigarette with maniacal nervousness.

She walked around Mrs. Horrigan's old, vaulted dining room and cringed from the fact of murder. Mrs. Horrigan came in from the kitchen and asked: "More toast? Bacon?"

"No, thank you," Connie said. She sat down, stunned.

The item read:

On the report of an airport mechanic who heard a shout and a splash, police fished a body from the river near the end of the bridge below the landing field. The drowned man was identified as Dick Hermann, a clerk in the Paulson jewelry store. Surprised at Hermann's weight, even if dripping wet, the police found his suit and topcoat pockets stuffed with gold pieces, the weight of which pulled him to the bottom like a shot when he fell, jumped, or was pushed to his death. Mr. Paulson could shed no light on where his employee acquired the wealth, nor the .38-caliber revolver found on him. Mr. Paulson has a gun permit, Hermann not.

Connie went up to her room, where she found that Mrs. Horrigan had already made the bed and tidied up and gone below to the kitchen to watch her light. She opened a new pack of cigarettes, lighted one, and after the first exhalation of smoke called quietly: "Ardanth!"

The sorcerer opened the door on the wind that whipped through the room and stepped inside. He looked around for whatever danger was besetting her, and asked: "What's the matter now?" She eyed him steadily and accusingly, until he prompted irritably: "Well?"

"You pushed that man into the river. You loaded him down with gold so that he'd sink to the bottom at once. I suppose you think you have a sense of humor, asking him whether he wanted a drink!"

"Is that all you called me for?" he demanded. "I told you not to call me unless you were in trouble."

"But you murdered him! Don't you realize that? What did you do it for?"

"What I do when I am away from here, young lady, happens to concern you nothing. And it happens that I was working on something very important when you called me away just now."

"And I kissed you last night. You murderer!"

"Listen to me," said the sorcerer. "I did jostle Hermann somewhat on the bridge, but he had it coming to him. It happens that he committed a murder himself three years ago, and he was never going to get caught."

"How do you know that?"

"I have ways of finding such things out."

"Two wrongs still don't make a right."

"Don't pull that schoolbook stuff on me," he said contemptuously. "I know what I'm doing. And what are you so worried about? There isn't the slightest possible chance of your being connected with it."

"Suppose there isn't! How about yourself? You can't go around doing things like that!"

"I can't, eh?" he retorted, smiling. "Believe me, some mighty peculiar things are going to go on before I'm done, and don't think you can do anything about preventing them. Just keep an eye on the newspapers, and I'll show you some sorcery that is sorcery."

"I'm going to tell on you."

"No, you're not. Anyhow, who'd believe you?"

"You're going to be awfully, awfully sorry."

"Somehow I doubt that."

"Ardanth, look; would you do something for me?"

"That," he said cautiously, "all depends. I can't keep on doing favors for you indefinitely if you're going to interrupt my work continually."

"Where were you when I called you?"

"This time?" he hedged. "The same place. Pretty far from here, and it wouldn't help you any to know the name of the place."

"What were you doing?" She was just keeping him now, struggling to decide how she should feel about him. He was such a big, handsome guy, and she would never meet anyone else like him. And he was champing at the bit after hinting that he might not answer her call next time.

"What I was doing," he said regretfully, "I am afraid, is a private matter. And I have to get back to it."

"Ardanth, look at me," she urged. "Look at me and promise that you'll never do anything like that again."

"I never heard a more preposterous proposition," he refused coldly. "Maybe I am obliged to you, but I've found it smarter not to be too scrupulous about obligations sometimes. Will you excuse me? Don't call me again unless you get into a real jam."

"Don't worry, I won't!" she said with sudden vehemence. "I hate you!"

"Really?" he asked. "And what difference does that make since I'm not in love with you? Not to say that you aren't unusually personable, which you are, as you know. In fact, your attractiveness is being wasted here. But you'd be surprised at the number of beautiful women in the world who are far more beautiful than you, and I'm in a position to take my pick of the whole shebang."

"Is that all you're interested in? Women?"

"One of the things," he corrected. "After all, I'm male, and human."

"I'm beginning to doubt it."

"Good-by, then," he bade her gently, sighing. "Back to the grindstone. If I fail you the next time you call, don't call me names. Something may have happened to me."

"If you know what's going to happen, can't you do anything about it?" she asked.

"There is absolutely nothing to do about it." He was in the hall; he waved his hand at her and closed the door.

"Wait a minute!" she called. She ran to the door and wrenched it open, but the hall was empty. She hurried to the front window and looked out, and waited, but he hadn't left the house in that manner.

If he didn't want to come around he didn't have to, and she didn't dare call him when she didn't need him, for fear of his getting really mad at her. The weeks went by; she got her doctorate without any trouble; school started, and she was promised the teaching job she wanted, young as she was. And every time she opened her purse the emerald, kicking around among lipstick, powder, handkerchiefs, cash and feminine odds and ends, reminded her of Ardanth.

One night in her room at Mrs. Horrigan's, while she was playing with it, she yielded again to the temptation. She didn't know whether she ought to see what the monocle would show her, if it worked. What would happen to her tomorrow, next summer at the lake, or twenty years from now. She was a very brainy girl and a sensible girl in most respects, and her life was planned as carefully as a prisoner's. But she was decidedly female even at the quickest estimation, and she didn't know whether she wanted to see what she looked like as a wrinkled old hag, if this wasn't a cruel hoax of Ardanth's.

With a piece of tissue she polished the lens until it glittered, and picked it up by the rim. Otherwise clear, the field controlled by the lens went black when she brought it to her eye. She turned the light off, and looked as though to see her reflection in the mirror over the dresser.

It did not work. There was still nothing to be seen, no shapes to make out in the flat blackness, though she counted a hundred beats of her heart. That was long enough.

From transparency the lens darkened to a wafer of unrelieved jet when brought to her eye, and that was all. That was what was tantalizing, for there was no reason why such an optical phenomenon should occur; if things went that far, they should have gone farther, but what secret the emerald contained she could not find out.

And it was spring, and the third quarter at Sherwood U. Dewey Hudson, deferentially known as the Duke, the man whom Connie had watched being fitted for an English garment at Millikin's, had acquired the habit of hanging around her office. He used the most transparent, little-boy excuses and confessed as much.

"You know," he said, "it's getting so I have to resort to the most transparent lies in order to get in here. For example, I wanted some help on the paper due in 317A tomorrow. It was an easy job, and it's all done, and I've got it right here in my pocket."

"Well, there isn't much opportunity to be resourceful," she admitted, eyeing him.

"The idea is," he continued with unblushing savoir-faire, "that I'm graduating pretty soon—it's damned near June already—and I won't be seeing you any more."

"What I can't make out, Duke," she said, "is what a personage like yourself sees in a cluck of a girl like me."

He screwed his face up in temporary pain, and suggested, "Maybe it's because you take baths, and your skin is not like that of an old persimmon. Look, Connie; you're away ahead of me on brains and all that, but as pupil to teacher, ain't I a pretty nice guy?"

"What a lovely red apple," she murmured.

"Don't you ever go out or anything?"

"Of course I go out," she said with sudden decision. "Let's go down to Stiffy's Green Lantern and get numb."

He stared at her , savoring the bait. "I wonder," he wondered, "if it would make any difference if the president of the Council got stewed in public."

"I'm risking more than you are," she pointed out.

"Let's go," he said. "Right after graduation I'm getting a job with a man who used to be a Presbyterian minister and he wouldn't like it much, but that's neither here nor there."

In the booth at Stiffy's she said: "No beer. It doesn't work fast enough."

"You really meant it?" he asked. "You honestly want to get skizzled? I thought it would be dinner and a movie, or a drive or something."

"Would you rather?"

"You wouldn't, by any chance, be entertaining any ulterior motives?" he inquired with elaborate shrewdness.

"Candidly," she said, "I have an experiment in mind."

"Lady," the Duke said, "ply me."

She instructed the waiter, asking for less sugar and more authority in the brand of cocktail she liked. "Bring it with a motor attached," she admonished. "Twin cylinder."

He grinned understandingly, and the first pair of drinks were planted on the table.

"What's this experiment?" Duke asked.

"Have you ever been drunk?" she countered.

After a moment he admitted: "Yes. Several times, but it's a secret. What goes on?"

"Well, look," she said. "Suppose we got really loaded with the royal essence of oojie-boojie tonight. Tomorrow morning, would you remember everything that happened?"

"Would I?"

"Would you? I'm serious."

"No. After a certain stage, I— No."

"That's taken care of." She sighed. "Let's get going."

After making the glasses kiss, Duke raised his, sighted across the rim and took down the contents in a swallow. Big man, big swallow. Next time, Connie told the waiter to mix a shakerful of the same liquid dynamite. It was a dry drink whose pale, cool taste resembled the innocence of lemonade, but had properties never found in any lemon ever grown.

Two, three, four, five, six, seven, with numbers three and six on the house. Connie and Duke looked up to see Stiffy himself bending over them.

"Professor Schoenbaum in the end booth having the London broil, with milk," Stiffy reported.

"Let him ride," said Duke.

"O. K.," said Stiffy, worried. "If you don't laugh your heads off at any jokes, he won't know you're here."

When Stiffy had gone, Connie eyed Duke speculatively. She said: "You're not even started yet. I'm beginning to buzz."

"It's not a buzz, it's a hum."

"Do you hum?"

"I hum somewhat."

"Take three in a row, or can't you do it?"

"I've done it before," he said, troubled, "but I don't know about these. They've got something in 'm."

Connie stared at him with nothing but interest. A shakerful of cocktails arrived, and methodically Duke poured and drank down three in a row. He leaned and twisted his head to look at his car on the street in front, and hinted cautiously: "Maybe I won't be able to drive."

"Give your key to Stiffy, and he'll put the car up in back. We'll take a cab."

"All . . . hp! . . . all right," said Duke. "Want one?"

"Still have one. Go ahead."

"I don't know," he said, enunciating carefully.

"Maybe I was wrong about you," she suggested, prodding him. "Go ahead; have another."

Her incredulity grew, but she was relieved when she saw his eyes glazing and partially unfocused after the thirteenth drink. She had stayed behind; he had gotten up to put some nickels into the record player, and when he got back she had lied, telling him that she had downed two. The flush in Duke's face had deepened, making his features rounded and boyish.

"Dance?" he asked.

"Wait a minute." She took the monocle from her purse and said: "Here's something I got from a novelty shop. Like this. Just look through it."

His hands held hers, and then he let them down slowly to the table edge. He stared, then screwed his left eye shut and squinted hard. His expression of happy inebriation faded and turned stupid and loose-jawed until he looked like a man who had been awakened by a thunderbolt.

He grabbed at her hand, and she jerked her arm back.

"Give me that!" he demanded. "How does that work?"

"It's just a gadget!" she protested. "What's the matter with you, Duke? There's no reason for getting excited."

His expression was still, flabbergasted. The red in his face was angry, and he said: "Give that to me, Connie; I want to see it again."

"You're drunk. What did you see?"

"There was a man in there who looked just like me, except that he was older, and he died. How did— Give that to me, or I'll take it away from you!"

"Oh, no, you won't." She jumped up.

Duke sprang erect and reached for her with both arms. She ducked, got out of the booth and ran for the front doors with Duke chasing after her.

Out on the sidewalk she looked for a cab, and there weren't any; she looked back and saw that Stiffy had grabbed hold of Duke Hudson. Duke pushed him off, threw him a bill, and came tearing toward the doors.

A cab swung around the corner and Connie ran into the street. The cab came to a violent halt and she climbed in, but not soon enough. With a crazy jump from the curb, Hudson made the running board and got in with her. With the slam of the door he ordered: "Along the river road."

The driver knew how to shift gears, and the cab went down University toward the river in a smooth leap. Duke immediately grabbed for Connie's purse, and she slapped his hands. The two most important things in a man's life were birth and death, and Dewey Hudson had seen the latter. His. And he was drunk and determined; he got athletic and turned her arms behind her back without any trouble.

"Don't!" she protested; and her face went white.

"I told you I wanted that," he said in a crazy voice. He took both of her slim hands in one of his big meaty ones, and when he reached for her handbag he gave her arms an unintentional twist.

Bent double by the armlock, Connie groaned: "Ardanth! Ardanth!"

The driver turned his head for a glance, grinning from ear to ear, and while he fumbled in Connie's opened purse Duke said belligerently: "Watch the road!"

The door on the right, nearest Duke, was yanked open as a tall figure appeared on the running board.

With the most unadulterated astonishment, because the hack was moving so fast, Duke blurted: "Hey!" Then, "Get the hell out of here, buddy."

He cocked a leg and drove it toward Ardanth's midriff, with great strength and velocity. Duke weighed two hundred and twelve pounds and played football, whereas Ardanth had only the same height. He accepted Duke's foot in both hands and twisted. Duke came off the seat with a yell, letting go of Connie, and came down on the floorboards on his knees. Ardanth swarmed on top of him, while Connie drew her legs up on the seat, and the sorcerer did something to the back of Duke's head with his quick hands.

The driver was getting bothered, so Connie said: "It's all right. We're all friends."

They turned into the river road, which was forbidden for love-making if love-makers got caught.

The hack slowed down to a crawl; Duke was limp and dreaming on the floorboards, underfoot. Connie pulled her skirt down over her knees, which were sticking up because her heels were on Duke's back.

"What's it all about now?" Ardanth inquired. "You took me away again."

"I took you away from what?"

"I was laying some fuses. Nothing is certain any more; there are some idiotic wars in the making, and I have to be sure that I'll be on hand next time. Do you understand? I was halfway across the Atlantic and was dropping bottles into the water when you called. I was filling them. The last bottle might be the one, and I have to make sure. So what's gone wrong now?"

She told him briefly, and he remarked: "A little streak of sadism in you, huh?" He sounded very much interested.

She protested, shaking her head and laughing with a touch of hysteria. "Oh, no, no," she said. "I showed him the monocle; I tried it out on him, and he saw something and wanted it, and chased me. He's drunk; tomorrow morning he won't remember anything."

"Yes, but what did you do it for?"

"I told you." She laughed again, running her fingers through her hair. "It doesn't work for me. It's just black. I can't see anything."

The driver turned his head and said: "How about it? The meter looks like we're going to Chicago."

"Stop for gas at the first station, and we'll start back," Ardanth said; and to Connie: "You couldn't see anything, nothing at all? That's very, very remarkable."

"I waited and counted up to a hundred, and there wasn't anything there at all. It was just all dark."

"Well, I'll be switched," said Ardanth thoughtfully. He took the emerald and glanced through it, gave it back to her. "That's the best sorcery there is, and it works, but you're just one of those people. The exception. It must be very dark where you're going to be, or you're going to get—"

He was going to say, "You're going to get blind."

Connie just sat, looking gloomily down past her round knees at the recumbent Duke Hudson. And Ardanth leaned back in deep thought, looking highly annoyed, moving his jaw around in his hand.

"Look," he said, "let me do something for you, and we'll call it square."

She turned her eyes to him and said: "All right; suppose you just stick around."

"I can't do that," he said apologetically. "I've got to lay some fuses. I don't know when I'm going to die, and the way things are now I don't know whether I'll ever be alive again, and I'm getting scared. It's getting to be a waste of time, burying bottles and manuscripts in the ground, because there's no telling where a bomb will land. I wouldn't want to show up in the midst of an explosion."

"Neither would I," she said faintly, looking out of the window at the night on the river. There was no wind, and the river was as smooth as a flow of gravy. Ardanth had drowned a man in that river.

They were approaching the outskirts of Thurston, and the U. Ardanth had the driver stop the cab, and hauled out the Duke onto the roadway.

"What are you going to do?" she asked.

"Just lay him in the bushes," said Ardanth. "He's big and husky, and he can walk home when he sleeps it off. So long."

"But you're coming back."

"No, I'm not coming back." His voice was echolike, and he was already out of sight in the darkness, dragging Duke. "So long. You'll get along all right."

"It's damp; you'll catch your death of cold."

She heard a pleasant, low sound that was either his laughter or the water bubbling over stones along the river bank. She smoked a cigarette, and got out of the cab to strain her eyes looking for him in the darkness.

Every time she called, he had answered, and she called him now after she had given him plenty of time to lay the Duke in the handiest bushes. "Ardanth!"

He didn't come back, and the hack driver turned around and said: "You want me to go look for him?"

"No, this is a habit of his," she refused. "I'll call him once more, and if he doesn't answer, it means that he's gone." She stepped on her cigarette, and wet her lips and looked into the darkness. Her voice was steady when she called, concealing a strangling panic: *"Ardanth!"*

The only answer was the laughter of the water on the stones.

She got back into the cab and hauled the door shut, and gave the driver her address. Puzzled, the driver got under way slowly, but shortly they were bowling along at regulation speed. They entered the city.

She still had the monocle, which was of no use to her at all unless she wanted to sell it as a precious stone. It wouldn't work for her, and the secret would remain a secret. For other people, yes, but not for Connie Ydes. She would never know until the time came, but she could imagine, and her imaginings wrapped her heart in cold.

What was going to happen to her finally would happen in the darkest night. Or she might be blind. There wouldn't be any light, and it would just happen and be over with, and Connie wouldn't be around any more.

On a dark night she would awaken in her bed and wonder if it was going to happen. When it didn't, there would be the next time, and the next, and in a dark place her heart would always pound with fear.

It was a platitude that a human being began to die at the instant of birth. She hadn't minded the fact of having to die sometime, but the matter had become specialized through the very failure of the monocle. It would happen in the dark. And it was the waiting—

Cape Verde Isls

St. Paul's Rocks

Fernando do Noronha

Lima

Coquimbo

Valparaiso

Rio de Janeiro

40°

20°

0°

20°

40°

80°   60°   40°   20°   0°

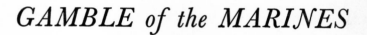

GAMBLE of the MARINES

Illustrated by
JACK MERRYWEATHER
and the Author

GAMBLE of the

ALBERT WHITMAN & COMPANY
Chicago

MARINES

A condensed revision for young readers
from the original manuscript by
CAPTAIN RAYMOND J. TONER, U.S.N.
made by MARY BARRETT, A.B., M.A.

Illustrations on front jacket and on pages 23, 55, 80,
103, 157, and 179 are by Jack Merryweather

Foreword

LIEUTENANT JOHN MARSHALL GAMBLE has the distinction of being the only Marine officer in American history to command a U.S. ship in combat. Gamble's commanding officer aboard USS Essex, Captain David Porter, U.S. Navy, captured several British ships off the Galapagos Islands. He placed one of the captured ships, Greenwich, under the command of Lieutenant Gamble. Shortly thereafter Gamble captured the armed whaler Seringapatam after a brisk engagement. For this action and the daring deeds recounted in this book, Lieutenant Gamble is considered the outstanding Marine of his era.

Against a backdrop of naval customs of yesteryear Captain Toner presents us with a thrilling sea adventure. The author has applied to his portrayal of Gamble an authentic background based on extensive research in primary source material. In this book, Gamble's story is amplified by nautical terms, vivid illustrations, and Marine Corps traditions which add to the authentic flavor of the whole work.

Young readers will here acquire an understanding of the role played by the Naval Service and by the brave men serving in it who contributed so much to our proud American heritage. This saga of the sea will undoubtedly encourage many readers to pursue additional historical studies.

JOSEPH GAMBARDELLA
Major, U.S. Marine Corps

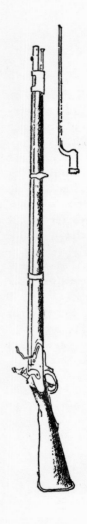

Above

Model 1808 Flintlock Pistol

Pistols generally were the private property of individual officers. This round-barrel, brass-mounted pistol was carried by a naval officer during the War of 1812.

At left

Model 1808 U.S. Musket

This musket, manufactured by U.S. arsenals and private companies, is typical of muskets furnished all U.S. military forces during the War of 1812. This model is .70 caliber and has a 41¼-inch barrel. A 16¼-inch bladed bayonet may be mounted over the barrel.

Acknowledgements

I WISH TO ACKNOWLEDGE the assistance given me by the Historical Branch, G-3 Division, Commandant of the Marine Corps, and the Office of Naval History, Navy Department, Washington, D.C.

Also, to my son, David Lawrence Shannon Toner, for data on muskets and pistols used by U.S. military forces during War of 1812.

The section on "Customs and Traditions, USMC," is reproduced by permission from *Marine Officer's Guide* by General G. C. Thomas, USMC (Ret.), Colonel R. D. Heinl, Jr., USMC and Rear Admiral A. A. Ageton, USN (Ret.); copyright 1956 by U.S. Naval Institute, Annapolis, Maryland.

The sketches of Marine Corps swords and emblems, have been reprinted by permission of the copyright holder, the Marine Corps Association, publishers of the *Marine Corps Gazette*, professional journal for Marine officers. Copyright 1950, by Marine Corps Association.

R. J. T.

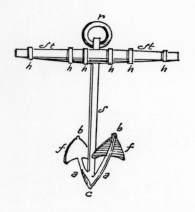

Parts of the Anchor

a   Arms
b   Bills
c   Crown
f   Fluke or Palm
h   Hoops (iron)
r   Ring
St Stock (wood)
s   Shank

Fishing the Anchor

A "fish hook" (h) is spliced to a "fish pendant" secured to inboard arm. Anchor is hoisted to gunwale (g). Stock remains outboard of hull. When secured for sea, anchor is lashed to fittings on deck and gunwale.

See page 73.

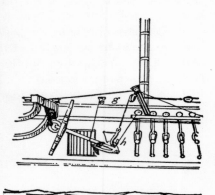

Contents

Contents

Pronunciation of Seamen's Terms

Seamen not only have a language and vocabulary peculiar to their calling, but they have through the centuries—particularly in English—radically changed the pronunciation of terms until sound and spelling have little relationship. In general, words are shortened and syllables run together.

The following are a few examples found in the text:

athwartship— (from side to side) athortship
boatswain— (a warrant officer) bo's'n
coxwain— (petty officer in charge of boat) cox'n
forward—for'ard
gunwhale—gun'nle
larboard— (left) larb'rd
leeward— (downwind) loo'ard
starboard— (right) starb'rd, sta'b'rd
thwart— (crosswise seat in boat) thort
topgallant sail—to'gan'sle
topsail—tops'le
windward— (upwind) win'ard

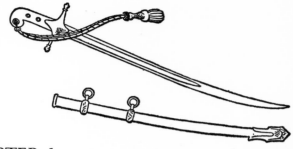

CHAPTER 1

First Command

THE FIERCE MIDDAY SUN of the equator poured down on the blue Pacific. Three ships, in line abreast, stood along their courses under easy sail. Astern, to the south, lay the dim shape of Albemarle, one of the Galapagos Islands.

The largest of the three ships, the Essex, was disguised to look like a whaling ship. Any experienced seaman, however, would have known by the trim set of her sails, the smart appearance of her boats, and the sleek lines of her hull that she was a man-o'-war.

The smaller ships were true whalers with rugged, simple lines. Each had a brick try-works amidships

where whale blubber was boiled, or "tried," to ex-
tract the precious oil.

The man-o'-war Essex was a United States frigate
of thirty-two guns. The smaller ships, the Greenwich
and the Georgiana, were formerly British whalers
but had been captured and were now prizes of the
Essex. The three had set sail from Albemarle Island to search for other British whalers reported
cruising to the northward.

On the windward side of the Greenwich quarterdeck stood her prize master, Lieutenant John M.
Gamble, United States Marine Corps, Marine officer of the Essex. He was twenty-three—a young
man in a young nation's service.

Gamble's face above the white ruffles of his neck-
cloth and the high collar of his uniform was deeply
suntanned. His features were regular and his mouth
was firmly set. Brown eyes peered through deep-set
lids. His legs were widespread to ride with the ship's
lift and roll.

The upward tilt of Gamble's chin and the straight
line of his back showed his pride in the Greenwich,
his first command. For an officer of the Marines to

command a naval ship was an unheard of thing. But Gamble had been lucky.

The Essex had captured so many ships of the British whaling fleet that her commander, Captain David Porter, U. S. Navy, could spare no more experienced officers to command his latest prizes. As a result, he had placed Gamble, the Essex' Marine officer, in command of the Greenwich when she was captured on May 29.

From his position near the stern, Gamble watched the members of his prize crew as they went about their tasks along the decks. He looked aloft to see that all sails were drawing properly.

"Sail ho!" came the cry from the masthead lookout.

Gamble snatched the speaking trumpet from the binnacle chest beside him and called up, "Where 'way?"

"Three of them, sir," came the reply. "One dead ahead, the other two broad on the larboard bow."

"Essex is making signals, sir," reported the quartermaster, who was watching the frigate through a long glass.

"Let me have the signal when you have it decoded," Gamble replied.

Turning to his second-in-command, he said, "Pipe all hands to handle sail, Mister Wilson."

The lookout's hail brought all hands tumbling up on deck. Even before the boatswain's pipe ceased to shrill, the sail handlers were swarming up the shrouds and laying out along the yardarms to loosen and set sail.

Under the added press of sail the Greenwich's deck began to heel. The wind blowing through the taut rigging took on a sharper sound. Her blunt bow, never designed for speed, rose and fell in a smother of foam, sometimes sending spray flashing over the bulwarks to wet the windward side of the forecastle.

"Ease her off a quarter point, helmsman!" Gamble shouted through the speaking trumpet. "We're starving her too much. We're already to windward of the Essex and all the strange sail."

Turning to his second-in-command, Gamble said, "I intend to engage the largest ship, Mister Wilson. We have a better chance of overhauling her than does Essex. Crowd on every bit of sail the ship will carry."

"Essex' message decoded, sir." The quartermaster touched his finger to his forehead in salute and pointed to the page of a signal book.

The signal read, "Engage closest ship."

Gamble nodded and smiled. He had sailed with Captain Porter long enough to know that he could expect bold action. He raised his long glass to observe the ship they were chasing.

She was definitely the largest of the strange ships. All three, now aware that they were being chased, had put themselves before the wind and were crowding on all sail. The Essex, with her greater spread of sail, had hauled ahead of her consorts toward the center ship of the three that lay ahead.

After a half hour's chase, it was clear that the Greenwich was rapidly overhauling the stranger. Because she was much to windward of the other ships when the chase began, the Greenwich was able to run down with a following wind on her starboard quarter.

The strangers, realizing that they could not out-
run the frigate Essex before the wind, had chosen
to beat to windward. This not only slowed them;
it shortened the distance the Greenwich had to run.

After more than three hours of chase, the Greenwich was nearly within long range of the nearest
stranger. Gamble gave the order to "Beat to General
Quarters." Men eagerly triced up the gun ports and
ran out the broadside guns.

The Greenwich carried only five guns to each
broadside. Even so, Gamble had barely enough crew
to man the guns of one broadside.

"Essex is hove to, sir. The ship she was in chase
of has hauled down her colors," the quartermaster
reported.

"Good!" Gamble replied. "But it will be some
time before Essex can beat to windward to help us."

Gamble noticed with pleasure that under the
capable direction of Lieutenant Wilson all was
ready for the attack. The tense excitement of a ship
about to go into battle was seen in the faces and actions of the men standing at their stations at the
guns. They often peered through the open ports to

sight the chase and glanced aft to watch their commander.

Gamble, too, was excited. For the first time he
felt the great responsibility of command. He knew
that he must not let the enemy captain outmaneuver
him. He had to justify the confidence Captain Porter
had shown by placing him in command of a ship.

Now the Marine officer raised the long glass and
studied his opponent carefully. He saw that she was
pierced for six guns to each broadside. That gave her
two more guns than the Greenwich. She also
seemed to be somewhat larger and carried a greater
spread of sail. Gamble knew that if the Greenwich
had not been to windward, she could never have
overhauled the stranger.

Suddenly Gamble noticed that the enemy ship's
headsails had begun to flutter. He could see her sail
handlers tailing out on the weather braces. From the
peak of the gaff English colors suddenly broke in the
wind. At the same instant the lookout hailed,
"Chase is coming about, sir!"

"So! They've decided to give us a fight before the
Essex can come to our aid," Gamble thought. He

seized the speaking trumpet and shouted to Lieutenant Wilson at his station near the foremast.

"Mister Wilson, man the larboard battery! I intend to round up and give them a broadside while her head is in the wind! Aim for her bulwarks! Hold your fire until I have the ship steady on her course!"

With a shout the men leaped to the guns of the larboard broadside. They adjusted the quoins and blew on the slow matches.

Gamble felt a momentary surprise that he knew so well what was happening. It was as though he were again watching the diagramming of single ship actions the officers so often discussed in the Essex' wardroom. He could predict what the stranger would do, and he knew what he must do to prevent her from gaining a windward position.

Gamble was tempted to round up and fire his broadside, but he did not. His opponent was almost into the eye of the wind. "Just a little longer now," Gamble said to himself, "and I'll be able to give them a raking broadside at closer range."

The quartermaster and helmsman, both manning the wheel, watched Gamble intently. The few sail

handlers who could be spared from the guns stood
ready to handle sheets and braces.

"Bring her head to north-northeast and let me
know when you are steady on course!" Gamble
called. "Trim braces and sheets as necessary."

The Greenwich's wheel spun in answer to Gamble's order. The shrill of the boatswain's pipes passing orders to the sail handlers rose above the sound
of water rushing along the Greenwich's lee side and
the creak of her running rigging.

"Steady on nor'-nor'east, sir," sang out the helmsman.

"All right, lads," shouted Gamble, "when you
have her bulwarks in your sights, fire!"

Gamble tensed, expecting an immediate response,
as though he had given an order for musketry
fire. The deck was responding to the motion of the
sea with a moderate roll and pitch. The guns of the
broadside were not yet bearing on the hull of the
chase. At last one gun roared, followed in an instant
by the other guns of the broadside. White gunpowder smoke swirled about the decks to make a
dense haze that hid the other ship briefly.

At first Gamble thought that the entire broadside had missed. The enemy ship had passed the eye of the wind and was paying off on the larboard tack. Then as the gunsmoke cleared Gamble saw the smashed bulwark. Two of the Greenwich's solid shot had raked the entire length of the other ship.

"Stand by to tack ship," Gamble shouted, "Ready about!" He turned and motioned with his hand to the helmsman to spin the wheel. As he did so, he heard a loud rushing sound that became a high whistle, then faded.

"Enemy fired his broadside, sir," reported the quartermaster. "No damage as I can see."

Gamble nodded, intent on the handling of the ship. "They fired their windward broadside," he reasoned. "If we can come about and steady on a course before they reload, I can hit with my starboard broadside."

Gamble turned his head to give the order to man the starboard broadside. He noted with satisfaction that Lieutenant Wilson had foreseen his order. The big naval officer, his red face streaked with powder, was stripped to his shirtsleeves. He was directing

the loading of the last gun of the broadside. The
remaining gun crews crouched by their guns, awaiting the command to fire.

After what seemed like an eternity, the Greenwich's head passed the eye of the wind. She began
to pick up headway as she laid off on the larboard
tack, running to the windward and almost parallel
to the other ship.

"Steady as she goes, sir," sang out the helmsman.

"Fire when she bears!" commanded Gamble.

Scarcely were the words out of his mouth when
the decks of the Greenwich shuddered under the recoil of all five guns of the starboard battery. Gamble
noted that Lieutenant Wilson was working furiously with the gun crews to reload the battery. Under his expert direction the men were sponging the
bores and ramming home the solid shot.

Again it was difficult to see how much damage
they had inflicted on the other ship. Gamble saw a
flash of flame and the plume of gunpowder smoke as
one or two enemy guns fired. Then the ship was lost
to sight as the second broadside roared from Greenwich's starboard side.

Realizing that Lieutenant Wilson and the gun crews needed no further attention, Gamble turned to keeping the enemy on bearing and his own ship as steady as possible. After the Greenwich had fired two more broadsides, Gamble noticed that the enemy was wearing ship—that is, placing his stern instead of his bow to the wind. The ship thus took the wind on the opposite tack.

This was a dangerous maneuver. Evidently the Britisher had had all the fighting he wanted, and was now trying to make a run for it down wind. Gamble saw at a glance what an opportunity this presented.

"Mister Wilson, hold your fire! Load all guns of the larboard battery. I shall come about, and when they present their stern to us we'll give them a raking broadside." Turning to the helmsman, Gamble ordered, "Steady as you go."

"Steady as she goes, sir," replied the helmsman calmly.

Gamble braced his long glass against the mizzen shroud to keep the enemy in constant view. He noted that some of her braces had been shot away and that she moved sluggishly. He forced himself to hold back the order to come about. The range must be closed further to do more damage. The minutes dragged on as the Greenwich closed the distance between herself and the other ship.

Raking broadsides are devastating when they hit. But a raking target is narrow because it presents either bow or stern, hence the need for close range.

"Ready about!" shouted Gamble. "We have her where we want her, lads. Hold your fire, and keep her in your sights."

The Greenwich responded readily to her rudder and headed into the wind. The sail handlers on the forecastle backed the headsails into the wind to make the ship's head pay off more readily on the new tack.

"Keep her full and by," Gamble called to the helmsman, who nodded and shifted his glance to the courses and topsails as they were trimmed to greatest advantage on the new tack.

"Full and by, sir," the helmsman finally called.

Gamble had kept the other ship in the field of his long glass. Her stern was now presented almost squarely to Greenwich's larboard broadside. Turning toward the gun crews, Gamble raised his arm, "Fire!"

This time the damage inflicted by the Greenwich's broadside could be seen at once. The enemy's mizzen-topmast swayed at an awkward angle, then crashed down on the quarterdeck. The entire bulkhead on the starboard quarter was stove in. A gun lay overturned on its carriage.

The Greenwich's crew gave a loud cheer as the red flag with the Union Jack in its quarter came fluttering down from the mizzen gaff of the chase. Gamble ordered all sail shortened and the main yard braced aback to heave to.

Suddenly a loud shout rose from the gun crews. Gamble spun about and put his glass on the enemy. To his amazement he saw that the other ship, after hauling down her colors, had crowded on all sail and was heading toward open waters between the Essex and the Greenwich.

"Mister Wilson," Gamble ordered through the speaking trumpet, "pipe all hands to make sail. Sheet home everything the ship will carry."

The standing and running rigging of the Greenwich creaked and groaned under the greatest press of sail she had ever carried. Whalers are designed for seakeeping qualities and for rendering whale blubber into oil. They are not made to carry guns. They are not intended to make the speed a man-of-war needs. Gamble was pleased to notice that for all her sturdy lines, the Greenwich was not sluggish.

The Essex, under a press of sail, was rapidly closing the gap through which the British ship was trying to escape. The sun was already low.

Shortly after sunset the stranger saw no chance to escape. Not wishing to risk a broadside from the frigate, she bore up and lay hove to.

A boat set out from the Essex, carrying a prize crew. As it pulled across the open waters between the ships, a signal fluttered from the frigate's signal halliards.

Gamble smiled as he lowered his long glass. No need for the quartermaster to decode this signal's meaning. Turning to the boatswain's mate, Gamble said, "Pass the word that Essex has signalled Greenwich, 'Well Done.'"

CHAPTER 2

Results of Victory

THE ENEMY SHIP Gamble had so successfully engaged proved to be the Seringapatam, of fourteen guns. She was one of the finest and best equipped of the British whalers. Indeed, it was she who had captured the United States whaler Edward.

Gamble and his men aboard the Greenwich saw the Essex' boat carry a prize crew to take over the Seringapatam. The boat then came alongside the Greenwich and two letters were passed up, addressed "Lieutenant John M. Gamble, USMC, commanding the prize ship Greenwich."

The first message was brief. Gamble scanned it quickly.

Allow me to return to you my thanks for your handsome conduct in bringing the Seringapatam to action which greatly facilitated her capture, while it prevented the possibility of her escape. Be assured, sir, that I shall make a suitable representation of the affair to the Honorable Secretary of the Navy.

Respectfully,

DAVID PORTER

Gamble felt a surge of pride. He opened the second letter. It was from an Essex officer who had stood near Captain Porter throughout the action. He wrote,

Captain Porter kept his spyglass as constantly employed as I ever knew him to. At one time, when Seringapatam tacked, Captain Porter became more anxious than ever; fearful that you would tack at the same time and receive a raking shot, he exclaimed: "Now, Mr. Gamble, if you'll only stand on five minutes then tack, I'll make you a Prince." You stood on for a while when he again exclaimed: "Now is your time"; just then we observed your ship in stays, which gave you the raking shot that did the enemy so much injury. So, my dear fellow, you stand a chance of being princed, knighted, or something else. The Captain was much pleased, put the spyglass under his arm, walked aft, and appeared to think all safe.

As he refolded the letters the young Marine lieutenant realized that he had met and passed an important test. He had accepted the responsibility of full command and proved his ability. Now it was time to turn his attention to his ship's needs.

As the Greenwich's men worked they speculated about the ship they had helped capture. Had her captain a letter of marque, the legal paper from the British government that gave her captain authority to take other ships? If the captain lacked such a letter then he was no better than a pirate and Captain Porter would not be obliged to treat him as a prisoner of war.

Later Gamble learned that this was the case. The British captain, unable to produce a letter of marque, was confined in irons aboard the Essex.

As dusk settled over the Pacific all the ships approached within signalling distance of the Essex to receive night orders. The two other enemy whalers

captured during the day's action were the Charlton
of ten guns and the New Zealander of eight guns.

In response to a signal from the Essex, all ships
stood to the southeast under easy sail.

In the days that followed, the Charlton proved so
slow that on July 19 Captain Porter made a decision
welcomed by Gamble and the other Americans.

All guns and equipment from the Charlton were
placed aboard the Seringapatam, while nearly fifty
prisoners of war were transferred to the slow whaler.
She was then returned to her original captain and
crew on condition that they land the prisoners at
Rio de Janeiro.

When the British prisoners learned their fate,
they protested loudly. They feared that in Rio
they would be forced to serve in the British navy, no
pleasant prospect for whaling men. They pleaded
with Captain Porter to let them sail in a small boat
to the Galapagos. The captain, however, convinced
them to follow his orders. As the Charlton sailed,
the men on the Greenwich heard their former prisoners raise three cheers for the ships they left behind.

A week later Captain Porter sent the Georgiana to the United States. Her full cargo of whale oil had a value of a hundred thousand dollars. But what interested Gamble most was that the Seringapatam's captain was dispatched with the Georgiana to stand trial.

Gamble had made an excellent report on Lieutenant Wilson's bravery during the Greenwich's action with the Seringapatam. As a result, Captain Porter chose Wilson to command the Georgiana on her homeward voyage. Her crew was made up of men whose enlistments were about to expire.

Now the remaining American ships, led by the Essex, made all sail for the Galapagos Islands to take on wood and fresh water.

Refitting the whalers was a slow business. The Essex cruised the nearby waters and on September 15 captured the Sir Andrew Hammond. Capable of mounting twenty guns, the Britisher had only twelve.

Welcome excitement came at the end of September. The Essex Junior, once a whaler, joined her sister ships at the Galapagos.

Captain Porter's officers, including Gamble, listened eagerly as Lieutenant Downes, the Essex Junior's commanding officer, brought news of home by way of Valparaiso, Chile.

"Mr. Madison has been elected President," Downes reported. But this news did not compare with word that a British frigate and two sloops-of-war had already sailed from Rio in pursuit of the Essex.

"Now," thought Gamble, "there's likely to be action. The British will want revenge for the damage we've done their whaling fleet. Suppose I were in Captain Porter's boots. What would I do?" Gamble turned several ideas over then decided, "I'd put more distance between us and those Britishers. The Essex isn't ready for a fight—yet."

As it happened, this was Captain Porter's reaction, too. The American ships set sail for Nooaheeva, a tropical South Pacific island in the Marquesas. There the Essex could safely be hauled up for scraping and repair.

For Gamble the next three weeks were the pleasantest he had known since the Essex had sailed from

Delaware Capes. That had been on October 28, not quite five months after the United States had declared war against Great Britain on June 12, 1812. "Nearly a year gone by," Gamble reflected.

The weather was fine. A steady trade wind out of the southeast carried the ships along their courses with scarcely the need to touch a brace or sheet. Each day was so like the one before that Gamble lost track of their passing.

Beneath the smooth surface of this three-week passage Gamble sensed hazards. He had lost most of the crew who had fought so well during the attack on the Seringapatam. Many of his comrades were now aboard the distant Georgiana, bound for home.

"It's true," Gamble reasoned, "that I have two excellent seamen from the Essex. But how far can I trust the other men? I wish I knew." He frowned, thinking of the British whaling sailors who had chosen to enlist in the U. S. Navy rather than to sail to Rio. There they would almost surely have been impressed into the Royal Navy. "That must be the worst service a sailor can think of," Gamble thought wryly.

As Gamble saw it, his problem was simply this: Would his crew remain loyal? Were there even now troublemakers quietly organizing themselves against their American superiors? He resolved to be alert.

On October 23 the island of Teebooa, one of the Marquesas, was sighted. Two days later the Essex and her consorts came to anchor in the lovely waters of Anna Maria Bay. Above rose the green mountain peaks of Nooaheeva.

CHAPTER 3

The Island of Nooaheeva

FROM HIS POSITION in the leading ship's boat from the Essex, Gamble scanned the beach ahead. So this was Nooaheeva, an island of the South Seas!

Gamble focused his attention on a group of natives, armed with spears, who were clustered about three white men. As the four ships' boats approached, the natives withdrew and disappeared among the trees and huts beyond the beach.

The three white men remained—a sorry crew, Gamble thought, in rags and tatters. One fellow appeared to be as completely tattooed as any native.

Earlier these same three white men had come out in a native canoe to speak to Captain Porter aboard the Essex. But the captain, assuming the men to be deserters, had refused to hear them.

"But one cannot accuse the captain of being unfair," Gamble thought. "He realizes how serious it could be to have the natives rallied against us, even by three white men."

Gamble now turned to the men in his Marine detachment. Armed with muskets, the musicians with drum and fife, the men sat tensely in the boats. They knew that the captain and their lieutenant counted on them for a show of strength to impress the island natives.

The bows of the boats touched bottom, and Gamble with his Marines and the seamen from the Essex leaped into knee-deep water. Muskets and powder cartouches held high, the men splashed to the beach. At an order from Gamble, the Marines fanned out.

One of the white men advanced. He spoke directly to Captain Porter. "Midshipman John M. Maury, United States Navy, sir!"

For an instant Captain Porter stared at the sunburned man in disbelief. Then he heard the story. Midshipman Maury and a friend, Lieutenant Lewis, had obtained furloughs from the Navy to sail to Canton, China, aboard a commercial ship. From Canton the men had sailed to Nooaheeva to collect sandalwood, highly prized in China.

After several months, Lewis had returned to Canton with a cargo. Maury had stayed to collect more sandalwood. The other two white men on the island were doing the same.

"You do not know that the United States and Great Britain are at war?" asked Captain Porter.

"At war?" Maury repeated. His surprise was too great not to be genuine. And here he had been helped for many months by a runaway Englishman named Wilson!

Midshipman Maury spoke without hesitation, "Then I beg you, Captain Porter, to let me join you so that I may return to the United States for reassignment."

The captain agreed, but his immediate concern was to win the cooperation, if not the friendship, of the natives on Nooaheeva. The men in his squadron could use fresh food and the chance to concentrate upon repairing the ships, unhindered by hostile natives.

Carrying out Captain Porter's original plan, Gamble ordered his Marines to attention. At his command they drilled smartly, every man aware of the curious eyes of the natives.

Work was immediately started to heave down the Essex, scrape the ship's bottom, and repair spars and rigging.

As this work went ahead, Wilson, the runaway Englishman, proved useful.

He had lived for many years among the Tayah tribe in this valley in Nooaheeva. He had, in fact, several wives among the island women. He spoke the Tayah language well and immediately became an interpreter for the Americans.

Gamble never felt too comfortable with Wilson. This was not a man to be trusted, however useful he might appear to be. Gamble shrewdly guessed that Wilson's only true devotion was to rum, and nothing else.

As the Greenwich lay at anchor day after day, Gamble requested permission from Captain Porter to exercise his men at drill on shore. This was given, and a small fort was built on a hill overlooking the bay. There, Marines stood guard.

Gamble was amused by the fascinated attention the natives paid to his men at drill. The young drummer in his scarlet jacket especially impressed them. The Tayah warriors never seemed to get over their surprise at seeing the Marines fire their muskets on command. How could so many men act as one?

In view of what was soon to come, it was well that Gamble had this time to drill his men. Long months at sea in close quarters aboard the frigate had almost made the men forget their primary role as "soldiers of the sea."

The first hint of trouble came when a party of Happah warriors from a nearby valley descended upon and attacked the friendly Tayahs. The Tayahs did not suffer greatly, but some breadfruit trees were destroyed. While this damage was slight, it suggested danger ahead.

As the days passed, Gamble and the other Americans began to learn something about the islanders and their customs. Several tribes lived on this island, each keeping to its own valley. A stranger who entered another tribe's valley knew the penalty might be death.

But there were certain men and women who were "taboo" and could travel freely about the island. These were persons who had married into other tribes.

It was through some of these taboo persons that the Happahs sent word that they had no fear of the Meleekees—their name for the Americans. They considered Captain Porter's friendly gestures cowardly. They would come down to the shore and take his sails—that is, his ships—from him.

Raiding parties of Happahs became more frequent.

"This cannot go on," Gamble thought. "The Tayahs are losing pigs and breadfruit trees. Their chief, Gaaneewa, feels we should punish the Happahs. On the other hand, who are we to get mixed up in native quarrels?"

"A few well-aimed musket balls, and we'd show them!" one of the Marines declared.

"Don't forget how they can disappear into the trees," reminded another man. "Like redskins, and I had my fill of them back home."

CHAPTER 4

A Dangerous Expedition

At last Captain Porter reluctantly decided to send an expedition against the Happahs. It was a colorful and strangely mixed crowd—some crewmen from the Essex Junior, a detachment of Marines armed with a six-pounder, and a disorderly mob of Tayah warriors with their chief warrior, Mouina. Lieutenant Downes commanded the party and Gamble was second-in-command.

Up the mountain bounding one side of the Tayah's valley the collection of Americans and natives went. The small cannon was heavy to drag, but the Americans counted on it and their muskets for a quick victory.

Hardly were the men over the brow of the mountain when they were set upon by screaming, tattooed Happahs. But well-placed fire from the six-pounder quickly sent the Happahs into retreat toward a log fortress. From this protection they hurled stones and insults at the Meleekees.

Lieutenant Downes paused to prepare the seamen and Marines for an attack. Just as the men were ready to launch the attack, a shower of stones and spears rained down from the fort. One stone hit Lieutenant Downes in the pit of the stomach, knocking him breathless. A spear pierced the neck of a seaman.

When the Tayahs saw Lieutenant Downes fall, they screamed with fright and fled. Only Mouina and a few warriors remained with the Americans.

Without hesitation, Gamble drew his mameluke sword and shouted, "Charge them, lads! Make them pay for this!"

With a cheer, the seamen and Marines charged through a second shower of stones and spears.

The first Americans to leap over the log breast-work fired into the Happahs, dropping several. But the Happahs continued to fight desperately.

One Happah warrior picked Gamble, the leader of the Meleekees, as his prize. He drew back his arm and hurled a spear which grazed Gamble's epaulette. Then the warrior rushed at him, wildly swinging a huge war club.

Gamble dodged the club. His mameluke sword clanged against the hardwood of the club as though it, too, were made of iron. The Happah, quick as a cat, spun about and raised his club to hurl it at Gamble. Just then, a Marine leveled his musket only a few inches from the warrior's head and fired.

The headless body of the Happah warrior fell back upon the bodies of his companions who had stayed to fight.

Leaping to the breastwork of the fort, Gamble shouted, "After them! Keep after them!"

The Marines and seamen rushed forward, but the fleet-footed warriors were fast disappearing into the wooded slopes of the valley. Nothing could be gained by pursuing them.

Gamble called the Marines to halt. "Fire!" he shouted, and they sent one volley of musket fire after the disorganized Happahs.

When Gamble and his men returned to the fort, they found Lieutenant Downes and the seamen setting up the six-pounder to defend it against a counterattack. But the Happahs for the time being had had enough of fighting. They sent a taboo man to sue for peace.

When Downes and Gamble reported their success to Captain Porter, he agreed to meet with Mowattaeeh, the Happah chief. It was arranged that the chief would pay a tribute in pigs and foodstuffs. Peace was declared.

The calm was short-lived. The most feared and warlike tribe on Nooaheeva were the Typees. Now they sent word that they would drive the Meleekees, together with the Tayahs and the Happahs, into the sea.

Porter sent offers of peace, but the Typees only replied by saying that they did not desire friendship with the Meleekees. The Happahs were nothing but cowards, the Typees claimed. Furthermore the Typees declared that their gods promised they would never be driven from their valley. They ended their message by calling the Meleekees white lizards, the most scornful name in their language.

The Typees began to send raiding parties at night to steal supplies. Both the Tayahs and the Happahs became restless. Soon their tributes to the Americans of pigs and fruits began to dwindle.

Captain Porter called Downes and Gamble to meet with him. He pointed out that since efforts to make peace with the Typees had failed, the only possible action was to attack. He had therefore decided that he would lead an expedition into the valley of the Typees.

Gamble was not ignorant of what this would mean. The Typees' valley was surrounded by high, steep mountains. The passes into the valley could be defended by a handful of warriors hurling spears at attackers climbing upward.

The valley was distant from the harbor. Any expedition moving overland would have to make a long, tiring climb to reach the passes. Against such odds Captain Porter hesitated to risk his men's lives.

But, the captain assured Downes and Gamble, he had learned from Mouina, the chief warrior of the Tayahs, about another route of attack. The warrior knew a secret path into the valley from a narrow beach on the other side of Nooaheeva. Here Captain Porter would make his attack.

Turning to his Marine lieutenant, Captain Porter said, "I put you in charge of all preparations for the expedition. Midshipman Feltus from the Essex will help you."

"Aye, aye, sir," Gamble answered briskly. He knew Feltus and liked the midshipman.

Although he was only sixteen, Feltus was one of the older midshipmen. Some of the reefers, as midshipmen were called, were mere boys. The youngest of the lot, who answered to the imposing name of David Glasgow Farragut, had joined the Essex two years earlier, when he was only nine years old.

Feltus was serious and likeable. He was so eager to please that he did the work of two grown men. With his help, Gamble was able to report on November 25 that the supplies for the expedition were loaded aboard the Essex Junior and all was ready.

On the afternoon of November 27, the Essex Junior, with Gamble, Feltus, and the seamen and Marines of the landing party aboard, sailed from Anna Maria Bay.

Captain Porter set out with five pulling boats, accompanied by ten war canoes of the Tayahs. They skirted the reefs of the island and rowed directly for the beach of the valley of the Typees.

At sunrise next morning, the Essex Junior dropped anchor off the beach.

"Let's go, lads!" Gamble called to his men, and the landing party went over the side into Captain Porter's waiting boats.

As the men pulled for the beach, Gamble saw ten war canoes filled with Happah warriors join the expedition.

"Good!" he thought. "We need all the men we can muster against the Typees."

Gamble shifted his gaze to the hills beyond the beach and saw more Happah and Tayah reinforcements gathered there. Still more warriors appeared along the beach.

The seamen and Marines landed. Immediately

Gamble and Captain Porter set out to investigate the secret path into the valley of the Typees.

Nothing that Mouina had said had prepared the two Americans for the surprise that awaited them. What was this secret path? Nothing more than the narrowest passageway through swampy, dense undergrowth.

Captain Porter cursed at not having sent an advance party. Gamble sized up the odds. They were not good.

"No wonder the Typees have never been driven from their valley," the captain muttered. "But we cannot turn back with the Happahs and Tayahs watching."

Captain Porter plunged into the pathway's narrow opening. Gamble motioned to his Marines and followed.

If the Americans hoped to move forward undetected, they were disappointed in this, too.

Spears and stones shot from enemy slings began to whistle about the landing party as the men darted along the narrow path.

The enemy could not be seen. The Typees did

not shout or chant. Only the snapping of an occasional branch and the constant rain of stones betrayed their presence. The path seemed unending. The men pushed on, one mile, two miles.

To have remained motionless would have been fatal to the landing party. To retreat would have admitted defeat and invited attack by the Tayahs and Happahs.

Mouina, who ran beside Captain Porter, at last gestured that the thicket would end shortly. It was none too soon. The seamen and Marines, nearly exhausted, burst into a small clearing along a riverbank.

A fresh shower of stones from the opposite bank greeted them. By some miracle no one was hit and a quick check showed no serious injuries suffered by any of the men in the difficult passage through the thicket.

There was no time to lose. Without waiting for a direction from Captain Porter, Gamble raised his sword and shouted, "Marines, aim! By volley, Fire!"

The volley crashed into the thicket on the other side of the river. It was answered by another shower of stones. At this close range and in the open, the stones did much damage. Men were hit and bruised. One stone, shot with great force, struck Lieutenant Downes, shattering a bone in his left leg. When the Typees saw the white man fall, they shouted triumphantly.

Gamble ordered a covering fire from the Marines. Downes and the other injured men were pulled back along the pathway. A small detail returned with them to the beach.

Now Captain Porter called to Gamble, "We cannot stay here. Have your Marines fix bayonets. We'll give them a volley, then clear the opposite bank with a bayonet charge."

Gamble held up his hand and nodded. He turned to his Marines and ordered "Fix bayonets. Load and prime." He knew that he could count on his men for speed. He would await the captain's signal for the volley.

At a sign from Porter, Gamble drew his sword and ordered "Fire!" Before the echoes of the volley died, Gamble was splashing across the river, his Marines close behind him.

This was not what the Typees had expected of the cowardly Meleekees. They fled before the charge. But they did not give up. As Gamble and his men forced their way through another narrow pathway in the thicket stones continued to fall about them.

Gamble set a fast pace of advance and soon his men reached a second clearing. Here they were stopped by the log walls of a fort some seven feet high that extended from one end of the clearing to the other.

Captain Porter overtook Gamble and the two men quickly reached a decision. The fort would have to be taken by storm. A sergeant interrupted to report that some men had exhausted their ammunition and the entire force had only enough ammunition for two or three volleys at the most.

"You are the only one I can trust, lieutenant," Captain Porter said to Gamble. "Take four men with you and return to the beach for ammunition. We can hold off the Typees until you return."

The beach was nearly two miles back. The long march to the beach and the frightful struggle back, loaded with heavy ammunition, was a nightmare for

Gamble and his men. Pushing through the thick undergrowth, with branches and thorns slapping his face and stones bruising his feet through his boots, Gamble felt a quiet pride in his men and in himself. They were nearly exhausted when they at last reached the second clearing where the rest of the men were waiting.

As the ammunition was being distributed, Captain Porter motioned Gamble aside. He said, "I've made my decision, lieutenant. We must return to the beach. There are not enough uninjured men left to take the fort."

Gamble bowed his head in disappointment, but he knew that any decision the captain made was a wise one.

"Take your Marines into the thicket behind us," Captain Porter continued, "and prepare for volley fire. The wounded will go with you. The seamen and I will pretend to make a hasty retreat. When we are through your lines, I'm sure they will rush us. Give them a volley and hold them with bayonet."

With the promptness of habit, Gamble raised his hat and replied "Aye, aye, sir."

The wounded started off down the path, with the
Marines hidden on either side. The seamen rose,
fired a few scattering shots into the fort, then ran in
apparent disorder into the thicket behind them.

Captain Porter had guessed correctly. The
Typees swarmed out of the fort, this time shouting
wildly. They raced across the clearing toward the
thicket.

Gamble had ordered the Marines to hold their
fire until they were certain of a hit. When the first
Typee warriors were only a few feet from the
thicket, the Marines' volley crashed into the closely
packed ranks.

Only a few warriors went on to reach the Marines'
bayonets. The rest fled to the safety of their fort.
Gamble gave the order to reload.

When it was clear that the Typees would not risk
another charge, Gamble silently signalled to the
Marines to move double-quick in single file along
the path toward the beach.

CHAPTER 5

The Typees' Challenge

DIFFICULT AS THE DECISION WAS, Captain Porter gave the order to embark the expedition aboard the Essex Junior for return to Anna Maria Bay. The men fit to carry a musket were too few to attempt to capture the Typee fortress.

After the Essex Junior put to sea, Captain Porter returned along the coast with the small boats.

As the Essex Junior stood into her anchorage the following day, a signal from the frigate directed Lieutenant Gamble to report aboard immediately. Within half an hour Gamble was standing before Captain Porter in the captain's cabin.

"Gamble," Captain Porter began immediately, "I cannot let things stand as they are. All the tribes will turn against us unless something is done quickly. The natives think the Typees defeated us."

"What do you propose to do, sir?" asked Gamble.

"I intend to proceed overland against the Typees," he replied, "with every man that can be spared from Essex and Essex Junior. We should be able to muster about two hundred."

The captain paused, and Gamble knew that he was considering carefully how to make the best use of the men he had.

"You, lieutenant," the captain continued, "will take the entire detachment of Essex' Marines, together with a landing party from the Essex Junior, and proceed over a trail that Mouina will show you to the top of the mountain. Avoid action if possible. I want you to clear the trail ahead of me to prevent ambush."

"Aye, aye, sir," Gamble replied.

"I will leave an hour after you with the main detachment from the Essex. We will have to manhandle the six-pounder over the steep mountain trails. This time I intend to teach the Typees a lesson they won't forget."

Gamble smiled approval.

The captain asked, "Whom would you prefer to have with you in charge of the seamen from the Essex Junior?"

"Midshipman Feltus, sir." Gamble answered without hesitation.

As the soft tropical dusk settled over Anna Maria Bay, Gamble assembled the Marines on the hard-packed sand of the beach. Feltus and the seamen from the Essex Junior joined the group. Gamble led the column in single file toward the path that led up the nearest mountain.

As the men marched, a full moon spread its light over the lovely valley. But Gamble and the long line of men struggling up the mountain behind him ignored the beauty of the scene. They were only grateful that the moonlight was bright enough to show the path.

After a weary two-hour march, Gamble and the advance party reached the mountaintop. Before letting his exhausted men rest, Gamble stationed them to protect the summit from attack.

After a tense wait of three hours, the first men of Captain Porter's group began to arrive. They appeared ready to drop in their tracks, for they had dragged the six-pounder with them. But they too deployed before resting.

During the next hour, Mouina and several Tayah warriors joined the expedition. They told Porter that it was about six miles to the valley of the Typees along the summit of the mountains. The weary men were roused to their feet. The march began.

Soon, word was passed to keep strict silence. A Happah village was close by. Porter did not want the Happahs to know his movements.

About midnight the Americans heard the beating of drums coming from the valley of the Typees. The warriors were noisily celebrating their victory over the Meleekees and praying to their gods for rain to make the white man's bhouies, as they called guns, helpless.

At last the expedition arrived at the pass. Gamble and a few picked men moved cautiously in advance, but they found no one defending this important entrance to the valley. All the warriors were celebrating.

Captain Porter halted his expedition at the head of a steep pathway cut into a sheer cliff. The Tayah guides knew that it was impossible to descend this path in the dark. The weary men were told to rest as best they could until daybreak.

Gamble had just dropped into a deep sleep when he was awakened by Mouina. The native pointed toward heavy clouds piling up along the summit of the mountain. As Gamble roused enough to realize what they meant, the large drops of rain began to fall.

"Mattee, mattee, bhouie!" Mouina kept repeating frantically. Gamble realized that the warrior was trying to say that the rain was death to muskets.

Gamble awakened his men and told them to protect their priming. The rain increased to torrents.

Wild shouts rose from the valley. The Typees felt their gods were answering their prayers.

A cold, piercing wind came with the rain, chilling the Americans to the bone. To make matters worse, the ground became wet and very slippery. The men dared not move for fear of falling over the steep cliff. Each man huddled in his spot, teeth chattering, as the biting wind and rain whipped him.

The rain beat without letup until sunrise. Even when it stopped, the steep pathway was too slippery to risk going down.

Turning to Gamble, Captain Porter said, "I want to warn the Typees that we are going to attack. They can remove their women and children. Have your Marines fire a volley into the valley."

As the sound of the volley echoed against the mountains, an answering shout rose from the Typees.

Porter then left a guard at the pass and with his other men returned to the Happah village for food until it was possible to get through.

The surly Happah chieftain did not want to bring food for the Americans. After Captain Porter threatened to have his men shoot every pig in sight, the chieftain finally agreed to feed Porter's men.

By the next morning the men were rested and the ground had dried. The march was resumed. The

Americans crossed the pass and descended into the valley without mishap. But when they reached the foot of the path, a strong party of Typee warriors awaited them. The natives lined the banks of a river before a fortified village, daring Porter to attack them.

Gamble took up the challenge and formed his Marines into line. They fired a volley into the ranks of the Typees. Then with bayonets fixed, Gamble and his Marines charged across the river. Waving their cutlasses and shouting, Feltus and his seamen swarmed after the Marines.

In the face of this fierce charge, the Typees retreated in disorder, leaving several dead and wounded behind. The Americans crossed the river and quickly took the fortified village by storm.

The Typees fled behind a stone wall on higher ground. But the Marines and seamen pushed on after them. The fighting was bitter. Natives traded a hail of stones and spears for every volley of musket shot. Three of Gamble's men fell wounded. Finally, the natives, several of them wounded, were dislodged and the stone wall taken.

Meanwhile fighting had begun on another front. Captain Porter dispatched men under Lieutenant McKnight of the Essex to capture a nearby native fort.

McKnight and his men managed to gain control of the fort. But they sent out word that they could not remain without reinforcements.

Captain Porter called Gamble to his side. "Lieutenant," he said, "take Feltus and a group of Marines to McKnight's rescue. His situation is desperate."

Even as he briskly answered, "Aye, aye, sir," Gamble was directing his men into marching order. They set out in double-quick time along a path toward the besieged fort.

A sudden rise in the ground gave Gamble a view of the long slope ahead. At the far end of the open ground he saw McKnight's party retreating from the fort, firing as they went.

Between Gamble's men and McKnight's there was a stone wall, slanting off to the right. Suddenly before Gamble's astonished eyes a large group of

Typees appeared from the thicket. They took up a position behind the wall, on Gamble's side, evidently unaware of him and his men.

It was soon plain that the Typees were intent upon setting up an ambush. Gamble prayed that none of his men would betray their presence by any sudden move. He waved to Feltus and indicated that he should lead the men off the path to the right. From this position they could advance as skirmishers.

Using signals, Gamble ordered the Marines to prime and aim muskets. Still the Typees were oblivious of danger. The seamen followed the example of the Marines.

When Gamble saw the leader of McKnight's party approach the stone wall, he gave the order to fire.

The Typees found themselves trapped in a cross fire between Gamble's and McKnight's forces. No matter which way they ran, they met heavy musket fire. Many of their warriors fell. Quickly the survivors disappeared into the thickets.

But fighting was not yet over for the day.

"The Typees deserve their reputation as valiant

warriors," Gamble thought. "They gave ground only under the heaviest musket fire. A single defeat could not bring them to surrender."

The expedition continued to fight their way through the entire valley, setting fire to each village they captured. Toward late afternoon, Gamble and his men, who had gone ahead as skirmishers, reached the far end of the valley. There the tired Marines and seamen stood gratefully beside a waterfall and let the cool waters drench them.

The main body of the expedition soon joined them at the waterfall, and Captain Porter allowed his weary men a half hour of rest.

Taking Gamble aside, the captain explained his plan to return to the ships by way of the mountains near the sea. These were less steep than those the men had just crossed.

Still the Typees continued to fight, although with greatly weakened forces. As the expedition made its slow way up the nearest mountain, huge boulders were suddenly rolled down. They plunged wide of their mark and did no damage. This proved to be the Typees' last effort at resistance.

Reaching the summit of the mountain, the Americans looked back upon the valley through which they had just fought. Smoke from many burning villages rose in the still evening air.

Victory had not come easily. Much as the Marines liked a scrap, they were glad they did not often have enemies like the Typees to face.

The next day the expedition returned to Anna Maria Bay. In the two days they had been gone, the men had marched more than sixty miles over high mountains. While no Americans had been killed, several suffered wounds and exhaustion.

The Typees were now very eager for peace. They sent a taboo man under a flag of truce to plead with Captain Porter.

"I will grant peace," the captain said, "only if you meet all my earlier demands. In addition, I ask a tribute of four hundred pigs."

The Typees held a council and accepted these peace terms.

For the first time in the memory of even the oldest men, all the tribes mixed with one another in peace. Fresh fruit, pigs, and other food flowed into the

fort which Porter had built on the shores of Anna
Maria Bay.

Precious time had been lost fighting the Happahs
and Typees. Captain Porter now turned all his attention to completing repairs. The Essex must be
made ready for sea.

To speed the work, Porter needed all hands on
board. He ended all shore leave. Gamble was told
to see that the order was enforced. Many of the men
were angry at this command.

The Essex and her consorts had now been in
Nooaheeva almost six weeks. Some of the crew
had taken wives among the native women. Now they
were angry at being kept aboard ship.

The native women treated the matter as a great
joke. Each day they lined the shores of the bay,
laughing and chattering. Some of them showed
mock grief by dipping their fingers in the sea and
touching their eyes, letting the salt water trickle
down their cheeks like tears. Others pretended
to beat themselves with grass spears.

The men, however, did not take the matter with
such good humor. They claimed that their situation

was worse than slavery. Robert White, a former British seaman aboard the Essex Junior, declared that when the time came to get the frigate underway, the men would refuse to weigh anchor. The threat of mutiny hung in the air.

On December 9, Gamble's Marines caught three men, including White, trying to swim ashore under cover of darkness. Captain Porter ordered them placed in irons. The three men were later spread-eagled at the gangway, and all hands were piped to see them punished.

The next morning Gamble received orders to report to the captain's cabin. As he entered, the captain was writing and waved him to a seat.

The cabin was peaceful. Only the ticking of the chronometers in their brass gimbals and the scratch of the captain's quill disturbed the silence.

Captain Porter got up from his desk and stood before one of the stern ports. He gazed for a moment out over the sunlit waters of the bay. Then he turned to Lieutenant Gamble.

"John, I must put a heavy responsibility on you," he said, speaking thoughtfully.

Gamble knew that this was a grave occasion. Never before had the captain called him anything but "lieutenant."

The usual sharpness of his voice was softened as he continued, "I must leave you here with four of the prize ships. I will sail the frigate, with the Essex Junior, to meet the British men-o'-war that have been sent to find us. I have prepared these written instructions."

Captain Porter picked up a bulky pack of papers from his desk and handed them to Gamble.

"I have set May 27, 1814, as the final date for the Essex to return to these islands. During the five and a half months until then you should, with the help of the natives, get in a good crop from the seeds I am leaving with you."

Captain Porter paced the cabin. Gamble followed him with his eyes, but said nothing.

"I am sorry that I can spare you only two midshipmen and twenty-two men. Some of the men are old and infirm, and six of them are being held prisoner for various offenses."

The captain paused in his pacing.

"But I am giving you Midshipman Feltus. He is a good man. Acting Midshipman Clapp is young and eager, but I think he has the makings of a good officer."

Clapp had been mastheaded—that is sent up into the tops as punishment—as often as any midshipman aboard because of his pranks. But he was deeply interested in learning about life at sea.

"Try to keep the good will of the natives," Captain Porter went on. "Keep a sharp watch on your own men, especially the prisoners. If they arouse the natives, you will be in serious trouble. White, as you know, is treacherous."

Gamble nodded.

"You will put all the whale oil from the other ships aboard the New Zealander. As early as possible she should sail to the United States to sell the cargo."

Gamble stood up and said, "Aye, aye, sir. I want you to know how much I appreciate the confidence you have in me."

"I know the ships will be in good hands with you in command. I shall miss you and the men I leave with you." The captain's voice was warm and friendly and he clasped Gamble's hand with a firm grip.

The lieutenant doffed his hat and turned to go, feeling both pride and dread at the burden of his new duties.

On the morning of December 12, all hands were piped to quarters aboard the Essex. Capain Porter ordered the seaman Robert White brought before him. Porter accused the Englishman of making mutinous threats aboard the Essex Junior.

The terrified Englishman denied everything. But several men swore that he was lying.

His face red with fury, Captain Porter raised his sword and shouted, "Run, you scoundrel. Run for your life!"

The sight of the captain's face was enough. White raced to the gangway. Without losing stride, he leaped into the bay and swam toward a passing canoe.

Captain Porter turned toward his crew.

"All who are ready to perform your duties as loyal men, man your stations!"

A loud cheer from two hundred and fifty throats

rolled across the still bay. The natives ran from their huts, amazed at the noise. The crew of the Essex Junior answered with another loud cheer.

In a moment the frigate's rigging was black with topmen laying aloft to loose topsails. The fiddler struck up the tune "The Girl I Left Behind Me." Willing hands grasped the capstan bars. Soon the anchor broke clear of its holding ground.

Gamble, Midshipman Feltus, and Acting Midshipman Clapp stood on the quarterdeck of the Greenwich. They watched as sail after sail was loosened from the frigate's yards and sheeted home.

As the Essex stood out of the bay with a fair wind, the clink of the Essex Junior's capstan pawls could be heard across the water as her topsails and topgallants were released from furl and sheeted home. A few minutes later she, too, was under way.

Gamble watched the two ships disappear below the horizon. He straightened his shoulders, took a deep breath, and turned to face his new duties.

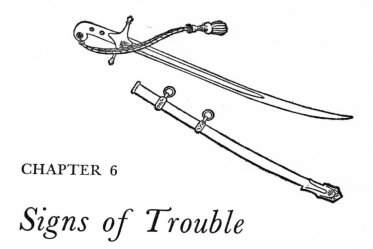

CHAPTER 6

Signs of Trouble

AT FIRST Gamble felt satisfied. The work went forward smoothly. The men began the transfer of whale oil from the other ships to the New Zealander. The natives brought aboard fresh fruit and meat each day.

Then without warning trouble struck Gamble. He had picked up malaria earlier in his voyage from the United States. For the past several months the young officer had been free of attacks. Now chills and fever hit him in full force. He knew the symptoms only too well.

Calling Midshipman Feltus to him, Gamble said, "You will have to take over, lad. I know that for the time being I am too weak to leave my cabin. Clapp can help you, but he is young and inexperienced. He will need your supervision."

"I'll do my best, sir," Feltus answered.

The midshipman was as good as his word. He kept the men busy at their tasks for two weeks while Gamble battled the fever and chills of malaria.

When Gamble was able to come on deck again and take charge, he noticed that a subtle change had taken place in the attitude of the natives and of some of his men as well. First the provisions supplied by the natives began to dwindle. Then they stopped altogether.

One day the watch on deck sighted natives breaking into the provision storehouses which had been built ashore. Gamble knew then that they were ignoring the peace Captain Porter had imposed on them.

He also realized that there were others besides the natives who could not be trusted. There was the

Englishman, Wilson, who had lived long with the natives. Gamble had never liked him. He could not abide the fellow's sly cockney voice and wheedling ways. Gamble was certain that Wilson had persuaded the mutinous seaman White to join with him. He suspected that the two of them were stirring up the natives against the Americans.

"I can handle Wilson and White," the lieutenant thought, "and the natives as well. But how many of my own men are trustworthy?"

He counted them off on his fingers—old John Witter, Gibbs, Thomas, Worth, Caddington, and, of course the midshipmen. There were not many. Most of the others had begun to grumble and scowl as they went about their work. They had become deliberately slow in carrying out every order.

"I must show the natives that we still have the upper hand here," he thought. "It will have to be done while I still have the prize crew of the New Zealander, before she sails for home."

Wilson and White could cause serious trouble if they aroused the natives. The best solution, Gamble knew, was to act quickly and put on a bold front.

He summoned Midshipman Feltus and explained
his plans. "You will take a boat's crew and go to each
ship. Load, prime, and elevate the broadside guns.
The old and infirm men will remain aboard with
young Clapp in charge. You and I, with Master's
Mate King of New Zealander, will lead a landing
party ashore."

Feltus answered eagerly, "Aye, aye, sir."

"On my signal from the fortified hill, the men remaining aboard the ships will fire the main batteries," Gamble continued. "We know that the
Tayahs, Happahs, and Typees are no cowards. We
have only a handful of men. Our only chance is to
catch them off guard and frighten them with the
threat of destruction from the ships' big guns."

Feltus raised his officer's hat—called by its French
name, chapeau-a-bras—and hurried to carry out
Gamble's orders.

"It will be touch-and-go if the natives have settled the quarrels among the tribes and combine
forces against us," Gamble thought grimly. "The
matter must be settled at once, or we are in for
even worse trouble."

Several hours later Gamble watched through his long glass as a boat shoved off from alongside the New Zealander and headed toward the Greenwich. "They finished sooner than I expected," he thought. "Young Feltus certainly knows his job."

The boat soon hailed the Greenwich, and Midshipman Feltus called, "All instructions carried out, sir. All guns are loaded and elevated. The men need only touch a slow match to the vents."

Gamble called back, "Proceed toward our rendezvous off the fort. I will follow immediately with the other two boats."

Feltus raised his hat in acknowledgement. Before the boat's crew took up their stroke, Gamble called a final warning, "Don't try to land until I join you. We need every fighting man we can muster!"

CHAPTER 7

A Risky Venture

THE SUN WAS SHINING into the Valley of Tieihuey as the three boats rode through the light surf of Anna Maria Bay and grounded on the shallow bottom. The thirty-five seamen and Marines, muskets held high, jumped into waist-deep water and waded to the open stretch of beach.

The moment they reached the beach, the men were aware of a strange quiet. Usually the natives rushed down to the beach when a boat came from one of the ships. Now the beach was deserted. Not even a child came forward to greet them. No sound

could be heard from the native village in the grove
of coconut palms.

Gamble's voice broke through the threatening
silence, "Mister Feltus, Mister King! Don't let your
men spread out. Check the priming of all muskets
and pistols."

Muskets and pistols were checked, and damp
priming was replaced. Gamble drew his Marine officer's mameluke sword from its scabbard. With the
firmness of command, he pointed it toward the hill
that rose above the storehouses.

"March directly, and in good order, to the fort,"
he commanded.

The landing party cautiously crossed the open
stretch of beach, Gamble in the lead. He had the
strong feeling that they were being watched. Yet not
a sound could be heard from the steep hills except
for bird cries and the rustle of palm fronds.

The men reached the hill and slowly climbed to
its top. There Captain Porter had built a fort with
four twelve-pounder guns emplaced facing seaward.

Through his long glass Gamble carefully inspected what he could see of the village and its sur-

roundings. He could find no sign of life. The village, usually so busy and full of movement, was deserted.

Gamble remembered a bit of advice Captain Porter had given him long ago: "Look out for trouble when they remove their women and children." This time Gamble was glad that the natives were gone, because he wished the firing of the ships' guns to be a warning, rather than a hurt, to the villagers.

Gamble ordered the "Blue Peter" broken from the flagstaff atop the fort as a signal to the ships. After what seemed like an endless wait, white puffs of smoke were at last sighted from each of the anchored ships.

As the smoke drifted upward through the rigging, the thunderous roar of the broadside guns echoed through the valley. This was followed by the sound of the round shot whistling overhead and the splinter and crash as the shot plunged into the coconut grove beyond the village.

For some minutes after the thunder of the broadside guns had died away, a strange, expectant silence filled the valley. It was broken only by the cry of a bird in the nearby coconut grove. Suddenly, in the path that led from the native village, a single stooped figure could be made out, coming slowly toward the fort.

Midshipman Feltus focused a long glass on the figure. After a moment he turned to Gamble, smiling. "It's Gattanewa, the high chief of the Tayahs! It looks as if he's had too much kava beer."

The old chief moved at a shuffling pace, keeping his balance with the help of a carved wooden staff. Finally he came within speaking distance of the fort. He held up his free hand and in a rasping voice called out, "Meleekee, Meleekee, Gattanewa, tayah." His eyes met the lieutenant's.

Gamble knew that "Meleekee" was the native pronunciation of "American" and that "tayah" meant friend, as well as being the name of Gattanewa's tribe.

Turning to Midshipman Feltus, Gamble said, "Tell the old fellow to come closer. I never thought I'd be happy to see his ugly face again. But it is a much pleasanter sight than a few hundred of his shouting warriors."

Feltus, who had picked up some knowledge of the native tongue, raised his voice and haltingly spoke a few words. The old chief came forward and made a low bow to Gamble, then spoke a torrent of words to Feltus.

"As near as I can make out, sir," Feltus said with a puzzled frown, "he says that some bad people stole the provisions and that he will punish them. He says that Gattanewa saw what the bhouies of your warriors did to the powerful and undefeated Typees. Even the Typees were driven from their valley and had their villages burned when they went against the Meleekees."

When Feltus finished translating, Gattanewa continued to speak earnestly. Feltus listened carefully. The midshipman then turned to Gamble and said, "He begs that we do not fire the great bhouies of the ships against his village. He promises that he will obtain more pigs and fruits and coconuts for us, to replace those that were stolen."

A great relief surged through Gamble. Their situation in the islands would soon be impossible if the natives decided to resist and withhold fresh fruit and other provisions. The prospect of enough food was an encouraging omen.

Turning to the old chief, Gamble spoke in slow, measured tones. He wanted to impress Gattanewa with the sound of his voice, even though he knew the old fellow could not understand him.

"Tell Gattanewa," he said, "that everything stolen must be returned, and that more pigs and coconuts must be brought to the fort. If the Tayahs do not prove themselves friends of the Meleekees, the great bhouies of the ships will kill their warriors and their villages will be burned."

Gattanewa listened intently as Feltus translated Gamble's words to the best of his ability. The old chief's skin, rough and scaly from the effects of continued drinking of kava, shook as he nodded his head to indicate he understood. He slowly turned to walk away.

"Mister Feltus," said Gamble, "please see to it that an armed watch is set. We will begin to transfer stores to the ships immediately. The pigs and other foodstuffs will be placed on board when they are returned to us."

Looking across the lush beauty of the Valley of
Tieihuey, Gamble sighed at the thought that every
Eden must have its serpent. Realizing that he still
held his mameluke sword in his hand, he returned
it to its scabbard. He motioned to the midshipman
and said, "Have the men launch the boats through
the surf, Mister Feltus. We shall return to the
ships."

CHAPTER 8

Perils Increase

DESPITE the old chief's solemn promises, Gamble soon found that he could not depend on the good will of the natives. As long as there were enough men to mount a guard at the fort, the natives returned the pigs, at least most of them. At first they also furnished coconuts and fruit. But as some ships prepared to sail and fewer white men were left, the supplies dwindled.

The greatest loss was the New Zealander. Following Captain Porter's instructions, Gamble had transferred the whale oil from the other ships to her and prepared her to sail for the United States. His log entry for December 28, 1813, read:

> At three bells in forenoon watch, Master's Mate John King, prize master of captured British whaler New Zealander, came aboard to pay his respects. Presented Mr. King with the written orders Captain Porter had prepared for him. Also delivered to him all mail for the United States and a copy of my report to Captain Porter, in the event he should fall in with him at sea.
>
> At six bells in forenoon watch, New Zealander underweigh, standing out of Anna Maria Bay loaded with 1,950 barrels of whale oil. We shall sorely miss the support of Master's Mate King and his crew; however I cannot justify delaying the sailing of New Zealander any longer.

After the New Zealander's departure, the supply of fresh provisions became dangerously low. Gamble thought that the other islands of the Marquesas might offer more supplies. He readied the Sir Andrew Hammond for sea.

Detailing a small guard under Acting Corporal John Witter to remain with the other ships and the storehouse, he sailed on February 8, 1814. The log entry for the day read:

> At two bells in afternoon watch, catted and fished the anchor, made all plain sail out of Anna Maria Bay. Course SSE to clear headlands, thence to Hivaoa Island of the Marquesas Group to trade scrap iron for fresh provisions. Provisions very scarce at Nooaheeva. Natives unfriendly.

Natives of all the Polynesian islands highly prized old scrap iron. From it they made knives, spearheads, fish hooks and ornaments. Gamble hoped to trade iron scraps left over from ship repairs for fresh provisions.

The expedition was a bitter disappointment. The Americans arrived at Hivaoa only to find that the natives were fighting one another in a savage civil war. The old men and the women who were free from fighting could supply only a few pigs and scarcely enough fruit and coconuts to replace the food which the Hammond's crew ate each day.

Gamble sailed on to other nearby islands. But nowhere was he able to find a large source of supplies.

On February 16, her mission a failure, the Hammond returned to Nooaheeva and came to anchor once more in Anna Maria Bay.

As if this were not misfortune enough, Gamble learned that Acting Corporal John Witter had drowned in the surf. Gamble felt his loss deeply. But Witter was not the last man he was to lose from his command.

One morning, shortly after his return, Gamble was awakened early by Feltus, shaking his shoulder.

"Sir! Sir!" he was repeating breathlessly.

"Yes, Feltus. What is it?"

"Our best whaleboat is missing, sir, and much of our ammunition. And most of our provisions are gone!"

Gamble's heart sank. The whaleboat they could spare, perhaps, and even the ammunition. But they needed every scrap of food they had.

Dressing quickly, Gamble went on deck. It took him only a moment to learn what had happened. Three British whaling seamen had been the night deck watch. They had voluntarily enlisted in the United States Navy to avoid being impressed into

the British Navy. They were now gone, together
with Isaac Coffin, a seaman who had been held prisoner for trying to desert from the Essex.

Gamble chose a few of his most trustworthy seamen to set out in pursuit, and ordered the longboat hoisted out. The deserters, however, had foreseen that this might happen. They had damaged the
longboat so badly that it could not be launched.
Gamble had to resign himself to the loss of his valu-
ble supplies.

Trouble continued. Only a few mornings later
Gamble was again awakened early—this time by the
sound of shouting and scuffling on deck.

He rushed on deck only to stop short at the
strange sight that met his eyes. Two of his men were
holding two struggling natives. Midshipman Feltus,
with a pistol, and Marine Peter Caddington, with a
musket, were holding six seamen at bay. The re-
bellious seamen were shouting vile names at Feltus
and Caddington. Feltus explained that the seamen
had been caught breaking into the Greenwich's
storeroom, and giving the natives several loaves of
bread made from the precious store of flour. The

natives loved the bread so much that they would trade almost anything for it.

Roused by the noise, several crewmen who originally served aboard the Essex rushed on deck.

"Arm yourselves, men!" Gamble ordered. As soon as they did, they seized the natives. Each was given a whack with the flat of a sword and motioned to dive overboard and swim ashore. The seamen who had been caught trading bread to the natives were spread-eagled. Each was given a dozen lashes with the cats, as seamen called the fearsome cat-o'-nine-tails.

All hands were then immediately turned to on ship's work. For a moment it seemed as if some of the former British seamen would refuse to do their duty. Finally, however, with much muttering and black looks at the American seamen under arms, they slowly went about their tasks.

It was evident to Gamble that he and the ships under his commmand could no longer stay in Anna Maria Bay. The unfriendly natives would not keep the ships in provisions. The seamen were growing more restless every day. He was afraid that even the men he could trust would be infected with the mutinous spirit of the British seamen. He must put out to sea.

Gamble decided that of the three prizes, the Greenwich, the Sir Andrew Hammond, and the Seringapatam, only the last two could be fitted for sea with the small number of men left in his command. Of the two, the Seringapatam was the better ship. So, on April 12, he set most of the men at repairs to prepare the Seringapatam for sea.

Noting the sullen attitude of many of his men, Gamble had all arms and ammunition taken from the Seringapatam and the Hammond and stored under lock in the Greenwich. Much to his surprise, however, the men worked quickly and apparently with a will. The repairs were soon made, and most property of value was transferred from the Greenwich to the other two ships.

About all that remained to be done was for Gamble to inspect the solid shot for the main battery of the Seringapatam. It was important that the shot be stowed in the lockers properly. If it broke loose in heavy seas and crashed on the lower decks, it could endanger the lives of the men and cause great damage to the ship. For this reason, the ship could not put out to sea until Gamble had inspected the stowage.

At four bells on May 7, young Clapp came to Gamble's cabin to report that the shot was stowed and that a boat from the Seringapatam had come alongside.

"Very well, Mister Clapp. Tell the coxswain to stay at the starboard gangway. I shall be on deck in a moment."

"Aye, aye, sir." Clapp turned to go.

"Sir," he asked, pausing in the cabin doorway, "may I go with you? I should like to see for myself how the shot should be stowed."

"Yes, Clapp, you may come along." Gamble smiled at the boy's eagerness to learn.

"Aye, aye, sir," the boy answered. He then clattered up the companionway to the weather deck, where Gamble could hear him repeating the orders to the coxswain of the boat through the speaking trumpet.

Gamble arose and stretched his arms to the accompaniment of a yawn. He had to watch his head however, for he had learned from experience that the low overhead of a whaling ship could inflict a very painful knob on the head if one stretched to one's full height. He pulled on his undress jacket and was about to reach for his scarlet sash and mameluke sword, which hung from double hooks near his bunk. Remembering that he would have to climb up and down several ladders to inspect the shot lockers of the Seringapatam, he decided not to wear his sword.

He unlocked the case containing the small arms, selected a pistol, then, after examining the pan carefully, primed it and thrust it into the leather belt about his waist.

He picked up his chapeau-a-bras, but on second thought put it down and picked up a head covering with a wide brim, similar to those planters in the West Indies use when out in their fields under the sun. The natives were very skillful at weaving and he and several of the Essex' officers had these very practical hats woven while the ship was undergoing repairs.

Glancing about the cabin to make certain that the small arms locker was secured and everything in order, he turned and disappeared up the companionway. The steady ticking of the chronometers filled with expanding sound the silence in the cabin.

CHAPTER 9

Mutiny!

GAMBLE WAS MET by Feltus at the starboard gangway of the Seringapatam. The boatswain's pipe rendered side honors, and the side boys, with young
Clapp, were dismissed. Midshipman Feltus walked
aft with Gamble toward the hatchway that led to the
berth deck.

There, an English seaman waited for them. Gamble remembered that he was one of the original
crew of the Seringapatam when she was an armed
British whaler.

The seaman knuckled his forehead smartly, in the seaman's salute.

"Served in the Royal Navy," Gamble thought, "to salute an officer so skillfully. The whaler must have shipped him as gunner." Acknowledging the salute, he said, "Please lead the way to the shot lockers."

"Aye, aye, sir," replied the seaman. He turned with military precision and led them forward along the berth deck.

At this moment one of the seamen clattered down the ladder from the weather deck. "Mr. Feltus, th' boatswain pre . . . pre . . ." the lad stammered.

"The boatswain presents his respects," said Feltus, trying to help the seaman. "What is his message?"

"Yes, sir," nodded the young seaman. "Th' boatswain asks as will you come on deck right away?"

Gamble turned to the lad. "Has anything happened?"

"No, sir," answered the seaman, ill at ease in the presence of an officer. "Th' boatswain, he just sez

I'm to ask Mister Feltus if he'll come on deck."

Gamble recalled the lad as a not-too-bright fellow who was the object of many jokes from his rough shipmates. In his dim-witted way the lad was pitifully eager to please his tormentors.

"Lieutenant," Feltus explained, "I told the boatswain that I wanted to inspect the repairs to the topgallant yard before it was swayed aloft."

"Very well, Mister Feltus," Gamble said, "I'll go ahead with the gunner."

As the gunner held a lanthorn above his head, Gamble's expert eye noted that the solid shot had been racked and secured very ably. "My compliments, gunner. A very ship-shape job."

"Thank'ee, sir," replied the gunner. "If you'll follow me, sir, I'll lead the way to the weather deck."

As he came on deck, Gamble's eyes smarted for a moment in the flood of brilliant sunlight. He noticed that Feltus was not in sight. Gamble took out his handkerchief to rub his eyes. At that instant someone leaped on him from behind and knocked him to the deck.

Throwing up his free hand, Gamble managed to half turn as he fell. He landed on his attacker and rolled over him.

Gamble struggled to his feet, reaching for the pistol in his belt. With a sharp blow the pistol was dashed from his hand. Several men leaped on him, pounding him without mercy. Under the rain of blows, he sank slowly to the deck, and was at once bound hand and foot.

"Take 'im to th' cabin," ordered the gunner.

Rough hands grabbed him, dragged him toward the companionway, and tossed him down.

A moment later, the door was opened and Midshipman Feltus, also bound hand and foot, was thrown in beside him. He was followed by Acting Midshipman Clapp, in the same condition.

"Are you injured?" Gamble asked anxiously.

"A bit bruised, sir. That's all," Feltus replied.

"I'm the same, sir," added Clapp. "But they've bound my feet painfully tight."

"Twist and pull on your bonds," Gamble said. "Maybe one of us can work a hand free."

For a few minutes the only sound to be heard was

the panting breath of the three men as they strained and pulled at their bonds.

"No use, sir," gasped Feltus, "they did too good a job."

They lay back, tired and helpless. Time seemed to drag on endlessly. The scuttle to the runway had been nailed down after they were thrown into its narrow space. The air was stifling. Each breath was an effort.

Once in a while they heard feet thumping across the deck above. Sweat trickled down their faces and dropped from their noses. Their clothes were soaked through.

Finally, a new sound reached them from above. It was the creak of boat falls—the sets of blocks and tackles used to hoist a boat.

"Listen!" said Gamble. "I can feel the cable being heaved in through the hawse pipe. They're going to sail."

The faint shrill of the boatswain's pipe could be heard, answered by the sound of running feet on deck. The tiller ropes rumbled as control of the ship's wheel was transmitted to the rudder-yoke.

Soon a gurgling noise indicated that water had begun to flow past the rudder. The deck heeled beneath the captives. They knew that the Seringapatam was standing out of Anna Maria Bay on the starboard tack.

After a while, the door to the runway opened and Feltus and Clapp were taken into the cabin. Gamble inched toward the open door, eagerly gasping for a breath of fresh air.

At last two men dragged Gamble, too, into the cabin. They unbound his feet and motioned him to a chair. A sharp pain shot through his feet as he tried to stand. With great effort, he lurched to the chair and fell into it.

Feltus was seated next him. Across the table was young Clapp, his expression twisted with pain.

A face appeared in the cabin skylight. "All right, laddies, all but one git up on deck and help handle sail."

Gamble recognized the sentinel who was left as the stupid lad who had brought the message to Feltus. The boy kept his pistol aimed at the lieutenant.

"There's no need to keep that pistol pointed at me. My hands are bound," Gamble said looking steadily at the seaman.

A foolish grin spread over the youngster's face, but he did not lower the pistol. Gamble was not used to being disobeyed. In his sternest voice of command, he said sharply, "Put down that pistol right now, and take your finger off the trigger."

The silly smile disappeared, and the youth lowered the pistol, mumbling "Mister White sez there's to be no talkin'."

"*Mister* White," thought Gamble bitterly. "He probably led this mutiny."

Each time Gamble or one of the midshipmen moved to lessen the strain of their position, the seaman raised his pistol. It was clear that he had never handled one before.

CHAPTER 10

Cast Adrift

THE SERINGAPATAM began to lift and heave to the motion of the open sea. She was obviously clear of the calm waters of the bay.

"Now that we're clear of the island," Gamble thought, "surely the mutineers will set us free to return." But the ship continued steadily on her course.

"Look out, you fool!" Feltus suddenly shouted. At the same instant the lieutenant heard a loud pistol shot and felt a searing pain in his left heel. He jerked backward and toppled off the chair to the cabin deck.

Immediately several heads appeared in the open skylight of the cabin.

"Who fired?"

"Shoot 'em all now an' be done with it."

"Move over. Let me take aim."

For an instant it appeared that a volley would flame down on them. The foolish seaman still held the pistol, muttering over and over, "It jist went off in my hand."

The men at the skylight cursed and withdrew. Gamble's wound began to throb, and his foot swelled rapidly.

Two men entered the cabin and bent over Gamble, examining his foot. One began to tug at his boot. Gamble cried out in pain.

"We'll have to cut off the boot," one said.

As the boot was cut away the pain eased somewhat. One of the men jabbed into the wound, and Gamble gritted his teeth to hold back a cry.

"Ball went clean through," the man said. "No bones broken."

Even in his pain, Gamble's habits of command took over. "You have done enough harm," he snapped. "Get muskets, powder, and supplies. Put us in a boat, before we get so far from land that we can't sight it in the dark."

"Charlie, go ask White what he wants done wi' the prisoners," one of the men said.

Charlie muttered and left the cabin. The men who were left waited in silence for his return.

Soon they heard the tiller ropes rasping, and the deck above came alive with thumping feet. The easy motion of the ship in the seaway stopped. She began to roll and pitch as she lay hove to.

Charlie thumped into the cabin. "White sez put 'em in a boat."

Gamble, Feltus, and Clapp were dragged up the companionway to the darkness of the deck. They gratefully breathed deep of the fresh night air.

A small boat bobbed near the stern. Water sloshed in its bottom. Two seamen, Worth and Lounsbury, had chosen to return to the island, and were already sitting in the leaky boat.

Gamble, Feltus, and Clapp were lowered into the boat. On Gamble's request, muskets and powder were sent after them.

" 'Ave a good time, Yank," a mocking voice called down from the darkness. "Remember me to th' girls o' Nooaheeva."

Feltus, Clapp, and the two seamen manned the oars and brought the head of the boat about. The looming mass of the Seringapatam became less and less distinct, until she was lost to sight in the vast darkness.

Gamble found the tiller and inserted it into the rudder. He steadied the boat on a course toward the jagged peaks of Nooaheeva, which he could just make out to the north.

The boat was leaking badly, and salt water swirled into Gamble's wound, stinging it mercilessly. He constantly bailed, using his woven hat that a mutineer, with contempt, had thrown into the boat after him.

Through the long night the men worked without stopping. They were soaked with spray. In the bottom of the boat, water sloshed about their feet. Their arms ached and their legs were cramped in the tight space. Blisters swelled, were broken, and raw flesh bled on the oar handles. Gamble was racked with chills and fever.

Toward dawn, the leaking boat with its ragged crew finally entered the calmer waters of Anna Maria Bay. The men took a deep breath and rested on their oars a moment. Picking them up again, they rowed with new energy to within several boat lengths of the Greenwich.

"Ahoy there," hailed the Marine, Peter Caddington.

"It's Feltus," the midshipman shouted back, "with Lieutenant Gamble and Midshipman Clapp."

"Thank God you're back," Caddington answered. "Wilson has boarded the Hammond and stolen everything of value. All our men are sleeping by the guns of the Greenwich to guard against attack."

CHAPTER 11

The Massacre

THROUGH THE LONG DAY and night that followed, Gamble kept all hands at work, preparing for an attack. At times he was burning with fever. At other times chills swept over him like huge waves, leaving him weak and gasping. Still he stayed on deck, giving orders.

The broadside guns of the Greenwich were reloaded with grape and canister. Netting was triced up to keep off attackers boarding the ship. All muskets and small arms were brought on deck to be at hand if the ship should be attacked in force.

The next morning broke clear and cloudless. A meager breakfast was prepared and eaten in shifts. Part of the small group of men aboard ate while the rest remained on watch at the guns. When all hands had breakfasted, Gamble beckoned to Feltus and Clapp to follow him.

The three men walked aft, Gamble limping painfully and dragging his wounded foot. When they reached the quarterdeck, Gamble leaned against the binnacle chest and spoke in a low voice.

"I must place heavy responsibilities on each of you," he said, pausing to look closely at the young, serious faces before him. "I don't want the men to know how desperate our situation is."

He paused again, then continued, "In fact, I regret very much that I have to admit it to the two of you."

The faint sound of chanting and the blowing of conch shells came to them across the water. Gamble looked toward the beach. Midshipman Feltus noticed that the officer's features were drawn, and a faint flush showed under the tan of his cheek. When Gamble spoke again, it was with great effort.

"I must tell you that I am very ill," he said, "and have little strength left." He turned to the older of the two midshipmen. "Mister Feltus, you are to take the most able-bodied of the few men we have and prepare the Sir Andrew Hammond so that we can put to sea with her at a moment's notice."

Midshipman Feltus nodded his understanding.

"Mister Clapp and I, with the remaining men, will somehow cover you with the guns of the Greenwich. You, Mister Clapp, must take over aboard the Greenwich if I should become too ill to carry on. Do you both understand?"

Midshipman Feltus raised his chapeau-a-bras in salute and replied, "Aye, aye, sir."

Clapp's boyish face was flushed with excitement as he, too, raised his hat. Consciously trying to imitate the quiet tones of the older midshipman, he answered, "Aye, aye, sir."

Despite his pain and fever, Gamble smiled faintly. He was proud of the two youngsters standing before him.

"Very well, gentlemen, you know what is expected of you. Mister Feltus, select your men and get them

aboard the Sir Andrew Hammond as soon as possible."

During the next few hours Gamble hardly knew
what was going on about him. His foot throbbed
with pain, and the chills and fevers of malaria shook
him. He was dimly aware of young Clapp's voice
directing the crew, and he noticed him working hard
to help the older men.

Late in the afternoon Midshipman Feltus returned from the Hammond. He brought with him
George Ross and William Brudewell. These two
were American traders who had been collecting
sandalwood and living on Nooaheeva awaiting the
return of their ship.

The Englishman Wilson had so stirred up the
natives against the Americans that the traders
feared for their lives. Leaving their valuable collection of sandalwood—the result of a whole year of
work—they sought refuge aboard one of the American ships.

Throughout the wakeful night that followed, the
hollow blare of war conches was heard from the
Valley of Tieihuey. The flames of giant bonfires

could be seen through the long glass. Everyone
sensed that serious trouble was coming.

Ross and Brudewell reported that Wilson had
joined the forces of the Typees and the Happahs.
Within a few hours they planned to attack the
ships.

At the first morning light, Gamble began the work
of transferring the few remaining supplies to the
Hammond. Only two boats remained to do the job.
One was the leaky boat in which Gamble, Feltus,
and Clapp had been set adrift from the Seringapatam. It needed constant bailing, and the work was
very slow.

"If only there were some way to speed the job,"
Gamble wished feverishly. "We must get away before the natives attack. With this handful of men,
we can never repel them."

Feltus came back with the second empty boat.
He boarded the Greenwich and drew Gamble aside.
It was obvious that he did not want others to hear.

In a low voice the midshipman said, "Lieutenant,
we are very short of powder and shot. With your
permission, I will take the whaleboat and make a

quick trip to the fort on shore. From there I can bring enough shot for several broadsides."

Gamble hesitated. He knew just how dangerous the mission was. On the point of refusing the midshipman's request, he stopped.

"Feltus is right, of course," he thought. "Without powder and shot we will be helpless against the hordes of natives."

"Very well," Gamble replied quietly, "select some of the best men. Don't remain on shore a moment longer than necessary."

Young Feltus smiled with pleasure that his request had been granted. He raised his chapeau-a-bras and said, "I shall not remain a moment longer than necessary, sir."

He hurried amidships and selected the men to accompany him. On his way into the boat alongside, he paused at the gangway and silently raised his hat in salute to Gamble. Then, with a quick wave of his hand to his brother midshipman, he disappeared over the side of the ship.

When the next boat was ready to leave the Greenwich, Gamble called young Clapp to his side.

"I will transfer to the Hammond with this boat-load," he said. "The next trip will be the last one. You, and the remaining men, will come aboard the Hammond on that boat."

The lad answered, "Aye, aye, sir. You can count on me to do the job properly."

When Gamble arrived aboard the Hammond, he forced himself to stay on his feet and direct the men in storing the transferred supplies. Dizzy and faint from the fever and the pain of his wound, he lost all track of time. He moved automatically, as if in a nightmare, barely conscious of the activity around him.

The boat returned from the Greenwich, with young Clapp aboard. Gamble was aware that the lad was telling him he would have to make another trip to the Greenwich. But in the noise and confusion, the lieutenant could not understand him. Suddenly, all efforts to try to understand were swept away by a great surge of fear and foreboding.

"Where is Feltus?" Gamble shouted. "The whale-boat should have been back long ago."

Without waiting for an answer, he grasped the

long glass. Steadying it on the taffrail, he focused on the beach. With relief he made out the tiny figures of Feltus and his men. They were launching the whaleboat through the long, rolling breakers of the surf.

Clapp was still standing beside Gamble, trying to make himself heard. Without removing his eye from the glass, Gamble broke in, "Inspect the priming of all broadside mounts. Train all broadside mounts that will bear on the beach and load with solid shot. We will cover the whaleboat until it is alongside." Clapp set off immediately to obey.

With part of his mind, Gamble noticed the sound of Clapp's retreating footsteps. But most of his attention was with the men trying to launch the whaleboat. The heavy weight of the shot it was carrying made the boat smash sluggishly through the combers instead of riding gracefully over them. A huge roller hit, nearly upending the boat.

Gamble sighed with relief as he saw the last of the tiny figures scramble aboard the whaleboat. The oars, looking like the many legs of an insect, took up the stroke.

Suddenly Gamble's heart pounded. Several warriors were running down the path that led to the
native village. Gamble could see them waving their
spears wildly. He drew in his breath sharply. The
beach within the field of his glass was suddenly
swarming with warriors racing toward the shoreline.
Through the windless air he could hear their wild
cries, softened by the distance.

Every muscle of Gamble's body strained in sympathy with the laboring oarsmen in the whaleboat.
The crew had quickened their stroke and were now
well beyond the crashing rollers of the surf.

In spite of the terrible efforts of the oarsmen, the
whaleboat barely moved through the resisting waters of the bay. Minutes dragged by like hours, and
still the position of the whaleboat scarcely changed.

Several natives had launched a light fishing outrigger through the surf. Gamble could see the glistening paddles rise in unison as they drove the
slender craft toward the laboring whaleboat.

The outrigger seemed to fly across the water. It
was now almost in line with the whaleboat. Gamble
tensed with fury. If he ordered a shot from one of

the broadside guns, it would almost certainly hit the whaleboat.

The distance between the two craft quickly grew smaller. Now only a few boat lengths separated them. Through the glass, Gamble saw Feltus rise suddenly to a standing position in the sternsheets. The lieutenant could barely see the shape of the musket which Feltus pointed at the outrigger. A puff of smoke rose as the primer fired the powder in the pan. Feltus bent down, raised a second musket, and fired again.

"Good lad!" Gamble shouted. Even in the excitement of the scene, he was proud that the young midshipman had remembered to bring muskets and to keep them primed and ready for firing. The outrigger sheered off. Two of its paddlers awkwardly sprawled backward in the boat, victims of Feltus' accurate aim.

Gamble was so intent on watching the battle scene before him that at first he did not hear young Clapp's cry of alarm. Only when the boy shook his shoulder did Gamble look around in astonishment. He shifted his gaze to the direction of the midshipman's outstretched arm.

There was no need for the long glass now. Gamble gasped as he saw two large war canoes clear the jut of land that had hidden them from sight. They flew across the calm waters of the bay toward the laboring whaleboat.

"Train all broadside guns that will bear on the war canoes!" Gamble shouted. "Elevate quoins one notch! Fire at will!"

Ignoring weakness and pain, Gamble heaved on the training tackle of the nearest broadside gun. The deck of the Hammond shuddered as gun after gun fired. The white haze and acrid smell of burnt gunpowder drifted along the deck in the still air.

"Reload all guns!" Gamble shouted at the top of his voice. He grasped the long glass again to see the effect of their broadside fire.

The gunpowder haze drifted maddeningly before the field of the long glass. At last Gamble could make out the tall geysers thrown up by the shot as they plunged into the sea. Then with sickening hopelessness he saw the dark shapes of the war canoes racing unharmed through the shower of

splashes. Could nothing stop them?

"Oh, my God!" The exclamation burst from the depths of Gamble's soul as he saw the leading war canoe range up alongside the whaleboat. As the warriors swarmed into the whaleboat, several puffs of smoke rose from discharged pistols.

Gamble saw the slender figure of Midshipman Feltus, pistol in one hand and sword in the other, standing in the sternsheets. There was a momentary flash of sunlight along the blade of his sword as it came down. Then the whaleboat was filled with a tangle of bodies as the second war canoe ranged alongside.

At that moment Gamble made the most difficult decision of his life. He knew that if the war canoes were not destroyed, they would attack the Sir Andrew Hammond. The natives could easily overcome his small crew. He also realized with a sinking heart that Feltus and his men were probably lost.

Gamble dropped the long glass and set to work feverishly with the nearest gun crew. They had just finished sponging and loading the gun and were now heaving it back into the battery.

Glancing over his shoulder, Gamble saw young Clapp staring at him in amazement. He knew what the boy was thinking.

"Get those guns to bear and fire into them. We must sink those canoes!"

Gamble glanced along the aiming notch of his gun and motioned to the men on the train tackle to move the breech slightly to the left. He raised his hand and held the glowing slow match to the powder vent. In an instant the gun roared and leaped backward in recoil.

Giving the order to reload the gun, Gamble focused the long glass on the whaleboat. What he saw was a scene of utter desolation.

The battered, barely recognizable pieces of one war canoe were drifting away from the whaleboat. He could make out heads bobbing in the water near it.

The other war canoe, minus several of its paddlers, was moving slowly toward several smaller canoes which had put off from the beach and were heading toward the Hammond. Only a few crumpled shapes could be seen in the whaleboat.

Deep anguish filled Gamble. Tears blurred his sight. "God have mercy on their souls," he prayed briefly, "they died as brave men."

Gamble's instincts and training as a Marine brought him back sharply to the terrible problems at hand. He glanced along the deck. Only a few of the sick and the older men could be seen. They were leaning against the guns or were stretched on the deck beside them, too tired to stand. Clapp and the few able-bodied men of the crew were nowhere in sight.

Gamble was sharply annoyed as he called Clapp and no one answered. One of the men pointed across the boarding nettings in the direction of the whale-boat.

Gamble leaped to the nearest gun carriage. He was astonished to see young Clapp in the sternsheets of the leaky boat. He was urging his three oarsmen toward the whaleboat.

As Gamble watched, the nearest canoes began to paddle along a course that would intercept the boat. Clapp, unaware of his danger, continued on his course.

"Give that after gun extreme right train. Put a shot between the boat and those canoes!" Gamble shouted. The gun roared in answer to his command.

"What is that young fool trying to do?" Gamble said. "They're all dead in the whaleboat. He's needlessly risking the lives of three men and his own, as well as our only remaining boat."

The man who had pointed out Clapp's boat to Gamble spoke. "I heard Mister Clapp sayin', sir, as he seen some men leap overboard from th' whaleboat. He made out their heads swimmin' toward us. I think he is pickin' 'em up now, sir."

Gamble jumped down from the gun mount and snatched up the long glass. He saw that the boat had put about and was heading toward the Hammond.

The shot from the broadside gun had discouraged the natives. They had turned about and were rejoining the large group of canoes that had drawn together for a council of war.

"Remove solid shot from the three after guns and reload with canister," Gamble called to the men on deck. "They will try to attack soon. I want to get as many as possible when they come within range."

Gamble was helping prepare the broadside guns for action when Clapp and his three-man crew brought their leaking boat alongside. With the help of some men on deck, they hoisted up two unmoving bodies.

Clapp glanced up as Gamble approached the group. There were marks where tears had run down his powder-streaked face. But his voice was steady, and there was a new note of dignity in it as he spoke.

"Worth and Caddington here are the only ones left, sir. Thomas Gibbs and the trader Brudewell were killed with Mister Feltus. Caddington is badly wounded, but Worth doesn't seem to be injured. He is dead tired from keeping Caddington afloat."

Gamble placed his hand on the young midshipman's shoulder. "That was a brave thing you did, lad. I shall see that you are remembered for it. Now, let some of the others take care of these two. I will need all your strength to help fight off the attack—which won't be long in coming."

Gamble had hardly finished speaking when the men at the guns called, "Here they come!"

"Hold your fire until I give the word," shouted Gamble. "After you fire, reload immediately with grape and canister."

A flotilla of war canoes, fishing outriggers, and smaller canoes was now heading directly for the Sir Andrew Hammond. Gamble could see the rhythmic flash of the paddles. In the larger war canoes, shouting warriors were shaking their spears and heavy clubs. The natives used these fierce gestures whenever they attacked to frighten their enemies. As the canoes drew near the ship, their converging courses drew them into a solid group.

"Stand by, fire!" shouted Gamble.

Once again the deck leaped with the shock of the guns' recoil. The drifting haze of gunsmoke settled on the crew. As they set about sponging, loading, ramming, and running out the guns for another broadside they looked like strange creatures from another world.

"Depress guns, full angle. Fire at will!"

A huge warrior, shaking a large club over his head, appeared at the ship's railing. He was instantly followed by another.

Gamble drew his mameluke sword and rushed toward them. He noticed that both warriors were struggling in the tangles of the boarding netting.

The second warrior grasped the netting, drew back his right arm, and aimed a spear at Gamble. The sharp report of a pistol sounded close to Gamble's left ear. He heard a hoarse cry as he drove his sword into the figure in front of him.

No more men appeared on the boarding netting. Gamble felt a concussion jar him as two of the nearest guns fired into the milling canoes at point-blank range.

Young Clapp was calmly reloading his pistol as Gamble moved away from the net. The midshipman looked up and smiled as Gamble approached him.

"Good shot, lad," said Gamble warmly. "Now back to your guns."

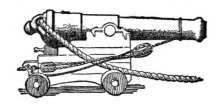

CHAPTER 12

Escape at Last

THE REMAINING CANOES gathered to prepare for another attack.

Gamble noticed that some of them separated from the group and headed rapidly toward the beach. At first he thought they were carrying the wounded, but they were travelling too fast for that. He swept the beach with the long glass and saw the reason for their haste.

Hundreds of natives were swarming over the hill on which the fort stood. The flimsy huts nearby which had served as the Americans' storehouses were being torn down. Already some of the islanders were streaming downhill, laden with booty from the huts. The warriors in the canoes, speeding toward the beach, were more interested in booty than in fighting.

Gamble could see several men, one of whom was Wilson, working at the guns in the fort. They were trying to remove the spikes so that the guns could be turned on the natives.

"Here they come again, sir!"

Gamble shifted the long glass towards the approaching canoes. There was no wild shouting or waving of war clubs now. The warriors who had not returned to shore came on silently and grimly to a fresh attack.

"Stand, men. Wait until I give the order to fire."

Soon the sound of the canoes and the stroke of their paddles could be heard.

"Fire at will!"

Two broadside guns crashed in response. Gamble could see the spatter of canister tear into the nearest large canoe.

When the powdersmoke cleared, only a few shattered remnants of the huge war canoe could be seen among the bobbing heads of the survivors. Two smaller canoes and an outrigger were badly damaged. Their crews had leaped overboard. Some swimmers were struggling toward shore.

Another gun of the Hammond's broadside roared. It was soon followed by still another.

The native craft withdrew and grouped for another council. Gamble noticed that the Hammond was gradually swinging to her anchor cable in response to the light airs that had sprung up as the heat of the setting sun lessened.

"Do not reload the starboard broadside," he called to the men working about the guns. "Remove the solid shot from all but two of the larboard broadside and reload with grape and canister."

While this was being done, Gamble noticed that the canoes had begun to separate. Suddenly they changed course and headed for the Greenwich. Fortunately, that ship had been much slower in responding to the shifting airs. She lay almost stern to the Hammond, thus closing the range between the two ships. Gamble noted with satisfaction that the Greenwich was well within canister range.

"Stand by to fire the shotted guns," Gamble called.

"Only two guns are ready, sir," Clapp replied, "and both are loaded with solid shot."

"Fire!"

In the light air, the powder smoke drifted away rapidly. Gamble saw the first solid shot plunge into the sea in the middle of the advancing canoes, causing no damage. The second shot, however, plunged into an outrigger. At one instant the craft had been moving rapidly across the water. At the next instant it had disappeared as completely as if it had never existed.

When the natives saw that they were well within range of the Hammond's guns, they turned and headed toward shore.

The men were reloading the guns when young Clapp appeared at Gamble's side.

"Lieutenant, I was trying to tell you before the action began that I must make another trip to the Greenwich."

Gamble looked at him questioningly.

"John Pittinger, who was confined to his bunk

because of illness, is still aboard. He is too weak to move, so we will have to carry him off. While we are aboard we can bring off the chronometer. It is the best we have left."

Gamble's heart sank. It was a dangerous mission. But there was no choice. They could not leave a sick man to be murdered in his bunk.

"Very well, Mister Clapp. Have the boat bailed and prepared for the trip. However, you must stay aboard the Hammond. You and I are the only ones aboard who know anything about navigation. If anything should happen to me, these men would be helpless at sea."

The young midshipman began to protest, but Gamble held up his hand. "I know you are willing, lad. You've more than proved today that you have a man's courage. My order is painful but necessary. Now, be off with you, and see if there are any men capable of pulling an oar."

"Aye, aye, sir," replied Clapp, lifting his hat in salute.

In a few minutes Clapp returned. "William Worth is recovered, sir. He and two others are ready to shove off for the Greenwich."

Gamble was amazed. The last time he had seen
Worth the seaman was unconscious. Gamble walked
to the gangway alongside which the boat was lying.
Worth looked up with a wide smile.

"Do you feel fit to make the trip?" Gamble called
down to him.

"Aye, aye, sir," replied Worth, knuckling his forehead. "Th' weakness has left me, an' I'm ready for
another tussle wi' th' heathen."

"Very well, then," replied Gamble. "Make all
speed to the Greenwich. Load Pittinger into the
boat. Then detail one man to put as much oakum
in the paint locker as it will hold. Here is a list of
the items I want you to bring off with you. When
everything is in the boat, set fire to the oakum in
the paint locker. Then return to the Hammond
as fast as you can. We will get underway immediately."

"Aye, aye, sir," answered Worth, with another
knuckling of the forehead. Turning to his two oarsmen, he gave orders to shove off.

The men remaining aboard the Hammond

watched anxiously as the small boat crept across the open space between the two ships. The natives were too busy ashore to notice, and no canoes put off in pursuit.

Throughout the day the looming peaks of the mountains had stood out sharply against the deep blue of the tropical sky. Now the westering sun softened their sharp outlines in its golden light. The slight land breeze began to blow down through the Valley of Tieihuey. It brought with it the fragrance of flowers and green tropical growth.

While the small boat lay alongside the Greenwich, Gamble and the men standing beside the broadside guns of the Hammond could hear the threatening sound of conch shells. More warriors were being called to the scene. The distant shouts and chanting meant that another attack was being prepared.

"They are pulling away from the Greenwich now, sir!"

"Good," said Gamble. "Now, Mister Clapp, we will man the capstan and heave 'round the anchor cable to short stay."

Only three men were strong enough to tackle the job. With all their strength they thrust their weight against the capstan bars. It was not enough. They could not heave in the heavy anchor cable.

"It's no use," Gamble panted, leaning against a capstan bar. "Even if we could hoist and cat the anchor, we don't have enough hands to fish it. Mister Clapp, get an axe and scramble down to the hawse pipe. When I give the word, cut the cable."

Clapp disappeared down the hatch leading to the cable tiers. Soon Gamble heard Worth's voice calling from alongside. With the aid of a single-whip block and tackle, which had been used in the Hammond's whaling days, the sick man was hoisted aboard. He was laid on deck.

"Worth, take two men and hoist the jib. When I give the word, tell Mister Clapp to cut the mooring cable." Gamble took his station at the ship's wheel. The remaining seamen made the painter of the boat fast.

Slowly, with short upward jerks, the jib was hoisted along its stay. Finally, its leech was stretched as tightly as Worth and two helpers could manage.

Gamble noted that the jib was fluttering loosely in the wind as it was hoisted.

"That's all right, Worth," he said. "Sheet home the jib and tell Mister Clapp to cut the cable."

The jib ceased to flutter as it was drawn against its sheet. Worth, who had leaned against the cat-head timber to observe the hawse pipe, straightened up and waved.

"The cable has been cut, sir."

"Very well," Gamble called, "Now all of you aft set the spanker, then hoist in the boat."

Although the breeze was light, it was enough to bring the Hammond's head around. Gamble could hear the faint, welcome sound of water rippling past and splashing against the small boat towing alongside. The breeze was blowing from the star-board quarter, and Gamble was able to steady the ship's head for open sea.

Gamble glanced astern and saw a bright flare of flames leaping upward through the Greenwich's tarred rigging. As he watched, the flames raced along the ship's wooden decks and beams, well seasoned with whale oil. Soon the entire ship was a raging mass of yellow and red leaping flames.

Although the open sea to the east was still light with the setting sun, the mountains had thrown their shadows across the inner bay. The great light of the burning ship scattered these shadows and lighted the near slopes of the mountains.

Shouts of alarm drew Gamble's attention to the larboard quarter of the Hammond. There Clapp and four helpers had set the spanker and begun to hoist the boat. Clapp turned toward Gamble, cupped his hands to his mouth, and called, "The boat just broke in two. She was half full of water. The weight of it must have broken her back."

Gamble started to call out in anger. Then he realized that it was unfair to blame the men because the rotten hull of the boat had given way. When he replied, the tone of his voice was even. "Very well. Hoist the two pieces aboard if you can. We may be able to repair the boat later."

Now that the crisis was over, Gamble noticed his weakness and fever. For the first time since the action began, he was aware of the painful throbbing of his injured heel. He knew that he could not stay on his feet much longer. Yet he was thinking, through his pain and exhaustion, "Get more sail on her. Get her clear of the reefs."

Gamble was aware that young Clapp had acknowledged the orders to make more sail. He could hear the men calling to one another as they tried to do the work that usually took the strength of four times their number.

The lieutenant lost all sense of time. He was aware only of the struggle to keep his eyes focused on the compass card. He concentrated all his strength on holding the lubber's line on the east-southeasterly course that would carry the ship clear of the surrounding reefs.

He was dimly aware that Clapp had brought him some quinine pills and water to wash them down. Finally he understood that Clapp was saying, "We're clear of the reefs now, lieutenant. We're on the open sea."

Gamble nodded and managed to mumble, "Hold her steady-as-you-go."

He dragged himself to his cabin and threw himself, fully clothed, across the bunk.

CHAPTER 13

The Sea

GAMBLE SLOWLY opened his eyes. He realized that he was lying in the bunk of the captain's cabin of the Sir Andrew Hammond. He listened for a moment to the slight creak of the running rigging and felt with pleasure the slow lift of the ship in response to the sea.

Turning his head, he saw the slight figure of Acting Midshipman Clapp. He was bent over the table, studying a spotted and rumpled chart.

A warm feeling of affection and respect filled Gamble as he watched the boy's serious face. He had certainly proved himself a man yesterday. The boy had taken over as second-in-command as though he had held the post all his brief life.

Gamble knew that he would have to depend more and more on Clapp, since Feltus was gone. With a pang, Gamble put the thought of Feltus' death from his mind. He noticed that young Clapp looked puzzled.

"What's the matter, Benjamin?"

Clapp looked up, startled. "Lieutenant Gamble! I'm glad you're awake again."

Before the young midshipman could continue, Gamble asked, "How is Caddington? And the sick men?"

"Caddington is a tough Marine, sir. In spite of his wound he ate a full breakfast this morning. So did the sick men. How do you feel, sir?"

"Very weak and a little damp," Gamble answered. "Perhaps a pot of tea is called for."

"Yes, sir. I'll have Worth get it for you. He has taken over as cook."

"And could you send someone to help me out of these damp clothes and bring some water for me to bathe in?"

Gamble bathed in a tub of sea water. He changed to dry, clean garments. He slowly climbed the companion ladder to the deck. A comfortable couch was made for him of coils of line and spare canvas. The sun, fresh sea air, and hot tea revived him.

Gamble noted that the ship was close hauled on the starboard tack. "What course are you holding, Mister Clapp?" he asked.

"The best we can do is northeast by east, sir. After you fell asleep last night, we were able to loose and sheet home the fore and main topsails. Getting more sail was beyond our strength. We also had to cut away the only remaining anchor, as we were unable to cat and fish it."

"That was wise," Gamble said. "The anchor would have caused serious damage in heavy weather if it couldn't be secured for sea."

"There is more bad news, lieutenant. We have only six solid shot for the broadside guns left."

"That *is* bad news. But we can do nothing about that now. My greatest worry at the moment is that we cannot lay a southeasterly course. I had hoped to sail to Valparaiso, Chile, and rejoin the Essex."

Clapp said, "I understand that the trade winds blow almost constantly from the southeastward. If that's the case, I don't see how we can work the ship to windward with the few men we have left to heave on a line."

Gamble nodded agreement, and studied the frayed chart before him. It was an old, well used general chart of the South Pacific. After a few minutes, Gamble folded the chart and lay back against the canvas cushion. He closed his eyes and considered the possible courses of action. Clapp and the others went quietly about their work.

Gamble drifted off into a fitful sleep. When he awoke, he called to the helmsman, "Lash the wheel, and bring Mister Clapp to the quarterdeck."

Gamble smiled, thinking again how much he had to depend on this boy for the safety of them all. Clapp appeared, and Gamble motioned him to sit on the deck beside him.

"Mister Clapp, the only thing we can do is to put her head before the wind and run the trade winds down until we reach the Sandwich Islands. They are actually nearer than Valparaiso. Owhahoo, in the Sandwich Islands, is the main rendezvous of ships in the Canton trade."

The Sandwich Islands was the name given to the Hawaiian Islands by Captain Cook.

The young midshipman looked puzzled. "But, sir, won't we have trouble with the natives there?"

"No. I've heard that Kamehameha, king of the Sandwich Islands, is friendly to all trading vessels. His capital, Kailua, is near Honolulu, a busy port. We may be able to ship a crew from those who served their time in the Canton ships. If we can obtain a crew and additional supplies, we can sail this ship back to the United States."

"That would be wonderful, sir," the midshipman said eagerly. "To sail a prize ship right into New York harbor!"

Gamble smiled. "We haven't even reached the Sandwich Islands; much less rounded Cape Horn and avoided scores of British men-o'-war blockading our east coast."

Clapp nodded ruefully.

Gamble continued, "Let's see. We can muster only eight men. One is a cripple confined to his bunk.

One is dangerously wounded. One is sick and one is a feeble old man recovering from scurvy. Then there is myself, unable to lend much assistance. That leaves you, Worth, and Ross the only three able-bodied men."

"Yes, sir. I figured it that way too. So last night I assigned myself and each of the able-bodied men to a watch. I thought that if an emergency occurred we could call the others. Perhaps in bad trouble, some of the sick could lend a hand."

Gamble said, "We'll continue with that arrangement. I believe that is Roberts Island on our larboard quarter. Lay off a course for Owhyhee in the Sandwich Islands. Then ease your lee braces and put her head before the wind, Mister Sailing Master."

The young midshipman smiled with pleasure at the hinted promotion. He stood up.

"Aye, aye, sir," he replied smartly, doffing his hat in the best man-o'-warsman manner.

As Clapp turned to go, Gamble called to him, "What is the date?"

"The tenth of May, sir," was the reply. "And I

hope we'll be back in the States before the snow flies."

Gamble leaned back against the piled canvas. He immediately fell asleep again.

When he awoke, the sky to the west was filled with the glory of a perfect tropical sunset. It was a sight that Gamble would remember the rest of his life. The sun was a huge, golden red ball. It was beginning to flatten as it entered the haze above the horizon.

Great cumulus clouds scattered across the sky were turned fiery red by the sunlight. The ship's sails looked as if they were made of copper as they strained against their sheets, filled with the southeasterly trade winds.

Gamble was content, almost perfectly happy, as he felt the easy lift of the sea under the ship. He watched the sun continue to flatten against the horizon until the last glowing bit of its disk disappeared. The deep colors of the afterglow still shone in the sky and stained the sea.

Gamble remembered the phrase "wine-dark sea" which the ancient Greek writer Homer used to describe the Aegean. This, too, was truly a wine-dark sea.

Young Clapp broke in on his thoughts.

"I'm glad that you're awake, sir."

"I must have slept several hours," Gamble said smiling up at the young face above him. "It looks as though you have everything under control."

"Yes, sir," said Clapp, responding to Gamble's smile. "Some of our sick men even felt strong enough to do some light work about deck."

"I have noticed, Benjamin, that when a ship puts to sea, the crew still has land weariness in their bones for a while. Then a fresh strength seems to come, as though they had been fed by the sea itself."

Clapp nodded at this bit of sea wisdom.

"Speaking of being fed, sir, here is some tea that Worth prepared for you."

Gamble lifted the steaming cup and sniffed its fragrance. Mingled with the scent of the tea was the smell of something stronger. Gamble smiled as he recognized the aroma. Worth had strongly laced the tea with rum, the sailor's remedy for all ills.

The tea and rum were refreshing. When Midshipman Clapp suggested that he be carried below, Gamble shook his head. "No. It's very pleasant here. Would you please ask Worth to bring me whatever food he has prepared. I'll eat here and watch the night come on."

When Clapp returned, Gamble motioned him to sit down.

"Benjamin, I'm very happy with the way you have taken hold."

A pleased smile crossed the boy's face, but he said nothing.

"I know now that you are a capable man. But we can't expect that the sea will always be as calm and pleasant as it is tonight. Do not hesitate to waken me at any hour of the day or night if you are uncertain of what to do."

Clapp nodded his understanding.

"I also want you always to remember never to take chances with the sea. Always be prepared for the worst that can happen. It often does. Don't try to carry more sail than you and your two healthy men can handle."

"I know what you mean, lieutenant," Clapp replied in a newly mature voice. "A few weeks ago I would have thought it a lark to be able to make and take in sail as I saw fit. But when you are responsible for the entire ship, it makes you stop and think ahead before you act."

"That's one of the first qualities an officer must acquire, Benjamin," said Gamble quietly. "The Naval Service calls it 'forehandedness.' "

Worth appeared on deck, carrying two steaming bowls. "Here's some chowder, lieutenant. I made it from some fresh fish as was caught today. It's tasty, if I do say so."

The chowder was indeed good. After they ate, the Marine officer and the young midshipman sat silent. They watched the slow lift and roll of the ship as the sails, spars, and rigging blotted out, then revealed, the brilliant stars scattered in the sky.

CHAPTER 14

Owhyhee

"LAND HO!" the masthead lookout's hail rang out. It was May 25, 1814, and the distant shape of the island of Owhyhee, of the Sandwich Group, had been sighted on the starboard bow.

Gamble experienced a deep feeling of relief and thankfulness. The only prayer of thanks he could remember to offer was the grace which he had heard at the table as a boy. "We thank Thee, dear Lord, for this Thy gift, which we are about to receive."

The men dashed to climb the rigging for a glimpse of land. The island peaks that could be clearly seen from the masthead would not be visible from the deck for some time.

Gamble leaned against the taffrail, watching the hazy blue shape of the island appear on the horizon.

"How very lucky we have been," he thought.

They had met no heavy blow. The trade winds had been steady. After the first week, Gamble's fever burned itself out. Even Caddington recovered quickly from his wounds.

Gamble turned his mind to the problems that would face him when the ship reached Owhahoo.

The first problem would be to anchor the ship. Both ship's anchors had been cut away in the desperate escape from Nooaheeva. Then he would have to ship a crew to man the ship. Finally, he would have to get enough fresh water and provisions for the long voyage to rendezvous with the Essex or to round the Horn and sail to the United States.

As if in answer to his thoughts, Midshipman Clapp approached quickly, calling as he came, "Sir, we found a spare anchor! It was hidden under a pile of staves."

"Excellent. We should have thought to look there

sooner. The staves are left from the Sir Andrew
Hammond's whaling days. The anchor must have
been buried a long time indeed."

Whaling ships often sent part of their catch home
in another ship or stored whale oil in warehouses
ashore. Barrels were needed for this transfer, but
because barrels took up so much precious ship room
they were built on board as needed from staves
which did not occupy so much space. The staves
were likely to be stacked wherever there was an
empty spot—on top of anchors or ropes or anything
not in use at the time.

Some of the seamen were able to rig a block and
tackle. All hands heaved together, and the bower
anchor was slowly hoisted on deck. The mooring
cable was led outboard of the shrouds and spliced to
the ring of the anchor.

There was plenty of time for these preparations
for anchoring off Owhahoo. The ship was reaching
the northern limits of the trade winds, and each day
the wind became more light and variable.

The island of Owhahoo was sighted on May 28.
Late the next evening the Hammond steadily neared

the island. Gamble ordered the main- and mizzen-topsails clewed to their yards. This shortening of the canvas slowed the ship. With so few able-bodied men in his crew, Gamble did not want to reach the anchorage in darkness.

All through the quiet night the men stayed on deck. Some of them napped on folded canvas. Lights on shore shone clearly. By the bright light of the half-moon several ships could be seen lying at anchor.

At dawn, the Hammond approached the anchorage in Whytetee Bay, as Waikiki was then called. Most of the southern shore of the island was exposed to the open sea.

Anchoring in Whytetee Bay was easier than Gamble had dared hoped. The helm was put down and the ship rounded slowly into the wind. As the headsails ceased to draw, they were let go "on the run."

The men dashed from the pinrail where the jib halliards were secured. They eased the lee sheets and braces, then tailed out on the weather brace of the fore-topsail yard. The yard backed easily into the wind, slowing the ship's headway.

When the Hammond was almost dead in the water, Gamble signalled to Clapp. The midshipman let go the bower anchor. The fore-topsail was clewed to its yard and the headsails were placed in a loose furl.

At last Gamble had a chance to look away from the ship work and notice the scene around him. He was amazed to see a huge native boarding the ship from a canoe, and coming toward him. The man was not wearing the usual native tapa cloth. Instead, he was dressed in figured cotton. He was carrying a wreath of fragrant flowers. Gamble was surprised to hear him say in English, "Dis lei for you, cap'n," as he placed the wreath around the lieutenant's neck.

"Thank you. You are very kind," Gamble said. "How different this is," he thought, "from the treatment we had from the last natives we met."

The big native explained that he was Kalanimoku, a subchief in the court of King Kamehameha. In the name of the king, he welcomed Gamble and his ship to Owhahoo.

Gamble noticed that, as he spoke, the native was curiously looking over the ship and her sadly re-

duced crew. Gamble did not, however, explain their misadventures in Nooaheeva.

The native asked what supplies were needed.

"We must have fresh fruit and water now. Later, I will come ashore with a list of our other needs."

Kalanimoku called down to his canoe lying alongside. In a few minutes several woven mats filled with fruits and vegetables were hoisted aboard.

The big fellow smiled broadly as he said, "Dese are gifts from King Kamehameha to you, cap'n."

In return, Gamble gave Kalanimoku a small whale's tooth. The native took the gift with a delighted grin. Here a whale's tooth was valued very highly. In fact, it could be worn only as a badge of high rank.

"I bring you mo' gift, cap'n," Kalanimoku declared, beaming, as he left.

"We need a boat. All of ours have been lost. I will pay for it," Gamble said.

Kalanimoku nodded and called down to the men in his canoe in the native language. He turned to Gamble.

"You have big storm o' big fight, cap'n?"

Gamble smiled. Without really answering the question, he said, "Yes."

Soon after the native canoe paddled away, Captain Winship came aboard the Hammond. He was the master of one of the American ships in port.

The shipmaster could not hide his surprise at his welcoming committee. It was very strange that a lieutenant of the United States Marines should be in command of a ship. It was stranger still that his second-in-command was a midshipman. Hardest of all to understand, the ship was a whaler bearing the signs of a long, hard voyage, and she had a very small crew.

Gamble took Captain Winship to the Hammond's cabin. He soon felt that he could trust the bluff, plain-spoken New England shipmaster. He told him the entire story of their misfortunes, holding back nothing.

When Gamble had finished his tale, Captain Winship sat quietly for a few minutes, puffing on his pipe. He took his pipe from his mouth and spoke.

"Most of the shipmasters in port are Americans or of neutral nations. I am sure they will join me in doing everything we can to help you."

Gamble had thought of his needs so often that he needed no list to remember them.

"I need anchors and another twenty men if I can get them. And provisions, fresh water, and powder and shot for the guns."

Captain Winship nodded. "I don't think you will have any trouble getting a crew. There are several men here who have served their time in the Canton trade and want to get back to the United States. I expect they will sign with you."

"The sooner I can get them, the better, captain. There is so much work to be done."

"I'm sure that is true. Now, as for supplies. We will give you what we can. But since you are a United States officer, I am sure King Kamehameha can help you even more. He will take your note for payment by the United States government for all the supplies he furnishes you."

"But does a native king have the supplies of a ship chandler?" Gamble asked with surprise.

"King Kamehameha has built up a big business, furnishing supplies to the ships in the Canton trade," Winship said, with respect in his voice. "I am sure he can fit you out with everything you need from the stores he has on hand."

"But I have seen no warehouses. There seem to be only native huts ashore."

"Oh, this is Kailua, where the king and his court live. The warehouses are in Honolulu. I'll take you there tomorrow."

Captain Winship rose and thanked Gamble for serving him tea. He kindly added, "I expect you have had that tea a long time, lieutenant. I'll send you a canister of fine tea from a Canton ship."

Gamble thanked him, and the two men climbed the companionway to the deck.

The next morning Captain Winship came in his boat to take Gamble to Honolulu. Just as he was going over the side, Gamble saw Midshipman Clapp looking wistfully at the distant beach. Gamble called, "All right, young man. Into the boat with you."

The midshipman's face lighted up with surprise and pleasure. "Yes, sir!" he shouted happily.

Clapp barely paused to salute the quarterdeck before he scrambled over the bulwark into the boat.

Gamble's first thought on seeing Honolulu was how very different it was from Nooaheeva. In the thirty-six years since Captain James Cook had landed there, a busy settlement had grown.

The main industry was outfitting ships and storing cargoes. Some of the cargoes were the tea, silks, and spices of the ships in the Canton trade. Sandalwood, too, was stored in the warehouses for later shipment. It was gathered from the South Sea Islands and traded in China where it was highly prized.

Many whaling ships also put in for fresh water and provisions. They stored whale oil in Honolulu for transfer to ships sailing for the United States and European ports.

The most recent trade was from ships carrying furs. They came from Russia, Alaska, and the Oregon Territories. Most of them were owned by an American, John Jacob Astor.

As the men walked along the busy waterfront, Gamble noticed the strange construction of the tall native huts. They were made of thatched palm fronds. Each one had a round hole near the peak of the roof, and each had a very low rectangular door.

The natives hardly noticed the three white men. In Nooaheeva, conches would have been blown to announce their coming. Scores of men, women, and children would have crowded around to look at the strangers. In Honolulu, however, the sight of a white man was no longer unusual.

"Except for the appearance and dress of the natives," Gamble thought, "we might as well be in any large seaport."

Gamble spent the day talking with American and English merchants. He was amused to note that even though England was at war with the United States, English traders were eager to sell him supplies.

CHAPTER 15

Aloha, Aloha!

IT WAS DARK when Gamble returned to the ship. He was tired after a full day in the streets of Honolulu. But there was something he could put off no longer. It had been on his mind since he left Nooaheeva. First his illness, then his duties aboard ship, had kept him from it.

Gamble turned up the wick of the lanthorn set in gimbals above his desk. He took off his uniform coat and sat down to the painful duty of writing to Midshipman Feltus' parents.

For a time he wrote fast, his quill hardly pausing except to be dipped into the inkwell. He kept the letter as formal as a report. He reviewed their service aboard the frigate. He told of their dreadful experiences on the island. Finally, he wrote of the attack by the war canoe.

Gamble held the quill poised above the paper. "How do I end this letter?" he thought. "How can I comfort those parents for such a loss?"

The chronometer ticked steadily in the quiet cabin. The distant booming of the surf came through the open stern ports. Gamble continued to search his mind for the right words.

With a sigh, he dipped his quill in the ink, and wrote:

> No words of mine, I know, can lessen your grief. But perhaps they may, in some degree, make bearable his loss. He, and the others in the boat with him, gave their lives in the line of duty. I loved and esteemed him not only as a brother officer, but truly as though he were my younger brother.
>
> In that brotherhood, of which we are all a part under the Eternal Father, may I have the honor to subscribe myself,
>
> Your grieving son,
> JOHN M. GAMBLE

The bitter task finished, Gamble fell into his bunk and was soon asleep.

During the next few days, several seamen who had served out their time in the Canton ships signed articles to ship aboard the Sir Andrew Hammond for the homeward voyage to the United States. With these added hands, the work of readying the ship for sea went forward rapidly.

Kalanimoku was cheering as well as helpful. One morning he climbed over the Hammond's bulwarks with his usual ease, despite his great bulk.

"Where Cap'n?"

Clapp pointed to the companionway leading to the captain's cabin.

Kalanimoku's huge frame completely filled the cabin as he came in.

"Cap'n, I t'ink I get you all salt horse you need!"

Gamble looked up from his desk with a smile. He liked the big fellow, and the news he brought was very welcome. Salt horse, the salted beef stored in barrels of brine, was the sailors' main diet on a voyage. Fresh provisions spoiled too quickly, and the men had to depend on dry or salted food.

"That's fine, Kalanimoku. When can the salt horse be brought on board?"

"Not here in Honolulu. You get from king of Windward Islands. He live on island of Owhyhee."

"That fits in with my plans. I must leave from here on a southerly course which will bring me close to Owhyhee."

"And, Cap'n. One t'ing mo'," Kalanimoku said, a wide smile spreading over his handsome face.

"Yes?"

"Kona wind blow now from mountains. Sea very bad for canoes. You take people and canoe to Owhyhee. They get you salt horse."

"I will be glad to take them; but why do they want to go to Owhyhee now?"

"To bring gifts to king of Windward Islands. Only Kamehameha, de great king, mo' powerful dan king of Windward Islands."

"The ship is almost ready for sea. I want to sail as soon as possible."

"One, two day, then they come. First, all have big luau. Eat, sing, dance. You come."

In the bad times that soon followed, Gamble sometimes recalled the big luau, a dinner of delicious native foods.

On the day of the luau, Gamble and Clapp came ashore in midafternoon. They were met by Kalanimoku who said, "Great King Kamehameha say receive you today. Bid you aloha."

"We are honored to be received by his majesty, the great king," Gamble replied. "Please take us to him."

Gamble and Clapp were joined by Captain Winship. The three followed Kalanimoku between rows of huts. Gamble noticed that as they approached the men remained where they were, but the women moved away.

"It is the taboo," Winship answered his unspoken question. "Kalanimoku is a subchief. If a woman were to touch him, or even if her shadow fell on him, it would mean death for her."

The men arrived at a large hut. In front were several tall carvings of manlike creatures resting upon carved palm trunks. A boy ran forward and handed Kalanimoku a cape made of bright feathers and a helmetlike headpiece. The subchief placed the helmet on his head. Then he crouched low to enter the doorway, which was only three feet high. The others bent down and followed him.

The hut was so dark after the blazing sunlight outside that at first the men could see nothing. A small hole near the peak of the hut let in only a dim light. As their eyes became used to the halfdark, the men made out the huge shape of the king.

He was seated on a mat, surrounded by women. Warrior guards were standing behind him. They held the shafts of long spears in their hands.

Kamehameha and the nobles of his court were much larger than the other natives. Some of the women were so huge that they had to be helped to their feet from a sitting position.

Kalanimoku spoke to the great king in the native language. Kamehameha turned to Gamble, and spoke with quiet dignity.

"Kalanimoku tells me you return to your country. I send greetings to your great king."

Gamble bowed and thanked the king for receiving them. He promised to give Kamehameha's greetings to President Madison.

"I hope," he said, "that the American people and the people of Owhyhee will always keep their friendship and good will."

Gamble bowed to the great king again. Kamehameha said, "Aloha, captain, and a pleasant voyage to your country."

They went out of the royal hut into the bright sunlight. Kalanimoku led them along the beautiful beach called Whytetee to a grove of palm trees. More than a hundred natives were gathered there for the feast.

Men and women carried food wrapped in large leaves from an oven of hot rocks buried in the sand. A long strip of palm fronds on the ground was the banquet table.

The sky turned to brilliant red in the sunset. Kalanimoku motioned Gamble, Captain Winship, and Clapp to positions of honor. He seated himself near them, crosslegged. Kalanimoku tore off a piece of roast pig. He dipped a finger into a dough called poi served in a coconut husk, and said, "Now we have luau!"

A dozen young warriors leaped forward and

formed two rows, facing one another. Drummers began to beat on hollow gourds. Conch shell blowers blew in rhythm with the gourds. Singers began to chant in time with the music. The warriors began to dance in graceful movements that imitated fighting.

The food was delicious. The dancing was fascinating to watch. The sunset faded and the soft dusk of evening was lighted by fires on the beach. Still the luau went on.

A group of young wahines, or women, moved to the center of the beach and began a graceful dance called the hula. There was no violent action in this dance. Instead, each dancer stayed in the same spot. Every movement, especially of the arms and hands, told a story from Polynesian legends.

The scene would always remain in Gamble's memory. He would never forget the lovely firelit movements of the dancers. A soft, fragrant wind blew down from the mountains. He felt perfectly contented. Above, a full moon raced through white clouds, flooding the picture with bright light.

CHAPTER 16

His Majesty's Ship Cherub

THE SAILING of the Sir Andrew Hammond from Honolulu was far different from her arrival. As the ship gathered headway from her anchorage, scores of natives moved about her deck.

A large canoe had been hoisted aboard. It held food, handiwork, and even several squealing pigs— all tribute for the king of the Windward Islands.

Passengers on deck were calling alohas to friends paddling in canoes or swimming in the crowded water alongside the ship. The air was filled with the squeals of the pigs, the beat of hollow gourds, and the calls blown on conch shells. Even with his speaking trumpet Gamble had trouble passing his commands to the helmsman and the sail handlers.

With the help of many natives, the anchor was catted and fished and secured for sea.

The canoes and swimmers were slowly left behind as sail after sail was set. The shores of Whytetee Bay glided past, and the noise dwindled away.

The natives made themselves comfortable on the decks. As the ship moved out of the lee of the mountains, the kona wind filled the sails and the ship began to respond to the motion of the sea.

Gamble turned to the young midshipman.

"Well, Benjamin, we're homeward bound!"

"Yes, sir, but I won't really feel it until we are in the Atlantic."

"True. We have a long, hard journey still before us," Gamble replied. He checked the compass in its binnacle and observed the trim of the sails.

"This course should carry us clear of the islands of Lanai and Kahoolavi," he said. "If the wind holds, we should make the island of Owhyhee."

"Yes, sir, we should do it without making a single tack."

Gamble nodded. "Let's hope you are a good prophet. Keep her head southeast, one quarter east. She seems to be riding easily, and the wind should hold for some time. Call me if you need me. I am going below for a cup of tea."

In the cabin, Gamble enjoyed his China tea and felt satisfied that all was well. The long, dangerous voyage to the Sandwich Islands was over. The ship was stocked with new stores and equipment. He had a full crew of prime seamen for the homeward voyage. Soon he would have the salted provisions they needed.

"All that remains," he thought, "is to deliver the natives and their canoe, load the provisions, then . . . homeward bound." He smiled.

"I'll put into Valparaiso," he reasoned. "If Captain Porter isn't there, he will have left instructions for me with the United States consul."

Gamble remembered that the Essex had earlier been warmly received in Valparaiso.

"I can expect a friendly welcome from the Chileans," Gamble thought.

The lieutenant's taste of peace did not last long.

Shortly after four bells in the forenoon watch of the next day he heard the cry "Sail ho!"

He rushed to the weather deck, where Clapp was waiting. He handed Gamble the long glass and pointed toward the island of Lanai, broad on the larboard bow.

"There she is, sir. She just cleared the headland of the island."

Gamble raised the long glass. In its circular field Gamble knew in a flash that she was a British sloop-of-war. His heart sank. He looked around at his own decks, cluttered with natives and their canoe. He glanced at his guns, so far fewer than those on the British sloop.

Feelings of anger and helplessness filled Gamble. There was no chance to fight or run. Such an unequal contest could have but one outcome. To risk the lives of his native passengers and his own crew for one moment of resistance was unthinkable. He had to assume the responsibility of command, no matter how bitter it might be.

Under her press of sail and a quartering wind, the sloop-of-war bore down rapidly. The red jackets of her marines could be clearly seen, shining among the crewmen.

Within three cable lengths of the Hammond, she bore up smartly. Her windward sheets were let go on the run and her courses clewed up to their yards.

A single gun fired, raising a splash ahead of the Hammond. The white ensign with the cross of St. George broke from the sloop's gaff and streamed out in the fresh breeze.

Gamble gave the order to put the Hammond's head into the wind and to back yards on the mainmast.

A quarter boat was lowered from the sloop and pulled toward the Hammond. As Gamble watched the boat approach, he was aware of young Clapp standing quietly beside him. The boy had not said a word. He had carried out quickly and well the orders Gamble had given him.

"I'm sorry it had to turn out this way, Benjamin," Gamble said, remembering the lad's boyish excitement at the thought of sailing a prize ship into the port of New York.

"Even so," the midshipman answered, without

taking his eyes from the approaching boat, "we are more fortunate than Mister Feltus."

Gamble was surprised at the dignity and maturity of the remark. He made no answer, but gently placed his hand on the boy's shoulder.

"Ship, ahoy!" The clear hail came from the figure of a midshipman standing in the sternsheets of the quarter boat.

Gamble picked up the speaking trumpet and answered, "Sir Andrew Hammond, prize ship to the United States frigate Essex."

Turning to the midshipman he said, "Mister Clapp, prepare to receive the boarding officer of the British sloop."

The head and shoulders of a midshipman, not much older than Clapp, appeared at the starboard bulwarks. A moment later he was on deck.

The British midshipman stood there, legs spread apart and arms crossed on his chest. He gazed coolly about. Two seamen, with pistols in their belts and unsheathed cutlasses in their hands, joined him.

"Who is in charge here?" It was clear from the boy's tone that he was proud of his role.

The natives crowded about the boarding party, talking and laughing among themselves. The British midshipman ignored the small group of men standing near the helmsman. He seemed to expect someone to come forward and identify himself.

"I said, who is in charge here?" The young voice was sharp.

Gamble felt Midshipman Clapp, standing beside him, jerk forward in anger. "Steady, now," he said.

One of the British seamen moved close to the young boarding officer and said something to him in a low voice. The youngster looked at last toward Gamble and Clapp. Without moving from where he stood, he called, "Are you in charge here?"

Gamble fought down the surge of anger he felt and forced himself to speak evenly. "Young man, you are impertinent."

No sooner had Gamble spoken than he heard Clapp say angrily, "You're only a midshipman. When you speak to a commissioned officer say 'Sir'!"

The British midshipman's face flushed. He pointed his finger at Clapp and said, "Seize that man."

Gamble's mameluke sword flashed in the sunlight. The two seamen who had started toward Clapp stopped dead in their tracks.

"If you so much as touch him," said Gamble, a quiet fury in his voice, "there will be bloodshed."

The British seamen looked at their midshipman.

The natives were crowding into the rigging to get a better view of this contest between the white men.

After a short pause, the British midshipman spoke. "You will surrender your sword to me . . . sir."

"I am a first lieutenant, United States Marines!" Gamble said firmly. "I will surrender my sword to no midshipman. Now I suggest, young man, that you have my gear put into your boat. Load Midshipman Clapp's gear also, as he will accompany me."

Worth stepped forward and grasped a handle of Gamble's sea chest, motioning to one of the Hammond's seamen to take the other handle. One of the British seamen picked up a small bag and moved toward the bulwarks. Gamble sheathed his sword.

The British midshipman said nothing. When Gamble followed Clapp over the bulwark, the midshipman did raise his chapeau-a-bras. Gamble raised his only slightly in return.

Before he got into the sloop-of-war's boat, Gamble unbuckled his sword belt. He held it, with his sword, in his hand as he descended.

The British midshipman appeared at the bulwark and told the coxswain of the boat to proceed to Cherub, which was the sloop-of-war's name. He told him to inform Captain Tucker that he would need more men for a prize crew.

"Ask him, too, what should be done with this large canoe filled with provisions," he added.

Shortly before the quarter boat arrived alongside the sloop, Gamble removed the boat cloak which he had worn to protect his uniform from the salt spray. They came alongside, and Gamble mounted the Jacob's ladder and passed through the gangway.

The lieutenant faced aft smartly and lifted his chapeau-a-bras in salute to the quarterdeck, then again to the officer-of-the-watch. The officer-of-the-watch returned the salute and said, "Please follow me."

Gamble followed the officer-of-the-watch. He made a great effort not to limp with the pain of the wound in his heel.

Standing on the weather side of the quarterdeck was an officer in the uniform of a Captain, Royal Navy. Gamble supposed he was the Captain Tucker whom the British midshipman had mentioned.

Gamble came to a halt before the captain. He raised his chapeau-a-bras smartly.

"Sir, I am First Lieutenant Gamble, United States Marines, late of the United States frigate Essex, and until recently prize master of the Sir Andrew Hammond, the ship under your lee."

"Well, sir, you have led us a devil of a chase," said the British captain, making no effort to return Gamble's salute.

Gamble continued to look steadily at the British officer's face. He said nothing.

"The Essex has been captured, you know," Captain Tucker continued. "I must say she put up a good fight. I have this to show for it."

He held up his left arm. Gamble noticed for the first time that it was bandaged.

"When did this happen, sir?" Gamble asked quietly.

"On the twenty-eighth of March, last. The frigate HMS Phoebe, Captain Hillyar, and my ship had been blockading the Essex in Valparaiso harbor. During a period of strong winds, the Essex tried to put to sea. Her main-topmast carried away off the Point of Angels. She put about, and we engaged her in the harbor."

"She was in action against two British men-o'-war, then, sir?"

"Quite."

"Is Captain Porter . . . ?" Gamble hesitated, seeking the right word.

"Captain Porter, Lieutenant McKnight, and some midshipmen were the only officers not killed or wounded," Captain Tucker replied. "Of her ship's company of some two hundred and fifty-five, only seventy-five were unwounded. Some fifty-eight were killed, and others died later of their wounds."

Gamble felt the words like a blow. "And the Essex Junior, sir?" he managed to ask. "What became of her?"

"She was captured, too. Captain Hillyar made her a cartel, sailing under safe conduct for the exchange of prisoners of war. The remaining officers and men were given their parole and returned to the United States in the Essex Junior."

There were many questions which Gamble wanted to ask. But before he could speak, Captain Tucker said, not unkindly, "You seem to be sick yourself, lieutenant. The officer-of-the-watch will see that you are assigned a stateroom. If you will go with him to the wardroom, a glass of port may help to make things seem a little brighter to you."

Gamble doffed his chapeau-a-bras in salute. Captain Tucker doffed his in return. Gamble limped toward the companionway after the officer-of-the-watch. He noticed that Clapp had been taken in tow by a British midshipman. As Gamble descended the companionway, he heard the boatswain's pipes calling away the prize crew to man the Hammond.

CHAPTER 17

Semper Fidelis

GAMBLE STAYED in the wardroom for nearly an hour. He grew impatient. Limping up the companionway, he stood on the lee side of the quarterdeck where he would not attract attention.

The Cherub and the Hammond were still lying hove to. The sloop's boats were passing between the two ships. One of the boats came alongside the sloop, and a full net was hoisted aboard.

When Gamble saw what was in the net, he was amazed and furious. It was full of the gifts the natives were taking as a tribute to the king of the Windward Islands.

Gamble immediately went to Captain Tucker who was talking to the officer-of-the-watch.

"I beg your pardon, captain. But I think there must be some mistake."

Captain Tucker turned and looked steadily at Gamble.

"Indeed, lieutenant. What mistake?"

"I have just seen a net hoisted aboard containing provisions and gifts that belong to the natives."

"Quite so. I have directed that this be done."

"Captain Tucker, I was only taking the natives to Owhyhee. The sea was too rough for their loaded canoe. Surely their property should not be taken. They have no part in the war between England and the United States."

"I do not agree, lieutenant. Maritime law states that *everything* found in a prize ship belongs to the captor."

Gamble flushed with anger. But he checked his words of protest. He was too well trained in the Marine tradition to be disrespectful.

Gamble doffed his hat, then turned and limped toward the companionway. The set of his shoulders was a reproach for the theft of the natives' property.

In the weeks that followed, Captain Tucker was to find that he had judged wrongly. He was to learn a good lesson in international relations.

At first, all seemed to go well for the British sloop. After putting a prize crew aboard the Hammond, the Cherub stood to the northward. The course was set for the island of Atooi, in the Leewards.

Gamble learned, from wardroom talk, that Captain Tucker expected to meet American whaling ships near these islands. The captain had learned from British whalers that American whaling ships preferred to store their whale oil in warehouses protected by the king of the Leeward Islands.

The British sloop made the approach to Atooi under cover of darkness. With the first light of dawn she stood in toward the open roadstead.

A cheer sounded along the Cherub's decks when a whaling ship was made out. She was anchored close inshore.

The Cherub hove to several cable lengths to seaward and hoisted out a boat to board the whaling ship. She proved to be the American ship Charon.

The British joy was short-lived, however. The men aboard the Cherub soon learned that the Charon had sent her entire cargo of whale oil ashore. There, it was stored under the protection of the king of the Leeward Islands.

Gamble knew that whale oil was much needed in England because the Essex had cut off her supply from the British whaling fleet in the Pacific. Many new factories were springing up in England, and they needed the oil for lubrication. Fuel was also needed for the new whale oil lamps.

Captain Tucker, too, was well aware of these things. He sent a landing party ashore to demand the whale oil cargo of the Charon as a prize of war.

But the king of the Leeward Islands had already heard that Captain Tucker had seized the native gifts when the Hammond was captured. He was in no mood to go along with the British captain.

The king refused to give up the Charon's whale oil cargo. He also refused to surrender the whale oil cargoes of several other American ships.

Captain Tucker threatened to bombard the island. He said he would invade with seamen and

Marines. Finally, he tried flattery. To all of these, the king of the Leeward Islands firmly answered, "No."

Finally, on July 15, 1814, the Cherub set sail from the island. Left behind was a large amount of whale oil still in the protective care of the king of the Leeward Islands. This whale oil, badly needed in England, was a thousand times more valuable than the native gifts Captain Tucker had taken.

Gamble was careful not to mention to the British that Clapp was merely an acting midshipman. Thus, both Clapp and Gamble were berthed in some comfort. Gamble was in the wardroom mess; the midshipman in the steerage mess.

The enlisted seamen and Marines, however, were roughly treated. They were permitted on deck only once every twenty-four hours.

Gamble protested strongly about this to the captain. He pointed out that his few men were no threat to the ship's company of a sloop-of-war.

The lieutenant was angered by another discovery. All the personal belongings of the men who had served in the Canton ships and signed aboard the Hammond for the voyage home were seized. Most of these men had served several years in the Canton trade. They had put all their savings in silks and spices.

Captain Tucker paid no attention to Gamble's protests. He repeated that *everything* aboard a prize ship belonged to the captors.

"As for the men," he said, "they are prisoners of war and will be treated as such. In my opinion, they are getting better treatment than most prisoners do."

The Cherub laid her course to pass through the usual whaling grounds, hoping to meet American whaling ships. Day after day she stood to the south and eastward in the sparkling blue seas. Still the same endless horizon lay ahead, empty of any sail.

Gamble spent most of his time reading everything he could find on board. He read newspapers nearly a year old, novels, textbooks, and those two great monuments of the English language, Shakespeare and the King James version of the Bible.

Each day Gamble managed to exchange a few words with the Hammond's men when they were

brought on deck. He tried his best to encourage them and cheer them in their misery. He also made a point of meeting Clapp on deck every day.

During the first few weeks of their captivity, he noticed that young Clapp's face was often bruised. Gamble knew that in any steerage mess a midshipman often had to defend his rights and views with his fists. Being a captured enemy probably did not improve the situation. However, young Clapp did not mention the matter. Since he did not seem badly hurt, Gamble said nothing.

The Cherub put into the island of Otaheite, as Tahiti was called, for fresh water and provisions. Gamble looked at the island from the deck of the sloop. He thought it the most beautiful, and its people the handsomest, of any he had seen in the Polynesian groups.

The harbor was empty of ships, and there was no news of any. After a short stay, the Cherub once again laid her course toward the constellations of the southern skies.

After an uneventful voyage, the Cherub raised the South American continent in the latitude of Coquimbo and stood to the southward. The Cherub's course lay to seaward of the northerly set of the Antarctic Current, now called the Humboldt. These dark and cold waters ran strongly from the Antarctic seas to the Galapagos Islands on the Equator.

At last, the Cherub anchored in the harbor of Valparaiso, Chile. She had not sighted a single ship, except for small coasting craft flying the Chilean colors. During her stay in port, the British frigates Tagus and Briton arrived, empty, from Nooaheeva. They had been sent there to capture Gamble's prize ships.

Gamble was able to get word to the United States consulate in Santiago of the situation facing the Americans aboard the Cherub. Through a neutral consulate, Gamble and his men received heavy clothing for use in the cold latitudes, as well as some wine, fruit, and other personal articles. But Captain Tucker would permit no visiting and kept the Americans in strict confinement.

Voyage repairs were made. Fresh water was taken aboard, as well as a store of excellent Chilean wine and delicious fruit from the country's central valley. Then the Cherub departed, and laid her head southward toward the howling gales off Cape Horn.

As she ran her southing down, an icy, penetrating chill began. Gamble remembered the heavy going the Essex had experienced from the westerly gales in the February of 1813. The westward passage around Cape Horn was so rough that Captain Porter had thought of trying to reach the Pacific by sailing around the world by way of the Cape of Good Hope.

The eastward rounding of Cape Horn, however, was much easier. The westerly gales sent the Cherub scudding along before them.

On December 15, 1814, the Cherub came to anchor in the beautiful harbor of Rio de Janeiro. She saluted the flag of the British admiral in command of the Royal Navy squadron at the Brazilian station. All hands were paraded at quarters, with the fifers and drummers sounding off. Even Gamble had to admit that it was smartly done.

The British admiral ordered all American prisoners landed immediately. Gamble was relieved to get his men off the ship where they had been so mistreated.

None of the men had any money or property. The lot of the Essex' seamen and Marines was bad enough. But they would receive their back pay for almost two years' service. The men from the Canton ships, however, had lost everything. All they could expect was the Navy pay due them from the date of their signing aboard the Hammond.

Gamble went to the United States Navy agent in Rio. The two obtained clothing for the men. Some of the men needed medical treatment as well because of the lack of proper diet.

One man died of smallpox shortly after the Hammond's crew landed. Luckily, none of the other men caught this dread disease.

Gamble and his men were all still prisoners of war. The British admiral refused to grant parole. He did not want any seamen to return to the United States, even though they promised not to bear arms against England. This made it impossible for the men to ship on a merchantman and make their way home.

The quarters ashore were much more comfortable than those aboard the Cherub. Still, life in Rio became tiresome.

Gamble and Clapp took long drives about the beautiful capital of the emperor of Brazil. They made some friends among the Brazilians and the few Americans in Rio. This made their captivity more bearable than it might have been. But the weeks and months dragged on with no promise of change.

Gamble still suffered from malaria. Toward the middle of March, 1815, the wound in his heel began to fester. His leg swelled. In spite of the fine medical care of an English doctor, his condition became worse. Finally, Gamble was in bed, only partly conscious. His recovery from the infection was long and slow.

By late April, he had enough strength to limp about his quarters. In early May, he was at last able to take short drives in a carriage.

Gamble's illness did have one good result. His doctor went to the British admiral and told him that Gamble could not remain in a tropical climate.

Much to Gamble's surprise, the admiral granted his parole. He told him that he was free to leave for the United States aboard a Swedish ship bound for Havre de Grace, Maryland, leaving Rio de Janeiro May 15. When he received this news, Gamble sent for Midshipman Clapp.

As the midshipman came across the patio of Gamble's quarters, the lieutenant noticed that many changes had taken place in the young man. Instead of a boy, a tall youth came striding toward him. Although Gamble had given Clapp a new uniform in Valparaiso, the midshipman had already outgrown it. His arms dangled below his cuffs.

The midshipman's face was firmly lined and deeply tanned. But the smile that lighted it was the same as it had always been.

"Good afternoon, sir. Congratulations."

"You know, then?"

"Yes, sir. News travels fast in this warm air."

"Sit down, Benjamin," the Lieutenant said, motioning to a wicker chair. "I won't give you lengthy instructions. In fact, none are needed."

The midshipman murmured his thanks.

Gamble continued, "I shall see the Secretary of the Navy and urge that your acting appointment be made permanent, effective as of the day the Essex sailed from Nooaheeva. In view of your fine performance, I am sure this will be done."

The midshipman started to speak, but Gamble held up his hand. "No need to say anything, Benjamin. You have earned any reward you may be given."

Gamble continued, "I shall strongly recommend to the Secretary that you be ordered to a billet aboard one of the large forty-four gun frigates. Now, I am turning over to you command of all United States seamen and Marines who formed my independent command. I know that I leave them in capable hands. God bless you all."

Young Clapp's eyes were bright as he arose. He stood before Gamble and doffed his chapeau-a-bras. "I accept the command, sir. And I . . . I wish you to know that I'm proud to have served under your command."

The young midshipman turned and walked quickly across the sunlit patio.

Several weeks later, far away, a cool breeze blew
in from the Narrows. It was a welcome relief after
the blazing sun of the August day just ended.
Through the open window of Gamble's room the
unending background noises of the busy port city of
New York could be heard. But the officer concentrated on his work.

Gamble read over the several pages he had filled
with his fine script. Then he dipped his quill in the
ink and continued his report:

> On the 15th of May, by the advice of a physician
> who attended me, I took my departure from Rio de
> Janeiro, in a Swedish ship bound to Havre de Grace,
> leaving behind acting midshipman Benjamin Clapp,
> and five men, having lost one soon after my arrival
> at that place with the small-pox.
>
> No opportunity had previously offered by which I
> could possibly get from thence, the English admiral
> on that station being determined to prevent by every
> means in his power American prisoners from return-
> ing to their own country.
>
> On the 10th instant, in latitude 47 degrees North,
> and in longitude 18 degrees West, I took passage on
> board the ship Oliver Ellsworth (Captain Roberts)

fifteen days from Havre de Grace, bound for New
York.

I arrived here last evening and have the honor to
await either orders of the Navy Department, or the
Commandant of the Marine Corps.

I have the honor to be,

JOHN M. GAMBLE

To the honorable the Secretary of the Navy, Washington.

Gamble put down his quill. He sat quiet in the chair
for a long time, unaware of the bustling city about
him. Shadows filled the room as darkness began to
settle on the city. Other shadows stirred within him
—memories of friends, and of life and death on distant seas and in fragrant islands. They were shadows
which would remain with him all the days of his
life.

Traditions and Customs of the United States Marine Corps

"The thin line of tradition"—the traditions of the Marine Corps, its history, its flags, its uniforms, its insignia—*the Marine Corps way of doing things*—make the Corps what it is.

BATTLE COLOR OF THE MARINE CORPS—The Corps as a whole has one battle color entitled *The Battle Color of the Marine Corps.* This color is entrusted to the senior post of the Corps, Marine Barracks, Eighth and Eye Streets, Washington, D.C. Attached to it are all the battle honors, citations, battle streamers, and silver bands which the Corps has won since 1775. (At present these include thirty-five streamers from the Revolutionary War Streamer to Republic of Korea Presidential Unit Citation Streamer.)

BIRTHDAY OF THE CORPS—The Marine Corps was founded by the Continental Congress on 10 November, 1775 . . . Although the Marine Corps joins the other services each May in observing Armed Forces' Day, November 10th remains the Marines' own day—a day of ceremony, comradeship, and celebration.

COLORS, FLAGS, AND STANDARDS—*National Color or Standard:* This is the American flag. When the flag is displayed over Marine or Navy posts, stations, or ships, its official title is the National Ensign.

Marine Corps Colors and Standards: The Commandant issues to every major Marine unit or organization a distinguishing flag which is carried beside the National Color . . . A Marine Corps Color bears the emblem and motto of the Corps and the unit title, and follows the color scheme of the Corps, scarlet and gold.

Guidons: These are small swallow-tail flags, made in the Marine Corps colors, carried by companies, batteries, or detachments, or used as marker flags for ceremonies.

Personal Flags: Every active general officer displays a personal flag. Marine Corps personal flags consist of a scarlet field with white stars according to the general officer's rank, arranged in the same manner as the stars on Navy personal flags.

DIVINE SERVICE—Divine services for Marines should always include the Marine Corps prayer:

O Eternal Father, we commend to thy protection and care the members of the Marine Corps. Guide and direct

them in the defense of our country and in the mainte-
nance of justice among nations. Protect them in the hour
of danger. Grant that wherever they serve they may be
loyal to their high traditions, and that at all times they
may put their trust in Thee; through Jesus Christ our
Lord. *Amen.*

It is also customary for Marine Corps divine services to
conclude with the traditional naval hymn, "Eternal Father,
Strong to Save."

GLOBE AND ANCHOR—The Marine Corps Emblem, as we
know it today, dates from 1868. It was contributed to the
Corps by Brigadier General Jacob Zeilin, seventh Commandant. Until 1840, Marines wore various devices mainly
based on the spread eagle or fouled anchor. In 1840 two
Marine Corps devices were accepted. Both were circled by
a laurel wreath, undoubtedly borrowed from the Royal
Marine's badge, but had a fouled anchor inscribed inside,
while the other bore the letters "USM." In 1859 a standard

center was adopted—a U.S. shield surmounted by a hunting horn bugle, within which was the letter "M" . . .

General Zeilin's U.S. Marine globe displayed the Western Hemisphere, since the "Royals" had the Eastern Hemisphere on theirs. Eagle and fouled anchor were added, to leave no doubt that the Corps was both American and maritime.

LEATHERNECKS—The Marines' long-standing nickname, "Leathernecks," goes back to the leather stock, or neckpiece, which was part of the Marine uniform from 1775 to 1881. One historian has written:

> Government contracts usually contained a specification that the stock be of such height that the "chin could turn freely over it," a rather indefinite regulation, and, as one Marine put it, one which the "taylors must have interpreted to mean with the nose pointed straight up."

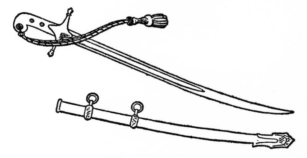

MAMELUKE SWORD—The Mameluke sword gets its name from the cross hilt and ivory grip, both of which were used for centuries by the Moslems of North Africa. The Marine

Corps tradition of carrying this type of sword dates from First Lieutenant Presley Neville O'Bannon's capture of Derna, Tripoli, in 1805, when he is said to have won the sword of the governor of the town . . . The Mameluke sword, carried by Marine officers to this day, symbolizes O'Bannon's feat.

MARINE CORPS COLORS—The colors of the Corps are scarlet and gold. Although associated with U.S. Marines for many years, these colors were not officially recognized until General Lejeune became thirteenth Commandant . . . In addition to scarlet and gold, forest green enjoys at least semi-official standing as a Marine color . . . when forest green was adopted (1912) for the winter service uniform.

MARINE CORPS MOTTO—"*Semper Fidelis*" ("Always Faithful") is the motto of the Corps. That Marines have lived up to this motto is proved by the fact that there has never been a mutiny, or even the suggestion of one, among U.S. Marines. "Semper Fidelis" was adopted in 1868 as a motto at the same time as the Emblem. Before that the Corps had had two mottoes, neither official. One was "By Sea and by Land" . . . the second, before 1847, was "To the Shores of Tripoli," in commemoration of O'Bannon's capture of Derna in 1805. In 1847, in Mexico City, this motto was revised to: "From the Halls of Montezuma to the Shores of Tripoli" . . .

MARINE'S HYMN AND MARINE CORPS MARCH—"The Marine's Hymn" is what its name implies, the hymn of the Marine

Corps. "Semper Fidelis," one of John Philip Sousa's best-known works, is the Corps march.

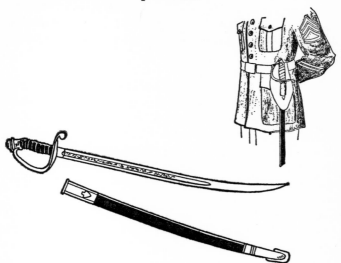

NONCOMMISSIONED OFFICER'S SWORD—Noncommissioned officers of the Marine Corps, corporals, sergeants, master gunnery sergeants, etc., are the only noncommissioned officers in any branch of the regular United States Armed Forces who still have the privilege of carrying swords. This sword is identical to the sword worn by Marine Corps commissioned officers during the Civil War.

QUATREFOIL (The cross-shaped braid atop officer's frame-type "barracks" caps.) —Tradition says that during the War of 1812, when U.S. and British Marine officers wore similar uniforms, this braid was adopted to identify the U.S. officers to their own riflemen posted in ships' rigging. Whether this is strictly true or not will probably never be known, but the device itself has been worn for many years, and, 1812 or not, is today a tradition in its own right.

RUM ON NEW YEAR'S DAY—Every New Year's Day since 1804, the Marine Band serenades the Commandant at his quarters and receives a tot of hot buttered rum in return. This occasion marks the last surviving issue of "grog" in the Armed Forces.

SHIP'S BELL—All Marine posts (and even some camps in the field) have their ship's bell, usually from a warship no longer in commission. The bell is mounted at the base of the flagpole, and the field music of the guard has the duty, between reveille and taps, of striking the bells—and also of keeping the bell in a high polish.

"THE PRESIDENT'S OWN"—Founded in 1798 (more than a century before the bands of the other three services), the Marine Band has performed at the White House for every President except George Washington, and was especially sponsored by Thomas Jefferson. Because of its traditional privilege of performing at the White House, the band is spoken of as "The President's Own." Another of the band's traditions is its scarlet special full dress blouses—the only red coats worn by American forces since the Revolution.